REVENGE IN THREE

THE COUNT OF MONTE CRISTO

LAURY SILVERS   JIBRIL STEVENSON

J. AUSTIN YOSHINO

Revenge in Three is published by Fresh Pulp Press.

https://freshpulpmag.com/ and @freshpulp

ISBN paperback: 978-1-7775313-8-6

ISBN e-book: 978-1-7775313-9-3

"It is necessary to have wished for death
    in order to know how to live."
        — Alexandre Dumas, *The Count of Monte Cristo*

REVENGE IN THREE

Love, money, power, betrayal… revenge. The Count of Monte Cristo has enthralled generations of readers the world over. Now three Muslim authors offer their interpretations of this classic tale. From the seedy underbelly of a medieval plague fortress, to the lawless borderlands of the Wild West, to the darkest depths of outer space, each novella delivers a full dose of adventure and excitement while exploring different aspects of society, politics and religion.

Rat City • Alt-Medieval Noir • Laury Silvers

In the walled city of Aman Kala, the grisly murder of a sacred Rat Keeper pulls Detective Derya Mack into an investigation that threatens to expose the power struggles that guarantee the very safety the fortress offers from the plague world.

The Pasha of Texas • Western • Jibril Stevenson

A botched robbery lands Eddie Dawson in a Mexican prison. His friendship with a Muslim prisoner opens the door to repentance and faith, if he could only let go of the ghosts of his past.

The Spatial Condition • Science Fiction • J. Austin Yoshino

Mohsin Dawoud, 3rd mate on the interstellar cargo freighter "Nightshade", has been preparing for life in space with his betrothed, Solmaz. When the Nightshade is attacked it draws him into a conspiracy of jealousy and greed among Earth's most powerful that could destroy the life he spent years building.

CONTENTS

RAT CITY

LAURY SILVERS

ACKNOWLEDGEMENTS

My gratitude to J. Austin Yoshino, Jibril Stevenson, Karen Heenan, Ahmed Saleh, Shaheen Ali, Michael Quinsey, Kathleen Self, Jenna Richards, Rachel Schine, Cyrus Zargar, Ali Olomi, Kecia Ali, Ash Geissinger, K.B. Wagers, Jonathan Lawrence, Yerusalem Work, Gülce Oral, Rana Mikati, Marwan El-Asmar, Leigh Kern, Zach Grant, the work of Mariame Kaba, and most finally, the detailed assistance of Cathal Keegan, Nadeem Ahmad, and Justin Stearns.

THE WORLD OF AMAN-KALA

The year is 986H/1578CE and Derya Mack lives and works in Aman-Kala, a plague fortress between Arab, Persian, and Turkic lands. Seven-hundred years earlier, the Zanj army—a rebel force of mainly enslaved Africans—toppled the Abbasid Caliphate, outlawed slavery, and turned regions and large cities into client states. The Zanj armies were able to resist the Mongol invasion in the 7th/13th century well enough to keep control of Iraq as well as some Persian and Turkic lands to the north and east. But thus weakened, they lost significant surrounding territory to Buyids and others to the east, the Qarmatis to the west, and the Fatimids further west through North Africa. The reduced Zanj Caliphate governs from Baghdad, backed up by the force of their caliphate-wide army. Regional militaries are outlawed and distant cities are left to govern themselves without police or jails. In Aman-Kala, private detectives solve crimes, large and small. Derya Mack is one of those detectives.

The Mosque is the city government and oversees administration of The Treaty.

The Treaty is a constitution outlining power-sharing and principles of justice.

Power is shared between The Treaty Holders: The Mosque, The Elders Assembly, The Guilds, and The Merchants Congress.

Justice is based on the Quranic and Prophetic principles of self-accounting and victim-centred recompense. Neighbourhood Elders mediate disputes and wrongdoings, and lead wrongdoers in self-accounting. If disputes or wrongdoings cannot be resolved at that level, they go before the judicial arm of The Mosque government.

The Tribunal is the recompense-based judiciary. A religious Judge leads hearings in which guilt is admitted or denied. If admitted, the case goes before a sentencing mediation hearing led by a judge, an elder, and the victim or their representative. If denied, the judge leads further investigation with the help of a detective.

Detectives are licensed and paid by The Mosque, but operate independently.

Crimes are divided between wrongdoings and violations. Wrongdoings include all crimes, even murder. Violations are reserved for breaking bright-line boundaries of The Treaty. Imprisonment of the guilty is outlawed except when holding over suspects for a hearing. Capital punishment of any sort is a last resort and only if the victim or victim's family insists after a lengthy process of mediation. Treaty violations result in banishment of the guilty, and at times, their extended families.

The Guilds are formerly criminal organizations that agreed to share power when The Treaty was formed, with the proviso they may carry on ventures such as smuggling in their territories and within limits. To break these limits would be a violation and result in banishment. Treaty sanctioned ventures are thus no longer crimes, but a way of keeping power and peace among all the city stakeholders. The Treaty affords the guilds the right to "smuggle" imported goods by paying a nominal bribe to officials, thus avoiding the city's onerous import tax, but they must abide by the same strict quarantine as other importers. Although guild ventures are no longer legally crimes and The Guild amirs have a public role as Treaty Holders, the guilds still act as shadow powers.

The Plague is ongoing, transforming the world since a particularly virulent wave was introduced by Mongol invasion, and ultimately took hold of the world in the late 6th/13th century. The Mosque government of Aman-Kala responded by building fortress walls around the city's surrounding farmlands—shutting off Aman-Kala from the world on its completion only three decades before the time of this novel—and creating a system of quarantine for people and goods entering.

The Rat Policy was instituted by the mosque, despite being controversial initially, it became a well-regarded system of breeding and supplying rats to the city, providing an endless stream of rodents to die of plague infested fleas that would otherwise bite and infect humans. The rat policy was written into The Treaty, thus making any wrongdoing against the Rat Keepers a violation of The Treaty.

Rat Keepers breed and supply these rats to the city. They are governed by The Rat Keepers Council, an arm of The Mosque government, and are paid by a special tax. Though The keepers are now seen as sacred, a few city-dwellers continue to protest the actual need for them and decry the cruelty to animals.

Aman-Kala and its denizens exist in an alternative medieval world. No such city exists. While many of the people, places, cultural forms, and situations in this novel are rooted in the history of the early to late medieval period in Muslim lands, I also make use of anachronisms past and present.

1

DAY ONE

DERYA MACK PRESSED the tip of her boot into the flesh spilling out from under the dead woman's short tunic. The Rat Keeper's skin was ashen. Sunken eyes and a gaping mouth smoothed the deep lines of her face. Her nose was a bruised knot from a life of hard drinking. A blood-stained sky-blue turban lay across the floor. She was ugly dead. She would have been even uglier alive.

Wada came up behind Mack. "Have you looked in a mirror?"

"Stop reading my mind."

"That's some other kind of jinn." She flicked her slender, lavender hand. "You are simply too obvious."

Mack wanted to object, but knew herself to be old, ugly, and, to Wada at least, obvious. She was not so different from the keeper, splayed out in a garish and humiliating pose. Same except in the colour of her turban and her refusal to accept the torture of rats so the city could live. Well, that and she did not have a shank sticking out of her neck. She faced Wada. "What happened?"

"I was tending the bar. But what I hear, and what you will hear, is that Joe cheated at cards. A man knifed her for it. But that's not why I sent for you and you know it."

"Do you know the killer?"

Wada raised a perfectly arched eyebrow. "I am certain that no one will know who he is."

"That's not what I asked."

Mack looked over at the three half-sobered witnesses, sitting in shadow on a bench along the mud-brick wall. An Arab woman and two men. One, small and barrel-chested with something Andalusian to his body language. The other was a big fellow with a smashed nose. All of them were middle-aged or older. They kept trying to get up to leave, then changing their minds and sitting back down. Once Wada told a person to want a thing, they could not resist. The woman, dressed like a stable-hand and smelling of it, had her hands open and was muttering, looking up to the sky like a fool. The Andalusian stared at the body, stunned, while the larger man watched Mack curiously.

He was handsome and nodded to her in that way some men do that make women soften their voices and round their hips. If Gad were alive, he would have walked over and slapped the look off his face. She missed the old bull in moments like this. But there was something else about this man getting her back up. Her head ached and she put it away.

A round card table was on its side next to the body, stools scattered, a fallen oil lamp stamped out, ale cups in pieces around it. Wet stains had spread out, mixing with blood, and raising the stench of long-spilled drink lying in wait in the wooden floorboards. There was not enough light to see all the blood spatter, but with a knife in the neck like that, it would be everywhere. She drew closer to the witnesses. They had got their share.

"What did you see?"

None of them answered, but the big one one spread his legs, settling comfortably into Wada's hold on him, and shook his head.

"We're not leaving." Mack gave out an exaggerated sigh.

The Andalusian tried to scoot forward on the bench but rethought it and sat back, irritated. He answered Wada rather than Mack. "Joe cheated. She always cheats. The man got mad. He told her. She told him. He stabbed her in the neck."

Wada replied, "Talk to the detective," and left for the bar.

"The money from the game is still on the floor here." Mack pointed. "He didn't want it?"

"Who knows? He looked at her body for a moment, then left."

"The killer didn't touch her otherwise?"

"No."

"Who is the man?"

"I've never seen him, but he sounded like an outsider." The Andalusian seemed honest enough in the saying of it, but the headache settling in had her on edge, clouding her judgement.

Mack glanced behind her, expecting Wada to return with an "I told you so," but she was talking to a customer at the bar.

"What did he look like?"

"Nothing special." The larger man finally spoke, but in a strangely accented caliphal Arabic rather than Aman-Kala's dialect, a patois of Arabic, Persian, Turkic, and the fair words adopted by any other immigrant to the city. "He looked like a red-haired Arab, but wore a Sogdian turban. Like myself, he was a well-built man."

By this point, Gad would have threatened to make them talk and at least one of them would have. Mack wished for a moment that she had it in her. But one of Wada's qiyan had pulled her out of bed just before she had drugged herself to sleep and her head was throbbing now. She set her jaw. "Joe plays cards here a lot?"

The Andalusian answered, "Once a week."

"And she cheats," Mack prompted.

He shrugged. The other two remained silent.

"No one cares?"

The woman replied in a thin, shrill voice, "She's a Rat Keeper!"

"I can see that much from her turban."

Mack needed a drink. The rats were chattering away under the floorboards, their voices tapping at her skull. A "subhanallah" here and there. One moaned in a corner, "Ya Shafi." But the divine healer would not be around to save it. That rat would be dead of plague tonight and the others not long after. If killing the Rat Keepers would stop this misery, she would kill them all herself. But there were always people ready to step up for the money and the honour of raising and delivering rats for the plague fleas to bite instead of the human animals. And few cared but her, the only one cursed from birth to hear their language of misery. She closed her eyes for a moment to control the urge to give the keeper a swift kick.

Mack hated that Wada let Rat Keepers in her place at all. But even if Wada wanted to turn their kind away, she could not. One complaint and The Keepers Council would shut down The Water Wheel. The denizens of Aman-Kala, even the poorest of the poor, paid the Rat Policy tax to support them. Those who disagreed still had to give the keepers whatever they wanted or find themselves on the wrong side of the law. The death of a keeper in her friend's tavern was no small matter.

She took out her notebook and stylus from the linen bag strapped across her thick chest. "I need your names and where you live."

The woman stuttered, "Marwa, Farm Amila, South Quarter."

"Mubarak ibn Abdurrazzaq, Zanbak Kocha, South Quarter."

But the larger man paused for a moment as if he were wondering what name to give, then said, "Jabal ibn Abi Faria. Hostel Ibn Battuta, just down Janub Kocha, I do not know the name of the alley."

They had no obligation to answer her truthfully, other than wanting to remain in Wada's good graces. And if she found the killer and the case got to The Tribunal, they could simply disappear. Nothing anyone could do about it. Mack yelled over her shoulder, "Wada, let them go!"

A moment later, they found they could stand without reconsidering it. Mack waved them out and leaned against the wide arch between the games room and bar, watching them go, one by one, spilling shards of light through the swinging tavern doors and into the darkened alley.

2

"WE'RE CLOSING!"

A few rough labourers were still lounging on low couches at The Water Wheel. A mukhannath in an elaborately wrapped turban and robes to match Wada's qiyans in allure had draped theirself over one, holding the man's drink. They were arguing and ignored Wada's announcement.

Anahita leaned over the handrail halfway up the stairs, her loose gowns caught up in her hand. "Not the rooms, too," she complained. "I've got trade waiting on me. We won't come down until you say so."

Behind the bar, Wada turned to look up at her. Mack could not hear her answer, but Anahita nodded and went to her client.

Sal came out of the storage room with a bottle in each hand and another under their arm.

Mack called out, "Sal, bring me some of that Indian rum," then turned to deal with the body.

She stepped around a trembling pool of jellied blood and squatted beside the keeper to pat the body down. The keeper's sky-blue waist sash had already come undone and her short, quilted robe was open, exposing a thick wool tunic and the usual coin purse strapped across the chest and tucked under the arm where not even a skilled pickpocket could get at it. Mack pulled her small dagger from its sheath and cut the purse's thong. It was full.

Purse in hand, Mack stood, grunting in sympathy with her old joints. She held one of the coins up to the light and whistled at the warm glint of pure gold. These were not Zanj caliphal dinars paid out for large trade or the Rat Keeper's salary. These were over seven hundred years old, from the days before the Zanj rebellion had brought down the Abbasid caliphate. Only once before had she held Abbasid gold.

The Mosque had brought in four of the best detectives in Aman-Kala to look into the heist of a chest of Abbasid dinars. The detectives assumed one of the two guilds was involved in the theft and their investigation was a sham to keep the peace between Mosque and Guild. But the job paid well, so the detectives took the money, expecting no results. She and Gad worked their end of it for a year, surprised when they recovered twenty-three coins on a dead body no one would claim. The others found nothing.

The coins could be from among those she and Gad had returned to The Mosque Exchequer's office. While the Exchequer received the gold from them with grave acknowledgment for their service, he was not happy about it. Who knows what he did with them? She dug through the purse and counted them: fourteen. Why did the keeper have Abbasid gold?

She should talk to Mehdi. He was the only one still alive other than her who had been on that case. Maybe he remembered something, or maybe he would have wisely forgotten. No one wants to get in between the Guild and The Mosque.

As Mack cinched the purse, Wada came into the games room with a glass in hand. "Got what you need?"

"You got what I need." Mack drank down the contents in one gulp, then coughed. "What the…".

"Aman-Kala's finest grappa."

Mack coughed again, but her headache eased a bit and the voices quieted. "Better than nothing." She held out the purse. "Put this in your safe for me?"

"Of course." Wada took the purse and a small oil lamp from a niche in the games room wall and disappeared into her office, her embroidered red robe trailing behind her.

Mack called to her through the open door, "Tell me your side."

"I heard the fight, Joe's threats, the patrons yelling." Wada returned, closing the door behind her. "I didn't rush. Let them have a bit of trouble. Keeps the place lively. But before I got around the bar, the killer walked out, calm, but blood all over him." She gave Mack a dramatic look. "As if nothing had happened."

"Why didn't you hold him here?"

"Not my job."

"Wada."

"I sent for you to make it go away."

"And how do I do that if you won't help?"

"Fine. I've never seen him before."

Mack snorted.

"No, Derya. He was new."

Mack looked for Wada's tell: a slight tension in her cheek brought out a dimple from the pleasure she took in mischief. Even Muslim jinn loved their little lies, but this time, Wada was serious. "Okay, then. What did he look like?"

"Big man, dressed like a labourer. Short, undyed rough wool robe. No lapels. Work belt. He had a thick red beard. A summer wheat complexion. Sogdian wrap to his brown turban."

"One of the witnesses called him an Arab."

"Never. A Sogdian, one of your people."

Mack nodded, wondering how anyone could miss the difference, then crouched to examine the knife sticking out of the keeper's neck. It was a cheap brass shank. The kind sold at most corner shops. Made from shards of scavenged metal wrapped with rags and wound with twine for a handle, anyone could have one for a copper fals. And most everyone carried them for protection. She tugged it out, feeling the flesh pull against the blade.

Wada hovered over Mack. "Need a cloth to wrap that?"

Although it was untraceable, and she would have preferred to leave the body so insulted, she agreed.

"Why do they keep playing cards with her if she cheated?"

"I back them." Wada chuckled, handing her a cloth.

"Of course." Mack wrapped the knife and put it in her bag to hand over to The Tribunal, then stood, grabbing the table to help herself up this time. "The keepers get away with whatever they want."

"I backed them because I back her work."

It was not the first time they disagreed about the keepers, but with a headache and voices looming, she did not want to hear it and grunted in reply.

"You'd rather human beings die than the rats."

Mack took the bait like she always did. "You don't hear the hissing and moaning when the fleas latch on. There have to be other ways to control the plague, but this city made it a sacred duty to torture rats." Mack waited for Wada to snap back, "Better them than us," as if the plague could touch a jinn.

Instead, Wada reached out and put a hand on her arm.

Mack shook it off and pressed the sides of her head with her palms. One glass of grappa was not enough. She had let it go too long. "Give me a drink so I can blot out the interminable prayers of these creatures you are so happy to let suffer."

They left the body for the bar. "Sal, get the good detective another glass of grappa."

Sal stood behind the bar in their trim, rajula's turban, quilted work coat buttoned right up and tied off with a leather belt, dagger at the ready. They put their gnarled hands onto the polished teak and leaned in to see the games room. "Can I send in Farhang to clean?"

"It's for Derya to say." Wada spoke over her shoulder as she went to bolt the entrance shut.

"Not yet," Mack said, and with that, her head cracked and the cacophony of voices took hold of her. Rats and mice screeching as they fought for food clashed with a donkey's rumbling, sleepy sigh. Every muscle in Mack's face was so stiff her teeth ached. She pulled herself up onto a tall stool and slumped over the bar, barely able to hold her head up.

Sal bent below the counter and brought out a long-necked glass bottle with a stopper and filled her glass to the rim.

Mack lifted her head enough to take the glass and sucked at the grappa, not wincing at the harshness of the alcohol this time, but grateful for its medicine. Sal watched and poured her another, then another, until Mack held up her hand. The voices retreated and her skull stitched itself back together, quiet again as long as the drink stayed in her system.

Mack leaned her elbow on the bar and rubbed her jaw until her teeth agreed to stay in her head.

Wada took the stool next to her.

"Why no rum or local wine?" Mack asked.

"I'm waiting for a delivery of wine, but there's a shortage of smuggled rum and I'm not paying for taxed imports."

"I'd pay the taxes rather than drink this swill."

"Swill or not, you got your quiet."

"Fair." She sighed. "Tell me, why do you say dressed 'like' a labourer?"

"His work belt didn't hang easily on him. He had a beard the length of a mulla, but he was no scholar. No ink stains on his fingers. Didn't hold himself like one of them, either."

"You want to be my new partner?" Mack quipped.

"The woman?" Wada tapped the bar with a knuckle. "She's a mulla. Comes in here wearing the clothes of her stable man. She's got ink on her fingers."

"A scribe at The Mosque? A government functionary?"

"I've seen her coming and going out of The Treaty Mosque, white mulla's turban piled up atop her skinny head and neck."

"Does she know you know?"

"I doubt it. Anyway, she only comes when Joe does and drinks and gambles on my coin."

"Do you think they knew each other?"

"I think she's cheap."

"Typical. The Mosque gouges us in taxes, pays their mullas in gold, but those scholars won't spare a fals, not even for their sin." Mack straightened. "What do you want from me?"

"Tell The Tribunal that it was a random act, not gambling, nothing to do with The Water Wheel."

"Why don't you just have someone drag her down the alley? Leave her for the rats to gnaw at." Mack huffed. "Fitting."

"Mack." Wada's plea had a frantic edge.

"Fine. You call in someone from the night watch to get the word to The Keepers Council to come and get the body. I'll send a letter to The Tribunal claiming the case in the morning." She stood. "Now, let me get myself home to a cup of Teddy's poppy tea and bed before this burning piss grappa wears off."

3

DAY TWO

Derya grabbed her coat and linen bag off their hooks and shuffled out of her bedroom. The sinking soft ease of last night's poppy seed tea had worn off, but the voices were quiet still. The grass mats covering the floor were kicked out of place and a jug of wine sat on a low table strewn with paper. "Plague be fucked," she muttered, seeing she had left the ink pot open. She kicked the mats somewhat back in line, then lifted the wine jug, revealing a red stain on the paper beneath. Mack sat down to drink the wine, leaving just enough to bring the ink back to life. Although she had fresh paper somewhere, she decided to write her letter to The Tribunal on the wine-stained sheet.

The thin wood slats of her door shook with a hard knock just as she sealed the letter.

"Derya, it's Anahita."

"Come on in."

Wada's fair-skinned qayna was deathly pale. Smeared kohl blended with the dark circles under her houri-round eyes. She gave Mack a weak smile. "What's the craic, Derya?"

"Mighty," she answered. "We'll make an Irish of you yet."

Anahita shivered, pulling her wrap around her more closely. "Only if I get an Irish man with money enough to get my back off of Wada's beds."

Mack winced. "Come in, I'll call down for some food. No trouble."

"No, I need sleep."

"There's a bed here. Come on. It's yours."

Anahita withdrew onto the landing, offering an exhausted half smile.

"Better tell me, then, so you can get some sleep."

"Wada sent me to say that a witness from yesterday came back and spent the night. He's ready to talk."

"I thought she closed the place."

"As soon as you left, she opened the doors again."

"Of course she did." Mack only hoped she had blocked off the game room until the orderlies sent by the Rat Keepers Council took the body away. On second thought, the idea of drunks stepping over the keeper's body lightened her mood. "Wada tell him to talk?"

"Who knows? This one has a taste for jinn, so maybe he enjoys being controlled."

There were plenty who did. Wada would warn them first, but after a taste of what it would be like under her spell, they begged for it.

"I'll be there as soon as I get my things together."

Mack stood in the doorway and watched her go down the uneven mud-brick stairs and into the alley.

The apothecary door opened at the bottom of the stairs. Teddy stuck his head out, offering Anahita a quick nod as she passed. Seeing Mack, he greeted her. "Labas sana?"

She nodded that all was well. "Labas?"

"Alhamdulillah. Late night?"

"A Rat Keeper was killed at The Water Wheel."

Teddy murmured the prayer for a keeper's soul, then asked, "How are you faring?"

"I'm only taking the case because Wada asked me."

"It's good of you." But the face of the old Habash told that he wished she had not.

Mack shrugged off his concern. "That jinn and I are always in debt to each other." She gestured behind her. "I've got to get my things and go."

"I was hoping to catch you. A small thing, but I wanted to mention it."

"Be right down." Back in her rooms, she kicked off her leather slippers and pulled on her boots. Her quilted woollen coat buttoned up and belted, Mack slung her linen bag over her chest and patted it to make sure her flask was there. She shoved her black and brown striped detective's turban over her short, greying red hair and was halfway out the door before she remembered the letter.

Teddy was waiting for her at the bottom of the stairs.

"Yeru was on a case yesterday," he said as she descended. "Pippo. You know him. He tried to pay her for healing his infected foot with a gold fleck."

Mack woke up. "Where does a man like Pippo get gold?"

"That's what we wondered. My daughter refused it, of course. The Mosque provides."

"Did she ask him about it?"

"Yes. He said the fleck was an inheritance."

"That man has no family but his grandson."

"Exactly."

"Did he have more?"

"He must have. Why offer his only fleck?"

"All right, thanks Teddy." She clasped his shoulder.

As she turned to leave, he said, "Thank God, they got that case of plague under control, sah?"

She stiffened. "What case?"

"In the West Quarter." He tipped his head back in surprise. "You haven't heard? Health moved the family into quarantine and sealed the home. If they live, they'll be back in a few weeks."

The old, animalistic fear overtook any relief she might have felt that the exposure was under control. It did not matter that outbreaks were to be expected from time to time. Brutal cycles of plague for two hundred years had transformed the world and broken its people. It had been thirty-one years since the Aman-Kala sealed itself off from the cycles, but the plague haunted her all the same, just as it did anyone else old enough to have lived through those days.

"There do not seem to be any more cases, for now," Teddy assured her. "But, if so, Health will find them."

Mack walked through the unpaved alleys in the cold light of the morning until her fear turned into something like numb acceptance.

She had been just another squalling infant found among the bodies of her parents and siblings. She survived again in the orphanage when it seemed like every other child died of plague or some coughing or shitting sickness. Then, her plague family. Little Danyal died and Rivka moved to Baghdad, leaving her with only the Mac Aodhagáins at the farm as family to her. But they, too, ended up being eaten by the pus-filled lumps. Little Tom died in her arms.

Yet she kept living.

This world was nothing but a grindstone that kept turning her through for another go at crushing her, and there were days when she begged it would.

She tore off her turban and pulled at the buttons on her coat, needing the cold bite of the fall air on her skin to bring her back to the case. But the wine had not been enough; the rising chatter of the birds' prayers as they scraped for seeds in the dusty road and a camel's bellowing in thanks to God as her heavy udders released their milk filled her with dread. She had to get another drink before she heard the rodents cry out to God in suffering and death.

4
___

A STRONG TANG of vinegar hit her as she walked through the swinging doors at The Water Wheel. Mack stopped short. Old Farhang was bent over, washing the floors with a large rag in his hands, sweeping the cloth back and forth, and into the bucket to rinse.

The old Persian stood up, hand on his back. "You can always walk on my wet floors." He called out behind him, "Lady Wada, Detective Mack is here."

Wada appeared from the card room. She had cast off her luxurious red robe and wore a simple gown of thick wool, its narrow sleeves rolled up, a faded wrap tied around her waist. "Labas sana, Derya?" To Farhang she said, "We need another jug of vinegar back there."

"Labas?" Mack replied perfunctorily as she walked behind the bar and pulled out the bottle of grappa.

One eyebrow raised, Wada said, "To your health."

"I owe you." Mack poured herself a glass and sipped it, the dregs-wine burning away fear and old hurts on its way down. She topped off the glass and took it, her turban in the other hand, to a spot on the kilim-covered couch nearest the cold hearth.

Wada ignored her and pushed a few black curls off her forehead. "I don't see why I am bothering to get the blood up. It adds character to the place. Perhaps I should hire a storyteller to grace the customers with a tragic tale of the stabbing?"

"You should use natron first, before the vinegar."

Wada sunk down onto the low couch next to her. "Didn't have time to dress this morning?"

Mack thumped her turban back on and buttoned her coat. "Anahita told me to hurry. Where's my witness?"

"Still upstairs. But the other one is here, too. In the games room."

That dimple of hers. "Which one?"

"Jabal ibn Abi Faria."

"He have something new to say?"

"Perhaps we all have something new to say."

Here it comes, thought Mack.

"The killer has green eyes."

Mack turned her hand up in questioning frustration. "Did you forget that when you could have told me earlier?"

"I dreamt it last night."

Mack sat up and stared.

"It came to me once I relaxed, Derya."

"Anything else?"

"His eyelashes were long. He used kohl."

Anahita teased as she descended the stairs, "Wada, what kind of dream was this?"

"I'll never tell." Wada's eyes were intense with desire.

The sun was barely up and Mack had had enough.

Jabal emerged from the games room and stood in the wide archway, watching them.

Most look worse in the light of day, but not this one. Grizzled beard and all the marks of age, he was still brutishly handsome. A long nose, flattened and off-kilter from being broken too many times, set off the plain intelligence of his face and sharp eyes. Those eyes, rich brown and kohled under a midnight blue turban flecked with green. *Bah bah*, she thought with pleasure. But there was something else there, a vulnerability, as if she could see the boy in the man. A charmer, this one; but she did not mind that he stirred her old body. Then Mack huffed, realizing. It was his kohled eyes that had sparked Wada's memory and she went cold at the thought of them together.

Wada touched Mack's face to bring her attention back and she flinched, wanting to slap her hand away.

The jinn smirked. "Oh, and the killer wanted to drink sharbat."

"Not alcohol? Who got the sharbat?"

"Sal."

"Where did Sal go?"

"What does that matter?"

She took another long drink of the grappa, this time out of plain irritation, and coughed again.

"Still no rum, my apologies."

Sal came over as if called. Mack pulled her empty flask from her bag and set it on the table. Sal took it to fill.

Mack stopped them. "Where did you get the sharbat last night?"

"Ben Yacoub."

"Why not Humayn's? It's closer."

"Better sharbat."

"Did he ask for Ben Yacoub?"

"No, a sharbat Ben Yacoub made for him."

The killer had been there before and Ben Yacoub could answer some questions.

Jabal moved out of the doorway to sit on a couch across from them. He spread his legs and threw one arm over the back of a high cushion.

Mack was stuck between wanting to punch him and put her hand up his thigh.

Wada followed Mack's gaze and sighed with pleasure.

"Tell me about the two regulars," Mack deflected.

"Room Rose. He wants to talk to you. The third will have to come to you."

Holding back made no sense. It was more than jinn mischief. "You called me for this job."

Wada mocked her with an innocent face.

"I'm done, then." Mack pushed herself up off the low couch with a grunt. "The Tribunal will send someone by." She patted her bag with the letter inside. "I haven't informed them yet, so there's no trouble."

Sal returned with her filled flask.

Wada gave an exasperated moan. "Derya, you are so tiresome."

Jabal stood and Mack watched as he walked towards them, his eyes on her. His body was powerful and fluid, the movements of a man who loved to fight and more. She did not look away.

"I'll be coming with you," he said in that strange accent she could not place.

"Didn't you hear? I quit the case."

He turned away to smile at Wada like he wanted to lean down and take a bite out of her. "You two, stop playing."

"Fine." Wada touched her finger to her lips, then stood with them. "I'll be good, Derya. Go up and see your witness." She gave Jabal a lascivious glance. "I'll hold this one captive for you until you get back."

"I'm going with her to question the witness, my dear."

His eyes were on Mack when he said it. Again, there was that touch of vulnerability in his gaze, making her want to bring him along and see what he had in mind for her. But that was not why she would ask him upstairs. She wanted to watch what he would do, find out why he wanted to come at all.

They climbed the stairs side by side, but he made her feel as if he were following her lead. Of all the men she had bedded in her life, none had tried that angle, and she admitted she liked it.

Without knocking, Mack opened a door painted with a single rosebud. Mubarak ibn Abdurrazzaq was sitting on the edge of the bed naked, his legs spread and flushed like a milk-drunk baby. Muna was pulling on a robe, done with him.

"So you have a taste for silat," remarked Mack. "Is it the shape shifting or the cruelty?"

"How is that your business?" Mubarak eyed Muna hungrily as she walked past him without so much as a glance.

She slipped between Mack and Jabal on her way out and whispered, "Cruelty."

Jabal chuckled. Mubarak dressed, pulling on his underclothes, pants, tunic, a short vest, then his long quilted coat. Made of fine wool, it had no embellishment; it was the clothing of a rich man who imagined he blended in with the poor. Better, it was now spattered with blood.

"Fine costume," commented Jabal.

Mack let him talk.

"Your sleeves are neither practically narrow nor luxuriously wide," he continued. "The hem hits mid-calf. A minor concession to the clothes of the poor who have no use for wide sleeves and robes that drag on the ground, getting filthy and in the way of work. Yet, you err. The poor are as keen on embellishment as wealthy."

Mubarak replied wearily, "You've caught me."

"The woman did better wearing an ostler's clothes," Jabal remarked to Mack.

Jabal's attempt to impress her was clumsy, not what she expected. Ignoring him, she addressed Mubarak, "Wada said you wanted to talk."

Dressed, Mubarak stood before her, wide-legged. But it only made him look like he was about to take a shit. "I am not married, nor is my brother unaware of my nights out. If you want to threaten me with exposure, on that point, you are going nowhere."

Mack laughed out loud. "You want threats to talk?" She gestured to the open door. "Should I call Muna back to get the information out of you? Because, I assure you, this is not my kink."

Mubarak's lips quivered at the mention of Muna and gave up the act. "The man started the fight. When he challenged Joe for cheating, she made it clear she was a Sacred Keeper. Told him to fold and go or keep giving her his money. He put his shank on the table, demanding his money back."

"Did Joe take it seriously?" Mack asked.

"We all took it seriously." He gestured to Jabal to back him up. "The man was calm. Terrifying. An angry man is dangerous. A calm man, more so."

"Go on," Jabal said.

"The rest of us stood to leave. Hajja Marwa," he added derisively, "our resident mosque scholar in disguise as a stable hand, stood first and we followed her. Joe apologized, and pushed all the money at the man. It was then he picked up the shank and stabbed her in her neck."

"And where were you all?"

"Backing away across the room." He touched his coat. "Still, I am covered in blood."

"Don't let your servants wash it out."

He nodded as if it were sincere advice.

"Why didn't you tell me this last night?"

"He could have been outside, waiting for us. We were all afraid." He looked expectantly at Jabal again.

"I, too, was afraid," Jabal conceded.

She very much doubted that and turned back to Mubarak. "So you slept here where he could find you?"

"My chances were better here than in the road. I came back after you left and joined Muna for the night."

Then he looked at her as if he had a sweetmeat to share, pausing long enough for her grunt at him to get on with it.

"Sometimes Joe came in with a man who was not her husband."

This was something.

"Know who he is?"

"She called him her Alp."

"Turk. Old, young, what?"

"Her match, but he was big enough to make a woman like that seem small in comparison. Bowed legs like a horseman. Sparse grey beard with a drooping moustache. He would sit on the bench and watch her play without saying a word. When she won, again, she would say, 'My Alp, my love, look!' Afterwards, she would hand him the money."

"How often did he come?"

"Often enough that he was taking home the bulk of her winnings."

"Maybe he just carried it for her?"

Mubarak shook his head. "One night when he did not come, she complained her Alp was bleeding her dry, but could not give him up. Said her husband complained about the money he thought she was losing at gambling."

"But he wasn't here last night?"

"He didn't always come." He clapped his hands once. "Now, I've told you everything. Go to The Treaty Mosque and ask for Hajja Marwa, your third witness. She will confirm what I have said."

Mack's eyes widened. "Marwa is her real name?"

"Yes."

"And yours is real, too?"

"Of course."

Mack rolled her eyes. "Well, at least I know where to find you. Wherever Muna goes, you will follow."

Before they left, she insultingly thumbed toward Jabal. "How often has this one gambled with you?"

"Last night was the first time."

Jabal pursed his lips.

She waved Jabal and Mubarak off, and left them for Wada downstairs.

"Got what you need?" Wada asked as Mack circled around to the bar.

"Did the keeper have a lover?"

"Alp. Old Turk. Came with her often. Costly man."

"How come he wasn't here last night?"

"I don't know him well enough to know, Derya."

Mack turned around and leaned on the bar with her elbows behind her and watched Mubarak walk down the stairs and leave without a care. Jabal took a stool beside her. Wada was unhappy about it.

"You did good in there, Jabal." Mack said, glancing at Wada, hoping to prick the jinn's jealous nature. "Want to work this case with me?"

"I thought you would never ask." He gave her one of his smiles.

Wada tried to stand between them like some poor girl who has pinned her hopes on a man for the first time. Mack would have told her not to worry; Jabal wanted something other than the chance to jump on the dried-up belly of an old woman, and she was going to find out.

5

MACK AND JABAL turned out of The Water Wheel's alley onto the cobbled main thoroughfare. The shops had raised their shutters and customers pressed against wide counters set into half-doors and haggled over goods. At the next alley leading off Janub Kocha, Humayn's sharbat stall was still closed. Three alleys further down, Ben Yacoub's stall was shuttered, too.

"I'm hungry. Let's get some food. It's going to be a long day getting out to the rat farm and back." Mack did not wait for him to agree, but walked ahead down the steep road until she turned into an alley that opened onto a small square. Off to one side stood a donkey, overburdened with sacks filled with clay pots. Hearing his discomfort, she approached and laid a hand on his cheek. The donkey softened to her. His prayer of thanks for her kindness touched her through the drink, and she swayed with it.

A hand steadied her. She spun around to find Jabal holding both hands up.

"Back off," she grumbled and went ahead of him to the food stalls set up in a circle around a large shared grill.

The greasy scent of meat searing on the grill turned her stomach, and she focused instead on a large simmering pot. Mack gestured to a free table against a wall not yet in sunlight. "Over there. I'll get the food."

"You must let me pay," Jabal insisted. "A lady should never pay for her food."

"I'm not a lady. Sit down."

He laughed with pleasure at her retort and went to sit.

An older man in a belted kirtle and wool cap saw her and nodded, knowing what she wanted, but she put up a finger and shouted over the men ahead of her, "François! Your pottage and one mutton!"

Keeping her back to Jabal, she set herself to thinking without thinking, letting her mind wander around him. There was something there, but when she touched it, she only found a bodily pull to him.

Francois' boy came around holding a blackened clay bowl with flat bread draped over it and more of the same bread wrapping chunks of meat, dripping with fat and sprinkled with fresh herbs.

"Pardon, Detective Mack!"

There it was. The accent. Jabal had a Frankish accent buried in his caliphal Arabic and a touch of something else. Persian? Mack dug out an extra copper fals for the boy in thanks for the information. She held the stinking meat away from her as she made her way back to the table. He stood as she approached and she put down her bowl, watching to see if he would recognize Francois' bean, pea, and onion pottage. He did, but only for a moment before turning to his meat. Maybe he had spent time in France, but he was not born there. He looked like no Frank she had ever seen. Not another word was said during the meal. No flirtatious banter. No questions about the case.

"Bah bah," she sighed, and pushed the bowl away. She stood easily, feeling better for the food and having caught him out in something. "Let's head out. The Boundary Wall is a far ways."

"The Boundary Wall? Can we return without quarantine?"

There was a tremor in his voice. Like every other outsider entering Aman-Kala from the plague world, he had been locked up alone in a thick-walled cell with nothing but dried meat and barley soup for forty days. Quarantine in the boundary walls was meant to protect the city from plague but also discourage outsiders from wanting in, and it did its job.

"We are crossing the city gates, not the gates at the Boundary Wall. But the Rat Keepers' farms are out there, so don't wander off."

She turned the corner without looking and bumped into a broad-chested Persian man, old like her but still fit to fight.

"Mehdi!"

"Mack! Well met, I've got something for you." He glanced at Jabal.

"Give me a minute with Mehdi, Jabal." She smiled to reassure him.

He stepped aside, frowning, leaning against a wall in the rising sun.

"Where's that one from?" Mehdi asked, unimpressed.

"Someplace where they don't know not to move in and out of shade."

Mehdi chuckled. "I heard you have The Keeper case."

"Fuck's sake. I haven't even sent in my letter yet."

"Word travels. Listen, Mack." His tone became serious, with a look of concern she was unused to in him. "Someone is smuggling behind Amir Pasha's back. There's a lot of gold changing hands in his part of the city. Folks running goods who never did before."

"Teddy told me there was some gold where it shouldn't be." She furrowed her brow. "Wada claims the smuggling is drying up, though. She's only serving local swill at The Water Wheel."

"I've heard the opposite, more goods, and cheaper. New runners." He hesitated, then said, "I just wanted to warn you if the amirs are coming to blows. Hard to believe Amir Alami would move in on Amir Pasha's territory."

Mack tucked her head back. "No one would violate The Treaty on that scale." The Mosque, The Elders Assembly, the Guilds, and the Merchants Congress divvied up power in a treaty negotiated over seven hundred years ago and never once had anyone threatened it. Each held a corner of the cloth that kept this city safe and if one let go, Aman-Kala would be torn apart. "I don't believe it."

"God willing, you're right." Mehdi tugged at his beard. "Better someone within Amir Pasha's guild, siphoning off Pasha's goods and reselling them. But a lot of folks will suffer, starting with the fool thinking he could best the amir, down to the child who carried the goods, and everyone who ate out of the money the kid brought home. The Tribunal would turn them all out of the city into the plague world with nothing."

"If Amir Pasha doesn't kill the fool first." She looked around. "It would save a lot of lives. Pasha would show mercy to the rest."

"Wouldn't be the first time The Tribunal looked away from a Guild correction."

"Mehdi." She checked to see if Jabal was listening. "What if the new smuggler is connected to my case? The gold you're talking about, is it Abbasid?"

Eyebrows raised, he asked, "You found more?"

"The keeper had fourteen Abbasid dinars in her purse. I thought it wasn't connected because the killer didn't take it off the body. But now?"

"Why would the keeper have them?"

It made no sense, but given what he had just told him, she said it anyway. "The rat farms are at the boundary walls."

"Paying out all that gold to bring in goods through the rat farms? Just to get around bribing the tax collector? The bribe is a pittance compared." Mehdi touched her arm. "That would mean going around quarantine, risking an outbreak. Who in Aman-Kala would do that?"

"No one from Aman-Kala," she said, keeping herself from glancing at Jabal.

"If the keeper found out about the fool siphoning goods from Pasha," Mehdi offered, "it might've been a payoff to keep quiet."

"But she couldn't keep her mouth shut." Mack rubbed her chin. "Still, killing a keeper?"

"We have to go back to the cost. No one's making any money bringing goods through the farms at the wall." He sounded like he was trying to convince himself. "We never knew what happened to the gold. Someone could have stashed it out there along the wall and she found it."

"And her death has nothing to do with the smuggling."

"We have to remember what Isiib taught us: don't ascribe a

conspiracy to something that is better explained through stupidity or passion." He nudged her arm hopefully as he left. "Someone within Pasha's guild is stealing from him. That's the only thing that makes sense. And remember, Mack, the smuggling's not part of your case."

Mack wanted to accept that Mehdi was right. God knows, Isiib always had been. *Think of the cost*, she told herself. But she could not shake the idea that the Abbasid gold meant the smuggling and the death were related. She would keep an eye out at the farm for unusual camel sacks or crates.

Mehdi may have been able to talk himself out of panicking over this, but she was not so sure she could. She waved Jabal over and considered his involvement. What better way to protect himself than chat her up and make her bring him along?

6

Local merchants, their wares loaded onto the backs of donkeys and camels or in carts, headed out the wide gates in the old city ramparts for the export market within the South Boundary walls. At the other gate, a porter waited beside a heavy sack of local goods coming in while the mukhannath who had hired him showed their papers to the guards. Carts, camels, and people crossing into the city lined up behind them.

Jabal pulled a letter out of the pocket in his sleeve. Mack took it from him and opened it without asking. "You don't need your quarantine release letter."

"The guard at the gate won't ask for it?"

"Only going back in."

She handed it back to him. "Your name really is Jabal ibn Abi Faria."

"At your service." He bowed ceremoniously.

She imagined that was typical of the Franks, because they, sure as the plague took your mother, did not do that here. Despite herself, she laughed at his gesture and heard the voice of her old partner, Gad, warning her to be careful. She shook it off, assuring herself that she knew where to draw the line.

The gate opened onto a large, dusty square with a stand of trees along one side. Donkey carts lined up beside them to head out to the farms. Other carts and camels carrying imported goods cleared by quarantine trundled in toward the South Quarter market tax warehouses. A burly porter gestured an insult at a merchant, dropped the sack from his back onto the ground, and walked away. The merchant threw up his hands and called for another porter, and several scrambled to get to him first. A water carrier walked among the crowds, leather sack slung over his shoulder, his brass cup jangling on a chain.

Mack took a long swig of grappa as they approached the donkeys, hoping to muffle their complaints to God. But she heard enough to pass by the first and the second to the third. The first two drivers cursed her, but she waved her badge at them and they withdrew, muttering. The third driver jumped onto the wide seat and picked up the reins. Mack hauled herself onto the seat next to him, grunting in pain as her old body objected. Jabal leapt onto the back on top of a pile of dusty camel sacks.

"Where to?"

"Rat Keeper Farm Gulnar."

He clicked the reins and they took off, the cart jerking with every bump on the hard earth, but as the donkey attested, he was an easy driver and they worked as a team, not master and beast.

It wasn't long before they were into the farmland. The sun was warm, but the cold bite of fall was on the wind. Mack set her eyes at the endless land dotted by farmhouses, barns, and stables. Farmhands and their oxen moved slowly through the stubbled fields, preparing to sow winter wheat and barley. Far in the distance, the imposing stone ramparts held Aman-Kala in its arms, amazing her still that they had been built at all. People said that there was a longer wall being built in China, but she found it hard to believe. Breathing was easy in this cloistered expanse. Out in the farmlands, the thrum and scratching of the wildlife was soft on her and she asked herself, again, why she didn't come outside the city more often.

The driver shifted in his seat. They had been silent for too long.

"Good harvest," she said. "Exports will be high this year."

"An easy plague year outside, too. They've got money to buy." His hands busy with the reins, he raised his eyes to the heavens instead. "Ya Allah! Make the outsiders safe, so that we will be safe." Looking over his shoulder at Jabal, he asked, "What about that one? Will we take him to the border when we're done at the farm?"

"No, back with us."

"Where you from, outsider?"

Jabal looked past him to the boundary wall in the distance. "I am from everywhere. I was a sea merchant, now a trader."

A trader. The smuggling looked too easy on him.

"Better I ask where your women live." The driver chuckled.

There was a long pause, then, "France."

Mack said nothing, hoping the driver would ask instead, and she was not disappointed.

"Long way. What does a Frank have to sell to us, we who have everything?"

"Everyone talks about the city that mastered the plague and I wanted to see for myself."

"You'll never leave Aman-Kala now you know what it means not to fear the plague years. Bring your family to us and raise your children among our honourable people. Ahlan wa sahlan!"

Mack turned, watchful for any longing for a woman left behind, but there was nothing.

He returned her gaze. "Maybe there will be family here for me instead."

The driver laughed again. "Our women are the most beautiful and virtuous in the world."

Mack faced the front, feeling sick at her ugly, old self, and wishing the game he was playing would not tug on her loneliness, and, truth be told, the last shreds of her vanity.

"And you, Detective Mack?" Jabal asked.

She shook off her thoughts. "I lived a good part of my young days out here in the farmlands with an Irish family, immigrants escaping the plague."

"You took their name?"

"Mac Aodhagáin, yes, but no one ever called me anything but Mack."

"A good life?"

It had been the only peace she had ever known, but she rarely shared that secret and deflected with another grief. "Coming out here meant leaving my family in the city behind."

"Your mother must have missed you," he prompted.

"That family died of the plague long before. By family, I meant the two I survived with in the alleys of Aman-Kala before the city was safe."

"What happened to them?"

"One died. The other, Rivka, never forgave me for abandoning them and left Aman-Kala before the boundary walls were closed. Rivka says she's still angry, but comes back here from Baghdad to see me often enough."

"And the one who died?"

"Danyal. He died." She said it flat, like it did not matter, but the driver gave her a sharp nod, sharing in the pain they all carried from those days.

The Boundary Gate came into view. The keepers' farm was not too far off along the boundary road. The farms were well-thought out; she gave the city that. Nestled against the wall on one side and encircled by tall, swaying cypresses on the other, the farms were protected from wind in the winter and sun in the summer. The rat hutches would be stacked high among the trees and she readied herself for them.

On the lane leading into the farm, two men loaded cages of rats onto a horse-drawn truck, while another tied the cages down with rope. The donkey became upset when they got close, and Mack touched her flask for assurance.

The driver stopped short of the farm. "I'll let you off here. Shahzadati doesn't want to go any further."

"We need you to wait for us."

"I'll be at the sharbat stalls beside the Gate."

They got down and waved the driver off. Mack turned away from the truck, but had already seen there were too many rats in each cage. They were clambering over each other, biting at the wire, noses pushed out, claws grasping, whiskers twitching. The chattering closed in around her and she bunched her shoulders against it.

The lane ended at a large, dusty courtyard set among the trees, the house, and outlying buildings against the wall. Towers of wood and wire rat hutches loomed within the trees. These, at least, were quiet and not overcrowded.

A tall, slim man in dusty work clothes, head uncovered except for his skull cap, stood up from a grouping of stools and a shabby low couch set out in the shade of the trees. A small ceramic brazier kept a kettle of water hot while a small teapot balanced on top.

He made his way over to them. The three other men did not give him a second look, carrying on with their conversation while sipping from tea glasses. They did not behave like men helping a friend grieve. One seemed out of place in his finely wrought clothes; his bright blue and green turban threaded with gold stark against his Norse complexion. Mack could just hear him regaling the others with the details of a profitable marriage he had arranged for his useless daughter.

She pulled out her badge before the man approaching could speak. "Assalamu alaykum. Hisn al-Madini? May I talk to you about Joe?"

On seeing her badge, he reached behind a dismantled rat hutch, pulled out a dusty sky-blue turban, and placed it half-cocked on his head. "Not Joe here. Her name is Jaleh."

Mack dutifully repeated the prayer instated by The Mosque as the rat policy went into place. "May the Sacred Keepers enjoy the shade of God's throne."

"Amin." His voice cracked with emotion and he wiped his eyes with the heel of his hand, smearing dirt across an already dirty face. With the smear, his tears, and his lopsided turban, he looked the mess a man in mourning should.

"We're investigating her murder, sir. I'm Detective Derya Mack." She gestured to Jabal. "This man, Jabal ibn Abi Faria, is helping me."

"Don't 'sir' me. We're not like that out here. I'm Hisn to

everyone." His face screwed up as he fought back tears. "Those mullas won't let me see her."

"They have to prepare her for the funeral procession tomorrow."

"Jaleh left here for town and never came back. I was preparing meals for the rats and never got to say goodbye. I should be able to see my woman and not just shrouded and under a velvet drape before they put her in the ground."

"I wish I could help."

Hisn jammed his turban on straight. "You want to sit?"

The men on the platform showed no inclination to move, but the one with the useless daughter kept his eye on Hisn.

"We've been sitting on a donkey cart for too long." She slapped her rear. "It's fine."

Hisn punched out a laugh at her gesture, then sniffed. "What can I do?"

"What's her full name?"

"Jaleh Dokht-i-Feryedun." His eyes softened.

Mack reached out and put a hand on his arm. "I'm sorry. I have to ask. You knew she was gambling?"

"Jaleh liked that jinn tavern."

"You didn't mind?"

He shrugged. "She had her half of this place. I have mine."

"They say she won a lot."

The man with the useless daughter snorted.

"She didn't?"

Hisn eyed the man behind him, then turned back to her, his resentment clear. "She lost all of this year's gold before I spent my first fals."

"How did she keep gambling, then?"

"Guild loan."

Mack let herself hope. An unapproved and usurious guild loan, then killed for not paying it back. The amirs would hand over whoever committed a violation of this magnitude. One did not loan money to a keeper one handed it over when requested as required charity. But that would not explain why the killer left her purse.

"Who did she go to for the money?"

"Musfik, Amir Pasha's dahbashi. She cursed his name day and night as if it wasn't her who gambled."

She knew Musfik. Old guild man. As a child, he had worked under the Pasha's father but never rose higher than a minor dahbashi in all those years. He was reckless enough to order the killing of a keeper. The case was looking better every moment.

Jabal walked away, inspecting the hutches as if it were his job.

"What's he doing?" Hisn pointed, still angry. "Detectives don't inspect us. We keep this place right. We've got our license."

"Just curiosity." But she wondered herself. Turning back to Hisn, she started, "Where…"

"You!" He yelled at Jabal. "You're upsetting them!"

The rats screeched and scrambled at Hisn's yelling. Mack pulled out her flask and took a swig.

Jabal lifted his head from a hutch with a look of apology. Backing off, he wandered over to where the men were seated and spoke to them. One man laughed. Jabal sat down and took tea when offered.

Hisn seemed unhappy with that, as well, but returned his attention to Mack.

"Where did she keep her money?"

"I told you, Jaleh was broke. A Council man was out here with one of those Mosque mullas to take their share of her inheritance. They broke open her strongbox. I told them, but they had to see for themselves there was nothing in it."

Mack edged towards the open front door of the house. Maybe there was smuggling going on, but now she also wondered if he was hiding more of that Abbasid gold. "Who owns the farm now?"

He followed, trying to get in front of her. "Rat Policy says it all comes to me." He got in the door and faced her. "This was my father's place."

"Your father was among the first awarded a farm?"

"He was. It's our family's legacy."

"How did she get half of it?"

"Demanded it in her dowry."

"And your parents agreed?"

A cloud passed over his face. "We met later in life, but Jaleh demanded a dowry like she was a prized virgin. I almost lost her because of them." He teared up again. "She was a tough one. More a rajula than a woman. I fell hard for her. And somehow she wanted me."

And the dowry, Mack thought, but said, as she looked past the door for signs of smuggling, "Sounds like a good woman."

"I wouldn't say that." He chuckled, wiping away tears with the back of his hand, and stepped towards her little by little, walking her away from the door. "But we had a good run."

Hearty farewells came from the seated men. Jabal was standing.

Mack considered asking about the Alp, but was sure he knew. This kind of woman would rub it in his face. He had motive. She had seen many a man honestly grieve over the wife he had killed. The Norse one with the useless daughter was still eyeing them. If Hisn had done it, she would have to come back when his friends were not around to get that story out of him. And she was going to come back to get inside that house.

"Do you know what happened?"

Putting her hand over her heart and bowing her head, she said, "I think a card game gone wrong, but I may need to return to tie things up."

"Always welcome," he replied, bowing his head but keeping a hard eye on Jabal as he made his way to them.

Once Mack and Jabal were beyond the trees on the lane back to the boundary road, she said, "I got two good leads. She owned half the farm. Took it out from underneath the family. The husband or the family could have killed her for it, the Alp, or both." She looked squarely at Jabal. "Not once did he ask me who killed her. Then there's also the matter of unpaid guild loans."

"I was finding out about the couple from his friends," he interrupted excitedly, "and I can tell you for all his tears, that man did not love his wife."

7

DAY THREE

JABAL SAT on a bench beside Ben Yacoub's stall, drinking sharbat from a hammered copper cup, looking as if he'd had a long night. With Wada, probably.

"Enjoying that?"

He raised the cup to Ben Yacoub, standing at the ready inside his stall. "This delicious cordial is all a man needs."

Swallowing a retort, Mack turned her attention to Ben Yacoub. "Labas sana?"

Jabal got up and stood beside her.

"Alhamdulillah, Detective Mack. Labas?"

She gestured "only a little" with her fingers. "Two nights ago, someone from The Water Wheel came by here for a sharbat."

"Sal. They ordered basil seed."

"Why did they come here? Not Humayn?"

"A special order. I knew who for immediately. Basil seed and lime, no rose. Humayn wouldn't make it without rose for the man." He looked down the alley toward Janub Kocha as if he could see Humayn's stall from there. "Stubborn. He'll lose his trade."

"How often does this customer come here?"

"Every day for a week now. A large young man with striking green eyes, kohled. Always waiting for me to open. Didn't come today, though."

"Did he give you a name?"

"Never. But he held himself like a guild man, despite being an outsider."

"What made you think outsider?"

"I had to speak caliphal Arabic to him."

"Anything else?"

"He had a hard face. No caring in it." He gestured toward Jabal. "A fighter like this one. But this outsider here, he has some caring, and he understands a bit of our patter."

Jabal shifted. She glanced at him and saw anger flash across his face.

"Did this man kill the keeper?" Ben Yacoub asked.

"You heard about her murder?" Jabal asked as if he were catching the old man out.

Mack winked at the sharbat seller.

Ben Yacoub inclined his head. "You're not from these parts, so you don't know everyone'll be at her funeral prayer and procession today. May The Keepers enjoy the shade of God's throne."

Jabal was mollified, but Mack wanted to know why being complimented in that way made him angry. She had known men who travelled the world who would have received an acknowledgement of a caring nature with humble gratitude.

"If he returns, what do I do?" Ben Yacoub asked.

She could not imagine a hired killer remaining in the city and, so, within the reach of The Tribunal. "He won't come back, but if he does, treat him as usual and send word to my office or The Water Wheel." She put her hand over her heart. "May God reward you."

Mack looked up at the sky, then at Jabal. "We're late. The Keepers Funeral Prayer will be called soon. We can still make it if we hurry."

Jabal asked, "How are we going to find Hajja Marwa?"

"Every last scholar on The Mosque payroll will walk behind that bier. We can pull her aside or go to the grave and find her there."

The call came sooner than she hoped. It began from The Treaty

Mosque, one lone angelic voice lying to her, echoed by other callers, blanketing the city with empty promises of another, better life. But this call, altered by The Mosque when the rat policy came in, added another layer of bitter piety. "Hurry to The Keepers Prayer. Hurry to their Blessed Return."

People streamed from every part of the quarter on their way to Treaty Mosque, choking Janub Kocha. It would be the same in the other quarters of the city. The crowd moved inch by inch. Jabal was at her back, his arms out on either side, protecting her from being groped, as if she had no practice elbowing a man in the chest. She reproached herself not coming earlier, knowing it would be like this. Now she would have to use her badge to force their way into the courtyard and get close enough to the procession to pull Hajja Marwa aside.

The crowd stopped moving, but they were still too far away to see the procession. She held up her badge at the price of curses and shoves, but they made it to the courtyard encircling the mosque.

Thousands of people stretched out around the vast courtyard and down Janub Kocha, all in their best clothes and well-doused with rose and orange water. They were under no obligation. They came in gratitude to the keeper for her work, no matter what kind of woman she had been.

A headache was coming on and Mack pulled out her flask, not caring that she was on mosque grounds.

Around her, voices hissed, "Haram sana!"

The next call to stand in line for the keeper's funeral prayer came and she held up the flask to disapproving stares and took a long drink. Those near her moved away as the crowd shuffled into concentric lines facing the mosque and not Mecca.

"My God," Jabal exclaimed. "Is the mosque Mecca in this city?"

"Only if a keeper's body is inside." She took another sip. "Do you know how to do a funeral prayer?"

He leaned in close. "Yes."

Her ear tingled with his whisper and, warmed by the grappa, she shivered with pleasure.

Callers stationed on platforms staggered from the mosque down to the kochas below carried the imam's prayer from within the mosque to the furthest worshipper. The four takbirs were called and their arms rose and fell in unison with each "Allahu akbar." Then they held their hands out in supplication, sealed the prayer with greetings over each shoulder, and it was over. At least the funeral prayer was quick.

The procession would begin at the southern entrance as a gesture to the poorest region of the city, so Mack and Jabal would not have to wait long for Hajja Marwa.

First out of the mosque were two Zanj Guards of the Empire, the Walinzi wa Himaya, dressed for battle in gleaming mail and helmets, swords by their side. They stood for a moment in the grand blue portico beneath the carved honeycomb muqarnas, then separated, moving to opposite sides of the entrance.

Following them, Amir Pasha and Amir Alami did the same. Pasha was dressed in his finest. Despite the distance, Mack could see the glint of gold in his guild turban. Alami may have dressed more respectfully, but it was Pasha who took care of the poor, whereas Alami stayed just within the line of brutality permitted by The Treaty. People said Alami's mother was a jinn, but that kind of shortsighted greed was entirely human. Pasha's father had been the same. She reconsidered the idea that Alami was breaking into Pasha's territory.

The four leaders of the Mercantile Congress followed, two by two, stopped under the muqarnas, then took their places beside the amirs.

The four Tribunal judges emerged in the same formation, each wearing black taylasan cloaks over white robes, with black hoods covering their white turbans.

Jabal gripped her shoulder so hard Mack gasped. But she had seen her, too. Not Hajja Marwa. Qadia Marwa. Marwa was no simple scribe or scholar, but a Tribunal judge. Impossible. She searched the others' faces. Qadi Abu Mu'min was missing and Marwa stood in his place for the South Quarter Tribunal. Was old Abu Mu'min sick?

They had expected her to be one of the straggling minor scholars, easily pulled out of the procession to be questioned. The only way to her now would be to demand a meeting in her office under some pretence and hope she would talk. She should. Unless she planned to step aside, she would be a witness to the very crime she would lead through an admission hearing, then sentencing mediation.

The four governing Imams, two Shia and two Sunni, had come out and each stood hand-in-hand with a community elder. The eight wore matching white turbans and black wool robes with right lapels so wide they were thrown over the left shoulder, symbolizing the merciful veiling of sin.

All turned to greet the body. Four Keepers Council leaders walked beside the pallet carried by men from each quarter of the city. Joe's husband, Hisn al-Madani, walked behind them. The crowd swayed at the sight of the keeper's body draped in the heavy velvet embroidered with verses of the Quran in gold thread. Hands held up to the heavens, they moaned prayers for the keeper's soul. The other leaders followed the procession of the body down the encircling stairs of the mosque; behind them were lesser city officials, scribes, administrators, minor scholars, and all those who had prayed within. The procession would circle the mosque itself, stopping at each portico, before making its way to the graveyard.

Without Marwa to interview today, the loan was the only lead to follow. But Mack would not question Musfik himself, rather his superior. Reckoning that Amir Pasha's amirzade would not be at the procession, but standing in Pasha's stead until he returned, Mack would ask her why one of their dahbashis made a loan to a keeper or worse.

If the killing came down to an illegal loan that ended in murder, the amirzade would hand over Musfik to The Tribunal, and the killer, if he was still in the city. She reassured herself it did not matter if Marwa did not recuse herself; the judge would be ordered to handle the case only one way. There would be secret diplomacy between The Guild, The Mosque, and The Keepers Council establishing the murder as a grave anomaly to be resolved by banishment of the perpetrators and the judge would be forced to go along.

And if Hisn killed his wife over the Alp? No worry there, either. Straightforward case.

But she did worry, and could not ignore that Jabal was unlikely to be following her around and tickling her ear if the keeper was killed over jealousy or a loan.

Hisn was hiding something at the keepers' farm. The smuggling nagged at her. Abbasid gold to keep the mullas from taking their share? What could Jabal have to do with all that? The only thing Mack knew for sure was that she needed time to clear her head about Jabal if she was going to sort this out.

"I've got to do something on my own," she told him.

"Not on the case." His voice was a low growl. "Not without me."

She gave him a smile that amounted to a pat on the head. "Go back to The Water Wheel. I'll find you there."

8

MACK LEFT Jabal behind without waiting to see what he would do. Walking down Janub Kocha, she turned in the opposite direction of Amir Pasha's compound. There was a deep alcove a few doors down and she hid in the shadows, watching to see if he came after her. People streamed past, but Jabal never appeared. She stepped into the stream and took the next turn to head back up to the heights of the city, and the compound, using only alleys and narrow passages between buildings.

The unpainted door to Amir Pasha's compound was like any other. Only an elaborate calligraphic "P" painted at eye level on the splintered wood gave a clue to what might lie beyond. One might still not know, except for the young guard in a leather cuirass standing beside the door, a battle-ready sword on his back and a dagger meant for close fighting at his hip. Mack held out her badge and he let her through without a question.

Inside the dimly lit reception hall, another guard stood facing the door. He was a small, sturdy man, the kind who could do a lot of damage.

"Yes?" The guard settled into a relaxed, but ready posture.

Mack held out her badge again. "I am here to see the amirzade."

"What is your business?"

"Do you think the amirzade would want you to know my business?"

The guard rolled his eyes and gestured to another standing beside the wide, arched entrance to the courtyard.

"Take her to Dahbashi Musfik's office."

Mack stiffened. "I'm here to see the amirzade."

"Everyone is at the funeral. You may speak to one of Dahbashi Musfik's sarbazen or leave."

So Musfik was not there. That was something at least, but she was not prepared to question his men. She protested, "This is an odd way to treat a badged detective. The amir has always had his people open their doors to us."

"We are opening a door." He gestured toward the courtyard. "The dahbashi's door."

The guard beside her made ready to show her out should she decline. She needed a lie, another case or question to present to the sarbazen, or she would have to leave now. There was no asking them about the loan. Or was there? It would not be clean and easy like speaking to the amirzade. It would be dirty, and maybe that was better. Dirty might make someone expose themselves without realizing. She could let slip that smuggling was involved or that Jabal had a hand in this. It would not be diplomatic, but if the amir wanted diplomacy, his guards should have treated her badge with more respect.

Mack nodded in agreement and was led to a tiled courtyard open to the cold, clear sky above. The sun shone on the deep pond at its centre. The water was still, but she could see and feel the iridescent fish trapped beneath. A gnarled pomegranate tree, heavy with fruit, grew nearby. Pots of flowering plants were arranged near a pallet covered with carpets and pillows. Doors lined the arcades, with one grand arched double door at the far end, leading to where Amir Pasha would sit on sheepskins and hear the pleas of supplicants. Kurban, one of Musfik's sarbazen, stepped out of a nearer door to meet her. She grinned. Kurban was a fool. If anyone was going to make a mistake exposing them all, it would be him.

"Detective Mack. Ahlan, ahlan." Kurban bowed his head as she passed into the room.

Finely upholstered couches were set against plastered and limed walls. Small inlaid tables topped with copper trays stood before each. Four men lounged by steaming glasses of tea arranged around a backgammon board. They were deep into the game. An Indian man with long brown curls and a red-threaded black turban was near to winning. The seated men looked up, but did not bother to greet her.

She opened, "Playing games on such a day? And hardly a tear among you for the keeper."

Kurban moved past her into the room and remained standing so that she could not sit. "So pious! Isn't the keeper's husband still alive and breeding rats? This one, that one. What does it matter? We live plague free." He turned to the men. "Stand up and greet our respected detective."

They rose, two of them half-heartedly. The Indian man lifted his hand to his heart, then sat back down with the others.

"Brothers, this detective is one of the last from the old days." Kurban asked Mack, "Just you and Mehdi now? These young people today, upstarts all of them, never having tasted the plague, are still learning to respect The Treaty." He said the last as if she needed a reminder to keep within its boundaries.

In response, she reminded him of his place. "You were not born to the plague years in this city, and I knew you when you were an upstart."

Kurban slapped his chest. "No longer. Some day, I'll be Dahbashi, then Amirzade, then the Amir himself."

This one was nothing if not reliable. "Don't say that too loud," she scolded, "or you'll end up a dead sarbaz."

"Wise words, dear detective." He put his hand over his heart dramatically. "But no one is here to listen. Our beloved lady amirzade is in the funeral procession, taking up the rear." Kurban laughed. The men looked uncomfortable, but chuckled all the same.

She waited until the room quieted, then asked, "Where's Musfik?"

"Our illustrious dahbashi is off enjoying the pleasures of the flesh."

"Ah." She bowed her head. "Since you'll be Dahbashi Kurban soon, I might be better off talking to you."

Raw pride erupted on his face and he shifted to a stance as if he had the balls of a lion. "You are here about the keeper."

With no invitation to sit, Mack positioned herself near the door, a hand ready to grasp her dagger. "Who killed her?"

"The keepers are off-limits." Kurban gestured with a mocking expression of innocence. "We abide by The Treaty."

"Word is she was a gambler who got in over her head. Took out loans she couldn't keep up."

The mood changed in the room.

Kurban's mouth twitched, but he replied with a high hand, slipping in and out of caliphal Arabic. "Absurd. Amir Pasha would have given her whatever she needed out of his own pocket."

"It seemed an odd claim to me, too. But word is also that she was a proud woman. Would only use money she earned."

A sarbaz interrupted. "How is money you borrow money you earn?"

"If she gambled and won," the Indian sarbaz explained, "then paid back the loan, she will not have borrowed any money in the end. Better a loan than a handout."

The questioner nodded slowly. Another idiot. Handpicked by Musfik, no doubt, just like Kurban. She wondered how the Indian had got a place among them.

"The minds of women," Kurban offered. "Always a mystery."

With a half-cocked smile, she quipped, "I'm sure your mother would agree."

Kurban moved on her. Mack relaxed, her legs bowed and ready to let him fall under his own ill-thought power if needed. But he stopped short before her dagger was out of its sheath and laughed in her face as if he had submitted her instead of the other way around, then retreated. "You should apologize for mentioning my mother."

"I am sorry, deeply."

Kurban accepted it despite her mocking tone and crossed the room to sit down. She took it as an invitation and sat on the couch closest to the door.

"No one would be foolish enough to loan her money," Kurban said. "And harm her? It would mean banishment, or worse, if our amir handled it in-house."

"Fair." She brushed the matter off with her hands. "Well, you must have some opinion of who killed her. Tell me."

Kurban leaned in. "Irfan."

She did not place the name in the guilds. "Someone under Amir Alami?"

"Irfan is not his real name." He sat back, pleased with himself. "I cannot believe you are not in league with him. He and his gang hate the keepers as much as you."

Then she realized who he meant and did not like it. "Why would Irfan kill a keeper? Like you said, there's always one to take the place of another."

One of the sarbaz offered, "Symbolic act."

She saw the sense in it. Irfan despised the suffering of the rats as much as she did. But he was irrational in his idealism, as if standing on corners decrying the horrors of rat farming would convince The Mosque to change its approach to controlling the plague. All Irfan ever got for it was a mouth full of dung. But that also made him the perfect scapegoat for the murder of a keeper.

"I'll look into Irfan," she said. "But here's the thing: the keeper's husband said it was your dahbashi, Musfik, who loaned her money. He was named."

Kurban did not react with disbelief or anger. He reached over for his tea and took a sip. The air grew thick as everyone waited on him. He put his glass down. "There's money to be made in rat keeping. Perhaps Musfik put her in debt to get his hand in it." He smiled. "Alas, Irfan killed her."

The one who had said Irfan did it as a symbolic act gave Kurban a look like he wanted to smack the words back into his mouth. It seemed the Indian man was not the only intelligent one in the room, after all.

Kurban failed to notice the censure. "I wonder if our dahbashi will lose his position over it?" He gestured to the men in the room. "What will his poor sarbazen do without him?"

Putting the keeper in debt and taking a percentage would not amount to much, but most of their rackets were petty grifts that added up. And even if it were Musfik's plan alone, his sarbazen would pay the price along with him. "This is dangerous business for so little. You all are young enough not to know what plague was like, but old Musfik lived it and he's risking your lives to the plague world."

"We grew up reciting the names of lost family in our prayers each night and listening to the stories of the plague years at home and in madrasa like any other child of this city." She felt Kurban's sincerity. "We honour your generation and would not violate The Treaty."

"Kurban, do you believe that if Musfik goes down, you won't go with him? Arrange for me to see your amirzade. Musfik will be done for, and I'll tell her you helped me catch him."

Kurban shook his head. "Go get Irfan."

"You just implied you want Musfik out."

Instead of denying it, he said, "That's not the plan."

The one not so stupid after all stood up. "With all respect, Detective, go. Now." His advice was not only directed at her, but at Kurban, to keep his mouth shut.

She stood, not to leave, but to risk forcing Kurban to go further. "One last thing."

Kurban ignored his man's warning again. "Ask."

"There's someone trying to break into Amir Pasha's smuggling quota, eating into his territory, paying runners in gold."

The men fell still as one, so quiet she could hear their shallow breaths. Kurban's eyes woke up to what she had said and darted to his fellows, but they had nothing for him.

"If this is part of your plan to become amir someday, Kurban, you'll never survive it." Mack held up her hands. "I'm not breaking that case. But I'm not the only one who suspects the threat to the Amir is from within."

Kurban found his voice. "The Amir is well aware of who threatens him."

"If not you, who is it?"

"The Amir is well aware," Kurban repeated.

Then she understood. "Your game is to take advantage of the fall-out when it comes." Something flickered across his face before it settled into the hardness that comes before violence. She got him. Instead of backing from the room with her hand on her dagger, a desperate, unthinking urge drove her to find out if Jabal was involved. "Tell me if outsiders are in this. Tell me who is paying out the gold." She stepped towards him once more. "Tell me if the keeper's death is connected."

The Indian man was up in a shot and between them, leaning into her with a look of warning that he could not protect her if she stayed a moment longer. He gripped her arm and opened the door with his free hand, then pushed her out. Mack stumbled into the waiting guard outside, who pulled her arm up so high she tripped over feet as he dragged her through the courtyard and out to the alley. The reception guard sniggered as she passed.

9
————

Mack had yet to catch her breath, let alone come to terms with the forces that she had put in play with her reckless questioning, when a boy clutching a package almost ran into her. She stepped back to get out of his way, steadying herself as he regained his balance. But the package fell, the jar within breaking broken, exposing its contents.

"Eudes, what are you doing?"

The filthy, poorly clothed boy did not answer. He grabbed at the rough cloth, trying to cover the broken jar and its contents, but the pungent scent pervaded everything. Passersby ignored them, except some who sniped at them to move. Only a young scholar emerging from a small prayer hall shot a pinched-nosed look at the lump of loamy grains spilling out of the jar, seemingly not grasping its value. No Treaty-bound importer, city or guild run, would give a boy even a few grains of costly musk to carry to a buyer.

Nearly in tears, Eudes got the package tied up and turned to run away, but she grabbed him by the back of his robe. "Who has you carrying that?"

"No one!"

She reached for the package.

He twisted around, keeping it out of her hands.

"We're going to your father. He'll tell me."

Hand on the back of his collar, she drove the boy ahead of her down Janub Kocha. They threaded through the crowd only having to move aside once for a woman leading a camel laden with wares. As they passed the alley leading to The Water Wheel, she kept her eyes straight ahead, hoping Jabal was not nearby.

Suspects had got close to her before and she had no trouble keeping her head. Half the work was cultivating trust, whatever it took, and when she was younger, she did what she had to do and she enjoyed it. There was no need for Gad's voice to tell her she had gone too far. What was she doing, taking such a risk with Kurban to see through her suspicion about Jabal? There would be retribution for exposing Kurban, a message sent for her to keep quiet and it would not be pretty. And all to find out if Jabal was playing her for a fool?

One alley after another, they carried on, Mack reproaching herself and keeping a tight grip on Eudes' collar, until they reached a passage so narrow the weakened mud-brick walls of the buildings on either side touched overhead.

The boy moaned. "Let me go."

A woman with a basket under her arm saw them coming and ducked into an alcove so they could pass. As they drew near, Eudes twisted and broke her hold. Mack lost her balance and stumbled into the woman, both of them falling back against the door in the alcove. Eudes ran ahead, turning the corner to his parents' sliver of a home, no doubt to warn them she was coming.

The woman stared aghast down the passage as she brushed herself off. Folded squares of threadbare cotton were now a jumble in her basket. Some had fallen out and lay dirtied on the ground. Mack reached out to help, but the woman slapped her hand away, cursing, "Over the wall with those Franks!"

She left the woman sputtering over the dirty cloth and wishing Eudes and his family dead. Mack was short of cursing them herself. Letting the boy get involved in unsanctioned smuggling? It made no sense. Mathieu, the boy's father, was a nimble pickpocket, but conservative. He only worked the West Market, where the upper classes did not pay strict attention to their purses. The family never indulged with his gleanings, preferring to stretch what he got from one day's work as long as possible. Vero took in laundry. The children helped. Like everyone else in Aman-Kala, they paid their taxes before they ate. Little was left, but they made do.

Mack stopped at a low arched door with a fading outline of a light blue fleur-de-lis and hammered her fist against the rattling planks. The sound echoed through the alley. Josse opened the door partway. The girl was wearing only a thin tunic that did not cover her knobby knees, but her face and hands were smeared with grease and she smelled of mutton, rosemary, and garlic. The family was taking gold, but not in deep yet. Eat first, buy warm clothes later. Josse licked her fingers and Mack's stomach turned.

"Labas sana, Detective Auntie?" She greeted Mack in a sing-song voice as if her little brother had not just run in there and let them know she was coming.

"Get your father for me."

The girl left the door open and disappeared behind the mud-brick vestibule wall. "Papa! Detective Auntie Mack is here!"

Mack strained to listen to the voices within, but a couple of wasps flew past her out the door and their humming praise for having fed off the meat muffled the family's words. Pulling her flask from her bag, she took a sip and looked up, searching for their nest.

Vero appeared in the vestibule instead of Mathieu, her wrap hastily drawn around her, and put one hand on the jamb to block her way. "What do you want?"

"Tell him he is not in any trouble."

She heard shuffling.

Mack yelled through the door. "You're not in any trouble!"

There was thumping on the stairs. Vero leaned back to watch her husband escape, her hand still blocking the door, then faced Mack, smirking.

"Over the roof?"

Vero nodded.

Mack sighed. He could run roof to roof until he was halfway across the quarter.

"Did Eudes get here before me?"

"What about my son?"

Mack took a step forward. "Let's talk inside."

The woman did not move. "I said, what about my son?"

"Your son had a package."

"And?"

"Give me the name of whoever hired him to carry it."

Vero's only response was a look of bitter skepticism.

"Let me explain. You are smuggling outside Treaty sanctions. When The Tribunal gets hold of the case, it is going to come down on the smuggler and anyone who carried for them. No neighbourhood elder is going to be able to mediate your release."

Vero took a fearful step back.

"You know what a Treaty violation could mean. No coming back."

Still no answer.

"Walla, I'm trying to protect you." Mack paused, frustrated. "Have I ever done anyone wrong around here?"

She waved Mack into the vestibule, but no further.

"How did Eudes get that job?"

"Mathieu," she whispered. "He asked Eudes to run it for him. Mathieu carries, not the boy, that was only today."

"How did Mathieu get the job?"

"The man who ran the goods before, he died of plague, so Mathieu rushed to take his spot."

Mack froze. It had to be the same family Teddy told her about.

"Where did this man live, Vero?"

"West quarter, near the market."

The unsanctioned goods must be going around quarantine. If the musk deer had carried plague, the musk pod would, too. Eudes. She told herself that the boy had only just touched the grains, or maybe not even that. Mack frantically tried to remember. Maybe he had only wrapped it back up and never touched them at all. And she had only grasped him by the collar.

She reached out to Vero, then pulled her hand back before touching her. "Vero, go wash Eudes down. All of you. Wash your clothes. And don't touch that package."

Vero's face blanched, understanding. She rushed inside the house. Mack heard the children complaining, Vero yelling, a slap, then water sloshing. There was no time to heat water. The three could die of a chill trying not to die of the plague.

If Jabal is involved in any way, she thought, her fear turned to seething, *he will pay by my hand before I drag him before The Tribunal.* It became quiet within and she waited for Vero to return, anger giving her the clarity she needed for her next move.

Shivering and wrapped in a blanket, Vero seemed surprised to see Mack still there and tried to close the door on her. "You've warned us. We've washed. Now go."

"The musk has to go to Health. I have to call them in."

"And what do you think will happen to us if we don't deliver it? They'll think we stole it and then we're dead, anyway." She spat on the ground in fearful anger. "Might as well be plague!"

"You cannot deliver it. It's too dangerous."

"Don't you look at me like that. I'll put it in a new jar and take it to the man who bought it myself."

"Not the jar, Vero. The musk itself might be infected," Mack said through gritted teeth.

She understood and spat on the ground. "Mathieu!"

"I have to inform Health. They'll come immediately. Tell me where Eudes picked up the package. I'll go there and explain."

Vero's eyes hardened as she grasped just how far in her husband had got them wedged.

Mack wanted to drag the lot of them to the farmlands, the sweet air and wide-open spaces, and set them free into it. With the musk there, Health would report unsanctioned smuggling to The Tribunal. The questions would begin.

"Who is Elder here now?"

"Maha."

"She needs to mediate for you. I don't know how far this will fall out, but it's always better if your Elder walks in with you to Tribunal rather than be brought before her already sitting next to the judge."

"What can Elder Maha do? You said it yourself. No coming back." Eudes and Josse came up behind her and held onto her legs.

"Eudes, tell me where you picked the package up."

He looked to his mother for guidance.

She shook him off her leg. "Tell her."

"Behind the West Market," he said, his voice cracking. "A warehouse beyond the wool stalls. The door is green with a white rose."

"Vero," Mack said. "When the quarantine ends, if nothing comes of this, take whatever gold you've got left and get the family outside the city walls. Rent a small farm, tend your own animals, tend a fire with a full belly."

The woman pulled Eudes back to her, looking at Mack as if she were mad, and shut the door without another word.

10

Mack hurried to the nearest Health stall. She needed time. Time to accept the possibility there might be plague spreading in the city. To trust that Health would contain it. To consider what it would mean for The Tribunal and Health to corner the amirs. To gauge the risk to herself by having exposed Kurban's plan. And to answer what any of this had to do with her case.

The Health clerk leaned over the narrow counter, laughing and sharing barbs with the paper seller across the road. When he caught sight of Mack storming towards him, he straightened and disappeared. By the time she got there, he had returned with paper and a stylus.

"Assalamu alaykum." There was no humour in him now. "Suspected exposure?"

Mack showed him her badge, gave him the names and address, and told him about the musk.

His eyes widened as she explained. He answered with barely contained anger as he lifted the counter and unlatched the half-door. "I'll start quarantine. We've been told to take any suspected cases to the Director at Health."

"That's unusual," she said, concerned.

"Every last one involved will wish their mother had never lived."

She left him to it. But reporting suspected exposures to the Director was not standard practice. There had to be more outbreaks that were being kept quiet. If they did not already suspect the outbreaks were tied to smuggling, they would now. Health, backed up by The Tribunal, would knock on the amirs' doors within hours.

She allowed herself to hope that the Health and Tribunal investigation into the guilds would thwart whatever Kurban was planning to shut her up.

As for Jabal, Mack did not know how she would get him to talk. She hoped that when she saw him, it would fall into place, and set out to find him at The Water Wheel.

The afternoon call to prayer rang out as she entered the tavern. Resting her hand on the painted wheel on the swinging door, she let the noise of the drunken people within, their hard banter and raucous laughter, crowd her head with a near-deafening bliss.

Mack wove through a cluster of men and one woman to reach the games room. The woman was covered head to toe in a heavy wrap, as if she was going to the mosque and not a tavern, but she was holding her own with the men from the sound of it and made no move to heed the call. Instead, she lay a hand on the shoulder of one man to steady herself and cursed Mack for disturbing them. "May the plague snatch you!"

Mack was not insulted. She wanted nothing more than to pull the woman into her arms and bless her for being alive. All these people. The crowded, awful mess of them, alive and, she hoped, safe from the plague. She touched her heart in apology and went into the games room.

There was only one table of players and no Jabal. With nothing to do but wait, she returned to the bar. Every stool was full. Sal caught her eye and told a man at the bar to move. No one disobeyed Sal and Mack was grateful for the kindness. She needed a drink. Now. Sal poured a glass half full of grappa as Mack settled in. She gulped it down and handed it back.

Sal filled it again. "I've got to go in the back to pray. You okay to wait for another?"

"Go. May God accept your prayer."

The man next to Mack got up. She turned and found Wada taking his spot.

"How is the case?"

"Where's Jabal?"

"So you desire him after all." There was more than a touch of jealousy in Wada's voice.

"Talking about yourself?"

"Tetchy." Wada sucked her teeth, but conceded the ground. "Sal praying?"

She leaned over the bar and got the bottle out while Wada wiped the edge of the man's used glass with her hand. Mack dug around in her linen bag for her flask and touched the letter; she still had not sent it in.

"I will admit," Wada said as Mack filled her flask, "there are some men who make me long for attachment. Then they reveal a little thing about themselves and it passes. And so, Jabal is gone."

"Gone?" Mack sat up straight, feeling a tug that had nothing to do with missing her chance to force the truth out of him.

Wada took pleasure in her surprise. "Oh! Something more than desire!"

"Fuck's sake, Wada. He has a hand in this case somehow."

"That's why you are taking him everywhere with you?"

"You think that man was going to answer a direct question?"

Wada nodded in understanding. "No, not him."

"So what little thing did he reveal that you are happy to see the back of him?"

"I do not care for a man who acts as if he is the owner and judge of all that he sees."

"Then you must not like most men."

She laughed wryly. "This was different."

"How?" Mack sat forward.

"Why don't you tell me about the case instead?"

Mack wanted nothing more than to lay it all out for her, but no matter how many years they had shared between them, she always took care with what she revealed. In the end, there was no trusting jinn, and with Wada's attachment to him, no matter what she said, Mack certainly would not share her suspicions about Jabal.

"Tell me." Wada touched her hand. "Walla."

She smiled fondly at Wada's workaround. "Making an oath without the promise attached?"

"My oath is that I'm here for you. Not for myself. Not for Jabal."

Even a jinn could not break an oath without consequences, but "here for you" might mean almost anything and so changed nothing. She left Jabal out of it. "We questioned the keeper's husband. He told us she'd been getting into debt."

"How is that possible?"

"All her coin went to her Alp. Wouldn't take a handout."

Wada nearly spit out her drink. "She took handouts from me!"

"Did she know you paid the players to lose to her?"

"No one wins like that, not even professional gamblers."

"People lie to themselves. You capitalize on it."

Wada's dimple showed. "Who loaned her the money?"

"The husband said Musfik, Amir Pasha's—"

"Musfik, that grizzled letch!" she exclaimed, then leaned in, gleeful. "Amir Pasha will tear him to pieces."

"I love when the blood-hungry old jinn breaks through the surface."

"You do love me." Wada winked. "Now, tell me about the husband."

"I took him to be sincerely grieving. Said she was a hard woman, but he seemed to have a taste for that kind. She demanded half-ownership of the farm for her dowry and he gave it to her, though it was his family's to give."

"Good on her. She was due it."

Mack had not considered it until that moment, but Wada was right. It gave a shred of respect for the keeper to get a substantial dowry when so few women did. "But Jabal talked to the man's friends. They said her husband did not love her at all."

Wada sat up at that. "He must have killed her over the dowry and the Alp."

"He wouldn't be the first man to kill his wife, love her or not."

"Exactly." Wada sat back, pleased with herself, as if she had solved the case.

"There's something else." Mack could not give up on the smuggling angle, despite it being well out of her hands. "The gold coins."

Wada perked up, not in the least sorry that she had not solved the case after all.

"Mehdi said there is a new smuggler working outside Treaty boundaries and paying in gold."

"More gold has been coming through The Water Wheel than usual," Wada offered.

"How much?"

"A few chinks and flecks."

"You have any here?"

Wada stood. "Come with me."

They walked through the games room to her office. Wada lit the lamps set into niches in the wall and the old felted wall hanging came into view.

The strange animal depicted there moved with the light and shadow. A lizard stood tall, its scaled forelegs grasping a staff, while a snake-like tongue slithered out and stubby wings extended to fly. She had asked Wada about it before, but she only said, "Something I came across in Babylon," and Mack never knew if she meant the animal or its depiction.

The key turned in the safe and in a moment, Wada placed a casket on the table between them and opened it.

Mack dug through it and pulled out one gold chink after another. "Only a few, sah?" But most were rose-toned Zanj gold, mixed with copper. There were three large chinks that were not, just like the Abbasid gold. She looked at them in the light, but the chinks were too small to tell if the imprints were Abbasid or from another region of the world. "These recent?"

"No way to tell."

Mack took it as a yes.

"I don't believe this talk of unsanctioned smuggling," Wada said. "Why would I serve you local grappa if I could get cut-rate Indian rum? There's no smuggler. Nothing is coming through."

Time slowed as the meaning of what Wada said hit her. Mack straightened. "All the smuggling has dried up because the amirs are trying to isolate the illegal smuggler. Only one source of goods to track." She turned to pace the room. "Of course the amirs were aware of unsanctioned smuggling. Kurban, one of Musfik's sarbazen, as much as told me. He said that Amir Pasha knew, and when I asked about the smuggling, it did not go well. Musfik is involved, but he cannot be at the top or this would be over already. They would have killed him." She put a hand to her forehead. "I haven't had a minute to think. Of course, the amirs know. Health and The Tribunal have to know, too. They are all working together and none of us have heard a thing."

"Wait, Kurban?"

Mack backed up. "I tried to get in to see Amir Pasha's amirzade, ask if she approved of Musfik loaning money to a keeper, but only got as far as Musfik's sarbazen. Kurban was doing all the talking. He said a lot, but I only now understand what he meant."

"But you said Musfik killed her over the money!"

"Cases, Wada, they take what turns they take."

"Now her death is connected to the smuggling?"

"I can suspect what I like, but I can't do anything about it."

"Why?"

Mack decided to give her something. "There have been plague outbreaks."

Wada stiffened.

"They are contained," she fibbed, depending on Health to control them. "But the point is that the infection may have come from someone taking smuggled goods around quarantine."

Wada let out a shaky breath. "You are right. The amirs cannot be involved. They would never permit it. So who is running Musfik?"

Mack held back, but the jinn read it on her.

"You suspect Jabal."

"Involved somehow." Mack trod carefully despite Wada's insistence she was done with him. "He's a trader."

"But Mack, the man has no respect for our system. He thinks we are too soft on those who commit wrongdoings. Why would he say that if he were a wrongdoer himself?"

"It doesn't matter. Whoever it is will be caught now." Unless the smuggler had already left Aman-Kala. "Wada, how long has Jabal been gone?"

"Not long. He came back here after the procession. We fought about Aman-Kala, like I said. I told him to get out."

It was not enough time to reach the border walls, but he would be through before long. She had no reason to think that the border walls had been closed. There was no chasing after him. Mack only hoped he had not left.

"Listen," Wada added, "If you find Jabal before they do, bring him to me. If he's done something, I'll make him admit to it. Then we'll turn him over to The Tribunal."

She was done with him, after all. Mack let down her guard a little, welcoming Wada's offer. "Agreed."

The first signs of a headache that alcohol could not control were coming on and she stood to go. She needed to lie down and be quiet. She needed Teddy's poppy seed tea. It was too early to sleep, but she could not see her next move.

Wada stood with her, looking stunned. "God help us and our city." She held Mack's hand for a moment before pushing her out of the office and shutting the door behind her.

11

———————

Mack trudged home. The sun was low on the horizon. It would be dark soon, and there would be quiet. There would be poppy tea. Her headache was becoming the kind that comes with spikes driven in behind the ears and sometimes straight through the top of her head, but it was not there yet. She could still make it.

But as she got closer, the chittering and screeching prayers of the animals turned into cries, but not of their own suffering. A few alleys away from home, the cries of people drowned out the creatures. She broke out into an old woman's plodding run, out of breath before she started, and finally came around the last corner.

Several families wailed and scrambled to collect their possessions, clothes, pots, bags of bulgur and beans, and the few pieces of furniture they owned. Teddy, his daughter, Yeru, and others tried to help, but the neighbours were grieving and furious. Teddy put his hands out, hoping to calm one man, but he would not accept it.

A call came out. "There she is!"

To a one, they turned toward her. Several ran to Mack, others followed, surrounding her. One woman grabbed her by her lapels. "You did this!" Mack teetered under her force, but someone behind her pushed her back up. Each of them screaming, accusing her of putting them out.

"Selfish woman!"

"Where will we sleep?"

"My children!"

"Sell us out for information, will you?"

This was Kurban, striking at her through her neighbours, destroying their trust in her, all because she let him know she saw through his plan to unseat Musfik. It was her fault and she took it from them.

Mack shook in their hands. Spit dripped from her face. Someone ripped her turban off and threw it down the road. Teddy stayed on the edges of the crowd, trying to reason with them. She wanted to tell him to stop; she deserved whatever they would bring to her for this hurt and more and welcomed the humiliation for everything she had ever done and had never righted. But Yeru took hold of the women, one after the other, until she had a firm grip on Mack's arm.

"I've got you!"

Crushing guilt drove the spiking pain straight in, cracking her head open. She fell to her knees, then onto her side. Yeru followed her down, forcing the women back with her body. Mack's cheek pressed into the gritty earth. She wept soundlessly, her mouth slack and drooling. Hands were on her. Her head in a lap. Then a blessed drop of poppy seed oil fell onto her tongue, then another, and another. The droning voices became more distant. The pain of their pain slipped away and the creatures' voices retreated under the floorboards, into the rafters, and scuttled around corners.

"Derya." A voice came from afar.

She lay in the embrace of the poppy and did not answer.

"Derya."

Yeru's voice. Her eyes focused. Those who had attacked her now sat in a circle around her. Touched by the near-setting sun, they shimmered golden in its light. Behind them, a Sufi stood in shadow. He had thrown his head back to the heavens, his arms stretched to encompass the world, his palms open in prayer. The golden light fell upon him, and his prayer rose, luminescent, and swept through them all. Its touch reached her and she met it with skepticism, wondering why those Sufis kept trying, thinking they wanted her among them, when if they knew who she really was, they would throw her to the side of the road. She tossed the prayer away. He lowered his hands and shook his head sorrowfully.

"Derya," Yeru whispered her name.

"I'm here," she answered.

Yeru put another drop of the poppy oil on her tongue and the muscles her neck softened and unclenched.

"I can sit."

The two nearest supported Mack as she raised her head from Yeru's lap, then sat up.

Yeru placed a hand on her cheek. "Let's get you home."

Those with their hands on her rose to leave. Mack searched their faces. Despite their care and support in her collapse, their distrust remained plain on their faces.

One spat on the ground now that she was back to herself.

"Come now," Yeru said to Mack, drawing her away.

They left the neighbours, some still cursing her, others back to gathering their things, and passed the young Sufi who had prayed over her. He leaned against a wall, watching her go.

Choking on the words, she called back to him, "Tell your shaykh I'm never coming back."

"We will wait for you!"

She gave her back to him just as she had done when his shaykh, all those years ago, had tried to pull her away from Rivka with promises they could teach her to hear the voices without pain. It was a gift, the shaykh said, a blessing, an opening onto the reality of reality itself.

The shaykh had taken hold of one hand, and Rivka pulled at her other. Seeing she was torn between them, the shaykh offered them both a warm place to sleep, food, and safety.

But Rivka hissed, "There'll be a bed, but no safety in it!"

Unwilling to abandon Rivka, Mack refused, only to leave her and Danyal a few years later to work on the farm.

She had rejected the Sufis. She had betrayed Rivka and Danyal. Every investigation exposed secrets and harms. Now she had betrayed her neighbours. This was her lot.

The Sufi brother must have prayed for her again; she felt the prayer's fingers touch her shoulder and brushed them off.

A man appeared beside them. Mack turned a poppy-muddled head to look at him. It was Musfik's sarbazen, the Indian man with the curls and red-threaded black turban.

"I never got your name," she said, her tongue only slightly lolling.

Yeru tugged at her, but Mack stopped.

"You got our dahbashi's message."

"Musfik, not Kurban?"

"Kurban only told Musfik what he wanted him to hear."

"And Musfik shut me up."

The sarbaz did not answer her question, only saying, "Musfik will see you, now you understand."

"Understand he'll put innocent people out on the road?"

"You did that."

There was no answer to what was true.

"Nadeem," he said.

"What?"

"My name." He looked at Yeru, then at Mack.

She unwound her arm from Yeru's and kissed her hand. "Go."

When Yeru was far enough away, Nadeem leaned in. "The amirzade wanted me to tell you, quietly, that Amir Pasha will not stand for his men breaking The Treaty."

"Kurban already told me this."

"I was asked to assure you that the Amir knows about everything and everyone."

He said it like she knew everything and everyone, when all she had were suspicions.

"He has a sarbaz who reports to him in every dahbash crew."

"And you are one."

He did not acknowledge it, but affirmed again, "The Guild will respect The Treaty."

"Has Dahbashi Musfik been informed?"

Nadeem recited a verse from the Quran. *"They thought they were deceiving, but it was God who deceived, indeed, God is the best deceiver."*

She smiled at how apt the verse was for this whole cursed thing and sealed the recitation with the words, "And God speaks the truth."

"Let's go, then?"

Still unsteady, she reeled back from it and he caught her. With a hand at her elbow, they carried on to Amir Pasha's compound.

As he reached for the door to the compound, she asked, "Will my neighbours ever trust me again?"

"You must mean will they be put back in their houses?"

"Yes." Trust was something else.

"That depends on you."

12

———

The reception guard was different. This one looked like Mack in her youth, broad shouldered with brutal hands, ready for anything. She took no notice of Mack and waved them on without a word. The other one was there as they entered the courtyard and watched as Nadeem led her along.

Musfik sat on one of the low couches, one arm thrown over a cushion, the other stroking his hennaed beard. He declined to greet her, raising a hand to Kurban. "Tea."

Kurban bowed and exited the room without turning his back.

Mack stepped past Nadeem into the room, asking, with a poppy-loosened tongue, "You made him tea-boy. So you heard Kurban went too far?"

Nadeem murmured a warning.

"Kurban was out of place to speak for me when you visited. Everyone needs a guiding hand now and again." But he looked at her with meaning when he said it. "Let us begin again, formally. Detective Mack, marhaba bik."

Yet he did not stand, as would befit a formal greeting. She remained standing until Nadeem pushed her suddenly into the room, and she made an instinctual, but clumsy, attempt for her knife.

"No need for that." Musfik gestured to a spot on the couch diagonal to him. "Please sit, Detective Mack."

The seat he chose required her to crane her neck to speak to him. Musfik did not need this performance to put her at a disadvantage; what he had done to her neighbours achieved that. She craned her neck as he desired, not shifting to sit more comfortably, and waited for him to tell her what she would have to do.

"I understand you have the keeper's case."

"Yes."

"You came here to ask questions, so ask them now."

Mack bit down to articulate her question politely. "Why did you loan Joe money to gamble? Please."

"You understand now that while your badge is respected here, there are limits to your influence. We owe you no more than what I will answer." He leaned forward to emphasize his words. "We commit to The Treaty, but the lines of its boundaries are not always bright. As long as nothing threatens power sharing between the guilds and outright violations are avoided, we are free. You, too, Detective Mack. You, too, work around it."

Of course she did. Everyone did. The language of The Treaty assured it. Everyone was meant to look the other way as long as The Treaty's principles were not affected, but this did not include loaning money to a keeper, let alone killing one. She chose her words with care. "By The Treaty, you had an obligation to give her the money. Loaning her money is grave wrongdoing, possibly a violation."

Musfik's eyes shone with satisfaction. "Yes. I loaned her money, but she paid me back."

"She complained to her husband about owing you."

"Because she was not aware."

Before Mack could ask what he meant, Kurban returned with steaming glasses of tea on a hanging tray and placed two before them, then retreated to stand beside Nadeem. Musfik gestured for her to go ahead. She picked one up, thumb on the lip, one finger on the bottom, afraid she would drop it, but she took a sip without trouble and put the glass down.

"Her 'Alp', as she called him, is one of my men. He gave back to me all she had borrowed. I let him keep what was not mine."

"Her winnings."

"Yes."

"Why did you put a spy with her?"

"He was no spy. They were true lovers. You would see him among us if not for his grief."

"If I understand, Dahbashi, Joe showered money on him and got into debt. She came to you for help. The cycle began."

"Yes." He sat back, tea in hand. "I did not have her killed for not paying her debt, as there was no debt. We agree The Keepers are a bright line of inviolability The Guild would never cross."

All the while, he made Joe believe she was in debt to him. Without crossing that bright line, he put her in a position where she could not refuse a request to smuggle through the farm wall. But Mack could not press him on that and if she wanted her neighbours to get back into their homes. Instead, she lowered her head in deference. "Respected Dahbashi, I am worried about my neighbours—"

"There is more," he interrupted.

Misunderstanding, she asked, "What can I do so they can return home tonight?"

"No." He looked as if she were a child. "I mean, there is more to give you. I asked you here to deliver Joe's killer to The Tribunal."

She stood suddenly, confused.

Musfik rose with her. "Nadeem, go get the man."

Nadeem returned in only a moment and there he was, just as Wada had described. The intense, kohled green eyes, red beard and Sogdian turban. Wada was right, the man was Sogdian through and through, and no labourer, either. His clothes were merely a costume for the job.

"Meet Turghar," Musfik said.

She asked, "May I ask why you have him or should I leave that to looking the other way?"

"You were told to question Irfan, that street preacher for the salvation of rats. Irfan hired Turghar to kill her. He wanted to put all the keepers in a state of fear for their own lives until they refused to breed rats." Musfik gestured to Kurban. "After you left, Kurban went to the preacher and convinced him his plan to terrorize the keepers would never work and to hand over the hired killer."

This was a lie. Mack would have to question Irfan all the same, but she was sure it would come to nothing. Musfik or someone he was covering for hired had Turghar and it was connected to the smuggling. This was no poppy-blurred supposition. She knew it in her bones.

Musfik leaned in. "Irfan agreed to give up his plan only if we assured the judge that the killing was over a card game, no more. That is not our wish. But there is always a way around things. As long as you do not say that Irfan hired Turghar to kill the keeper, there is no harm in saying he is associated with the preacher."

The dahbashi did not even try to hide the fact that turning in Turghar and throwing suspicion on Irfan served his needs. There was nothing Mack could do about it now. She would have to agree to say what Musfik wanted. "I can honour that."

"You should. Especially now you understand what happens when you challenge us."

"When I do this, you will put the families back in their homes tonight?"

"Yes. I will send Nadeem with you to be certain you follow our instructions. He will handle the matter of your neighbours."

With Nadeem there, she could not risk warning the court when they dropped Turghar off at Tribunal House. Instead, she would go to The Mosque before The Tribunal hearings began in the morning and see Qadia Marwa in her office. See how she reacted to the information and get her talking.

Nadeem took Turghar by the arm.

"Will he confess?" she asked Musfik.

"I am assured he will."

Nadeem and Mack left the compound with Turghar and turned onto the now darkened roads. The killer ambled along with them as if he were on his way to a tavern to relax, not to Tribunal House, where he would be held overnight for his hearing the next day. Even though his hands were bound, Turghar had a casual rolling walk and

Mack almost expected him to break out into song. To be sure, he acted like his family, wherever they were, were being paid handsomely for him to turn himself in. Perhaps he had friends waiting nearby to release him. Nadeem seemed ready if they attacked, but she doubted the two of them could hold off this man, let alone if he had accomplices. She kept an eye out as they walked up Janub Kocha, but alley after alley, there was nothing. They reached the wide-open space of the mosque courtyard. Still nothing. He had to be paid off by Musfik or for someone else's sake above him. The man would be banished, and head home pockets full of money.

Mack snuck a look at Nadeem, wondering if she could chance a question about the smuggling without harming her neighbours any further. She got what she wanted to say straight in her head and cut back to walk on Nadeem's other side as they crossed the courtyard toward Tribunal House.

"I have a question. I don't want any more trouble and I assure you I am not interested in the guilds."

Nadeem looked at Turghar, then back at her, nodding that she should get back on the other side of him.

"Quit the act," she replied. "The man is being paid to turn himself in."

He stopped playing his role in the performance. "Ask."

"Only if it is safe."

"I've got no interest in making things worse for you."

She nodded gratefully. "The keeper had gold on her from the days before the Zanj Caliphate." She watched him for any reaction, but Nadeem gave nothing away. "There's a lot of gold being paid out to runners. People say it's a new smuggler not associated with the guilds. I'm wondering if there is a connection to my case. What do you have on that?"

"No more than you." He kept his eyes on Tribunal House.

She would not have expected him to tell her if he had, but she pressed on, hoping for a reaction. "Can you at least tell me if an outsider named Jabal ibn Abi Faria is involved?"

He looked at her. "Is that why you are dragging Wada's lover around with you?"

"That doesn't answer my question."

"I can't answer your question."

"Can't or won't?"

"What's the difference?"

"Fair," If fair meant she had taken the matter as far as she could and still get those families back into their homes tonight.

They reached Tribunal House and approached two guards standing next to a wall-mounted torch.

She asked Nadeem, "You ever take anyone to Tribunal House before?"

"Once," he replied.

There was something behind how he said it, but Mack did not ask. She held up her badge to a guard. "This man is to be held over for a hearing."

She went ahead of Nadeem and Turghar into the reception room. The secretary rose from the floor where he had been reading from a Quran and whispered a prayer, then sat behind a writing desk. A large book lay open with an ink pot and pen ready to hand in carved notches at the top. "Assalamu alaykum, Detective Mack."

"Wa alaykum assalam, Dabir Roshan."

He coughed for her to continue.

"Turghar." She turned to the killer, asking him in caliphal Arabic, "Where are you from?"

"Tashkent."

His Sogdian-accented voice was unexpectedly gentle, and she glanced at him again.

The secretary said as he wrote, "Turghar Tashkenden," then looked up. "Local or outsider?"

Mack replied, "Outsider."

"Wrongdoing?"

"Murder of Jaleh Dokht-i-Feryedun, Rat Keeper, Farm Gulnar. He will confess to guilt."

Nadeem nudged her. "Irfan."

"Please note to the court that it is reported he associated with Irfan." She realized she did not know Irfan's full name and looked at Nadeem, but he shook his head. "Irfan, the street preacher."

"Noted. Turghar Tashkenden will come before Qadia Marwa bint Yusuf ibn Asaf ash-Shami in the morning. First case."

"Light schedule?"

"It's the murder of a keeper. I'll make the others wait." He addressed Turghar. "Go sit over there. Someone will be along soon. You will have a meal and a bed waiting for you before long."

Nadeem let him go and Turghar did as the secretary ordered, dropping onto a couch with a satisfied grunt.

"Forgive me," she said to the dabir as she pulled out her letter. "I forgot to submit my claim to the case." Then she dug in the bag again. "And this. The murder weapon."

The dabir gave her a scolding glance, but took them both, then waved her off.

"That's it?" Nadeem asked as they walked out.

"I thought you said you were here before."

He paused. "As a child."

Mack did not reply, giving him time to decide what he wanted to share of that story.

"I followed when you and your partner walked my father here."

She winced.

"They executed him in the end."

"I'm sorry. The Tribunal couldn't mediate any other recompense?"

"Don't be sorry. We demanded nothing less."

The grim memories of that day fell into place. Mack was grateful that the poppy oil still lingered. Soaked in his mother's blood, the boy would not leave her body. His father stood nearby, his rage spent, ready to admit what he had done.

"I didn't know you had followed us."

"My aunt and uncle took me from my mother. But I escaped my aunt's arms and ran after you. I wanted to see him put in Tribunal House myself."

Mack remembered the boy trembling as he spoke at the sentencing mediation. "You told them exactly what you saw, so they understood why your family would only accept execution."

"I looked back at you," Nadeem said. "You nodded to me and I knew I was safe."

They remained in the awkward silence of his revelation until they reached her alley, her feeling shame rather than gratitude she had helped once.

Two of the families were sleeping in the cold, huddled against walls of their homes with their possessions. The others were gone; she hoped, with family.

Nadeem walked ahead to them. "Your homes are yours again! Detective Mack is innocent!"

They got up, heads down, and snatched up their things to get inside before he changed his mind. A woman came back out for a bundle and faced Mack. A floral wrap, washed within an inch of its life and not warm enough for a cold autumn night, covered all but one eye and clung to her broad body. Shoulders back, she pulled the wrap away from her face and gave a look that said Mack would not want to see her come morning.

Nadeem admonished, "Do not blame Detective Mack."

But winning their trust again would take more than words.

Alerted by the noise, Teddy came out and took her arm.

She turned away gratefully from Nadeem and the families as they moved the last of their things, asking Teddy, "Have you heard of a new exposure? Here in South Quarter."

"No." He searched her face. "Is there one?"

"I reported it to Health myself."

"Bad news rides a swift horse. Us healers would have heard if so." He looked down the alley as if plague were coming around the corner. "But if Health has it, there is nothing to worry about."

She nodded. But why had news of the exposure not been shared with the healers? They were best positioned to spot an outbreak. First, new exposures were being taken straight to the director of Health, now this? How many had there really been?

Teddy's arm tightened, and she realized her knees had nearly buckled underneath her.

"This case," he said, "Let's get you upstairs."

But she held back. Having gotten the neighbours inside, Nadeem was returning to her side. She tightened her hold on Teddy, not knowing what he might say.

"One last thing." He looked at her straight on. "Because of that day, know I will always do what I can to protect you."

13

DAY FOUR

BANDS OF MORNING light moved slowly through the high arched windows across the carpets. Mack shifted restlessly adjusting her position against lime-washed wall of The Tribunal courtroom, and rubbed her eyes. The poppy oil worn off, the case, her confusion over Jabal, and the guilt over her neighbours set her on edge. She watched for Marwa to emerge from the mosque's interior. Earlier, the judge's secretary had refused to admit her, despite Mack's note that her message was urgent. Putting up a barrier of denial and relying on everyone's discretion was a risky move on Marwa's part. One word by anyone involved at the hearing or the sentencing mediation and she would be exposed.

Mack muttered to herself, "On your head, Qadia Marwa. On your head."

Through the open courtroom doors, she watched the worshippers in the main prayer hall, caught in arches of light or shadow, rising and falling in private prayer. A man among them rose from prayer and walked towards the courtroom. It was Mehdi. The sight of him leaving prayer irritated her even more. All these years she thought she knew him, yet he had hidden that he was a praying man.

Mehdi tipped his chin to her as he came into The Tribunal room and sat down beside her. "Labas sana, Mack?"

"Shouldn't it be 'assalamu alaykum'?"

He joked, "I'll keep you in my prayers."

Mack grunted. "You here on case or just observing?"

"A case. Yours delayed us. You found the killer?"

"Musfik handed him over to me. He is the one who did it. But Musfik or someone else hired him."

"Did you find a connection between your case and the smuggling?"

"Nothing that proves it." She wanted a swig of grappa to wash the harsh mood out of her mouth, but took a few breaths and tried to answer him as if he were the old Mehdi, the one she thought she knew. "Just too many people talking around the smuggling when the keeper comes up." She gestured toward Hisn and a Keepers Council representative coming around the corner from the Council offices. "What do you know about a case of plague exposure coming through the West Market?"

Mehdi furrowed his brow. "Health quarantined a family in the West Quarter last week."

"That's all?"

"There's another exposure?"

He turned his body to face her, and she wondered if he was whispering a prayer behind that thick beard. He should. There was still no word out about Mathieu's family. It seemed impossible.

Mack asked, "You ever heard of a reported plague exposure going more than a day before we all knew about it?"

Hisn and The Keepers Council representative entered and sat down on the carpets near the clerk shuffling papers on his low desk.

Mehdi became agitated. "What are you saying?"

"That exposures are not being reported and the plague is coming in with the smuggling." She looked him in the eye. "Pray it is not."

"I'll nose around is what I'll do."

Finally, Marwa and her chamberlain emerged from her office. Shafts of light broke across them as they passed through the prayer hall toward the court.

Everyone stood as she drew near.

Marwa paused under the arch, her judge's hood pulled low over her face in a ritual act of humility.

The chamberlain stepped within the courtroom and announced in caliphal Arabic, "In the name of God, the Most Merciful, The Most Compassionate, the Prophet Muhammad and his Way, God bless him and peace, and those with knowledge who walk in the Way, and thus in the Way of The Blessed Treaty, Qadia Marwa bint Yusuf ibn Asaf ash-Shami will now hear your plea."

Marwa entered and sat on a thick pile of sheepskins without the usual backrest.

Mack rolled her eyes as they sat back down. It was either another performance of humility or she had not yet been a judge long enough to admit how exhausting it was to sit through plea hearings and sentencing mediations all day.

She spoke, palms open in prayer, "May God prevent me from disobeying His commands, the Way of the Prophet, alayhi salam, and the Way of the Blessed Treaty." She wiped her face with the prayer. "Amin."

The clerk stood. "Turghar Tashkenden."

A side door opened and a guard walked Turghar to the front of the court to stand before the judge. The man still looked as if he was being taken for a basil-seed and lime sharbat instead of admitting to murder, and he did not blink upon seeing Marwa on the judge's seat.

Mehdi leaned in. "He seems unbothered."

"Someone has his back," she whispered, turning to look at Hisn's reaction to seeing his wife's killer.

The Council representative put her arm around him as he shook and wept.

The clerk asked, "To the murder of Jaleh Dokht-i-Feryedun, what do you say?"

In that strangely gentle voice, he said, "I am guilty of stabbing to death Jaleh Dokht-i-Feryedun."

Qadia Marwa replied with a bow of the head, hand over heart. "We are grateful for admitting your guilt before The Tribunal. It is the first step towards reconciliation."

He bowed in return.

The clerk said, "Detective Derya Mac Aodhagáin."

Mack stood and took her place to the right of Turghar.

"What did your investigation reveal?"

Switching to caliphal Arabic, she replied, "Turghar Tashkenden stabbed Jaleh Dokht-i-Feryedun over a gambling dispute. There are three direct witnesses." Mack paused.

The clerk prompted, "The names of the witnesses?"

Mack looked expectantly at Marwa, who gave nothing in return. She seemed certain that Mack would not give her away. And she did not. "I took the testimony of three witnesses, only one of whom gave his real name. Jabal ibn Abi Faria. An outsider, a trader visiting from France."

The clerk sat down to write Jabal's name.

"Will he be present to testify in one week's time at the mediation? Marwa asked.

"He may have already left Aman-Kala."

Relief touched Marwa's face. "As Turghar Tashkenden has admitted his guilt and you are a Badged Detective, The Tribunal will accept your testimony of their accounts of the crime."

She had broken with procedure, and the clerk and the chamberlain looked at her askance. Turghar could use such a breach to negotiate a sentence more to his liking.

The clerk cleared his throat. "Qadia Marwa. In the admission note, Detective Mac Aodhagáin added that Turghar Tashkenden is 'associated with Irfan'."

Marwa flushed, and she raised her hand to her face. "It is noted." Then she said to Mack, "Thank you, that is enough."

The clerk and the chamberlain exchanged glances at her extraordinary behaviour. Mack marvelled. She was expected to follow it up.

Marwa then addressed Turghar, "The court accepts your admission of guilt. As you are an outsider, we will assign you an elder to support you through sentencing mediation." Then to the clerk, "May God correct my judgement if I have erred. This case is carried over to sentencing mediation in one week."

Mack joined Mehdi as Turghar was led back to Tribunal House.

"What was that about Irfan?" Mehdi asked.

"Let's get out of the courtroom."

They passed by the seated clerk, the chamberlain, and Qadia Marwa, hands over their hearts and never showing their backs.

A small, distraught family waited outside the door with their elder.

"Your case?" Mack asked.

He shook his head.

Once well away from the courtroom, she answered, "Musfik claims Irfan hired Turghar to kill the keeper."

"The one always yelling about the rat policy?"

"The same."

"What do you think?"

"I think I need to ask Turghar myself."

Mehdi laughed. "If you think that man is going to jeopardize his payoff by telling you who hired him, you've lost your touch."

"The judge doesn't want to hear it, anyway." She turned to face him. "Our judge was a witness."

His eyes widened, and he whispered, "Let's get outside."

They walked around the wide circular steps away from lone worshippers and a constant flow of people seeking audiences with Mosque or Tribunal administrators.

"Who do you think hired Turghar?"

Mack grunted as she sat down. "It depends on what role the keeper plays. Irfan hires him for a symbolic killing against the rat policy, or, as Musfik suggested, to threaten other keepers. That story ends with Turghar's conviction and the capture of Irfan. If Musfik hired Turghar because Joe was going to give him away, then it's either like you said, Musfik is siphoning off Pasha's goods and reselling them, or it's like I said, Musfik is smuggling through the rat farm. But either way, the motive behind the smuggling seems to be to upset the power balance in the guilds. Along those lines, Kurban could have hired a killer over the unpaid debt to put the blame on Musfik, get him out of the way and take his place. But anyone could have hired him, including an outsider, for any reason. Finally, the husband, for all the usual reasons, or perhaps he is in on smuggling and she got in the way."

Mehdi pulled on his beard. "My call is Musfik. He has always been a fool and an ambitious one." He shook his head in disbelief. "Musfik probably thought pinning the killing on Irfan would shake Pasha off his throne."

"I don't get it. Why? Who is Irfan to Pasha?"

"Mack, Irfan is Pasha's son. Irfan is not his real name."

She leaned over, elbows on her knees. How did she not know?

"It's Anwar, his youngest."

Mack sat up slowly, light breaking on the case at this news. She let herself hope it meant that Jabal was not involved. All these theories. Nothing made sense until now. The smuggling. The power plays within Amir Pasha's guild. Only one thing did not fit. The Abbasid gold.

"Let's try this," she said. "Hisn, Joe's husband, is allowing unsanctioned smuggling through his house at the border. Musfik had been paying Hisn and Joe for the use of their farm. She threatened to talk, wants more money, something like that. Musfik pays her off in gold so she won't suspect that he is planning on removing her as a threat. That explains why Joe had the gold on her when she died. Killing her was not originally part of the plan, but he realizes it works to his advantage. He can pin the killing on Irfan and it furthers his goal to bring down Amir Pasha." She paused. "But why does Musfik have Abbasid gold?"

"We talked about this, Mack. No one would pay so much to smuggle around quarantine. It makes no financial sense. The tax is so high, it's cheaper just to pay off the quarantine guards to get around the tax."

She slapped her thigh. "Plague be fucked. If—"

Mehdi ignored her, continuing, "Amir Pasha must know and already informed The Tribunal about all of this." He stood, pointing toward the mosque. "That's why that judge brushed off the mention of Irfan's name. Not because she is a witness, but because The Tribunal is protecting him for Amir Pasha. Walla, The Tribunal will bring Musfik down and this will be over soon."

Mack rose stiffly. "That works. All The Treaty Holders know and are bringing it to a close."

"It's done then."

"No, listen. If Musfik's goal is to destroy Amir Pasha, then the money paid out to smuggle through the wall is worth it. It's not about making money. It's about the plague."

"Tell me what you mean," he demanded.

"If I'm right about smuggling through the rat farm, then Musfik went around quarantine knowing there was a risk of plague. Maybe bringing in select infected goods intentionally. He wanted to take down Amir Pasha by accusing him of exposing Aman-Kala to plague. Musfik was paying Hisn and Joe not just to let him use their land, but to stand as witnesses. Say that Pasha hired them to do it. In this story, Musfik would be the hero, and Pasha and his family would be banished with nothing." She looked out over the city again. "But none of this explains why Abbasid gold."

"Mack, this is not like you. It's too complicated. It's always the simplest explanation."

"Listen. I, myself, turned in a suspected exposure connected to smuggling. But the one confirmed case is a man who was running goods for the new smuggler."

He had no answer to that, and they turned to gaze out over Aman-Kala. The warren of houses. The shops lining Janub Kocha. The road stretching out to the city walls, then beyond it the farmlands, and the vast boundary walls.

"It doesn't matter even if you are right," Mehdi insisted. "We're agreed, The Tribunal knows. Health knows. They'll have whoever is involved in hand soon, if not already. Let them handle it."

She held back a retort, only because there was nothing more to say. But her irritation that he was advising her to back off pushed up against the resentment that he concealed his praying. The question came out before she could stop it, making her sound like a petulant child. "Why did you never tell me you pray? You fast, too?"

Mehdi frowned in disbelief. "Who hides their worship? You just never noticed." He pulled a disk of hardened clay from his sleeve pocket with a chuckle. "This, too. Now you know all my secrets. I am Shia."

His friendly chiding stung her heart as he left to go back to court. It was true. Here she was thinking that this man she had known most of her life, who had trained with her under Isiib, was more than a fellow detective to talk over cases. But when had she ever tried to make it more? When had she ever noticed anything about him or even asked? She only knew Mehdi was married because her old partner, Gad, had once mentioned his wife. The distance between them was of her own making. And he was not the only one.

Mack stood on the steps of the mosque a while longer, watching families come and go, friends holding hands. A chill ran through her as she took broken-boned steps down to the bustling city, an old woman unable to recover from the choices she had made.

14

Mack should have gone straight out into the streets to find and question Irfan, but all she wanted was sleep. Her fear for her city, the harm she had done to so many, the puzzle of Jabal and the gold. It was all too much. As she walked the alleys toward home, where she would once have received warm greetings, she got dirty looks, even from those well beyond her own neighbourhood. Nadeem's assurances had meant nothing, and she did not know how to turn it around.

Mack stopped at a stall jammed in-between two houses, knowing they carried wine, and leaned over the counter. Nothing needed to be said. The shopkeeper, her face and body veiled with a black wrap, poured out a jug of wine from a large amphora and passed it to Mack, taking the coin she left on the counter.

Thinking of nothing but drinking from that jug until sleep took her, Mack trudged up to her rooms. But she had barely got the door shut and her bag on the hook when she heard footsteps on the stairs.

"Derya!" Yeru entered before Mack could turn around. "There's a man downstairs waiting for you. I've got to run." She left the door open, her boots slapping the stairs as she flew down and out into the alley.

Mack followed to stand at the top of the stairs. Jabal was leaning against the wall across from the apothecary door, looking up at her with those kohled eyes. She wanted the weight of him against her, not caring what he had done if he could fuck the brittle isolation out of her.

"Come up." She poured wine for herself, then grabbed a cup off the shelf and put it on the table next to the small water jug. "Sit," she said, pouring water for him as he walked in. Mack looked up and sighed. The man seemed eager, but not for sex. "I'll send for some food."

He glared and she gave up on her half-hearted hospitality, sat down across from him, alone again, and took a deep drink of wine.

"Where are we at in the case?"

"The killer is in Tribunal House."

He frowned. "Impossible."

"Dahbashi Musfik turned him over. He was exactly as you all described, kohled green eyes and all. I took him to The Tribunal House last night and attended the hearing this morning. He confessed."

"But there's more to this than the killer," he insisted.

She leaned forward. "Anything new for me?"

"Nothing!" He paced the room, thinking aloud. "Her husband must have hired the killer. You did not investigate that further!"

There was something there. She could feel it. Something he would say if he were pushed. Whether a lie or the truth, either might expose him.

"What does it matter who hired him? Wada hired me to keep The Water Wheel clear of official censure. That's done."

Jabal opened his mouth to speak, then changed course. "Why would Musfik turn him over?"

She shrugged dramatically. "The guilds have to respect the sanctity of the keepers if they want to keep doing business."

He turned on her, saying through gritted teeth, "You know that's not why."

"Sit down, then, and tell me why you care who killed her at all."

"A woman was murdered!"

"And the killer will be held to account to Hisn's satisfaction."

"I was warned about Aman-Kala. A city with no justice, where corruption is openly practiced and you call it government." He opened the door and paused half-way through, as if he was waiting for her to ask him to stay. "When is the tribunal hearing?"

She pushed him to go. "Sentencing mediation doesn't need you as a witness."

He wavered.

"Marwa is keen to see it cleared up without asking too many questions." That tugged him back.

"Marwa." He spat the name as he shut the door and moved back into the room. "When is mediation, then?"

"At the hearing, when I mentioned witnesses, she did not admit to being one and dismissed the need for them."

"Are you incapable of answering a question?"

Knowing she was close, Mack let the tension build with a long pause, then moved in, softening her shoulders and her voice. "Tell me what's bothering you."

"You people may be happy when justice is had by putting a man to repentance, but I need to see his head on a spike."

"Wada said you were one for revenge." She replied sorrowfully, then stood, hoping to force his hand. "You've got no stake in this killing. If your business in Aman-Kala is done, why do you stay? "

"I have a stake."

She sat down. "Yes?"

"Joe is my mother."

He expected her to believe that, when he did not lift a finger to stop the killer? The mask of compassion dropped, and she barked out a sarcastic laugh. "Oh, yes, you were in a sorry state that first night. These past few days, too. I'd say you miss her terrible."

Jabal crossed the room in two strides, looming over her. "I do not need to prove my grief to you."

Mack slapped her thighs and said with a burst of finality, "If you stick to that story, then you'll have the justice you want. You and Hisn will go before The Tribunal mediation until you accept the sentence. Insist on execution. It could take weeks of working through, but if you don't back down, you'll get what you want."

Still leaning over her, he growled, "When is The Tribunal?"

"One week."

"Then we still have time." He returned to the couch and poured himself a cup of water.

"You don't understand. There will be no further examination of witnesses and evidence. The case goes straight to mediation."

"We've got one week to follow the coin. What about the smuggling?"

A cold shot ran through her. Wada told him when she said she would not. How else could he know? But Mack acted like she had told him herself. "You insisted Hisn killed her. Now you ask about smuggling?"

"I did not take you for one who gives up on the truth."

She leaned back. "You'll have to adjust your opinion of me."

"I guess your fine reputation was false."

"Haven't you heard?" she asked bitterly. "I'm the one who got my neighbours kicked out of their homes. That fine reputation is no more."

"Get it back by solving this case." He gestured forcefully toward the door as if all of Aman-Kala were just outside, waiting for her. "Tell them you saved Aman-Kala!"

"Saved Aman-Kala from what?" She had caught him out at last. "You are going to have to give me everything."

Jabal took his time before answering. "My mother fell pregnant alone. She wrote to her brother in Bandar Siraf, by the sea, to come and get me. He and my aunt raised me from an infant. When I was old enough, they told me my mother had died of plague and put me to work on merchant ships. I rarely saw them after that. When my uncle was on his deathbed, he wrote to me in France telling me, after all, that my mother was alive, and a keeper in Aman-Kala."

Mack examined him as he spoke, and Joe's features emerged as if they had been imprinted on his face. His flattened nose and beard had been enough to hide the resemblance before, but not now. It was true.

"I came looking for her. It did not take long to find out she gambled at The Water Wheel. I played cards across from her that night trying to find the words to tell her." He dropped his head into his hands. "I choked on every word I had imagined saying. Then, in a moment, she was dead." He raised his head, eyes glinting with furious purpose. "I could not act then. But I will avenge her murder now!"

It explained why he wanted in on the case from the start and why she had sensed his vulnerability. But while his story might be true, it did not mean anything else was. She did not accept that a man like Jabal would not have intervened in the moment.

She slid the cup over to him, offering a concerned expression. "More water."

He took a sip, then carried on. "Her marriage, the gold, the smuggling, are all connected to her death. They must be! If you won't help me, I'll do it myself."

"Do it yourself? What does that mean?"

"I'll track down everyone involved and kill them myself."

"I'll help."

"Kill them?" He jumped from the couch.

"No." Mack pushed herself upright. "I'll help you find them on the condition that you leave it up to our justice. Like I said, if you want them dead, you will have to sit through weeks of mediation and remain firm that execution is the only resolution."

A knock on the door startled them both. She reached past him to open it.

Sal stood in the doorway. "Lady Wada asked me to tell you word is out Irfan is being held in Tribunal House."

In her shock, Mack took a step back, muttering thanks to Sal, then shutting the door in their face.

"What is it?" Jabal demanded.

"Irfan is Amir Pasha's son," she explained, leaning against the door. "I do not believe for one moment that he hired the killer. Dahbashi Musfik wanted Irfan named at the hearing, to create trouble for Amir Pasha. But Marwa protected Irfan, maybe at Pasha's request. But now this?"

He sneered, "Aman-Kala, the city of justice."

She drank straight out of her wine jug and grabbed her linen bag from the peg. "Follow me."

15

MACK LED Jabal north on Janub Kocha toward the mosque at the city's centre, then, crossing the mosque courtyard, they left the South Quarter for the West. When they began the long walk down Gharbi Kocha to the city wall, he tried several times to start a conversation, remarking on the size and elaborate decoration of the quarter's Shia mosque, the wealth of the neighbourhood and the finer shops lining the main road. But she gave one-word responses, wanting to ask where all that emotion had gone.

They passed through the tiled, arched entrance to the market and cut down an alley to the left, passing the dried fruit and nut sellers, each with heaping cones of dried melons, dates, apricots, raisins, and every type of nut. Her stomach burning from a breakfast of wine, she stopped at one stall and bought a small sack of mixed nuts.

She offered the nuts to Jabal before taking any herself.

"Where are we going?" He popped a walnut into his mouth.

"Dry goods shop. To talk to a man and his wife from an old case."

The fruit and nut stands gave way to sellers of beans, flour, and barley, but everyone else in the city, including Mack, knew that from the back of their shops, they also sold smuggled, but sanctioned goods: Greek wine, Syrian araq, Marvi dried melons, and Indian and Chinese textiles. A small, wiry man with a Mongol wrap to his merchant's green and yellow striped turban was closing out a sale. When he finished, Mack called out, "Batu!"

He scowled. The old case had not gone well for them, but he greeted her as he should. "Assalam alaykum, labas sana?"

"Alhamdulilah. Labas?"

Hearing Mack's voice, Catalina came out from the back wrapped in an embroidered shawl with fringed edges, a thick black braid over her shoulder. "Local items only, Detective," she said sweetly, but Cathal would have said that butter would have melted in her mouth.

Batu pressed two fingers to his forehead. His wife had as good as admitted that there were unsanctioned imports in the back.

"That's not usual for you," Mack replied.

Batu crossed his arms.

Catalina smiled as if she were looking into the face of a daisy on a summer day, then tipped her chin at Jabal. "Who's that?"

"Jabal ibn Abi Faria," he announced, stepping forward. "I'm a trader."

"Then you should be aware," Batu said, "that imports are not available right now."

"I'm not a trader today. I'm helping the detective."

Batu snorted.

"Word is there is a new smuggler in town, moving goods well below price," Mack said.

Catalina moved in front of Batu and took a defiant stance, still with that stubborn daisy smile.

Mack murmured to Jabal, "I'm going inside. Stay here and grab them if they try to run." No one was going to run anywhere, but she did not want him following her.

Batu had already moved to the side, knowing Mack would go in whether or not they liked it, but Catalina stood firm.

Mack went nose to nose with her. "I'm not interested in you."

"I'll come for you," Catalina hissed, "if The Tribunal comes for my man."

"You have my word."

She stepped aside at that, but her smile turned menacing.

Mack entered the back room, Batu one step behind her. The nearest shelf was lined with familiar sanctioned goods, including a bottle of Indian rum she sorely wanted for herself. On a higher shelf, just out of reach, there were also two bottles of wine with labels tied around the neck. Lettering that she could not read. A large wheel of cheese of a kind she had never seen before lay on another shelf. The rind was mottled grey and brown with mould. It smelled strongly of the wheat straw she had been tasked with cleaning out at the farm. Her stomach turned. "Batu, why do you have rotten cheese?"

He sighed. "It's from France. I am assured it is meant to be eaten that way."

She gestured to the bottles. "And what's that?"

"Frankish, too."

"I have to know, are these unsanctioned?"

Batu did not answer, which was answer enough. She burned. Jabal. He must be involved in supplying these goods. Too much of a coincidence. *You plague-carrying piece of Frankish shit, be glad your mother is already dead.* Mack had to hold back from going out to grab him by the throat.

Batu took a fearful step back.

"You are not in any trouble," she reassured him, regaining control over herself. "Hold these back and don't touch them. They could be plague-infected."

"No need to worry." Batu sighed. "Health and Amir Pasha's men were here. They cleaned everything and moved the goods to that shelf. Amir Pasha even paid for it. We are to hold it until they come for it."

She was right. The guilds, Health and Tribunal were working together. But they were risking plague to track unsanctioned smuggling and it made her sick with fear for them all. Mack cursed-well hoped they knew what they were doing.

"Batu, where did you get all this?"

"A warehouse behind the wool sellers. A green door with a white rose."

The same place where Eudes had picked up the musk. The same

place the runner with plague got his goods. They would go there next. Mack pulled out her flask. "You got anything cheap back here for this?"

He snatched the flask from her hands and filled it from an amphora at the back. Mack put the expected coin on the shelf beside her and took the flask.

"Thanks. I'm going to tell him outside I didn't find anything. You act like that's exactly what happened."

Batu nodded and followed her out. Catalina walked away from a customer to give Mack a hard stare as they left.

"Nothing that shouldn't be there." Mack slapped Jabal's shoulder a little too hard. "Now we go to a warehouse with a green door and a white rose."

"Good."

The man confounded her. He was eager to go to a warehouse that was selling unsanctioned goods he had smuggled himself?

They left the market through a small square that led to the road for the wool market. Once they passed in front of stalls packed with raw wool, some hanging in clumps from pegs, the rest spilling out of sacks, the West Market warehouses were before them.

They checked the warehouse doors until they found the green door with a white rose. It was open a crack, and Mack entered first. The dirt floor was covered with straw, but the shelves were empty. Mack caught a flash of a bright red turban as an import guard ducked behind the wide gate doors at the back. She hurried over, Jabal right behind. The gates opened onto a wide tunnel leading through the city wall and out into an enclosed square with a gated entrance. The gate was open. They walked through it to a large arcaded square.

A young woman with a red turban stood under the arch of an arcade, looking at them straight on. While Jabal eyed the busy offices, guards, and porters moving goods on camels and donkey carts through to other gates as they approached, Mack was watching Jabal and the import guard. He seemed unconcerned, and she seemed not to recognize him.

"That warehouse," Mack asked her. "Who owns it?"

"The Mosque rents it out." She gestured to an office further down the arcade. "Saleh Bashruddin handles it for them."

"Does The Mosque know who rents their warehouses?"

"You would have to ask Saleh."

Mack headed to the office, Jabal on her heels.

"He's not there now," the guard called after them.

She spun around. "Why don't we ask you a few questions, then?"

"Where are all the goods that were stored in that warehouse?" Jabal asked.

The guard held out her hand, looking at them expectantly.

Mack gestured for Jabal to pay her. He slipped his hand inside his robe and dug into his purse, dropping a whole dirham in her hand. She would have talked for far less, but if this man was going to have to pay for what he had done, he might as well start with a dirham now.

"All sold."

"Nothing is coming in after?"

She raised her eyebrows. "Not so far."

"What kind of goods were there?" Mack asked.

"There were fresh things," she said with a gossipy smile. "Fresh meat, too."

"Fresh meat after four weeks of quarantine?" Jabal asked.

Mack glanced at him. The man could act, she would give him that. But everyone slips in the end.

The guard shrugged. "I said what I said."

Mack asked, "How did the goods get around quarantine?"

"The paperwork had a local goods seal."

"Yet no one worried they might be infected?"

"Health would handle an outbreak." The guard looked at her as if she were stupid. "What's the worry?"

"You're young." Mack pointed at her insultingly. "Plague has never touched you."

"Those days are over," the guard scoffed.

Mack grabbed her by the lapels. "There's been two exposures, both linked with this warehouse."

"It's not her fault." Jabal urged her back.

Mack let go, pushing the guard away.

The guard spat at her. "That dirham doesn't pay for her to handle me like that!"

"I'm sorry," Jabal said. "Just a few more questions." To Mack, he asked, irritated, "How is this the first I have heard of these exposures? How do you know plague is tied to this warehouse, these goods?"

"Informants," Mack replied smoothly.

Jabal pressed the guard. "Who moved the goods?"

"I didn't look." She eyed Mack warily.

"Just give us a description. We won't tell anyone it was you who told us."

"People have seen you talking to me!"

"Then it's too late already," Jabal said.

Mack interrupted. "Are Amir Pasha's warehouses empty, too?"

"Getting thin." The guard seemed relieved at the change of subject. "Nothing new has come in for him in a while, but nothing going out, either."

"You see a lot, after all." Mack said.

The guard puffed her chest out. "Someone's got to keep an eye open if they want to get paid." She held her hand out again.

Jabal gave her another dirham.

"Looks like a Norseman. Dresses like an amir, except he never changes his turban out. Always this large blue and green turban with real gold wire woven in it."

It was the man at the rat farm who had spoken about the useless daughter he was marrying off. Mack glanced at Jabal. He had a satisfied look.

The guard nodded at a few men standing against a far wall. "We joked we were going to take it off his head and sell the gold." She held out her hand again. "You want his name?"

Jabal patted his purse. "No need. I've got it." He turned to Mack. "We have to get back to the South Quarter, now."

The sun was getting low on the horizon; they would not make it out of the West Quarter and back into the South Quarter in time to knock on the man's door and get their knock answered. Jabal struck out ahead of her, not worried if she could keep up.

Mack caught up. "Where in the South Quarter?"

"I've got an idea."

I bet you do. Already breathless, she trotted with him back out to the market.

16

DAY FIVE

Nabil ibn Ulayq. Jabal had given up the man's name on the walk to the South Quarter. She recognized it. He was a retired guild man and ran his own business now, but he grew up in guild during the dirty days under Amir Pasha's father. Not Norse, but, as she remembered it, his mother had been enslaved from near to those lands.

By the time they had reached the South Quarter the day before, the sunset call to prayer had come and gone. Jabal wanted to push down Nabil's door if his household would not open it, but she insisted it would get them nowhere. He gave in, and she left him at his hostel.

She did not ask Teddy for poppy seed tea once she got home. There would no sleep until she sorted out how Jabal fit into what she had so far. Once the lamp was lit, Mack saw Teddy had got her a jug of wine and a bag of dates, and she thanked him from deep within her soul. With the dates beside her and a cup of wine in hand, she thought it through, finally warming to the idea that Jabal had supplied the smuggled goods without knowing the crew running contraband through the rat farm. But something went wrong. His mother was killed. And he was using Mack to get to them.

The matter decided, she went downstairs to get her tea and drank it down in one gulp. Teddy walked her out of the apothecary and watched as she made her way back up the stairs, one hand on the wall to keep from stumbling. Once in bed, she slept immediately and woke; it felt like only moments later, to first light and Jabal banging on her door.

Still in her nightclothes, she let him in and left him to dress and throw water on her face. He paced in the other room, stamping a bit. She hoped everyone was already awake downstairs.

When she was ready, Jabal left ahead of her and she followed, watching as the man who claimed the city's warren of alleys confused him suddenly found his way.

"You're walking this city like an old hand," she said, catching up.

"I suspected Nabil from that first day." He looked down at her. What do you think I've been doing while you were investigating without me? Drinking alone in my room, waiting on you? I stayed at the gate that first night. When Nabil returned to the city from the farm the next morning, I followed him to his house."

She smiled slightly, hating that her first reaction was relief he had not been with Wada at least one night.

Jabal walked ahead of her again, this time too fast for her to keep up.

"Slow down," she said. "Getting there too early is as bad as getting there too late."

He waited, hand on his dagger. She hoped he was not planning on killing Nabil because she knew she could not stop him.

"What did Nabil say that made you suspect him?"

They walked again.

"He watched you too carefully, half gossiping with the men, half listening to you question Hisn."

"And when you followed him, what did you find?"

"Wedding preparations at his house. Women going in and out. His wife screaming that he cannot sell their daughter into marriage. Guess who is to be the groom?" He smirked. "Musfik. Dahbashi Musfik is to be the husband."

"You could have told me earlier."

"And you have been telling me everything?" He looked her up and down, then walked on ahead.

She hurried to follow.

Turning the last corner, Mack saw there was no worry about waiting for the household to wake. The outer gate to the home was wide open. Jabal stood nearby, observing two young women in fine clothes weeping noisily into their hands.

Mack entered the courtyard garden to a chaotic scene. Several distraught women, young and old, were holding back an older woman who struggled against them, wailing. Her gown was rent at the chest, her face smeared with tears and snot. Nabil's wife?

Nabil, still in that turban, gestured wildly. "Stop that caterwauling!"

Unnoticed, Mack stepped up and grabbed his arm. "Come with me."

"How dare you!" He tore free, then realized who she was and noticed Jabal standing behind her. But there was nothing in his face suggesting Jabal was anyone other than a man he had met once before. Nabil brushed the taint of her grasp from his arm and reluctantly showed them into a passage connecting the inner and outer courtyards.

"What is all that?" Mack demanded.

"Amir Pasha's dahbashi, Musfik, came this morning and stole my daughter."

"What do you mean 'stole'?"

"He said he would never pay for what belongs to him."

His wife ran in and threw herself to the ground at his feet.

Nabil yelled at the women behind her, "Get her out of here!"

They dragged the wife back to the front courtyard, but her shrill cries were deafening.

"Jabal, take Nabil through to the inner courtyard."

But Jabal did more than direct him. He threw the man down onto the courtyard floor. Nabil hit his head on a large potted lemon tree, and his turban rolled across the tiled floor.

Jabal kicked it away and stood over him. "The warehouse."

Nabil got up, seemingly unimpressed by Jabal's violence, and stood to face him, his mouth a hard line.

Mack got in between them before anyone could get hurt. "Talk to us and we'll get your daughter back for you before he ruins her."

"What difference does her ruination mean to me?" He looked at them as if they were fools. "She was always part of the price. I want the deal respected!"

"Your wife would disagree," Mack said.

"Fuck the old hag. God knows she fucks who she likes. Women are made for deals and money and to give you children that will make you more deals and money, nothing else." He spat in her direction. "She'll quiet down or she'll see herself divorced with nothing but her dowry, and, given her behaviour, I do not owe her even that."

"Why is Musfik paying the dowry to you and not your daughter?"

"I said it was part of a deal."

Jabal tried to step in but Mack held out her hand. "What was the deal?"

"Musfik respects you," he said to her. "He told me so himself. Get him to cut me back in."

The man was a fool, as if she could do that. "Done."

Nabil tugged his coat straight. "My daughter was the price to get in under the new amir once he disposes of Amir Pasha. Musfik is the new amir's amirzade." He leaned in, greed glistening in his eyes. "As we speak, the new amir is being written into The Treaty and Amir Pasha is being written out."

"Who is this amir?" Jabal asked.

For a moment Nabil looked embarrassed. Then he recovered, straightening his back. "I will be told when he takes his place."

"I think we'll just take you to The Tribunal instead," Mack said. "What you described is a Treaty violation." She turned to Jabal. "Bring him in."

She moved toward the door, and Nabil went after her. "No! The judge, Qadia Marwa, she is in the new amir's hand. She has taken the matter to the highest advisor in The Mosque government. It is confirmed. There is no violation! Amir Pasha is out!"

"Qadia Marwa was removed from The Tribunal yesterday," Jabal lied.

Nabil squirmed at the news.

"To The Tribunal House." Jabal pulled Nabil's arm up behind him, forcing him to walk ahead out of the house.

His wife stood in the outer courtyard waiting, spent, eyes red and swollen. But as they passed, she leaped at him, scratching and shrieking invectives. Mack pulled her off and shoved her back inside, shutting the gate behind them.

Jabal looked at her for direction. She drew a picture of a wheel in the air and he nodded. Wada would hold Nabil until they needed him. But she also intended to ask Wada to make him talk until they got every last bit out of him.

As they marched him toward The Water Wheel, Nabil still tried to wheedle his way out of their grasp, promising them riches they could not imagine, status beyond the stars. He even tried to rededicate his daughter to Jabal. But once the tavern was in sight, Jabal stopped, asking Mack, "What will Wada do?"

Nabil twisted his head around, grasping he was not going to Tribunal House. "You cannot take me to that Jinn tavern! She'll eat me alive! Take me to Musfik at least!"

Mack spoke over Nabil's pleas. "She'll make him talk."

Hearing them, Wada came to the door and rubbed her hands. "For me?"

Jabal handed him over.

"Come." Her dimple showed. Nabil did as he was told and followed her through the tavern and into her office.

Sitting on the couch, surrounded by the three of them, he shook in terror.

Touching Nabil's chin, Wada urged, "Tell them the truth. Whatever they ask."

"Who is this new amir?" Mack asked.

"Walla, I don't know!"

Wada laughed. "My dear, you don't need oaths for them to believe you now."

"Who ordered the keeper's death?"

Near to tears, he squalled, "I don't know!"

"Why was she killed?"

"I don't know!"

"Make him tell the truth!" Jabal demanded.

Wada lifted one eyebrow. "He cannot lie at the moment."

"I'll tell you everything." He tried to reach out to assure Jabal, but then pulled back, afraid. "Two months ago, I was stopped in the west market and dragged into an office. It was Musfik and one of his sarbazen, Kurban. They gave me a choice. Make more money than I ever had in my life or die. They had a small bag of gold coins. Old gold from before the Zanj. They threw it at me and said there would be more if I went along. They rented a warehouse and brought contraband goods in through Joe and Hisn's farm. I went to the farm to supervise."

Mack wished Mehdi were there to hear it.

Jabal asked, "Supervise?"

"I made sure the goods got through the wall and hidden in the rat carts going into the city. After we dropped off the rats for distribution, I took the cart to the warehouse they rented. A hired man had all the local goods paperwork done, sold the goods, and paid the runners."

"What about the new amir?"

"After they saw I would do the work and take their money, Musfik told me the plan. The Mosque was paid off to scratch out Amir Pasha's name from The Treaty and write in the new amir. Musfik offered me a place in the new guild and unimaginable money. The only price was my daughter." He turned toward Wada and smiled. "She's a beauty, at least. I made deals with her as the prize, but she's refused every man I brought before her." He looked at Wada. "I was planning on selling her to you at a high price had Musfik not come along."

Wada leaned in, her voice dripping with derision. "And I would have freed her from your grasp."

He shrunk away from Wada, looking to Mack for help.

"But she agreed to Musfik?"

"I waived her right to decline."

"You can't do that."

"I did."

Wada looked like she wanted to eat him alive.

Mack asked him, "What else?"

"That's all."

"There's more here!" Jabal insisted.

Mack ignored him. "Wada, hold him for me?"

"With pleasure," she replied.

"Not too much pleasure, please." Mack pulled a still angry Jabal out of the office. "I'm going to get a drink. You get one, too, and get your head together. Then we're going to end this case. I have to take care of something, but I'll be back."

"I've heard that before."

"I mean it." She pushed him down on a couch and signalled for Sal to bring drinks for both of them.

17

———

MACK PUT her name in again to see Qadia Marwa and sat down on a bench outside her office. She watched the sun, shining through the high windows, move across the carpet of the prayer hall. The judge was going to try to ignore her, but if Marwa thought she could wait her out, she was wrong. Too old for a woman's excuse, the midday call to prayer would come soon and Marwa would have to pray in congregation. Mack could intercept her then. She wrote it out in a note and gave it to the secretary. Stiff-backed and disapproving, the secretary came out of Marwa's office and told Mack the judge would see her.

Marwa sat on sheepskins before her writing desk, surrounded by a large cabinet with pigeonholes holding rolled documents and shelves of books stacked on top of each other. She looked more like a child waiting for punishment than a judge.

"What were you thinking?" Mack demanded.

Marwa stammered half a word, then shut her mouth.

"Where do I begin?" Mack sat down in front of the desk. "You're framing Irfan for hiring Joe's killer. You're working for a new smuggler bringing plague-infested goods into the city as part of a plan to place a new amir in Pasha's place."

Gripping the edge of the desk, Marwa found her voice. "No, no! Irfan is only being held to keep him safe. I'm sympathetic to Irfan, understand. I, we… Together, we planned to overturn the rat policy. End the torture of rats!"

"What?" Mack's breath quickened.

"All I had to do was bury reports of unsanctioned smuggling that came through my office. But then The Tribunal transferred me to court when Qadi Abu Mu'min became ill. When reports came in without me there, my replacement put the cases into action. Every part of government became involved in finding the smuggler and controlling the outbreaks."

"How many outbreaks, Marwa?"

"Seven so far. All traced back to the smuggled goods."

"And those who are behind it?"

"The Mosque, like Amir Pasha's men, has been observing them."

"We're holding Nabil ibn Ulayq."

"Allah! No! You will ruin everything! It could still work! You can help. I know you feel the same way about the rats."

"Tell me everything." Mack said through gritted teeth, "Now."

The judge's face took on that screwed up look children have before they cry. Mack wanted to slap her out of it, but instead she smacked the desk, making Marwa jump. "Tell me!"

"Amir Pasha and The Mosque have been using you," Marwa said. "They hoped you would find the smuggler behind it all. None of those working for him have met him. He only uses letters and couriers. Even the couriers who paid out the gold have never met him." She put her head in her hands. "It's all lost."

Mack's frustration boiled. "I'll find him, Marwa."

"No. Don't find him." She lifted her tear-stained face. "The rats. We'll never be able to save them from their suffering now."

"What are you saying?" Mack wanted to shake her.

"The rat policy. Adil Abdulmanie, may God be well-pleased with him, fought it all those years ago. We nearly won his battle."

All she knew, all she had been told, was that Adil Abdulmanie, the scholar who had advised The Mosque on protecting Aman-Kala from plague, had devised the rat policy as the only way to keep them safe.

"No one knew, Detective. The Mosque does not want anyone to know. Back then, Abdulmanie only recommended that they build the border wall and quarantine goods and people for forty days."

"But," Mack argued, "Abdulmanie observed that fleas transmit the plague to humans when the animals die off and they need a new host, so the rats…"

"No." Marwa held up a hand. "He advised The Mosque to clear small mammals from making nests around our homes, keep track of them, so when they die of plague, Health could act in time. It would be enough. What did The Mosque do? They had us build up wooden floors over our earthen ones so the rats nested inside our houses!"

"This can't be right!" She leaned in. "Who created the rat policy, then?"

"The Mosque presented the idea to Abdulmanie. He fought it and lost. They began killing all the cats not long after that."

Mack remembered the hideous yowls as workers stuffed cats into bags and left them to be eaten by packs of dogs outside the city walls. "How do you know this?"

"Irfan. His grandfather, Amir Pasha's father, was a guild amir at the meeting when it was debated. When Pasha became amir after his father's death, he accepted the policy, despite knowing other ways to protect the city from plague, because he understood its uses."

"Uses?" Her breath caught in her throat.

"Fear." Marwa's voice became shrill. "Amir Pasha explained to Irfan that if the people believe that only the government can save them, especially through brutal means, they will accept whatever the government demands."

Mack's skin prickled hot. She stood unsteadily and pulled open her collar in a panic, mumbling, "Their lies. Their lies."

"They are keeping the plague alive within the walls! And they sanctified the Rat Keepers. They turned them into gods before God, without whom we would all perish."

Mack took deep breaths, pacing to get hold of herself, until she was able to distance herself from the horror of what the city had done. When she understood, she faced Marwa. "Taxes."

"Yes!" Marwa nodded.

"The tax to build and maintain the wall. Then The Keepers tax, the local goods tax, the import tax. They are using our fear to fill their coffers," Mack said.

"The taxes are more than most can bear. But no one revolts, not the even hungry or the barely clothed. They thank us when we offer them a bowl of stewed barley and a bit of gristle from our public kitchens." Marwa gestured to the mosque building surrounding her. "The Mosque! Our benefactor!"

"And when we want an import we can't afford because of the tax, we give our money to the smugglers. And even that costs more than before the walls closed around us."

Mack dropped onto a bench by the door, hands on her knees, letting it all come clear. Before the boundary walls closed around them and the rat policy was instated, revolts came and went with every season, every hardship. With the military and police disbanded by the Zanj, no one could quell the people in the streets. The government had to negotiate. This was the city's answer. They managed us into a corner then. They are managing us now. This case, too.

She lifted her head. It all made sense, everything except their plan. "Why would unsanctioned smuggling expose the truth about the rat policy?"

Marwa clasped her hands, hope returning. "Irfan brought an outsider to me. He said if we proved to the people that the taxes on their food are unnecessary, they might hear the truth about the rats. He promised the people would riot again and the government would be forced to suspend the rat policy. Force The Mosque to do what Adil Abdulmanie advised. He…"

The utter idiocy of the plan made the pieces fall into place. Mack interrupted. "Is the outsider the new amir?"

Marwa was breathless with admiration. "He is not an amir. He desires no power. Only to help us."

"And he insisted that the smuggled goods come through Joe and Hisn's rat farm?"

"Yes, but only dry goods less likely to carry plague. No fresh foods. No textiles."

Mack wanted to remind her that this plan was responsible for the seven outbreaks 'so far', but held her tongue. "And you gambled to keep an eye on Joe?"

"I already gambled there, so it made sense for me to watch her."

"Because Wada paid." Mack snapped.

Marwa lifted her chin, offended, but said, "He worried she might go to The Tribunal and tell them everything. I was to listen for any mention of it. Then that night Turghar came in and killed her." She started to say something, then corrected herself. "I feared it meant that our plan was falling apart. I prayed it was only that her husband was sick of her affair with the Alp."

"Is that what you were praying for?" Mack shook her head. "The Alp was Musfik's man."

"I only found that out later, and that Dahbashi Musfik hired Turghar."

"Say that again?" She had Mack's full attention.

"It is all such a mess." Marwa raised a dramatic hand to her forehead. "Musfik killed her rather than wait to see if she would talk." She leaned in. "I asked our man why he would hire such people. If his intent is pure, why involve these men Irfan and I would never approve of?"

"And?"

"Our man assured me—"

Marwa blushed so deeply that Mack had no difficulty sorting out the means by which he had convinced her, as well as his identity. A stab of jealousy hit her in the gut. She took a moment to steady her voice and changed course. "He seems like a good man. A rare man."

Marwa turned her face away, whispering, "And he loves me."

Jabal was a master. Despite wanting to throttle him and drag him beyond the wall herself, it hurt to hear. He had turned Marwa upside just as he had done her. Mack dug into the fight. "Marwa, why does this outsider care about Aman-Kala at all?"

"I can tell you," she said. "You must know, so you trust him, too. You can protect him."

"Tell me," Mack whispered.

"Born in Aman-Kala, he had to leave when just a boy, but Aman-Kala remained in his heart."

Which was the lie? Jabal's story that he left the city as an infant or a boy? She sighed. "And he paid for everything himself? The goods to bring in, hiring all these people, from a cache of Abbasid gold?"

"His mother's treasure." She gasped. "Just like the story of Moses and Khidr. She found a buried treasure where the boundary wall needed repairing and saved it for her orphaned son. He was lost to her, but she prayed he would return someday."

That was not how the story went, but why intervene? She could barely believe that Joe had found the Abbasid gold. It had to be one of Jabal's manipulations. "How did he get the gold from his mother?"

"His uncle sent on a letter from his mother to him, telling him everything, where to find the gold, where to find her. He came at once, but she had already died. In her name, he has devoted everything on our cause." Marwa concluded, "May God reward her with eternal bliss."

All these lies, lies which led to the truth. The manipulations unravelled before her. Until this moment, her suspicions had been easily deflected by her lonely desire for Jabal's attentions. What a fool she had been, not examining the source of that desire. It came from deep place drawing her to him. Jabal, the boy, was her Danyal, alive and despising her for abandoning him, now using her to some end she did not yet understand. Her culpability in abandoning him and losing him, again, crushed her, and she leaned into the wall to keep from collapsing. She fumbled for her flask and drank deeply until she could stand. Then she faced Marwa. "The third witness. The man who gambled with you all that night. He's your man."

"I, I barely remember the third man," Marwa stuttered. "I had so much ale."

"You don't have to tell me." Mack put her hand on the door. "Protect yourself, Marwa, so you don't find yourself on the other side of the wall."

Marwa blanched, trembling.

The call to the midday prayer came the moment the door closed behind Mack, and a long ignored inclination within her told her it was a sign from God. She shook it off as ridiculous and exited through the prayer hall as people wandered in to take their places, men in front, women behind, the mukhannaths and rajulas in-between, a jinn here and there among them.

Not only the worshippers in the mosque, but every creature nearby was answering the call. The sound of their praise came to her gently this time, pulling her to the edges of ecstasy, as if a drop of poppy oil had been placed on her tongue. Mack swayed with the joy of its enfolding quiet.

She searched for the old Sufi shaykh among those waiting for prayer. Only his presence could overcome her this way. There were hundreds of worshippers in the prayer hall and she could not find him. Mack refused him in her heart, feeling his sorrow at her answer as surely as if he were standing before her, and cloaked herself from his gift in the bitterness that kept her among the living.

18

———————

MACK HOPED Jabal had gotten tired of waiting for her at The Water Wheel. She was not ready to face him. The walk from the mosque cleared her mind, but clarity only made it worse. She needed to get some answers from Wada and make sure of herself before she acted.

The Water Wheel was half-full when she arrived. Jabal was nowhere to be seen. Old Farhang went in just ahead of her, carrying a hanging tray of steaming, lidded copper bowls of stew for the customers. Several qiyan lounged invitingly on the stairs. A man too drunk for so early in the day wandered over to them unsteadily. Sal waved Mack over to the bar, where a glass of grappa was waiting for her.

"Sorry, still no rum."

"I'm off imports. Only local swill for me." She tipped her head toward the office. "The man still stuffed away?"

"Yes. He complains, but there's nothing he can do."

"Where's Wada?"

"Back soon."

There was no point in talking to Nabil now he had given up everything. By the time Mack had finished her second glass of grappa, Wada came in through the swinging doors. She acknowledged Mack, but took her time coming over, stopping at each table. Wada sat on a knee for a moment here or leaned over a customer there, touching them lightly until they eyed the qiyan on the stairs. Mack rose from the stool, leaning her back against the bar, legs spread slightly, thumbs in her belt, taking up space.

"Not a welcoming stance," Wada quipped as she joined her.

"Who asked for me?"

Wada smiled broadly. "Are you to join my qiyan?"

"Who asked you to come get me the night Joe died?"

"Mack." Wada drew her head back. "You know I called you to deal with it so The Keepers Council did not shut me down."

"What I'm trying to say here is that your interests and someone else's interests were aligned. So tell me."

"Oh Derya, when you ask like that, you already have the answer, so get on with it."

"Jabal."

Wada held up both hands. "You got me."

"So why don't you tell me how that happened?"

She lifted a shoulder in a half-shrug. "The killer walked out and Jabal followed close behind. Jabal came back to the bar and asked if I had a detective I trusted."

"He didn't try to stop the killer?"

"Would that have been wise?"

"The killer's knife was in Joe's neck. Jabal could have taken him down, and you, Wada, you could have held him here." She did not ask why the son would not have avenged his mother there and then.

"Derya." Wada sounded exasperated.

"Why did he ask you to call in a detective? He's new to the city. How does he know how we do things?"

"Other cities don't have detectives?"

She didn't know how other regions and cities managed crime. The Zanj had come through all those years ago, released the enslaved, opened the prison gates, drafted the military and police into their own empire guards, and told the cities to sort it out. Their only instruction was to follow the Prophet, who had never taken recourse to police or jails, but urged recompense first.

"Did Jabal use my name?"

Wada's eyes sharpened, suddenly more interested in that question than avoiding the admission she had done Jabal's bidding. "How would he know to ask for you?"

Mack didn't answer. "Why didn't you make the killer stay?"

"I did, actually." Her lavender skin shimmered with anger. "But Jabal asked me to let him go in such a way I felt compelled and wanted to understand why."

"You see through everyone, why not him?" Mack sighed as she took a stool.

The shimmering receded into an expression she had never seen on the jinn's face before, embarrassment. "He said something to me."

"Tell me." Mack touched her arm, and Wada sat beside her.

She looked at her qiyan on the stairs rather than at Mack. "He said, 'Do these human beings know you love them?'"

Mack held back a gasp. This jinn felt for human beings. She knew that. But Mack had never considered Wada's loyalties and obsessions to be love, only amusement. Like with Mehdi, she reproached herself for not noticing, not asking.

"He took my hand and kissed each one of my fingers and said, 'Let me love you in return.'"

Kinship with Wada arose within her where before there had only been a friendship built on what they owed each other. Jabal had seen them as they were, alone, untouched by love, and used it against them. He had betrayed Wada, whereas she had only got what she deserved.

"I am a stupid old thing." Wada lowered her head. "How long have I been alive? I do not remember my creation, and here was the only man in all that time who has understood what it meant for me to live alongside you all. All your pride and vulnerability. I loved you for it and yet I was always apart, desired only out of perversity or greed."

Sal came and stood in front of her, but did not touch her.

"Wada." Mack took her hand. "Jabal knew me before he came to The Water Wheel that night. He used you to get to me."

Wada's head raised, her eyes flashing with jealousy.

"When I was young, there was a boy close to me. Danyal. Rivka and I found him in the roads, picking through garbage. We fed him and made him sleep between us to stay warm. He stole with us. His hands were fast. But he was a good boy, he didn't want to do it. He complained God would punish him and it was better to die than to steal to stay alive. We'd box his ears for it and put stolen food in his mouth."

"You've never mentioned him." Her jealousy subsided into concern.

"It hurt too much." Mack lay it all out before her friend. "I left Rivka and Danyal when the Mac Aodhagáins invited me to work on the farm. Rivka and I were eleven or twelve. Danyal was no more than seven or eight, if that." She let go of Wada's hand. "I chose myself. I left them to fend without me. Rivka did small jobs with the guild to support him. These were the old days when Amir Pasha's father was in charge. It was difficult for her. Then she came out to the farm to tell me Danyal had died. Rivka blamed me and she was right."

"My Derya," Wada said, leaning in to touch her, shoulder to shoulder. "I never knew what you carried from that time, only that you trust no one and look after everyone. I know your loneliness, but how did he? How did he know to use it to make you do what he wanted?" She faced Wada. "He sees right through us."

"Jabal sees through me because he is that boy. I sensed it the first day, but I never let myself think it. Rivka said he was dead, after all. I let the vulnerability I recognized in Jabal be a fantasy of him wanting me instead."

"It can't be." She pressed Mack's hand. "Why would Rivka lie?"

"When does Rivka not lie?"

Wada sighed. "She was angry you left them and lied to hurt you."

"I never saw him again. I was on that farm for nearly five years. I reckon he left Aman-Kala with her," Mack said. "I never returned to the city until the Mac Aodhagáins had all died and the farm got taken over. After that, Ibiis took me in and trained me to be a detective."

"And Rivka settled in Baghdad. He must have seen her again and she told him what you had become."

"How many times has she come to see me and never said a word?" Wada sucked her teeth.

"I just saw Marwa. He did the same to her as he did to us. It's too much to explain right now. But he's the one running the illegal smuggling. It's certain."

"The betrayals mount," Wada said, a protective growl running under her words.

Mack looked at Sal and raised her glass.

"That for the voices?" Wada asked.

"No, for me." She slugged back the rough wine. "If he knows our vulnerabilities, he knows the vulnerabilities of everyone involved."

"Nabil, his greed."

"Musfik, his arrogance and hunger for power."

"But how does he know them?" Wada asked.

"I can only guess. Rivka worked for Amir Pasha's father. Musfik and Nabil were child runners for the guild." She faced Wada. "But why would he want me on a case to discover he is aiming to take over Amir Pasha's guild?"

Wada sat up, with a look of having solved the case on her face. "Mack, he is using you to set them up."

That was it. Mack tapped her knuckle on the bar. "He was furious when I told him the case had ended. He wants them caught."

"What did they do to him all those years ago that he would do this to them now?"

"Wada, there's something else. Joe is his mother."

"I don't believe it." She tucked her head back.

"There's a resemblance. There were parents who abandoned their children back then."

"I can see Joe doing that," Wada replied savagely.

"He wants revenge on everyone who hurt him. That has to be it."

"Even his mother? Could he be responsible for her death?"

"He was a good boy, Wada. If his mother abandoned him, maybe he hates her like he hates me for leaving him behind? Maybe that's why he didn't intervene in the murder? He had Marwa watching Joe, never knowing she was his mother." She shook her head. "I cannot believe Danyal would kill his own mother. How could he have lost so much of himself?"

Wada jumped in. "Jabal was clearly distressed at first. I saw it. Then he came to me, changed, and said those things. He must have recognized it was his opportunity to get to the others."

Mack was willing to accept that explanation for the time being. "Jabal wants to kill whoever ordered his mother's death." She paused. "I wronged him. What does he want to do to me?"

"My Derya, he is using you no more. He can't want…" She took Mack's hand. "Be safe."

She stood, nodding. "Hold Nabil, will you?"

"Of course."

"One more thing. Can you go to Marwa? Tell her about Danyal. It will hurt, but tell her everything."

"Where are you going?"

"Out to the rat farm."

"Now? It will be dark soon."

"Now."

19

____

THE CALL to the afternoon prayer had not yet come, but there was not enough time to get to the farm before dark. Mack hoped to find the same donkey driver and convince him to take one last trip that night, but she would be lucky to find a driver at all.

"You look like you need help." A voice came out of the shadows.

She started, then saw Nadeem. "Amir Pasha tell you to follow me?"

"I promised to protect you."

This cursed mess. Here was a boy she had helped with a single look, trying to protect her on a case driven by a boy she had irrevocably harmed.

"What can I do?"

"Nothing." Mack walked towards Janub Kocha.

He caught up, walking just behind her. "I'm coming along."

Halfway to the city walls, he had not abandoned her. She finally stopped, turning to face him.

Nadeem put his hand over his heart and bowed his head in service.

She snorted at the gesture. "I need a donkey cart out to the rat farms."

Nadeem smiled and fell in beside her, but the whole walk down she wanted to grab him and wise him up on who she really was. All he knew of her was a look from a long time ago. She should tell him, see if he would still lend a hand or leave her. But she never spoke and reproached herself for that, too.

Outside the city gate, a line of carts coming in from the border wall raised dust into golden, choking clouds in the afternoon light. A heavily laden camel paced beside them. But only one cart stood in the square, ready to go back out to the farms. Mack took out her flask, and headed toward the waiting cart, sorry it was not her man and his cared-for donkey who would take them on the long drive to the farm and back.

Nadeem stopped her. "We have our own stables."

He walked her well beyond the square to a wide-gated building and approached a man working outside.

"Ho! I need a donkey and cart."

They followed the stable man inside the building. The ten stalls housed mainly horses, but there were three donkeys and several carts lined up in the main area. The stable man pulled a pliant donkey from her feed. Mack approached the poor girl and put a hand on her cheek, but she only heard the donkey's exhaustion with always being at another's behest.

Mack left the stables as the donkey was harnessed to the cart and leaned against the wall, looking out at the shorn fields. Tears ambushed her. She gasped for breath, shuddering under their weight. The cart rumbled out and she wiped her face, dragging her sleeves across her cheeks, and blew her nose out onto the dirt.

Nadeem stood for her beside the cart. He did not say a word about her tear-stained face. She let him help her up and recalled how Jabal had let her struggle to get up on the cart that day.

Once out on the road, he asked, "Will you let me in on your side of the case?"

It was time. "I know who is behind it all."

"We couldn't find out." He sounded surprised. "Amir Pasha was right. He told The Treaty Holders to let you keep investigating. How did you find him?"

"He found me. It is Jabal ibn Abi Faria."

"Truly?" He sounded as if Jabal were the last man he would have considered.

"I thought you suspected him."

"No. I only didn't like him around you."

"The smuggling is a setup to bring down everyone involved. Jabal has been leading me to them. I didn't realize until today. He has some old grudges against Musfik and Nabil, but there may be others." She paused, almost telling him that Jabal had a grudge against her. Instead, she said, "I don't know what he wants. Maybe for Amir Pasha to kill Musfik and Nabil for him, see their families disgraced and impoverished?"

"He's been successful there. I doubt Musfik will live."

"I know Musfik paid Turghar to kill Joe."

He nodded.

"Musfik took Nabil's daughter."

"Yes, he crowed about how he took her honour."

At least Nadeem said it like he did not like it. "What will happen to her when Musfik is killed?"

"It's up to Amir Pasha."

"There's more. Joe was Jabal's mother."

Nadeem whistled. "He'll want to kill whoever ordered her death."

Finally, she came around to it. "This is all my fault."

"Let's talk to Hisn now. We'll divvy up fault later," he said, not understanding, and she let it go.

They rode in silence for a time. As the sun went down, he began to hum. The hum rose and transformed into a single word, "mun," held for longer than a man should have breath, until the breeze took its last note and was gone. With his next breath, he traced out the word "mun" again and began a song in a language she did not understand.

"Mun tu shudam tu mun shudi,
mun tun shudam tu jann shudi
Taakas na guyad baad azeen,
mun deegaram tu deegari."

She took up the song, clapping in time. Then, he sang in the Arabic of the city,

"I have become you, and you me;
I am the body, you are the soul.
So that no one can say hereafter,
That you are someone, and I, someone else."

When the sun had set, he pulled the cart over and got down to pray beside the road. The donkey snuffled, grateful for the rest. A waning moon rose, giving them a bit of light as the day faded. Finished, he got back into the cart and pulled some dried meat out of a cloth he had tucked in his short belted robe and offered her some.

She waved it off. She was hungry, but not hungry enough to eat meat.

"Is it true what they say about you?" he asked. "You are a majdhub. You hear the animals talking?"

"I don't hear them talking. I hear their constant conversation with their Creator and their pain, pleasure, and frustration." She held up the flask. "This helps, but I can still hear our donkey is unhappy, though you are a gentle driver."

He looked at her with pain in his eyes. She was grateful the donkey mattered to him, but wondered how he could choke off this compassion to be the man Amir Pasha expected. And who would he be when he found out what she had done? The man who sang Sufi love songs meant for God, or a guild man settling scores?

It had been dark for some time when they turned off the boundary road toward the farm, but the lane was visible in the moonlight.

The donkey pulled up short partway down the lane and they got out there.

"I'm going to accuse Hisn of killing his wife," she said. "Follow my lead."

The farm was invisible behind the cypresses, but a small fire burned in the pit outside, sending shadows and flickering light through the trees. As they emerged through the trees into the farm, the rats in their stacked hutches were mainly and blessedly asleep.

Hisn stood over the fire, stumbling drunk.

When he saw them coming, he rushed into the house and returned with a sword, waving it around like a man who has never held a weapon in his life. "Who's there?"

She held up her hands. "Detective Mack. I'm here to bring you to The Tribunal House. You got someone who can watch the farm tonight and after?"

He glanced at the house.

Nadeem walked slowly around him to the door.

Caught between waving the sword at her or at him, Hisn stepped back to avoid them both, and Nadeem ducked inside. Mack heard a scuffle within, a woman screeching, then Nadeem returned holding a half-dressed young woman, her long black hair hanging in her face. She pulled at him, her shift nearly coming off, and broke away to hide behind the old man.

Hisn swung the sword wildly again and the woman screamed. The rats began their own screeching and clamouring in their cages. Mack took two hard pulls on her flask as they waited for Hisn to tire. The woman looked behind her and escaped beyond the trees into the darkness.

Exhausted, Hisn fell to the ground, snotting and wailing, "She was my woman. Mine."

Nadeem approached and took the sword from his hand.

Mack asked, "She was your woman, so you wanted her dead?"

"It's not like that." He sniffed hard and spat on the ground in front of them.

Nadeem dragged him over to the low couches.

"So what was it like?"

"She stole my manhood." He put his head in his hands. "Lorded it over me. Talked about her Alp's fine cock and the work he did on her. Telling me she went into debt for that cock and I was going to have to pay for it."

"So you killed her."

"I should have!" He lifted his head. "I took her insults. If it weren't for Nabil, she would be here, still mocking me."

"Nabil told you to kill her?"

"I did not kill her! Nabil helped me find my way back to being a man. He talked me through it. I tried to hit her one night like he said, but she just pushed me down and kicked me until I gave up. He saw me covered in bruises and asked why didn't I do something she had no part of?"

"What?"

He looked between them, drunk and exhausted, and Mack guessed no more energy to lie. "Smuggling." He gestured to the house. "There's nothing in-between the outer wall and our own. They broke through ours, then the outer wall, and stored the goods in the space between. They broke through ours, then the outer wall, and stored the goods in the space between."

"And she agreed?"

"She called me a traitor." He half-smiled, remembering. "But the worst of it for her was Amir Pasha's men doing it."

"Why?" Nadeem asked, sitting beside him.

"Bad history going back to the hard days of Pasha's father. Two of his runners beat her husband down dead when they begged for food. She and her boy were too weak to stop them. Joe lost her mind with grief, ending up in the bimaristan for the better part of a year. She never knew what happened to her son." He smiled at Nadeem. "I got the better of her that way. She had to deal with Pasha's men going in and out of her home."

Nadeem looked at her, mouthing, "Jabal?"

She nodded. This was how Danyal had been orphaned. Musfik and Nabil grew up in the guild. What could Jabal have against them, unless they were the ones who killed his father, sent his mother to the madhouse and left him on the streets, alone? Rivka ended up working under those same boys, forcing Danyal to eat from their hand. Killing them would not be enough. He wanted their lives ruined just as they ruined his. Mack's life, too. And none of this would have happened if she had not abandoned him and Rivka for life at the farm.

She barely heard Nadeem ask, "Joe did nothing to stop you?"

Tearing up again, he replied bitterly, "Always with her Alp."

Mack stepped in, desperate for it not to be true. "You told me she had no son and that's why her half of this place was reverting to your family."

"She wanted it for her boy." He wiped his hands off him. "We don't even know if the boy is alive. Why would I bring him up?"

"Hisn, when she died, she had fourteen Abbasid gold dinars on her."

Before she finished her sentence, Hisn was on his feet, his tears eaten up by fury. Nadeem took hold of him. "Settle down."

Struggling against Nadeem, he said, "We found that gold buried along the wall. She took it and hid it where only she could find it. For her boy, she said. She never let me have even one." Hisn spat the words in Nadeem's face. "Now I find out she spent them on her filthy lover!"

Nadeem asked, "Have you got what you need?"

Mack asked the still angry Hisn, "You got someone who can watch the farm for a while? Family nearby?"

"Where are you taking me?"

"Tribunal House. You'll be gone a while."

"I'm a keeper." He snorted. "I'll be back here by tomorrow night."

She did not think so, but she said, "Get someone in to feed the rats in the morning, then."

"Nazanin!" He arched his head back. "Nazaniiiin!"

She came through the trees, eyeing them warily.

"He's going to be away for a bit," Mack said to her. "Can you get a farm hand, family, someone to come and take care of the rats?"

She nodded, then ran past them into the house.

"A farmhand's not far away." He leaned in to Nadeem. "Her husband."

Nadeem grunted and pulled him up, walking him down the lane towards the cart. Mack followed, picking up two apples and a skein of rope. She handed the rope to Nadeem once Hisn was in the cart.

Once Hisn's hands were bound, Nadeem jumped into the cart and turned it away from the farm. The donkey was even more unhappy this time. Hisn began to moan. She tried to lay her part out before Nadeem. "Back then, I did Jabal wrong—"

"And he wants to harm you, too."

"I need you to understand who I am."

"I work as Amir Pasha's left hand. Imagine what I've done." He shut the conversation down, leaving her grateful she did not have to say more, and certain of his loyalty, at least for now. Then he asked, "So what are we doing with Hisn?"

"I've been thinking. Let's get Jabal and the other men and do what he wants."

"That could be dangerous," Nadeem warned.

"It's a good thing you'll be with me, then." She pulled out her flask. "Plague be fucked. It's empty."

20

DAY SIX

IT HAD BEEN years since she was awake all night for a case. She had slept part of the way back, trapped in a fitful dream. Jabal had killed them all, ending with her. He had her pinned with a knee, cracking her ribs one by one, his dagger at her neck. Each rib was an accusation she could not deny. "Remember me?" Danyal, the boy, asked. Then Jabal, the man, slit her throat.

Mack had set his desire for revenge in motion. Yet here she was, setting a trap to keep him from carrying out his plan instead of offering herself up in recompense.

She and Nadeem left the donkey and cart in the stable and entered the city.

The voice of guilt, overlaid with the chattering of the creatures, stabbed at her skull. White flashes of pain obscured her sight. Her body ached. Mack kept touching her flask as if it would fill miraculously and told herself to toughen up. She had lived with unrelenting pain right up until Cathal Mac Aodhagáin had poured her that first glass of poitín in The Water Wheel. "Look at that red hair, you're a right Irish cailín," he said, then invited her to work on the farm. This pain was nothing compared to the days before the farm. And there would be wine as soon as she got back to Wada.

As they walked up Janub Kocha, dragging Hisn behind them, they talked over her plan.

The idea was to bring together Hisn and Nabil, two men Jabal wanted exposed, and Musfik, the one he wanted to kill, and put them all in Jabal's hands. That he wanted her dead had to be considered. Her dream had told her he cursed well did, but she did not tell Nadeem. There seemed to be no other way to squeeze Jabal into revealing himself except to put herself in his hands, too.

They could not just walk up to Marwa's court. He would catch on and run. Drag him in bound? He would never admit a thing. Mack did not know even if Marwa would identify him. Irfan? Mack had nothing to go on.

She bet that if Jabal thought he was calling the shots, he would demand they all go before Amir Pasha himself. After all, Amir Pasha was the only one who could guarantee the humiliation and summary execution Jabal desired. She expected Amir Pasha would get a confession out of him and uphold The Treaty. Nadeem agreed. Musfik may not survive the Amir, but she trusted Pasha would have Jabal, Hisn, and Nabil dragged to Tribunal House.

If Jabal was going to kill her, it would come after he believed he had gotten everything else he wanted. They would be ready.

She recognized Jabal's hostel in the spare light of the setting moon; daybreak would come soon. Nadeem and Hisn stood back in the alley as she banged on the outer door. An old woman wrapped in a wool blanket opened it with a curse on her lips until she saw Mack's badge. "I'm here for one of your guests, Jabal ibn Abi Faria."

"Top of the stairs, on the right."

Mack knocked and opened the door without waiting for an answer. He was already pulling on his boots.

"I heard you."

"Meet me downstairs."

At the outer door, Jabal stopped cold seeing Nadeem and Hisn there.

"Hisn's confessed to the smuggling," Mack said.

"Who's that?" Jabal asked, gesturing to Nadeem.

"A friend. I needed some muscle to hold Hisn."

Jabal looked Nadeem up and down, disapproving.

Hisn tried to break away. Nadeem jerked him up.

"Did Hisn kill my mother?"

"No. It was Musfik who ordered it. Hisn will implicate him."

"And where is he?"

"At Amir Pasha's compound." She pressed her hand to her ear as pain spiked through it.

Jabal asked smoothly, "One of your headaches?"

"I'm out of wine."

"Nothing to be done about that now." Her suffering plainly pleased him.

Mack made her pitch. "That speech you gave about justice in Aman-Kala. I'm coming around to it. These men were behind your mother's murder and nearly brought the plague down on this city. I don't want to wait for justice to find its way. I want them dead now. How about you?"

"You and your 'muscle' go get Musfik and take them all to The Tribunal." He gave her a stony stare. "I've come around to your way. I'll stay in Aman-Kala long enough to demand execution at Turghar and Musfik's mediation hearing, like you said."

What was she thinking? He would not give himself away so easily by insisting they go to Pasha.

Nadeem intervened. "I'm afraid Amir Pasha might interfere. If we ask to take Musfik, they will have to ask the Amir's permission. He might have other plans for him."

Jabal was listening.

"I think," Nadeem wavered, "I think if you, as the murdered woman's son, came before him and asked for him to be brought to The Tribunal, he would be in no position to deny your rights under The Treaty."

"This one has a point," Jabal said.

Mack held her breath, waiting.

There was a slight curl at the corner of Jabal's mouth, then it was gone. "I will follow your lead, Detective Mack, but only if we end up at The Tribunal."

"You're right." She put her hand to her head. "This headache. I want everyone dead. Let's get you before Amir Pasha, and after, take everyone to The Tribunal."

Jabal waved for her to walk ahead, then stepped beside her. Nadeem pulled Hisn along behind.

"When we pick up Musfik, perhaps we can also free Nabil's daughter?" Jabal asked.

The pain was now running down her back and into her legs. "Let's not complicate things."

"You seemed concerned about her before."

"There's no going back." Mack turned on him. "Amir Pasha will find a place for her."

"In one of his brothels."

Through the fog of her pain, she gave him what she hoped was a contemptuous look.

Nadeem paused and called ahead to them. "I doubt he will give her up."

"The walls have mice, it seems," Jabal scolded Nadeem for listening in. "And how would you know?"

Mack answered, "He's training to be a detective."

"I will ask." Jabal leaned in to Mack, whispering in her ear as he had done before. "And perhaps the amir can also be convinced to restore your reputation?"

Repulsed, she lost her ability to play along. A night watch guard was ahead of them carrying a torch. She hurried toward him, showing her badge and telling him there was no worry. But Jabal caught up, and she forced herself to walk beside him as they had before.

By the time they got back to Janub Kocha, the call to prayer had come, followed by a brightening sky. They turned right and there was The Water Wheel. Mack pulled at the door, but it was locked. She pulled again, holding back a scream of frustration. Quick footsteps, then Old Farhang opened the door, his beard wet, ready to pray.

"Sorry to bother you so early," she managed, pushing past him.

A large rug had been rolled out. Anahita, Sal, and Farhang were taking their places on it. Wada walked in from the back, her hair covered and leaving wet footprints on the floor.

Nadeem indicated to Mack he wanted to pray.

Wada nodded. "Leave your captive on a couch. I'll make sure he does not move."

Mack took a bottle of grappa from the bar, slid to the floor and drank straight from the bottle until the sharpest edges of the pain subsided.

Jabal leaned over the bar and looked down at her, giving her one of his vulnerable faces. She pushed herself up, grabbed a glass to keep drinking, and faced him. "Thanks for coming to check on me."

"You'll get a long rest soon." He touched her cheek with tenderness.

There was enough drink in her at that point that she was able to lean into his touch and smile instead of run, despite knowing damn well what he meant by rest. She poured herself a full glass and gulped it back.

Wada and the others bowed, prostrated, and stood again behind Old Farhang. He recited the required verses from the Quran in Aman-Kala's rough accent, giving the words, *"guide us to the direct path,"* greater urgency than when recited with skilled, lyrical intonation.

The prayer completed, Wada left and returned with Nabil. He was bound at the wrists, bleary-eyed and defeated. Mack shot her a warning look. Letting Jabal take the man from her, Wada drew a finger across his arm, whispering in his ear, and snuck a wink in Mack's direction.

Jabal brought Nabil to Mack, looking like a man who would soon be served a grand meal.

"To Amir Pasha's?" she asked.

Nabil pulled back. "You said we were going to Tribunal House!"

"We're picking up Musfik on our way."

"Onward." Jabal jerked Nabil into submission, then opened the door for them all with a flourish.

Mack doubted he would try to kill her until after they met with

Pasha, but she stayed a half a step behind him so at least he would be out of balance if he turned on her.

Nearing the compound, Nadeem pulled out ahead, handing Hisn's rope to Jabal, and approaching the guard. The guard nodded and opened the door. That first guard was on duty in the reception hall, and at Nadeem's indication, once they were all inside, the guard moved to stand in front of the only way out of the building they could reach. There was no mocking today. His focus was on Jabal and the two men.

Nadeem said to Mack and Jabal, "I'll be back in a moment," and left for the courtyard.

Jabal tensed, looking back at the now-guarded door they had come in. "You said this man was training to be a detective." He let go of Nabil and Hisn, who looked around, confused and eager to escape. There was nowhere to go.

Mack put a hand on his arm and whispered, "Nadeem is my man on the inside."

"What's he doing, then?"

"Asking for an audience with Amir Pasha."

Jabal muttered harshly under his breath.

It was not long before Nadeem returned through the courtyard. "Amir Pasha welcomes us."

21

JABAL TOOK hold of Nabil and Hisn again, forcing the men in front of him as they followed Nadeem to stand before the amir. The two arched doors at the end of the courtyard stood open. Even though the sky was bright, the office was still lit by lamps. The amir sat on a pile of sheepskins, leaning against a backrest with his legs tucked beneath him. He wore a brocaded red robe, a simply wound red and yellow turban, and an expression that he had lost all his patience.

Nadeem bowed his head before the amir. They all remained standing, Jabal and Mack inclining their heads in turn. Hisn was trembling, but Nabil seemed to have regained his courage. A man entered through a side door and whispered to Pasha. He left and returned with Musfik, unbound but in a panic, knowing there was no way out. On seeing him, Nabil tried to lunge across the room at him, but Jabal kept a tight hold.

Amir Pasha addressed them. "The Treaty is a delicate peace. Each of us has to give up a measure of our greed. It is difficult to restrain yourself when so much more is within your grasp. But we do it for the greater good. And out of love for Aman-Kala and the safety the city affords us. The people must be reminded now and again, but we bring them to order with The Treaty's guidance."

Mack hung on every word, waiting for the one that would break Jabal's game wide open.

"Nevertheless," he continued, "there are times when one must take the guilty into the public square and beat them, both to convince them, and to convince others. Those whose wrongdoings have gone unnoticed, or ignored," he bowed his head toward Jabal, "should see it as a mercy."

Musfik shook, and Hisn fell to the ground. Jabal let him go.

Nadeem bent to haul Hisn back up, but Pasha gestured to leave him seated.

Mack glanced at Nabil, who gazed around the room as if he were the master of this moment.

They turned to face the amir again, expecting him to act, to order, to do something. But he remained quiet, his hands folded in his lap.

The door opened again. Nabil's daughter walked in on her own. She was beautiful, even in her despair. Her pale, delicate features were set off by a finely wrought red gown and an embroidered red and white cap and wrap, signalling the marriage had been consummated. Mack feared for her. She stood still for a moment, then, with a scream, she attacked her father. Her cap and wrap fell away, letting loose her long, blonde hair. She scratched at her father's face and spit on him, finally collapsing on the floor at his feet.

No one moved to help her, and Nadeem gestured for Mack to remain still.

Nabil did not even look at her, but wiped his face with his hand, smearing the spit and the blood she had drawn.

Amir Pasha addressed Nabil over his daughter's heaving breaths. "You have allowed your daughter to be shamed. She, in turn, humiliates you. What will be done with her now? Will her mother take her back?"

Unrepentant, Nabil said, "Her mother will not stand the shame of it."

"Then how will your wife stand the shame of you? There is a reason I rid the guild of you when I took my father's place." He paused. "And now this feeble attempt to take my guild from me?"

Finally, Nabil trembled, understanding what was happening.

"And you." The amir addressed Hisn. "You shame our most sacred profession, that around which the city endures, and the reason The Treaty survives. Without you, without the rats making this city whole, The Treaty would fail. You defiled your profession with your greed, all because your wife had a taste for other men. You gave up a lesser man's right to vengeance when you agreed to keep the rats."

Hisn crouched on the floor, whimpering, and covered his neck with his hands, thinking the sword would come for him.

Amir Pasha turned to Musfik. "I understand your ambition. Indeed, I herald it. I did not win this place without ambition. I drove my father out before his time. But ambition must be matched with wits and the ability to inspire loyalty, and you, Musfik, have neither." He paused, nodding toward Jabal. "Worse, you ordered the death of this man's mother to cover your guilt. She was not only a mother to this man, but a mother to us all, a Sacred Keeper."

A stink rose in the room. Musfik's pants went dark with urine and a puddle formed around his feet.

"Such crimes can only be redressed by your deaths and the humiliation of your families."

Mack looked from Musfik to Jabal. His face was an obscenity, slavering with hunger for what he believed must be coming, his revenge fulfilled.

Amir Pasha clasped his hands. "Alas, I must forgo that pleasure, as this is Aman-Kala, and we sacrifice our desires for the greater good. Thus, I am obliged to hand you over to The Tribunal."

Jabal rushed at the amir, but Nadeem and another man were there before he could reach him. He strained against them, seething. "After what they've done!"

Amir Pasha looked at Mack apologetically. "Not everyone understands our subtle language."

But she did and swayed with relief at his decision.

The amir addressed Jabal, speaking caliphal Arabic this time. "Danyal, those who have gone unnoticed or ignored should see it as a mercy."

Jabal froze at the use of his childhood name.

"I remember what these men did to your father, your family. We were all boys then. Like you, I never forgot. Because of that day, and so much else I witnessed under my father, such petty brutalities do not occur under my command. I have avenged you. Now it is time for you to forget. For your crimes, my men will make sure you leave the city today, never to return. And we will forget you. Do not test me or this city. Only God's mercy is infinite."

Furious in his defeat, Jabal took an unsteady step back. A guard moved in behind him, ready to take him in hand if needed.

Mack wanted to fall at Jabal's feet and beg for his forgiveness for what she had done long ago. But he was already kneeling beside Nabil's daughter.

"I have you," he said, taking her in his arms. "Come with me. You will be safe from these men."

She fell against him, weeping.

Mack shuddered at the thought of the girl leaving the city under his control and what he might do to her in unspent vengeance against Musfik. Instead of begging forgiveness, she begged for the girl's sake. "Let her go, please."

He replied through gritted teeth, "Should I leave her to their hands? Your hands? Is that how you do things in this city? Your Aman-Kala justice?"

Mack backed away until she came up against a wall, and watched, with sickened acceptance, as the end unfolded before her eyes.

Amir Pasha stood, indicating to his men that the girl could go with Jabal, then left the room, his robes sweeping it all away behind him. Nadeem organized the guards, who took hold of Hisn, Nabil, and Musfik. They would be taken to Tribunal House, where their banishment would, no doubt, be handled quietly. Marwa and Irfan would likely be forced into retreat, perhaps out to the farms. Health and Pasha's men would retrieve Jabal's smuggled goods from the shops. The outbreaks would be resolved, never to be mentioned again. The rats would suffer. And taxes would be paid. Aman-Kala, the just, once more at peace.

Nadeem shook her arm, breaking through her dark thoughts. "I have to go with the men to Tribunal House. Amir Pasha has asked you to stay in the compound until Jabal has left the city. He has assured your safety." He grasped her hand. "Amir Pasha will clear your name."

She barely heard him. Jabal stared at her coldly while he cooed in the ear of Nabil's daughter.

Nadeem started toward him, but Mack held him back. "Go, Nadeem. I'll be safe."

But he called over another guard from the courtyard to stay with her. He looked back at her one more time, then left.

In spite of the guards, once Nadeem was gone, it was as if they were alone. Jabal, the girl, and her. She had been given a second chance.

"Danyal." She approached him a step at a time. "Danyal, forgive me for abandoning you."

Jabal kissed the girl's hand and went to meet Mack. Their guards matched him. He stopped an arm's length away, signalling to the guards he would go no further.

Danyal the hurt boy stood before her. He softly answered her plea. "Be grateful I chose not to kill you."

AFTERWORD

Readers may interpret freely, but I do have intentions. I did not have COVID-19 mandates in mind when I depicted government fear-mongering at play with Aman-Kala's rat policy.

ABOUT THE AUTHOR

Laury Silvers is a North American Muslim, retired historian of early Islam and activist in the gender-justice movement, now writing novels inspired by her research and advocacy.

Visit www.llsilvers.com to find out more, including details about her first series, *The Sufi Mysteries Quartet*, murder mysteries set in tenth century Baghdad with a mystical backstory, and what is planned for the future. Keep an eye out for a new, light-hearted mystery series set in The Sufi Mysteries world: *Ghazi Ammar's Agency of Investigation and Implementation*. And a full-length novel of *Rat City* and more set in Aman-Kala in *The Rat City Chronicles*.

Bluesky and all Meta platforms: @laurylsilvers
Twitter/X: @waraqamusa

THE PASHA OF TEXAS

JIBRIL STEVENSON

PART I

LIFE AND DEATH

1

———————

SANTA CATALINA, TEXAS, 1893

SANTA CATALINA WAS a typical South Texas town, mostly adobe and clapboard, with a few brick storefronts in the business district. Main Street had been macadamized in '88, but the rest of the streets were still dust, or mud during the rainy season, and electricity was nothing more than a rumor blowing down from San Antonio.

The people were mostly Mexicans, always had been, since before the Texian Revolution. They were hard-working people—farmers, shopkeepers, artisans, laborers—as were most of the few Anglo-Saxons in town. But as was the case in every border town from Brownsville to Tijuana, Santa Catalina was known to attract that class of men who made their living on the fringes of civilized society, trusting in their ability to light out across the Rio Grande under cover of night if things went sour. It had its share of gamblers and con men, pimps and painted ladies, common thieves and road agents.

Eddie Dawson was one of the latter. He was a young man still, no more than twenty-one, but he'd been stealing chickens since he was ten and sticking up stage coaches at sixteen. He wasn't a bad kid, but life was hard for an orphan in the East Texas swamps he'd grown up in, and once he started robbing he knew he had a knack for it. He made a decent living at it and he'd never been shot nor seen the inside of a jail cell.

Eddie didn't think much about God, but he figured someone must be looking out for him.

That was before, though. Now Eddie was a new man. He had three things he'd never had before: a job, a home address and a girl.

True, Don Rigoberto barely paid him four bits a day to chop wood and clean up, but it was enough to cover his meals and rent a room at Doña Gertrudis's boarding house, which he supposed wasn't much of a home address either. But the girl, she was his everything.

Mariana Hernández ran the sewing machine in her father's haberdashery on Main Street. She was said to be of old Spanish stock, her family come over with Cortez or Coronado, to hear Don Pedro tell it, and Eddie supposed he could see a certain aristocratic line to her face. She had raven-black hair and olive-green eyes, and, when she smiled at Eddie, his heart melted.

He'd met her by chance when he stopped in to buy a new suit with his share of the loot from a Wells Fargo van up in Tom Green County. He was planning to hit the Double Eagle Saloon while he was in town and couldn't very well go in his trail clothes. Mariana had been busy sewing a serge coat and hadn't even looked up at Eddie, who was just standing there in the doorway watching her nimble hands guide the fabric under the presser foot at precisely the right angle while her foot worked the pedal with a rhythmic whirr. When she did look up, Eddie forgot all about saloon girls.

Then Don Pedro had come out to take his measurements, and Eddie had barely exchanged two words with Mariana, but he found excuses to visit the haberdashery every day that week. First he had to pick out some shirts, then the suit itself, then it needed hemming, and then letting out.

Eddie was a handsome kid, or so the saloon girls always said, and he had a certain natural charm. Soon, he and Mariana were chatting for fifteen minutes every time he entered the shop. Don Pedro was not blind.

"If you want to court my daughter," he said to Eddie, who'd come in to have some buttons replaced not five days after buying the suit, "I have three conditions. You must be a Catholic, you must have a steady job, and you must not go whoring about town."

Thinking of his family back east, Eddie vaguely remembered half of them were Cajuns, so he figured he was Catholic enough, though he hadn't been to church in a year of Sundays. After first meeting Mariana, he'd never made it to the Double Eagle, and he figured it would be easy enough to keep it that way. And a healthy young man could always find work, or so he'd heard, so he hired out to Don Rigoberto. Then he cleaned himself up, put on his new suit, and presented himself at Don Pedro's doorstep as a fully qualified suitor.

That was three months ago, and Eddie remembered every day of those three months with fondness.

But then Don Pedro had fallen ill, and the German doctor said it didn't look good at all. The old man, who Eddie had come to be pretty fond of, considering he'd never known his own pa, spent all day in bed, coughing and wheezing like a lifelong smoker, though he'd never had so much as a cigarillo. Now, instead of meeting at the ice-cream parlor or watching the Catalina Caymans play some other South Texas team at the new ballpark, Eddie and Mariana spent every moment of their leisure by Don Pedro's bedside, changing the cold compresses on his forehead and wiping the bloody spittle from his lips.

Don Pedro couldn't work, of course, so Eddie offered to quit Don Rigoberto's to come help out at the shop, but he didn't know anything about tailoring and they both knew it.

"Better your three dollars every Saturday than you ruin my inventory trying to learn to sew at your age," Don Pedro told him. "I'll be back in the shop soon enough, and, until then, Mariana can take care of things."

The former was blatantly untrue. Don Pedro could barely get out of bed, much less measure, cut, or stitch, and wasn't getting any better. The latter was true, as far as it went. Mariana sat at her sewing machine until late at night, until the whirring of its mechanism even featured in her dreams. She took in mending, too, but this was cheap work, and hardly made up for the lost tailoring business.

When Bob Dixon's Menswear and Leather Goods opened up at the other end of town, that was it for Hernandez's. If anyone came into the shop at all, it was more likely a creditor than a customer. Don Pedro authorized Eddie and Mariana to sell off the inventory at cut-rate prices just to pay his bills, but it was too little, too late.

Eddie came to visit Mariana one spring morning to find her crying over a letter from the Rio Grande Valley Real Estate Bank. If all arrears were not paid within thirty days, the bank would repossess the shop, to include the upstairs apartment she shared with her father.

"Can we talk downstairs?" she asked Eddie when she had regained her composure.

"Of course, my love."

"Eddie," she said, "I'm sorry."

"For what, Mariana?"

"I love you, Eddie, I do. You're a good man, and you've been so kind to my poor father. But…"

His heart dropped. Of course there was a "but."

"Eddie," she said, barely holding back her tears, "I can't marry you. My father is sending me to live with my aunt in Nuevo León. She has a little farm, a few goats and chickens, and things are looking up in Mexico these days. She's all the family I have left."

Now it was Eddie's turn to say, "But…"

"But nothing, Eddie. How can I refuse my father's dying wish?"

Eddie should have seen it coming. He couldn't even be mad at the old man. It was his own fault, wasting his time working for Don Rigoberto for pennies a day, months of labor with nothing to show for it. He bowed his head and made to leave.

But a thought was forming somewhere in the recesses of Eddie's mind, whispering its way to the forefront. He was only on the straight and narrow, working that rubbish job, to fulfill Don Pedro's conditions, wasn't he? If those conditions had changed, Eddie knew how to get money. He turned back to the weeping girl.

"Mariana," he said, his mouth working faster than his brain, "I got a way to pay off the bank. Just don't let your old man send you away."

"What do you have in mind?" she asked, probably suspicious of

Eddie's sudden confidence. "I know you have a past, Eddie. I never judged you for it. But don't go down that road again. Not even for me. It's not worth it."

"My family has some land back east," Eddie lied. "My cousin Pierre always wanted it to expand his spread, but my pa made me promise not to sell it too cheap. If I offer him a good enough price, he'll buy it, worthless swamp though it is. I'm sure I can pull in a thousand."

Mariana's eyes, almost dry now, betrayed incredulity, but she didn't voice it. "Whatever you're going to do, do it quick. Time is short."

"I will. *Bendición.*"

"*Dios te bendiga.*"

Eddie kissed Mariana goodbye, a sweeter, sadder kiss than they'd ever shared before. Then he headed out into the night, his feet tracing a path he'd resisted for months. Within minutes he'd reached the Double Eagle Saloon.

"Evening boys, ladies." He tipped his hat. "Anyone seen Frank Danger lately?"

2

SIERRA MADRE OCCIDENTAL,
MEXICO, 1893

So here he was now, dug in behind a pile of boulders somewhere in Chihuahua, Winchester in hand, waiting for a mule train to come into view.

This was rough country, bare rock and gravel with nothing but creosotes and yucca every few feet, not so much as a scraggly mesquite for shade. The whole area was crisscrossed with canyons and arroyos. Eddie was set up at the mouth of one of these canyons, where it opened up into a wider valley with steeply sloped—but not vertical—walls, so he could watch for his prey from on high, but still make it down without breaking his neck.

Chihuahua was hot, hotter even than West Texas in July, and Eddie could feel the back of his neck burning and blistering where his bandanna left a strip of skin exposed. He was sweaty on the bottom, where his body pressed against the hot stone from chest to ankles, and bone-dry on top, itchy from the salt left behind by evaporating sweat.

Behind another pile of boulders on the other side of the gorge was his partner, Frank Danger, a real bad customer if ever there was one.

His legal name was Francis Scott Key Dangleberger, but he was liable to shoot a man for calling him that, so Frank Danger it was. He wasn't much older than Eddie, but you wouldn't know that to look at him. Frank was about six-five and weighed two-fifty if he weighed an ounce, with a prizefighter's build. He was missing a few teeth, too, but those were from barroom brawls—he'd probably never fought a fair fight in his life.

Frank was from East Texas, too, somewhere up toward Texarkana. He and Eddie'd first partnered up for a mail stage outside Nacogdoches, and they'd done a few jobs together since then, including the one that had brought them to Santa Catalina. If Eddie had a knack for robbery, Frank was a downright genius at it, always knowing when and where to hit the stages for the biggest take. And this one was supposed to be the biggest of all.

A mirror glinting between the rocks told Eddie that his partner had spotted the target. It seemed like an hour passed, not a breath of wind to cool Eddie's sun-baked body, before he could see it too.

Two riders first, their upright posture indicating alertness even from a distance. Their sombreros and shirts looked gray, which might not mean anything. If they were *rurales*, though, this would be a little tougher than ambushing some untrained, poorly armed miners.

The mules were coming around the bend now. One, two, three...six of them, with a mule-tender ambling behind, his long whip resting over his shoulder. Another two—no, four—horsemen brought up the rear. As the mule train came closer, Eddie saw that each of the riders carried a carbine.

This wasn't Eddie's kind of operation. He liked stagecoaches because you could ride up in a gang, or pop up out of the brush all by your lonesome, and stick a gun right in the driver's face. And unless the shotgun rider or one of the passengers got cocky, you'd take your money and no one got hurt. If they did get cocky, well then you might have to shoot someone, but it was a fair fight, more or less.

This here was just murder. The only way Eddie and Frank could take out six armed guards, *rurales* or not, was to shoot most of them before they had a chance to shoot back. No "halt!", no "hands up!", no warning shot, just a .45 caliber slug in the chest.

The mule train was almost below them now, close enough that Eddie could make out the first riders' faces—tanned, heavy black mustaches—and their gray uniforms. Definitely uniforms. Definitely *rurales*. All the more reason to take them all out quick.

Another glint of the mirror across the gap. Eddie counted to three.

The Winchester bucked against his shoulder and, down below, two of the trailing riders tumbled from their saddles.

Two of their comrades raised their own rifles to return fire, but it was hard enough to shoot from the saddle, and harder still when you weren't really expecting a fight. Their bullets rattled in the rocks far enough from Eddie's position that he didn't sweat it too much. The other two *rurales* were dismounting, though, running for cover. These were trained men, all right.

Eddie shot one of them before he could duck behind the boulders that littered the canyon floor. Frank shot one of the two still mounted. Eddie sighted in on the last mounted figure and pulled the trigger. He pitched back, probably shot twice, just as his bullet ricocheted off the red rock a few inches from Eddie's head.

The mules continued plodding forward as if nothing had happened, but their driver was cowering by the canyon wall, out of Frank's sight most likely, but plainly visible to Eddie. He was fumbling with an old-fashioned pistol he'd had stuffed in his belt.

Eddie ignored the mule-tender. He wasn't much of a threat, the poor bastard, and there was still one armed *rural*, who had managed to hide behind some kind of cover and was now trying to pin Eddie down with aimed shots, the bullets kicking up dust not far from where Eddie was dug in. There was enough gun smoke in the gorge that Eddie couldn't quite make out where the shots were coming from.

He was well enough ensconced behind his boulders that the Mexican's bullets were unlikely to do him any damage, but he couldn't hit the Mexican either. And they couldn't very well sit there shooting at each other all doggone day. Was Frank going to do anything to break the impasse?

There it was, another flash of the mirror. Eddie counted to three then started popping off shots in the general direction of the *rural*'s hiding place. Frank scrambled down the opposite hillside, setting off a cascade of tiny pebbles and raising a big cloud of dust.

Eddie saw movement through the haze of smoke, the round shape of a sombrero poking out from behind a cluster of rocks. As soon as he thought the man's head must be exposed, he pulled the trigger.

Silence.

After a few seconds, Frank came into plain view and dropped to the desert floor. He had slung his rifle and unholstered one of his twin Colt revolvers instead. While Eddie kept watch with his rifle, Frank walked from body to body, shooting each one in the forehead to make sure it was dead.

Eddie cursed. He'd been so busy watching for the last of the rurales that he lost sight of the mule-tender. The mule-tender wouldn't be any threat to him at this distance, not with that single-shot pistol, but he might surprise Frank, shoot him point blank.

Still cursing, Eddie got to his feet, each joint cracking after hours of lying motionless, then he rushed down the steep slope as swiftly as he safely could.

A minute later, he was on the ground. He made his way over to Frank, trying to ignore the twisted bodies all around him. Frank gave the last dead *rural* the *coup de grâce*.

"Good work," Frank said, wiping the sweat from his brow with his sleeve. "Let's go round up the mules."

"What about the driver?"

Frank pointed to the mule train, the dumb animals still trudging eastward down the flattening valley, about a hundred yards away now. The Mexican was running after them, whip in one hand, pistol in the other, his straw sombrero flopping comically with every step.

They rounded up two of the horses and mounted up. The ground here was flat enough they made good time, covering the distance in a few seconds.

The mule-tender looked over his shoulder at the approaching horsemen, and in doing so tripped over a rock or bush, sending him into a face-first tumble among the mules. The animals attempted to scatter, though they couldn't make it far, being all strung together.

Eddie rode to the head of the team to get the mules back in line, while Frank dismounted right next to the Mexican, who was struggling to regain his feet. To his credit, the man still had the old pistol in his hand, but Frank had the drop on him.

The Mexican raised the pistol, his grip shaky. He was an old man, a stringy gray beard covering most of his weathered face. He said something in Spanish, his voice shakier than his hand. Begging for mercy, maybe, or praying for deliverance.

Frank had his Colt pointed right at the fellow's face, and he inched closer, his arm fully extended, until the muzzle was practically touching the poor man's forehead.

He cocked the hammer, the click echoing across the desert, despite the braying of the mules and the Mexican's unintelligible mumbling.

The hammer fell with a dry click.

Frank had shot the six *rurales*, and he hadn't reloaded or switched pistols. It wasn't like Frank to lose count of his shots, but it certainly was like him to grandstand the way he was now. He chuckled like a schoolboy who'd just played a prank on teach', almost doubling over with laughter as he holstered the revolver.

But then, swift as a raptor, he grabbed the old single-shot from the mule-tender's hand before he could get to thinking he might have a chance at surviving this situation.

"Let him go," said Eddie, as Frank turned the antique weapon around in his hand, checking it was serviceable and primed. "He ain't a *rurale*, just a damn teamster happened to be in the wrong place."

Satisfied with the weapon, Frank raised it just as he had the Colt, pushing it up against the Mexican's forehead. "Can't have anyone telling the *federales* who done this," he said.

The Mexican had finished mumbling his rosary and dropped to his knees, but Frank pulled the trigger before he hit the ground.

The old smoothbore pistol echoed like a cannon. The mule-tender's corpse landed knees first, then toppled backward into the halo of blood painted on the desert floor.

Overhead, the vultures were already circling.

3

CHIHUAHUA DESERT, MEXICO, 1893

FRANK AND EDDIE drove the mules about a mile down the valley before they found a brush-filled draw that offered a little concealment, where they could open up the saddlebags and take stock of their loot.

"Woooowee!" Frank hollered, peeking inside one of the saddlebags. "We struck gold alright!"

Eddie undid the buckle on another. Frank wasn't lying. It was full of gold ingots, each about as big as a brick, gleaming like the sun itself. Eddie took one out, weighed it in his hand. It was far heavier than a brick, maybe twenty pounds. The saddlebag held five of them.

He did some mental arithmetic—twenty-pound ingots, five per saddlebag, two saddlebags per mule, times six mules…

Twelve hundred pounds of gold! More than fourteen thousand ounces… That would be almost three hundred thousand dollars!

With that money he could buy Mariana a dozen shops, with a dozen sewing machines and hire a dozen seamstresses to run them. He could buy a ranch like Mariana's aunt supposedly had in Mexico, and they could live as God intended, masters of their own destiny.

Eddie would only get a third of the loot, of course. That was the deal. It was Frank's job and he'd cut Eddie in, when he could have picked any one of the other would-be gunslingers at the Double Eagle that night. Half for Frank, a third for Eddie, and the rest for Frank's contact in Mexico, who'd given him the intelligence on the gold shipment. Eddie didn't care. A hundred thousand dollars in gold was more than enough for him and Mariana.

"Let's go," Frank said. "The sooner we get back across the Rio Grande, the better. Even without witnesses, it ain't too hard to figure two gringos with a string of mules hauling a fortune in gold must've stole 'em."

"Those were *rurales* we killed," said Eddie. "If they sent *rurales*, they were expecting trouble. Even if they weren't, someone will be waiting for that shipment in Chihuahua City in four days. We won't reach the river for a week with these mules."

"True," said Frank, "but by the time the *federales* come after us, we'll be too far gone to catch up. What we got to worry about is running across any soldiers or *rurales* on the way."

They got the mules back in line and followed the maze of arroyos and dry gulches to where they'd left their own horses, hidden well out of sight among the craggy rocks at least a mile from the trail. Apart from the two they'd taken to chase after the mule-tender, Eddie and Frank hadn't bothered to collect up the rest of the *rurales'* horses. The others might still be milling around their fallen riders, or wandering in the desert, or they might have headed to the *rurales'* headquarters or back to the mine. If that was the case, the bodies were likely to be discovered sooner rather than later, and a pursuit organized long before the shipment was due to arrive in Chihuahua City. But it was equally dangerous to linger around the ambush site, trying to round up the horses. The trail was remote, but not so remote as to be completely untravelled.

He and Frank cut north across the badlands, which would be slower going than established trails, but it would hide their tracks and lessen the chance of accidental discovery. A team of six mules and four horses would always leave some kind of sign, but it would be harder to read on the bare rock than on the softer soil of the trails. They camped the first night among the rocks, forgoing a fire, though it hardly mattered in that heat. The next morning, they emerged onto the open plain of northern Chihuahua and joined a trail that snaked northeast toward El Paso.

The ride was monotonous. Unlike the craggy rock formations around the mine, the desert here was flat and featureless, an immense expanse of dust peppered with creosotes and the occasional cactus, distant hills and mountains barely a shadow on the horizon. They couldn't manage more than a walk with the mules loaded down as they were, and the air was just as oven-hot and still as yesterday. In such conditions, it was easy to drowse in the saddle.

Eddie didn't know how long he'd been asleep when a slap on the back startled him awake.

"You hibernating, Eddie?"

"Just nodded off," he replied.

Frank pointed to the western horizon, where a cloud of dust was visible against the late afternoon sky. "What do you make of that?"

Eddie shaded his eyes with his hand. The dust was close to the ground, not like the dust storms he'd seen up in the Panhandle, which looked like a whole damn mountain flying through the air, and making a horrible howling noise too. No, this had to be animals kicking up dust, and to be visible from such a distance, it had to be a lot of them. There weren't any more buffalo, if they ever ranged this far south, so it had to be horses.

"Mustangs?" Eddie suggested, sounding more hopeful than he was.

"I'd bet on cavalry," said Frank, voicing what Eddie already guessed to be true. "Probably from that new barracks at Nuevo Casas Grandes. Somebody must've found the bodies and sent a messenger. Maybe they even got a telegraph line now."

The dust cloud was growing faster than seemed possible. He and Frank were pretty easy to spot on the open plain. The Mexicans must have seen them and quickened their pace. There was no way to outrun good cavalry horses with these mules, especially laden with two hundred pounds of gold.

"As long as we're in the open, we're good as dead," said Frank. "If we can make the Peñones"—he pointed to a low rock formation way off to the east—"we might throw them off the scent."

"You think we'll make it?"

"We'd better try."

They rode hard, urging the mules on with the dead Mexican's whip, but the cavalry was catching up. It looked to be a few dozen men, too early yet to see if they were *rurales* or *federales*, or both.

Eddie and Frank were covering ground, though, and soon the Peñones loomed ahead of them, a jumble of rocky spires and arches jutting vertically from the desert floor. But behind the Peñones, the country became hilly again, offering the possibility of caves and canyons where a fugitive might hide or escape unnoticed.

The Mexicans were no more than a mile behind them when they reached the Peñones. Eddie could almost count them now. They were at least thirty, all in blue. A whole platoon of regular Federal Army troops. There was no picking that many off from a distance. He and Frank might take out a few, but enough would dig in behind the hillocks and boulders strewn around the Peñones to lay down covering fire while their compadres maneuvered up into the hills.

"We ain't out of the woods yet," said Eddie. "See them fanning out to try to surround us?"

"They ain't going to be able to box us in," said Frank, "as long as we keep moving. But they might still catch us up."

They were among the Peñones now, the misshapen spires towering over them like stone giants. Eddie guessed the Mexicans weren't too far behind, as they had been moving at a good pace, but at least they were out of sight.

"Let's split up," said Frank. "They can't catch us both."

"What about the gold?"

"You take three mules, I'll take three. If you make it out, you'll have more than your share. Ain't worth quibbling over now. If we both make it out, I'll look you up in Santa Catalina in a fortnight and we'll settle accounts."

Frank wasn't the most trustworthy fellow, but if he was willing to let Eddie dip into his share for expediency's sake, Eddie figured he must be on the level.

"Frank," Eddie said, suddenly remembering what he had come out here for, "if you make it and I don't, you got to take care of Mariana and her pa."

"Of course, kid. You think I would let that pretty girl of yours go hungry?"

Frank dismounted and cut the trace between the third and fourth mules. He tied it to the stirrup of the cavalry horse Eddie was leading, and then gave the horse a slap on the rump.

"Go on, then," Frank said. "You head north by northeast, I'll head east by southeast, and head back north after a couple days if they ain't caught me first. See you in Santa Catalina."

"Godspeed, Frank."

They parted ways without another word.

As Eddie led his little string of mules around and between the massive stone pillars, he heard Spanish voices echoing off the rocks. He tried to skirt around the left of each obstacle, to keep from crossing paths with Frank, but then he started thinking that would take him too far off his northeasterly course, maybe bring him out of the Peñones too early and into the open where he'd be easy prey for the *federales*.

He figured he'd be all right once he made it out of the Peñones and into a shallow valley between two ridges, but, after he'd been walking for ten minutes, he realized it was just a draw, and what he thought were ridges were actually just spurs of a larger ridge looming ahead of him.

In short, he was fucked.

Eddie got the mule train turned around, hoping he might get out of this dead-end draw before the *federales* found him, but it was too late. The first blue uniforms were already emerging from between the spires of the Peñones. He turned the animals around again, thinking he might make it up the steep slope at the end of the draw, and over the ridge to freedom.

But that was wishful thinking. There was sporadic gunfire behind him now. Puffs of dust erupted on the slope before him, not close enough to be too dangerous yet, but while he was playing the mountain goat, the *federales* would be getting closer, finding cover and taking aimed shots that wouldn't all miss.

Not a quarter of the way up the slope, Eddie's horse stumbled on the loose shale and slid a few feet before regaining its footing. He dismounted, careful not to slide downhill himself, and took advantage to return fire. This time he was not ensconced in a carefully chosen position, and his hands were shaky with nerves and exhaustion. He didn't hit a damned thing.

Ducking behind the animals just in case, Eddie cut the trace tying the mules to the police horse. He slapped the horse on the rump, sending it stumbling haphazardly down the hillside. Bullets kicked up dirt all around it.

With a heavy sigh, he did the same to his own horse, Spot, which he'd ridden all the way from East Texas. Spot was no derby-winning thoroughbred to be sure, but he was a good horse, and Eddie was sorry to see him go. But if he got himself shot to death in the desert it would be goodbye anyway, so he gave Spot a good shove downhill.

There was another burst of gunfire. Spot collapsed at Eddie's feet, a bullet in his flank, kicking up a big cloud of dust and screaming like a banshee.

Eddie ignored the poor animal, no time even to put him out of his misery. He tried to stay low and drag the mules up the slope, taking advantage of whatever concealment the dust might provide. It wasn't much. The shots were now close enough to hear the bullets whizzing by.

He was still a good thirty yards from the top of the ridgeline, thirty yards of steep slope without a twig of cover. Eddie clenched his butthole and carried on, thinking only about keeping the mules moving, ignoring the gunfire ricocheting all around him. At least the mules were more sure-footed than the horses.

The crest was only a few steps away when Eddie pitched forward into the dirt. He thought one of the mules had kicked him, but how would it hit his shoulder like that? He reached back to find blood oozing from the spot.

He'd been shot.

He was bleeding from the front of his shoulder too, so it must have been through and through, but that didn't make it hurt any less. His left arm flailed around uselessly, so he tried to push himself up with the right alone, but the bullets whistling overhead changed his mind for him. He managed to roll over enough to look back down the draw and see at least a dozen *federales* charging up the hillside while their comrades kept up a volume of fire from behind cover.

He'd lost his grip on the Winchester when the bullet hit him, and it had clattered over the rocks to rest against a yucca a few yards downhill. But he still had his revolver. As he struggled to draw from his awkward supine position, the mules walked right over him and up to the crest of the ridge.

They disappeared from sight just as the first Mexicans crowded in around him, their rifles at the ready.

Eddie was a good shot, but he only had six bullets, and the *federales* were ready to shoot him almost point blank.

He threw down his gun.

4

NUEVO CASAS GRANDES, CHIHUAHUA, 1893

THE JAIL CELL in Nuevo Casas Grandes was the most miserable hole Eddie could imagine, and he'd grown up in a tarpaper shack on the bayou. It was as humid as the damn bayou, even though the country was mostly desert, and while it was hot and sticky during the day, it grew cold and damp once the sun set. There was nothing in the cell but a bucket to shit in and a clay pot full of stagnant water.

The *federales'* surgeon had cleaned his wound with mescal and stuffed it with rags, and that was all the care he got. Which was more than he supposed he deserved after shooting six *rurales* in cold blood.

Eddie wondered why they were keeping him alive at all. He found out soon enough.

On the morning of his third day in jail, the jailer, a big, bearded man in peasant dress, opened the door to admit a lieutenant of *rurales* along with a sergeant and two troopers.

The lieutenant was a Spanish-looking youth, no older than Eddie himself, wearing a neatly tailored gray charro suit, adorned with silver lace and accented with a red cravat. He carried a clean, white towel.

The troopers were shorter and swarthier, their plain gray uniforms bleached almost white by the desert sun. The sergeant was the biggest

Mexican Eddie had ever seen, with a mustache like a boot-brush and an unreadable expression.

Eddie tried to get up, his left arm not cooperating, but the two troopers dragged him upright and held his arms, though they were already shackled, as were his feet.

The lieutenant wrapped the towel around Eddie's wounded shoulder and under his arm, addressing him in passable English. "You will probably be shot for what you have done," he said. "But first, you will tell us where the rest of the gold is."

The lieutenant stepped back. Without warning, the sergeant reached out and walloped Eddie across the face, hard enough to split his lip. He felt a trickle of blood oozing down his chin. More blood, warm and salty, welled up between his teeth.

"Sooner or later," continued the lieutenant, "you will tell us about your partners. If you tell us soon enough to find them and the missing gold, your stay in Nuevo Casas Grandes can be pleasant, and your execution swift and honorable, which is more than a bandit like you deserves."

"I ain't telling you shit." Eddie spat a stream of bloody saliva onto the dirt floor.

The sergeant hit him again, on the other side. No blood this time, but his whole face stung from the blow.

"Then your stay here will be miserable, and by the time they stand you in front of the firing squad, you will be begging for death."

The sergeant punctuated his superior's threat with a punch to Eddie's gut that left him heaving for several seconds.

But Eddie had been beaten before. When he was sure he wasn't going to puke, he straightened up as much as he could and said, again, "I ain't telling you *shit*."

The sergeant hit him again, of course, and again and again, every time Eddie refused to talk.

Eddie didn't know how long he could hold out. Sure, he'd been beaten before, but never continuously like this, not for any length of time. He'd been told that everyone had a breaking point, and he didn't imagine his would be too far off if these men were serious about it.

He had made up his mind to spill his guts when the lieutenant noticed that his wound was bleeding profusely. After a quick exchange in Spanish, one of the troopers ran off and returned with the surgeon.

Ignoring Eddie's new cuts, welts and bruises, the surgeon cleaned his wound again and re-packed it with rags. He admonished the *rurales* to have more *cuidado*, presumably if they didn't want their prisoner to die before telling them what they wanted to know.

"You must be hungry," said the lieutenant, as someone brought Eddie a pile of stale tortillas. "I'm going to dinner too. When I return, you better be ready to talk, or this is the last thing you ever eat."

Then the door slammed and Eddie was alone with his tortillas and his thoughts. He was bruised and bloodied, but without serious injury besides the gunshot. But if the *rurales* thought he wasn't going to be useful to find the gold, that was bound to change. So he had to be smart about it. He couldn't keep blustering and spitting and refusing to say *shit*. He would talk, but what should he say?

He could spill the beans on Frank Danger, of course. Frank was likely halfway back to El Paso anyway, and by the time word got out who he was and where he was going, and the Mexicans got a chance to organize a pursuit, he would be too far ahead to catch. But with six dead *rurales* and a hundred and fifty thousand dollars in gold still missing, the Mexican authorities were liable to plaster wanted posters all over both sides of the Rio Grande. They'd request the U.S. Marshals arrest him pending extradition and send an army of bounty hunters to track him down no matter how far north he tried to go.

Frank was hardly Eddie's bosom buddy, but they were partners and Eddie couldn't just turn him in. Besides, Mariana and her father needed Eddie's share of that gold. Seventy-five thousand would be more than enough to keep the shop open and a roof over Mariana's head until…

Until what?

Eddie wasn't going to kid himself. He was never going to see Mariana again. If he wasn't beaten to death in the next few hours, he'd be shot soon enough. There was no way to postpone his appointment with death.

Would she marry someone else?

Just the thought of it hurt Eddie more than the Mexican's punches and kicks. He doubled over in the corner of the cell, gagging on the dry tortilla he had been chewing.

But after a few seconds he calmed himself. She was a young girl, and beautiful. Of course she'd find someone else. And how could he begrudge her that?

"Just let it be someone who cares for her," he said to himself. "Not the first jackass who rides up to rescue her from poverty."

He went back to strategizing. If he couldn't tell the truth, he could spin a lie that would keep the *rurales* busy long enough for Frank to escape, long enough for Eddie's captors to lose patience and put him out of his misery. He just had to make it close enough to the truth that they'd believe him. He needed details to make the story stick. Names, places.

Instead of Frank Danger, his accomplice could be Francisco… Delgado. From Tucson. That would send them searching in the wrong direction for days. Eddie wished he'd had the presence of mind to come up with this idea before they beat him bloody.

He was putting the finishing touches on Francisco Delgado's physical description and life story when boots echoed in the hall, followed by arguing in Spanish. The jailer stumbled over to the door and began to unlock it while another Mexican officer, this one in federal blue, looked on.

"I am Capitán Villacorta," he said. "We are taking you to the federal court in Chihuahua for a proper trial. High banditry is no matter for *rurales* and local prosecutors."

"At night?" Eddie wondered aloud as the *federales* dragged him out of his cell, not worrying too much about the wound in his shoulder.

"The people here don't care much for *gabachos*," said Villacorta, "or for highwaymen. Especially not for *gabacho* highwaymen. It might not be safe to show your face in the daytime."

That was good enough for Eddie, and it wasn't like he had a choice anyway. The *federales* dragged him out into the street and threw him over the back of a waiting horse. As the platoon of *federales* set off, a chorus of shouts and Spanish curses followed them. The *rurales* had returned from supper to find their prisoner gone.

But the *rural* lieutenant must have known he wouldn't prevail against a regular army captain, for they did not pursue.

The trip to Chihuahua took three days, much of which Eddie spent slung across the horse's back like a sack of potatoes.

On the first night, they made camp in the shade of a cluster of live oaks. As the enlisted men pitched their pup tents, Captain Villacorta took hold of Eddie's collar and pulled him aside, out of earshot of the men.

"You have committed a grave crime, *gringo*," he said, "and you will surely be punished."

"So I hear."

"Surely you did not carry out this big robbery all by yourself."

Eddie shrugged. It was obvious enough he hadn't killed six *rurales* all by his lonesome, then misplaced half the loot.

"How many men did you have? You had three mules when you were captured. Two carrying gold, one carrying provisions for the voyage."

Though he tried to school his expression, Eddie's eyes must have widened.

"You didn't know that, did you, *gringo*? You thought you had half the gold. You know what that tells me?"

"What?" Eddie figured he might as well play along.

"It tells me you were only two men, since you each took half the mules. And it tells me you are not the smart one, not the boss."

In other circumstances, Eddie might have argued that point, but —well, for one, he knew it was true, and maybe it was better to let the Mexican believe it. Anyway, there was something off with this line of questioning. "Wait," said Eddie. "Didn't your men pursue us to the Peñones? So you already knew there were two of us."

"True. But now you've confirmed it. And once again you've shown me you're not the smart one."

Eddie let his shoulders slump as if he were truly crestfallen. "I guess you're right," he said, looking at the ground. "Francisco was always the smart one."

"Francisco? Your partner is a Mexican?"

"Of course. I don't know nobody down here. How would I find out about a gold shipment?"

"Listen," said Villacorta. "Mexico is a civilized country, no matter what you *gringos* think. You'll get a fair trial in Chihuahua. You tell everything you know about this Francisco and you might just escape the firing squad."

———

Captain Villacorta treated Eddie all right the rest of the way to Chihuahua City, offering up little privileges—a sip of water, a bean-filled tortilla roll, a cigarillo—in exchange for information about the imaginary Francisco Delgado. Eddie wasn't sure his story held water, but the captain showed no sign of doubting it.

They entered Chihuahua city the same way they had left Nuevo Casas Grandes, under cover of darkness. Eddie was thrown into a cell not much different than the one he'd left: cold, damp, dirt floor, shit-bucket, putrid water, stale tortillas.

In the morning, some soldiers dragged him out of the cell and led him down the street to a handsome colonial building. Inside the courthouse, the soldiers sat Eddie in a wooden chair and then stepped aside while a few Mexican gentlemen in frock coats talked in Spanish, occasionally pointing at Eddie. He figured one must be the judge and the others the prosecuting and defending attorneys, but he couldn't tell which was his since no one even talked to him.

After a while, Captain Villacorta came in and spoke to one of the men, who called for a clerk to take dictation. Villacorta spoke for a few minutes—Eddie could make out his own name, and that of the fictitious Francisco Delgado—and then signed the document with a flourish. The clerk applied a rubber stamp next to the signature.

Then, one of the attorneys read over the document, writing on a second sheet of paper as he did so. When he was finished, he drew a horizontal line at the bottom, and pushed the page across the table to Eddie, saying something in Spanish.

"*No comprendo*," said Eddie.

The lawyer pantomimed tracing a signature on the line. Eddie skimmed the text, but understood no more than he had of Villacorta's statement. He assumed this was to be his own testimony, but what was he testifying to?

"It says you confess to participating in highway robbery," Villacorta explained. "The robbery was planned by your partner, Francisco Delgado, a Mexican national, who then escaped with most of the gold. You were unaware that any *rurales* would be killed during the robbery, and you are willing to cooperate with Mexican justice to apprehend Señor Delgado. I have written the same in my statement, and have recommended clemency in your case, so you will be available for questioning should the need arise."

Eddie looked from the paper to Captain Villacorta and back. The officer's face betrayed no hint of his true thoughts or motives, but Eddie knew there had to be more to this story. During the trip to Chihuahua, Villacorta had questioned him about Delgado, but had hardly pressed him for details, had never picked up on any inconsistency. Villacorta was a captain of cavalry, not police, so maybe he just didn't know how to conduct an investigation, but if that was the case, why would he have taken the only suspect away from the *rurales*, who were already on the verge of obtaining a confession?

"Señor Dawson," said the attorney, "*su firma.*" He gave another flourish of his imaginary pen.

Eddie shrugged. It was prison or death, whether he signed or not. He took the pen offered by Villacorta and scribbled his name in nearly illegible block letters.

The attorney handed the paper to the clerk, who filed it in a leather-bound folder. The judge made a short pronouncement, and it seemed the trial was finished. Villacorta waved to a pair of *federales* standing by the door. They shackled Eddie and led him away.

5
―――――――

CHIHUAHUA STATE PENITENTIARY, CHIHUAHUA, 1893-4

THE CHIHUAHUA STATE PRISON, in which Eddie had spent a single night before trial, was a converted Spanish presidio, with three sprawling wings of prisoners' cells and a wing of soldiers' barracks arranged around a vast central courtyard. The courtyard, designed to accommodate battalions of drilling musketeers, was now planted with beans and peppers, which the prisoners tended mornings and evenings to supplement their meager rations of dry tortilla and weak broth. A bewildering assortment of machinery was arrayed around the edges of the yard, where the barracks' eaves cast some shade once a day.

Eddie would soon discover that the labor of the prisoners was the fabrication of cheap wool serapes. In the blistering heat, the men washed and carded wagon-loads of wool, bleached and then dyed it in steaming tubs of lye and God-knows-what, spun it into yarn, and finally wove it into patterned squares. It was hard work, harder than the little tailoring Eddie had picked up in Don Pedro's shop, but not as bad as the backbreaking labor some of his unsavory acquaintances had been obliged to perform clearing forests or digging ditches in American prison camps.

If it was just for the work, Eddie wouldn't have minded the presidio that much. For him, the worst part of prison was the prisoners.

The abuse had started the minute he crossed the threshold, pushed forward by the tip of a guard's club. *"Puto gabacho,"* he heard from one side and, *"gringo de mierda,"* from the other. He didn't speak much Spanish, but he knew all the cuss words, and he even understood when one brawny fellow admonished another that, *"ese güerito es para mí."*

Rather than putting him back in the tiny cell where he'd spent the night before his trial, the guard led Eddie to an open bay in the south wing, where blankets and straw mats were strewn haphazardly across the floor and dozens of hammocks hung between pillars and walls. Though it was the middle of the day, and a large number of prisoners had been hard at work in the courtyard, just as many lounged around the sleeping bay, chatting, playing cards or puffing on cigarillos that didn't smell like any tobacco Eddie'd ever smoked.

Although the iron-barred door was already open, it creaked when the guard walked Eddie inside. The prisoners fell silent, all eyes on him. Their card games stopped, their cigarillos burned away unsmoked. Then the chatter started up again, the same profanity and lascivious remarks as he'd heard outside.

Trying to ignore the commentary, Eddie looked around at his new accommodations. "Which bed is mine?" he asked the guard. *"¿Cuál cama?"*

The guard shrugged, gave Eddie one last shove, then turned and walked away.

The other prisoners sneered or turned away when Eddie got close, so he only gave a half-hearted wave of his hand, pretending he couldn't understand the threats and insults. He scouted out an area along one wall, not too close to anyone else's bed or hammock, where there was a sliver of shade and it didn't smell too much like piss, and lay down on his side, using his uninjured arm as a pillow.

He closed his eyes, but he wasn't about to sleep.

Sure enough, within five minutes he heard footsteps drawing near, and unintelligible whispering in Spanish. When a huarache-clad foot nudged him in the ribs, Eddie sprang into action.

He tried to spring, anyway, but with his lame arm, it took time to get to his feet, and by then the nudges had turned into kicks and punches. Eddie fought back as vigorously as he could with his one good arm, feeling his knuckles connect with ribs and jawbones, and once he was back on the ground—sooner than he had hoped—he kicked like a mule.

But it wasn't enough. They were too many, and Eddie was too weak from the gunshot wound and the beatings he'd already taken in the *rurales'* jail. He managed to fold his right arm across his face to keep his eyes, nose and teeth intact, but that left his stomach and ribs exposed to jabs and kicks that turned his dull ache into a spiderweb of sharp pains. When a particularly strong punch caught him in the shoulder, right where the bullet had gone through, Eddie felt the wound tear open and the blood oozing out, slow and viscous at first, then faster.

He lost consciousness.

———

When Eddie came to, he was lying on what felt like an actual bed, or at least a soldier's cot covered in wool blankets. His whole body hurt, his arms, legs and torso a mass of welts and bruises, his face swollen from blows he could not even remember. He opened and closed his mouth, ran his tongue over his teeth. At least none were missing.

He heard a voice nearby, deep and calm, questioning perhaps, to judge by the rising tone at the end of each sentence. It was Spanish, Eddie assumed, but it had a strange cadence to it. He tried to focus on the individual words.

"*¿Cómo te sientes?*" How do you feel, right? "*¿Puedes abrir los ojos?*" *Ojos* was eyes, so the man was probably asking Eddie to open his.

He tried to comply, but the left was swollen shut, and the right only opened enough to make out a dark, blurry figure against a bright background that must have been a window or doorway.

"*¿Dónde estoy?*" asked Eddie.

The man replied with something that sounded enough like

infirmary that Eddie figured he understood. He was surprised they even had an infirmary, and that they would bother trying to treat a prisoner who'd barely escaped the noose the day prior. They could have saved themselves the cost of his keep if they'd just let him die, but he supposed then someone would have to be held responsible. Maybe the warden just didn't want to waste a pair of hands that might still provide years of labor by letting him die on the first day.

Though every inch of him protested at the man's examination, Eddie didn't have any broken bones. His shoulder, however, felt like it would explode in flames when the man began to change the dressing.

"Shit!" Eddie exclaimed. "Sorry, doctor. Hurts like hell is all."

"*No doctor*," the man replied. "*No* English *tampoco*."

Eddie got a better look at the not-a-doctor when he leaned in to examine Eddie's swollen face. It wasn't just the sun at his back. He was Black, darker than any Negro Eddie'd ever seen back in Texas. Eddie'd never heard of a Black Mexican, and there was something in this man's speech that suggested he wasn't much better at Spanish than Eddie himself. Eddie thought of the Black Creoles in the bayous where he'd grown up, and tried to summon a half-remembered word or two learned from his Cajun relations.

"*Parlez français?*" he asked, though he didn't know what he'd do if the answer was yes.

"*Un peu*," said the man. "*Un peu français, un poquito español, más árabe.*"

"An Arab, huh?" Eddie had never met one. "What's your *nombre?*"

"Abdallah."

Eddie spent a week in the infirmary, at the end of which a doctor from a nearby military encampment made an appearance and pronounced Eddie fit for duty after a cursory examination. Though his official responsibilities in the infirmary appeared to be more janitorial than medical, Abdallah had changed Eddie's bandages daily throughout the week. They conversed at as great a length as might be expected during these short visits, in a mishmash of Spanish, which Abdallah knew much better than Eddie had given him credit for—though he did have a thick accent—and pidgin French, which he also knew much better than Eddie.

From what Eddie understood, Abdallah was from the Egyptian Soudan and had come over with the French army during their disastrous intervention in Mexico some thirty years prior. He didn't know, or couldn't explain—or maybe Eddie just couldn't understand—why he was still in a Mexican prison so long after the war had ended.

Abdallah's job was to clean the administrative section that took up the first floor of the northern wing, which also housed the guards' barracks. It was largely by chance that he had ended up caring for patients in the infirmary when the doctor wasn't around, which was most of the time. Of course, prisoners only went to the infirmary when they were seriously ill or injured, and most died shortly thereafter, so this additional duty didn't take as up much of his time as one might expect.

As soon as he was deemed fit, Eddie joined the daily work gangs in the courtyard. There were only so many tasks and only so much machinery, so just a quarter of the prisoners were selected to work on any given day. Eddie always strove to be among them. Working in the courtyard kept his hands busy, even if his mind was free to dwell on his past mistakes and his dead-end future, but, more importantly, it kept him in view of the guards and away from the worst of the other prisoners, who generally shunned honest labor.

Eddie soon found that the prison had its own hierarchy. At the top were the *caudillos*, bandit chieftains who had escaped summary execution to become the kings of the prison yard. There were only a handful of these—one for each of the three wings, to be precise—but each had his retinue of *bravos*: bandits, armed robbers and murderers who had been imprisoned along with their bosses or attached themselves to rising stars on the inside. Next were the *guapos*, those prisoners—usually horse thieves and burglars—who hoped to build a reputation by starting fights and picking on the *peones*, who were petty thieves and swindlers just trying to survive. Then there were the *putos*, who allowed their bodies to be used, no matter how reluctantly, for the pleasure of the other castes. Finally, at the very bottom of the ladder, were Abdallah and Eddie, the *chango* and the *gabacho*.

Eddie's position at the bottom meant that he was subjected to constant insults and curses, and the occasional shove or kick if he happened to be in someone's way. But, after the first beating to teach him his place, the *bravos* and *guapos* mostly left him alone. They fought to exert dominance and increase their stature against others of their own class, and to win the favor of the *caudillos*. There was little to be gained by beating up a lowly *gabacho*.

By devoting himself to the textile workshop during the day, and keeping to himself at night, Eddie was able to avoid serious abuse. There were only two men he really had to watch out for: Benito and Caneloso.

Benito was a *guapo*, renowned for the multiple murders he had committed both before and after his incarceration, but his open lust for handsome young men kept him from being accepted into the *caudillos'* inner circles. He was a short, dark fellow from somewhere way down south, with a wicked scar running from the corner of his lip almost to his right ear, where his cheek had been sliced completely open and sloppily sewn shut with thick twine. He'd supposedly fled north after killing an off-duty policeman in a knife fight, hoping to take refuge in Texas just as so many *gringo* ne'er-do-wells tried to escape to Mexico, but he'd been turned in just miles shy of the border by a hooker in Guadalupe. That, according to his self-proclaimed legend, was why he had sworn off women forever.

"Not only did she sell me out to the law," he'd tell anyone who'd listen, "but that slut messed up my face with her clumsy fingers."

Caneloso had been Benito's lover for years, serving him exactly as a wife would serve her husband, and even turning a blind eye to his dalliances with other, younger prisoners. He was something to look at, any man would have to admit, with soft cinnamon skin—hence the nickname Caneloso—silky black hair, and big, emerald-green eyes. But despite his beauty, Caneloso was a viper, ready to strike with poisonous swiftness to defend Benito against his many enemies or to defend his own position in Benito's affections should he feel it threatened.

From Eddie's first day in the presidio, when Benito had leered at him, saying, *"ese güerito es para mí,"* he knew there would one day be violence between them. He had not suspected that Caneloso might be just as much of a threat. Benito alternated between wooing, threats and sometimes outright assault, if he could catch Eddie alone at night. Eddie was the bigger man and stronger—once his wounds had healed—and walked away from their encounters with only a few bruises, but no sooner did Caneloso get word of it than he would come after Eddie, often with a razor or knitting needle.

Eddie ended up in the infirmary again, almost a year after his first visit, this time with a deep gash just left of his kidney, where Caneloso had stabbed him with a sharpened garden trowel.

6

___

CHIHUAHUA STATE PENITENTIARY, CHIHUAHUA, 1894

NOW THAT EDDIE knew enough Spanish to converse with Abdallah, he explained to the janitor-turned-nurse what had happened with Benito and Caneloso.

"*Zamb qawm Lut,*" said Abdallah with a look of disgust on his face. "Allah will punish them."

Eddie didn't understand half of what Abdallah had said, but he knew the word "Allah." He knew Allah was the Moorish god Abdallah prayed to when he disappeared all of a sudden, in the middle of work or dinner. Eddie had seen him before through the window of the infirmary, banging his head on the floor hard enough to leave a permanent bruise in the middle of his forehead, though it was hard to see given his skin tone.

"Why would your Allah care about a murdering infidel like yours truly?" Eddie asked without thinking.

"He is not *my* Allah only. He is Allah, Dios, God, the One and Only. My God and yours, whether you believe in Him or not."

"I believe in God," Eddie said tentatively, not sure he wanted to enter into such a weighty conversation in these circumstances. At least it would take his mind off his wound, which throbbed every time

Abdallah pierced it with what was probably an upholstery needle. "But it seems like he's punishing us all equally."

Abdallah jabbed him so hard that he howled. "Does the needle hurt?" he asked.

"Damn right it hurts!"

"Am I punishing you?"

"No…" Eddie stuttered. "I mean you're fixing me up, so I can't complain."

"This is what Allah does, my friend. When you think he is punishing you, it could be that he is healing you. And when you think he is rewarding you, it could be a punishment."

Eddie gasped as Abdallah pulled the sutures shut. "What do you mean?"

"Allah has every right to punish you for those men you killed. If you suffer for it now, perhaps he will recompense you in the hereafter. If you were to profit from your crimes like that Benito and the *caudillos*, and other robbers who are never caught, then your punishment would await you in the hereafter. You've only been in prison for a year, and you think you are suffering? The Fire is everlasting."

Eddie had heard such fire-and-brimstone talk before, from street-corner preachers in Texas and from the friars who came to harangue the prisoners every Sunday, but he had never heard an explanation like Abdallah's.

"Allah is Merciful," Abdallah continued. "He does not want to condemn any of his servants to the Fire."

"Even me?" Eddie asked, surprising himself with how seriously he was taking this sermonizing. "I've robbed and fought and whored around, and I've killed men in cold blood."

"Our Prophet"—he murmured something in Arabic every time he said this word—"said that Allah is happier with the repentance of a sinner than you would be finding your lost camel in the desert. He said that if you draw nearer to Allah by a foot, he will draw nearer to you by a yard, and if you draw nearer by a yard, he will draw nearer by a mile. If you come to him walking, Allah will come to you running."

"Well, tell your Allah he better run fast if he wants to catch me," Eddie joked, but his laugh rang false even in his own ears.

"Allah will always open a door for you," Abdallah said, shaking his head at Eddie's impertinence. "It's up to you to step through it."

———

Eddie resolved to take that step.

He was still in the infirmary on Sunday morning when the priest came round, which he took to be a stroke of Providence.

"Padre," he said, tugging on the friar's cassock, "I need to ask you something."

"What is it, my son?"

Eddie launched into a litany of the abuses he had suffered in prison, the fear he lived with each day, skirting decorously around the drama of Benito and Caneloso, so as not to offend the priest's sensibilities. He assured the priest he was a good Catholic, not a Protestant as one might expect given his nationality, and expressed contrition for his crimes.

The friar, a portly, red-faced Spaniard, waited patiently for Eddie to get to the point, his expression of studied beatitude both encouraging and discouraging at the same time. Eddie wanted to lay it out, to ask all the questions he had been holding in, about God and death, fate and forgiveness and divine justice.

"Would you like me to hear your confession, son?" asked the priest with a Castilian lisp, and the spell was broken.

"Sure," answered Eddie, "but I wanted to ask another favor as well."

"If it is within my power. The penitentiary is a secular institution. My influence here is limited."

"Just ask the warden to put me on the same cleaning detail as the Negro, here in the infirmary and offices. Get me out of the yard, at least, away from so many unrepentant sinners. I want to do right, I do, but I need your help."

"I'll see what I can do."

————

By Tuesday, Eddie was working in the infirmary with Abdallah. The doctor hadn't been around in weeks, and there were enough sick and injured prisoners that Abdallah spent more of his time nursing than cleaning.

Together they swept the floors and polished the furniture, washed the windows and even emptied the warden's outhouse when needed. Most days, the two of them made quick work of these tasks and spent the rest of the day treating patients.

Abdallah taught Eddie how to clean and dress wounds, and stitch them shut with needle and thread borrowed from the textile works. He taught him to set broken bones, to soothe burns with aloe and honey, and to break fevers with hot teas and cold cloths.

Sometimes they worked in companionable silence, and sometimes Eddie stayed silent while Abdallah recited Koranic verses in a melodious voice. Other days, they talked. They talked about everything, in more detail now that they could understand each other better.

When they got to discussing their lives, it turned out they had more in common than they had suspected, despite having grown up on different continents and thirty years apart.

Both were orphans, Eddie having lost his father in a drunken knife-fight and his mother to cholera a few years later, while Abdallah's parents had died of hunger in the famines caused by the Turkish invasion of the Soudan. They had both grown up in abject poverty, Eddie in the east Texas swamps and Abdallah in the Nuba Mountains west of the Nile. Both were single, having come to Mexico one way or another before they got the chance to wed.

Eddie supposed that was where the similarities ended, for after his parents' demise, he had made his way as a petty thief and bandit. Abdallah had been taken in by an aunt until his village was raided by slavers.

"They were horsemen from the north," he told Eddie one evening when they had finished their duties and sat together eating their tortillas in the deserted infirmary. "They called themselves Arabs though they looked more like us than the Egyptian Arabs I would meet later in the army. They called us *kuffar* and *mushrikin*—that means pagans—even though my village had been Muslim for a hundred years. We were blacker than them, which made us infidels in their eyes.

"A few of our men fought back with spears and knives, but the Arabs had scimitars and muskets. They killed most of the men and captured the women and children. They took us away to the slave market, strung together like mules, leaving only the old men and women and the smallest babies behind to survive or starve as Allah willed.

"I thank Allah that my mother had already died before that day, because the women and girls were sold off to warm the beds of rich Arabs. The few men left alive were taken to pick cotton and cut sugarcane for the Turks. We young boys—I must have been no more than eight or nine—were taken to a military camp to be trained as soldiers.

"It must seem strange to you, the idea of arming slaves. I have heard that your people always lived in fear of revolts and massacres, so you prohibited your Negroes from carrying weapons. But in the East, the sultans do not have big armies like the Yankees or the French. It is more like in Mexico during the war, when each side recruited bands of gunmen loyal to their own chiefs. These men cannot be trusted. They are liable to plunder the land they are meant to protect, desert on the eve of battle or even switch sides if the enemy pays better. So our sultans purchase slaves, with no ties to family or tribe, to train from boyhood to be soldiers. Slave soldiers are believed to be loyal only to the sultan, because they have no one else to turn to.

"This was my condition as a soldier for the Turks. As a boy, I spoke a Nubian tongue, but I have since forgotten it, and know only Arabic. My comrades were my brothers, in arms and in faith.

"The veterans among us told stories of campaigns in Equatoria and Abyssinia, but I never saw battle myself. One day we were ordered to board a steamship, which took us down the Nile to Cairo, a majestic city we were unable to enjoy, for we were immediately transferred to a barge that brought us by canal to Alexandria. Our stay there was hardly better. We were kept in barracks until it was time to board another, bigger steamer.

"This steamer docked in some European ports I don't know the names of, for we were not even allowed ashore, and then, eventually, we disembarked in Veracruz.

"The governor of Egypt had loaned us to the French emperor for his invasion of Mexico, but no one told us much of anything. When we reached Mexico, we learned that our task was to guard supply trains in the southern jungles, where the climate was unhealthy for those of your race. Many Frenchmen had already died of malaria, dengue and yellow fever. Many Soudanese would die of these things, as well, though the whites had assumed we'd be immune.

"Most of our losses were to disease, but a few men drowned in the treacherous swamps and others were killed by guerrillas and bandits, who sniped our men from a distance and ambushed the weakest platoons to capture our weapons and supplies."

Eddie was only vaguely aware of the French occupation of Mexico, which had ended before he was born, and he had never heard of the African cities and countries Abdallah was talking about. Still, he could imagine the life of those Negro soldiers, far from home, protecting mule trains on poor roads through mosquito-infested swamps like the swamps he'd grown up in. Protecting them from bandits, no doubt, from men like Eddie himself.

The guilt hit him like a wave.

"That's what I did to end up in here," he told Abdallah. "Killed three *rurales*, maybe four. Shot them down without so much as a warning, like they weren't even people. They were somebody's sons, though. Brothers. Husbands, maybe. Fathers. Like you told me before, I deserve whatever punishment I get. Hell is too good for me."

"Eddie," said Abdallah, "Allah's mercy surpasses His wrath. Never despair, not as long as you draw breath. If you are truly repentant, that is the first step toward Allah."

"I am, Abdallah, I am. What is the next step?"

"You must submit yourself to Allah, wholly and without reservation. Can you do that?"

For a moment, Eddie was overcome by almost abject terror. His trembling hands betrayed the fluttering in his heart.

Could he abandon his own religion to follow this foreign god? He'd never been a good Christian anyway—never went to church, never prayed, and he lied, cheated, stole, fornicated and even murdered like a regular old pagan, so what, exactly, would he be abandoning? Abdallah had told him that a Muslim abstained not only from pork, but from drink as well, and from all kinds of immorality. Was he ready to give up wine, women and song? But he had none of these things in prison, anyway. And he realized then the truth of what Abdallah had tried to explain before.

Prison was not a punishment for him, but a second chance. A chance he had to take.

"I am ready," he said, and knew at that moment it was true. His heart stilled and his trembling hands along with it, as he felt a sense of calm such as he had never experienced before, a tranquility so profound he could not imagine having been upset or frightened just moments before. And yet underneath he felt an upswelling of emotion he could not quite name.

"Repeat after me," said Abdallah, and Eddie did, first in Spanish and then, syllable by syllable, in Arabic.

"I bear witness that there is no god but Allah, and I bear witness that Muhammad is His servant and His Messenger. *Ashhadu al-la ilaha ill Allah wa ashhadu anna Muhammadan 'abduhu wa rasuluh.*"

The dam burst and all that emotion poured out, so strong and fast that Eddie could not make sense of it. He was so awash in these new feelings that he was barely aware of Abdallah speaking, clasping his hand and pulling him into a fraternal embrace.

"You are my brother now," Abdallah was saying when Eddie was able to focus on his words, "my brother in Islam. You are a new man, free from sin. Go bathe, that your body may be as stainless as your soul. Then I will show you what it means to be a believer."

7

—————

CHIHUAHUA STATE PENITENTIARY, CHIHUAHUA, 1894-1913

OVER THE MONTHS and years that followed, Abdallah fulfilled his promise. He taught his student to pray five times a day, to avoid swine and drink, to lower his gaze and watch his tongue. Abdallah taught him of the lives of the prophets, from Adam to Muhammad, Seal of Prophethood, some of whom were Israelite prophets he'd heard of and others Ishmaelites unknown to him.

Abdallah had decided Eddie should have a new name, a Muslim name, for he was a new man. The name he chose was Idris, the name of the wisest prophet of old, and close enough to "Eddie" that he would have little trouble remembering it. His surname would be Ibn Abdallah, the usual surname given to new converts, as it meant "son of a servant of Allah." However, the newly renamed Idris could not help but imagine that this name reflected the filial bond he shared with this particular Abdallah.

After he had learned a few short verses by rote repetition, Idris asked if he would ever be able to read the Koran he'd heard so much about, the way the padre would read to them from the Bible.

"Follow me." Abdallah led Idris to a supply closet in a lonely corner of the administrative wing, and, beaming, reached behind some bottles on the top shelf and produced an accountant's ledger. "You are clean?" he asked.

They had prayed *zuhr* recently, and Idris had not been to the privy or broken wind, so he indicated that he was. Abdallah handed him the ledger.

Idris opened it to discover that the first few pages were empty, but, starting from the back of the book, each page was filled not with columns of figures representing income and expenses, but rather with the loops and whorls of Arabic script. His eyes grew wide as he realized exactly what he had between his hands. "Is this…?"

"Yes," said Abdallah. "It is the product of nearly thirty years of labor, occupying every free moment since I was imprisoned here. I began with *al-Fatihah* in 1867 and I wrote the final *sin* of *Qul a'uzu bi Rabb in-nas* just before your arrival here, which I believe was in 1894."

"You wrote it all from memory?"

"I have recited one *juz'* daily since I was a boy. When I was a recruit in Khartoum, I recited the Qur'an silently while I practiced marching, loading and shooting. Reciting the Qur'an kept me sane during the voyage down the Nile and across the seas. When we were slogging through the jungle outside Puebla, I read the Qur'an as loud as I could to keep the spirits away.

"Here in prison, I recited every waking moment, out loud or silently. After a while, I decided I should have a *mushaf* of my own, so I began to fill this ledger, a few lines at a time. *Al-hamdulillah*, I have the Qur'an in my heart. You need this *mushaf* more than I do, and I want you to have it."

Idris had to wipe the tears away before he could respond. "Brother," he said, his voice still shaky, "I can't even read this."

"You will learn, *inshallah*. In prison you have nothing but time."

They started with the *surahs* Idris had already memorized, the short ones from the end of the book, which Idris discovered was toward what looked to be the front cover of the ledger. Idris traced the Arabic script with his fingers as he recited the words, while Abdallah corrected his pronunciation and showed him which shapes corresponded to which sounds. At the end of each *ayah*, Abdallah would explain its meaning in Spanish.

Soon Idris had learned to recognize the individual Arabic letters, though they looked completely different depending on their position in the word, and he had learned a few dozen words that tended to reoccur in the *surahs*.

Grammar and syntax were harder, but after a few years, with Abdallah's guidance, Idris was able to read and understand unfamiliar *surahs,* at least superficially, and he was able to converse with Abdallah on simple matters in his native Soudanese dialect.

———

Compared to the privations of his childhood and the violence and iniquity of his youth, Idris's years in prison with Shaykh Adballah were the most tranquil and—dare he say it—the happiest time of his life, surpassing even the momentary bliss he had felt during his few short months with Mariana. But that was before the cholera outbreak.

When the *peste* struck Chihuahua, it hit the penitentiary even harder than the city and its surrounding slums. The infirmary was overflowing with patients, with the worst cases left out in the yard where the stench of their shit and vomit would be less oppressive. So many of the textile workers fell ill that all the healthy prisoners, including the *bravos* and *guapos* who usually shirked honest work, were conscripted to keep the looms running and the prison's coffers full. The strongest among the sick were tasked with burying the dead in hastily excavated graves outside the walls.

The doctor no longer came by at all—he might have died for all Idris knew—and even the priest only walked through on Sunday to hear confessions and administer last rites. Abdallah and Idris worked tirelessly from morning until night, aided by a few patients who were well enough to walk but not hale enough to dig graves.

Idris fell ill first, on a Monday, three or four days into the epidemic. He woke in a cold sweat, with an overwhelming urge to shit. He spent the next five days stumbling from bed to privy and back, sometimes stopping along the way to vomit. Abdallah kept him covered with damp blankets to control the fever, and gave him boiled water with just enough salt to make it taste horrible, and prayed over him whenever he could get away from his other patients.

On Thursday night, Idris's fever raged. He dreamed so vividly that he was sure he was wide awake, if not dead and passing through *barzakh* or the trials of the grave. The dream started with him in his hospital bed, sweating and puking just like he had been for days. The stench was so strong, he could never believe he had dreamed it. He rolled out of bed to crawl toward the privy, but instead of the dirt floor of the prison yard, he found sun-baked stone and loose sand.

His hands and knees burned and chafed as he crawled over the strange landscape, along a faint path that wound between dunes and crags dotted with thorn bushes and clumps of dry grass, not unlike the desert where he'd ambushed the gold shipment. But after what seemed like hours of dragging his ailing body, lizard-like, under a scorching summer sky, Idris came to a rock formation that loomed over the surrounding landscape, nearly blocking out the sun, which cast an orange glow around its silhouette.

By the time Idris reached the mountain, the sun was overhead, and he could see that the path wound its way uphill to a cave, barely visible amid the boulders. Dragging himself with the strength of his arms alone, his lacerated legs trailing uselessly behind him, Idris crawled over and between the rocks until he gained the mouth of the cave. Inside, glowing with a light of its own, was a wooden chest full of gold.

Idris jolted awake. His hands and knees burned as if he'd really crawled across the rocky wasteland, but he could see no wounds. The morning sun cast an orange glow through the barred window.

"*Ya Abdallah!*" called Idris.

Abdallah rushed to his friend's bedside and placed a hand on his forehead. "The fever has abated," he said, relief plain on his face. "*Al-hamdulillah!*"

Idris told him about the dream, and his relieved expression turned to one of shock and then consternation.

"I am sure this gold will haunt me until death," said Idris at the end of his story.

"I do not think it is the same gold," Abdallah replied. "I know the mountain you describe, though you have never seen it yourself. I remember reaching it at dawn, as in your dream. It glowed with an orange halo like Jabal an-Nur, and I knew before we even climbed its slope that we would find a cave like Hira, where our beloved Prophet first received Revelation."

"So the treasure is not gold, but rather the treasure of Islam?" Idris asked, trying to work out the meaning.

"Perhaps," Abdallah replied. "I am not Prophet Yusuf, *'alayh is-salam*, to interpret such dreams."

The next day, Idris was up and about, having fully recovered, while Abdallah had taken ill. He called Idris to his bedside.

"I am not a young man like you," he said between bouts of retching, "and I expect my days in this world are coming to an end."

"Don't say that, brother. Allah is the Healer. *Inshallah*, He will cure you as He has cured me."

"Allah will do as He wills, brother. I cannot pretend to know His intentions. But I feel that I am near death. I have had a long life, and full enough, though I have spent more than half of it between these walls. Anyway, our Prophet, peace be upon him, said that this world is a prison for the believer, so this prison of bricks is nothing beside the prison of flesh I shall soon escape, Allah willing."

"Allah knows best," said Idris, holding back tears, for he could see Abdallah's diminishment and knew his words were true. "I only wish I had more time with you."

"He has given us the time we need, no more, no less. But before I go, let me tell you something that has been weighing heavy on my heart."

"Anything, my friend."

Idris helped the ailing man to sit up against the sack of straw that served as a pillow, and offered him a ladleful of water from the small jar he'd purified by boiling. Abdallah waved it away. "I'll just puke it back up," he said. "Maybe later, but first, let me tell you my secret, while I still have time."

"A secret?" Idris Imagined they had no secrets from each other, not after so many years.

"Not from you alone. I've kept this secret from everyone."

"My *shaykh*, if it is a sin, perhaps it is better to conceal it."

"The sin is not mine, my brother. You know my history with the Egyptian battalion. You do not know how I came to remain in Mexico, while the rest of my battalion returned to Africa, or so I've been told. Toward the end of 1866, by the Christian reckoning, the French emperor had announced that all French forces would be withdrawn from Mexico. French troops were streaming from all corners of Mexico toward Veracruz, carrying as much goods and equipment— their own and what they'd plundered from the locals—as their porters and livestock could carry. Everyone knew that Emperor Maximilian was bound to fall, and his Mexican troops were deserting like—what's the saying?—like rats from a sinking ship.

"Now Maximilian had amassed a huge treasure during his time as emperor, enough to put your lost gold to shame. He had Mexican pesos, Austrian dollars like we use in Egypt, gold watches and ladies' jewelry, ingots and bars, even ancient Indian relics the French and Austrians had dug up. I know this because a few of us Africans were tasked with loading this treasure into wagons and escorting it under arms to a port on the west coast. I heard we were to rendez-vous with a steamer out of Port Isabel, which was in American hands and said to be sympathetic to the Emperor.

"We never made it, of course. The whole west coast had fallen to the Republicans, from Baja California on down to Guerrero. There we were, a dozen Africans and three white officers—Austrians, perhaps, kinsmen to the Emperor—on a mountain road a hundred miles east of San Blas, surrounded by Republican guerrillas. When it was clear we would never reach the coast alive, the Austrians led us to a cave hidden among the boulders on a mountainside—the mountain you dreamed of, bathed in golden light like Jabal an-Nur—and there we hid the whole hoard. We closed the mouth of the cave with rubble, so completely that no one would know it was there.

"That's when I understood why they had chosen Africans for this secret mission. Mexicans might have deserted to the enemy. Frenchmen would have talked—if they ever got home, that is. We barely spoke Spanish and had no friends among the population, so we could be trusted not to mutiny and take the gold. And assuming we delivered it successfully, we would be returned to our unit and sent home to Egypt, never breathing a word to anyone who mattered. And if we found ourselves trapped as we did…"

"What?" asked Idris, when Abdallah's pause lengthened.

"We were expendable. Animals to be sacrificed. Those three Austrians unholstered their revolvers and shot us down with no more compassion than they showed the oxen that had pulled the wagons. I only escaped because my executioner stopped to reload. I ran, not stopping to think if any of my comrades had survived, ran until my legs quit working.

"The Mexicans picked me up many miles away and threw me in jail. They only knew that I was an enemy soldier, I suppose, perhaps a deserter. No one questioned me in any detail, and I did not know enough Spanish back then to volunteer information. Later on, whenever they transferred me to a new prison—which was pretty often right after the war—I thought about offering the guards some or even all of the treasure to set me free. But I knew that would never work. Once the treasure was recovered, they would shoot me down just as the Austrians killed my comrades, sacrificing me just as your friend tried to sacrifice you—"

"What?" Idris nearly choked at these last words. Frank hadn't sacrificed him. They'd agreed to split up to give each the best chance of escape, and Eddie—Idris, that is—had just had the bad luck to get caught. Right?

Abdallah continued, ignoring Idris's outburst. "And what would such men do with such great wealth? A prison guard suddenly in possession of an emperor's fortune? He would buy himself a generalship or start his own bandit army, or buy a great hacienda and live like a king while his peons labored in poverty and want. I could not see any future in which that treasure would lead to a better situation in this country, rather than increasing its poverty, exploitation and violence. So I kept it to myself."

"Why are you telling me, then?" Idris asked, his mind still reeling with unpleasant thoughts about Frank Danger and that day so many years ago. "Why not take your secret to the grave?"

"You are a good man, Idris. A Muslim. When you recover the treasure, you will give a fortieth of it in charity to the poor in my homeland, for *zakat* is your obligation. And you will make the pilgrimage to Mecca, once for yourself, and once on my behalf, Allah willing. There is no end to the good you could do with such a treasure."

"*Inshallah*," said Idris, "but what makes you think I will ever see this treasure of yours? I am no less a prisoner than you."

"My brother, the prison is changing. Mexico is changing. I am sure Allah will soon prepare for you a path to freedom."

PART II
REBIRTH

$$8$$

NORTHERN MEXICO, 1913-14

IT WAS TRUE.

Shaykh Abdallah was one of the last casualties of the cholera epidemic. Neither guards nor priest cared much what happened to his black corpse, so Idris was able to bury him on his own. He washed his friend's body with the last of the clean water, supplemented by his own tears, and wrapped him up in the only clean white sheet he could find. Then Idris buried his only friend in a secluded corner of the graveyard, his head facing the *qiblah.*

He performed the funeral prayer alone, following Abdallah's instructions as closely as his memory allowed, and then he returned to care for the few remaining patients.

The prison's population had been so thinned by the cholera that the prisoners could be crowded into a single wing of the presidio. The textile workshop was closed, as was Abdallah's infirmary. Idris found himself back among the general population, though he was allowed to partition off a space and keep a few beds for any prisoners who might fall ill.

Meanwhile, a new battalion of *federales* moved into the vacant wings, and their constant drilling filled the courtyard where the prisoners had once plied their spinners and looms.

Though Idris had feared returning to the open bay where he had once been in constant danger of being beaten or killed, he discovered that the climate in the prison had changed. The old *caudillos* had died off in the epidemic, and most of their *bravos* along with them. Benito had picked a fight with the wrong *caudillo* just before the cholera hit, and had been carved up like a Christmas pig. Caneloso, crazy with grief, had managed to kill three of the assassins before he too met his death.

There were a few new prisoners, mostly political types—socialists, communists, anarchists. Idris wasn't even the only foreigner anymore, as a few of these agitators were Spaniards, Germans and Slavs.

These newcomers brought news of revolution. President Porfirio Díaz, who had reigned in Mexico for as long as Idris could remember, had agreed to hold elections the previous year, but had resorted to gross fraud to emerge victorious. His opponent, the reformist Francisco Madero, had called for an armed uprising, and local businessmen, landowners and bandits throughout Chihuahua and other northern states were raising men to support him.

That explained the increased military presence in Chihuahua City. It didn't explain why the new battalion stayed in barracks while the rebels won victory after victory across northern Mexico, culminating in the siege of Ciudad Juárez.

When news came that Juárez had fallen and Díaz had surrendered the presidency, the prisoners partied for a week, cheering and beating drums, feasting as best they could on their scrawny chickens and stale tortillas, getting drunk on moonshine mescal and smoking marihuana day and night. But the soldiers didn't leave.

Soon the revolution splintered into factions and violence returned to the prison yard, only now the fights were not over drugs or boys, but rather between supporters of Huerta or Madero, Villa or Orozco.

Idris had little use for the conspiracies of Mexican generals and politicians. His mind was occupied with unraveling the conspiracy that had landed him in that hellhole so many years before.

Abdallah was right, but it had taken Idris a while to open his eyes to the possibility that he had been betrayed. Once he did, so many things made so much more sense.

He'd known Frank Danger had a contact in Mexico who had informed him of the route and timing of the gold shipment, and that person would get a cut of the take. Frank had told him that much, though he'd never shared the Mexican's name. His percentage, Idris remembered: one sixth, after Frank's half and Idris's—or rather Eddie's—third. So who was this Mexican? It made sense he'd agree to a smaller cut, seeing as he hadn't risked himself in the firefight as Frank and Eddie had, but when, where and how was he even supposed to get his cut with half the Mexican army after Frank and Eddie?

While Eddie had gone in blind, with no thought to the myriad things that might go wrong, Frank and his Mexican contact clearly could have foreseen the possibility of being pursued. Frank had done these kinds of jobs before, though never with so much money at stake, so he would have made a workable plan. He would not have stiffed his contact, not because he'd feel any moral imperative to keep his word, but simply because if he didn't deliver, his contact would go to the Mexican police and Frank would be forever in danger of falling prey to bounty hunters or Mexican agents. No, he would have to go back, either to pay off his contact or to kill him.

That led to another quandary. Frank couldn't just wander around Chihuahua, asking about gold shipments. He and his contact would have to be old associates. Anyone who knew Frank would know he was capable of killing in cold blood if he sniffed betrayal, so said contact would have to be confident of his own ability to face Frank if things went south. Probably someone in the police or army, someone who could count on his comrades to back him up in a fight.

Villacorta!

Of course... That would explain everything. Frank and Villacorta had planned to rob the shipment, but it was too big and dangerous a job for the two of them. Villacorta couldn't be part of the ambush itself, since his absence from barracks might be noted, but he could trust Frank not to abscond with his share of the loot or try to murder him. And it would explain why Villacorta and his men showed up under cover of night to pull Eddie out of jail before the *rurales* could interrogate him too much. No one at the penitentiary had ever come to question him about the robbery.

Villacorta's guilt was so clear, Idris couldn't believe he hadn't seen it from the beginning. But another question remained. Had the *federales* captured Eddie by sheer luck and Villacorta stepped in to limit his liability, or had Villacorta himself captured Eddie? And if so, did Frank know?

That was the part that bothered him most. Villacorta was a stranger to him, a foreigner he'd only met once, who had no reason to give him any more consideration than he'd given those faceless *rurales*. But Frank? Bastard that he was, Frank had been as close to a friend as Idris had ever had before he met Abdallah, back when he was still Eddie.

If Frank had planned to use him as a patsy from the beginning, as the evidence seemed to indicate, that betrayal would break Idris's heart.

Abdallah had tried to dissuade him from these thoughts during his last hours.

"Idris," he'd said, "forget about the past. You are a new man. Eddie's friends are not your friends. His life is not your life. If you trouble yourself with Eddie's affairs, you will return to Eddie's sinful ways, and you will burn in Eddie's fire."

Idris knew it was true, but he couldn't stop picking at the scab.

As the rebel factions battled back and forth across northern Mexico, the guns sometimes audible just outside Chihuahua City, Idris began to believe that freedom might indeed be possible, just as Abdallah had assured him.

Abdallah had described the location of the imperial treasure in minute detail, and made Idris repeat it until he could recite the description as easily as *al-Fatihah*.

Idris had faith he would find the treasure one day, and there would be no end to the good—or evil—he could do with such wealth.

In November of 1913, the *federales* packed up their gear and marched north to retake Juárez from Pancho Villa, but they were ambushed and practically annihilated before they got there. Chihuahua City was left in the hands of Orozco's nominally pro-government militia, who plundered the city for a week before retreating to the east.

On the third of December, Villa's División del Norte entered Chihuahua as liberators. They made a romantic picture, wearing white peasant dress and oversized sombreros instead of blue or khaki uniforms like the *federales* and other revolutionaries, but with bandoliers of rifle cartridges criss-crossing their chests. Most were mounted on fine Spanish horses probably requisitioned from local landowners, and they had machine guns and European artillery pieces unlike any cannon Idris had seen at the frontier forts in the States.

The last few guards had fled as soon as they saw the first *villistas* in the streets, but they'd left the gates chained shut, so Idris and his fellow prisoners stood on the rooftops to cheer on the victorious revolutionaries.

General Pancho Villa himself, who Idris recognized from newspaper clippings pinned up in their quarters by many of the inmates, noticed the cheering prisoners and dispatched a small contingent of soldiers to blast open the gates.

"Gentlemen," said the officer in charge of the detachment, "the Porfiriato was a criminal regime, and violation of its laws is, in and of itself, an act of revolution. General Villa welcomes you into the ranks of the División del Norte."

"What if we don't want to join?" asked one of the prisoners, a partisan of Villa's rival Obregón. "Will you leave us in here to rot?"

"Of course not," the officer replied. "General Villa does not have enough supplies to feed a bunch of counterrevolutionary criminals, nor men to guard you. In time of war, prisons are a luxury we can't afford. Firing squads, however, are plentiful, and ammunition cheap."

All the prisoners rushed to join Villa's forces. They gathered their personal effects and followed the officer to the tent city the *villistas* were setting up on the outskirts of town. A sergeant made them line up as neatly as he could—the ex-prisoners had long since forgotten their regimented existence before the cholera hit—and each man wrote his name or made his mark in a ledger and took a captured army rifle off the pile by the quartermaster's desk.

When one of the European prisoners, about five steps ahead of Idris in line, reached the desk, the quartermaster balked at his foreign name. "Schneider? What are you, German?"

"Yes, Sergeant. From Hesse-Darmstadt."

The quartermaster laughed until he started coughing. "General Villa hates Germans," he said. "Germany sends arms and advisors to the *federales*. Why don't you be a Pole? The general has Polish aviators in his air force. He likes Poles."

Idris didn't understand what an aviator was, but he got the gist of the conversation. He'd better steer clear of General Villa's prejudices if he wanted to survive in the División del Norte. He didn't imagine Villa had a positive opinion of Americans.

When it was his turn, the quartermaster gave him the same judgmental look he'd given the German. "Where are you from, *güerito*?"

"I'm a Turk," said Idris.

"You don't look Turkish to me."

"I'm from... European Turkey." He leaned down and wrote his name in the ledger in Arabic script. *Idris ibn 'Abdallah.*

"What do you know," said the quartermaster, looking down at the squiggles and dots, "a blond Moor!"

Writing Abdallah's name had almost brought tears to Idris's eyes, but he recovered his calm enough to quip, "How does General Villa feel about Turks?"

"He probably likes your lot better than the goddamn papists," the quartermaster retorted, laughing and coughing again.

Idris took a rifle off the pile and followed the other recruits to find himself a bunk.

———

Life in the División del Norte was not so different from life in prison, except that now Idris marched twenty miles at a stretch, for weeks at a time, before pitching another camp. Then it would be back to the same routine of tortillas, mescal and marihuana, though Idris only partook in the first.

Occasionally, they would meet with patrols—*federales, orozquistas, constitucionalistas*—and spend hours prone in ditches or kneeling behind boulders, exchanging potshots with enemies they could barely see. Even more infrequent were the real battles: Ojinaga, Zacatecas, Celaya. These were a wholly different affair, the opposing soldiers taking turns assaulting machine guns and artillery emplacements, sustaining hundreds of casualties in an hour or two. It was an unworldly experience, alternating between elation when Idris reached a trench or embankment and found himself still—miraculously—alive, his lungs heaving, heart pounding, and abject terror when the order came to fix bayonets and charge once more across no-man's-land.

Idris had heard that a Great War had broken out in Europe, where the same scene was repeating itself on a titanic scale, hundreds of thousands of men obliterated by bombs, shells and disease. But the European war meant little to Idris. The only thing that got him through the boredom of camp life and the horror of battle was the thought of Abdallah's treasure.

Celaya was the worst battle of all. Obregón's *constitucionalistas* were dug in around the city, well entrenched with bunkers and barbed wire, and machine guns and heavy artillery manned by European mercenaries. Having fewer heavy weapons, Villa was forced to go on the offense if he wanted to capture any ground. He tried to gain the initiative with daring cavalry charges, but his horses were soon shot to pieces, and after that there was nothing to do but launch massed infantry assaults like the French at the Marne.

On the fifth or sixth charge of the day, Idris found himself pinned down in a ditch in no-man's-land, a quarter mile from friendly lines, alone except for Luis Vargas, a peon from up north he only knew by sight. They hunkered down until the machine gun fire petered out, Luis reciting the rosary and Idris the last two chapters of the Qur'an.

When the heaviest firing had stopped, they got to their knees and tried to peek over the edge to get the lay of the land. Idris placed his oversized sombrero over the barrel of his rifle and raised it clear of the ditch. Nothing happened. After Idris retrieved the sombrero and crushed it back onto his pate, Luis poked his bare head up to see for himself.

Idris saw a muzzle flash in the distance, and knew instinctively that it was a sniper. He dove, pushing Luis down behind cover, and the bullet struck his right arm below the shoulder, not quite opposite where the *federales* had shot him so many years before. The crack of the gunshot reached his ears an instant later.

"You saved my life, Turco!" exclaimed Luis as the bullets began to fly overhead once again. "And you're wounded."

"It's nothing." Idris fingered the spot where the bullet had creased his skin, but done no significant damage. "Just help me to bandage it."

"Of course." Luis moved closer, taking care to keep his head low. "How can I ever repay you?"

"Don't mention it."

"I swear to the Virgin, if you ever ask me for anything, it's yours."

Just then, the bugle sounded and Villa's men launched another ill-fated assault against Obregón's lines, passing by Idris and Luis's hiding place on their way out, and sweeping them up on their retreat a few minutes later.

The battle was lost.

———

Just as he alternated between the exhilaration of battle and the fear of death and dismemberment, Idris alternated between fuming over Villacorta's betrayal—and Frank's?—and dreaming of the hoard that awaited him in a forgotten grotto in Jalisco.

He had wanted to retrieve the treasure after Zacatecas, but he had been unable to get away from the División. With Huerta and his *federales* out of the way, Villa and Carranza had ended their uneasy alliance, and Villa was on the lookout for any sign of disloyalty among his men, especially those who were not *norteños* by birth. He became even more paranoid after the disaster at Celaya, when some of his officers defected and many of the rank and file simply ran away, but there was little he could do to stop the rash of desertions.

Not long after the battle, Idris stumbled upon a trio of *villistas* whispering together in a shadowed part of their makeshift camp.

"Fuck off, *gringo*," said one, but another shushed him. It was Luis Vargas.

"El Turco is a good man," said Vargas. "Let him come along if he wants."

Desertion? This had been Idris's goal for a year now, and it would be much easier with a group. "I'm in if you'll have me. Where are we going?"

"San Blas," the first man said after a minute of contemplation. "And from there, anywhere your purse can take you."

Idris grinned. The route to San Blas would take him as close to the treasure as he was ever going to get.

They left under cover of darkness. Villa had lost so many horses at Celaya that he put the rest of the herd under guard, so they went on foot, carrying only what they could fit in their packs. Idris was reluctant to take anything more than the clothes on his back, for a Muslim should not steal, but Villa owed him almost six months' wages, and that should cover his revolver, some spare rounds, a small spade, a bit of candle, a full canteen and a few days' worth of tortillas and beef *machaca*.

Once they were safely away from camp, Idris pulled Luis aside to talk privately as they walked.

"What is it, Turco? Are you getting cold feet?"

"Not at all, my friend. I need to call in the favor you promised me."

"By the Virgin, I'll do anything."

"When we reach a town called Ixtlán del Río, some two days' march beyond Guadalajara, I need to take a detour into the mountains to check on a property for an old friend from prison. I swear that I will do nothing to endanger our comrades. You must convince them of this."

"Of course. Consider it done."

"There is more, and this part may be more difficult. You must wait for me in San Blas. While you're there, inquire about mules, as many as you can hire. If my friend's property is in good condition, I will find you within a week, and we will return to the Sierra to bring some goods to town. If I haven't appeared in seven days, assume I've been captured or killed. Your vow will be fulfilled and you can go wherever you please with a clear conscience."

"This is too little, Turco. Ask whatever you would of me. After all, you saved my life."

"If you do this for me, you will have saved my life as well."

———

The other two deserters looked askance when Idris parted ways with them in Ixtlán, but seemed to accept Luis's assurances that he would not turn them in.

The mountains were more thickly forested than in Abdallah's description, and Idris wished he'd thought to take a machete as part of his back wages, but he made do with the spade.

It was a full day's march to the nameless mountain he'd begun to think of as Jabal an-Nur, after Abdallah's description of it. The mountain was just as Abdallah had said, a near-pyramid of bare rock, with only the occasional shrub or yucca sprouting from the dry earth accumulated in its crevices. He worked his way around the base of the mountain, until the peak was directly up and ahead when he faced the *qiblah*.

He washed with water from his canteen, prayed *maghrib* and *'isha'* combined, and then wrapped himself up in his serape to await the dawn.

Idris awoke to see the sky reddening in the east, forming a halo of pink and orange clouds all around the contours of the mountain, just as Abdallah had promised. *Wallah,* it looked exactly as Idris imagined

Jabal an-Nur must, the whole mount illuminated by the *fajr* light. And there, exactly where the sun's disc first appeared over the edge of the mountain, Idris saw the cluster of long, flat boulders Abdallah had mentioned, framing what looked almost like a doorway into the heart of the Earth.

He spent the next few hours climbing up the steep mountainside to the spot he had seen from below. The cave entrance was easy enough to pick out if one knew where to look, but, as Abdallah had said, it was clogged with debris.

Soil had accumulated over the years, turning what must have once been loose rocks and gravel into a fairly solid wall of earth, but Idris was able to break through in the space of two hours, and in another two, he had widened the opening enough to squeeze through.

Once inside, he lit his candle and, cupping his hand around the flame to keep it from going out at the first breath of wind, began to explore the cave. First there was a sort of tunnel, barely tall enough to stand up in, but it soon opened up into a larger cavern.

Idris spent almost half an hour inching his way around the cavern, keeping one hand on the wall, until he had gone one hundred and forty-three paces, no more, no less. Then he took seventeen paces toward the center of the cave and began to probe the ground with the spade. It was solid rock.

"Of course!" Idris said aloud. Abdallah had been considerably taller than he, so his paces would have been noticeably longer. As he made his way back to the cave entrance to retrace his steps, Idris tried to calculate how much further he'd need to go.

He knew he took a thirty-inch step, as this had been drilled into him while marching with the *villistas*, but Abdallah, being over six feet, probably had a stride two or three inches longer. Over the course of a hundred and forty-three paces, two inches per stride would make a difference of about twenty-four feet, or nearly ten of Idris's paces. So he counted out a hundred and fifty-three paces this time, and eighteen toward the center.

This time the spade struck wood. As Abdallah had recounted, the treasure had been hidden in a natural depression in the floor of the cave, then the Soudanese soldiers had been made to break up the wagon to cover the gold with sheets of wood and finally hide it with a layer of rubble.

Setting the candle aside, Idris worked quickly to clear the rubble off the wooden planks, then he used the spade as a lever to pry up one side, heaving with all his might. The board came up, and Idris got under it to push it out of the way.

Finally, he recovered the candle and brought it close to inspect the contents of the pit. Even in this weak light, the glitter of gold was unmistakable. The entire trench was full of the stuff—coins, both gold and silver, bars, chains and watches, rings and bracelets studded with diamonds and sapphires, sacred chalices, pagan statues…

Ya Allah! How could so much wealth be concentrated in such a small space, hidden away while men fought and died for much less right outside?

Idris wanted to grab handfuls of gold and jewels and toss it in the air like confetti. He wanted to swim in the sparkling coins like a duck, feeling their metallic warmth against his skin. He wanted to dynamite the cave to destroy this golden calf.

But Idris did none of these things. He forced himself to act methodically, to still his pounding heart with cold calculation. He sorted through the coins, inspecting each by candlelight, until he had set aside around five hundred dollars in twenty-dollar and twenty-peso coins, and a handful of silver coins of lesser value. He made sure to choose coins of recent minting, though even the newest were fifty years old, so that the ancient coins would not give him away like the Seven Sleepers of the parable.

Ya Allah! Idris felt he might as well be one of the Seven Sleepers himself, after being shut away in prison for two decades, still surprised every day by how much the world had changed. He could learn to live with automobiles and aeroplanes, but what else had changed remained to be seen. What had come of Villacorta, of Frank Danger? What of his lovely Mariana? Would she be married now, a mother?

Idris pushed those thoughts away. He would find out soon enough.

Until then, there was little use in speculation. Anyway, he had work to do.

He met up with Luis in San Blas six days later, as promised. The Mexican had found a teamster willing to hire a string of mules for a rate that was not so unreasonable as to raise eyebrows when he agreed.

He also purchased a decent suit, and a regular, American-size felt hat. *Gringos* were scarce enough in this part of Mexico, but a *gringo* in a sombrero and tattered peasant dress was sure to be marked as a *villista* deserter. He bought a notebook and a few lead pencils too, figuring if anyone asked, he could say he was a newspaperman.

"Do newspapermen write in little notebooks with lead pencils?" Luis asked.

Idris shrugged. He'd never actually met a newspaperman, but he supposed most folks he was liable to run into out here hadn't either.

Idris would have liked to buy or hire a couple horses, but they were scarce, with the *constitucionalistas* and *villistas* requisitioning as many as they could, and the rest selling for so much that it would be a red flag for a stranger to pay such an inflated price. Maybe a foreign newspaperman could get away with it. Idris didn't know how much money they made.

He and Luis made the trek back to Ixtlán, more slowly this time since they had the mules with them, and then up the overgrown path into the Sierra.

On the way, Idris told Luis what to expect, watching the man's reaction closely. Though Luis's eyes widened at his description of the gold and jewels, Idris saw no hint of malice or cupidity.

"You will take a share of the gold," Idris told him, "and don't try to refuse. You can spend it on your family, or on the people of this country, as you see fit. I would give you more if I could, but I have other obligations."

Idris had no idea how much the treasure would be worth in dollars and cents, nor did he know how much he would need. But he would have to pay for passage to Arabia, and he would spend in charity there, and he would spend on Mariana and her family, even if he found her married to another. That had been his purpose for chasing *haram* gold so many years ago, and he would fulfill that purpose now, God willing.

With Luis beside him, it was easy enough to retrieve the treasure bit by bit from the cave and pack it into the mules' saddlebags until each one was liable to collapse under the weight. They left a few of the larger pieces in the cave for some lucky peasant to find, or perhaps for a future archeologist to stumble upon and wonder how such disparate artifacts could exist in the same time and place.

While driving the mule train down from the Sierra, Idris was at times assailed by the irrational fear that he would be gunned down by bandits, as had befallen that other mule team so many years ago. He held his breath through every mountain pass and cringed at the curious stares of the peasants and townspeople they passed on the way to San Blas, but there was no need to fear.

Within a week, they reached the port, and a day later Luis had departed for his hometown with enough gold to feed the whole population for a year, while Idris and the rest of the treasure were aboard a steamer en route to Los Angeles.

9

____

MEXICO CITY AND SANTA CATALINA, TEXAS, 1915

GENERAL VILLACORTA WAS NOT an easy man to pin down, but Mr. Benson Abbott, attorney-at-law, representing the interests of the Texas Petroleum Company in Latin America, was able to secure an appointment with uncharacteristic ease.

As he rolled down the private drive in his Cadillac Type 51, chauffeured by an Asturian named Xavier, Abbott took the time to appreciate the manicured shrubs and well-watered lawn of the general's estate. Of course, beyond the park-like grounds of his villa, the general's lands extended for miles in every direction, comprising thousands of acres of coffee, maize and fruit trees, and grazing land for a thousand head of cattle. A platoon of uniformed constitutionalist cavalry patrolled the perimeter of the estate, while at least a half dozen dismounts guarded the villa itself.

A young secretary in a smoking jacket and cravat met Abbott at the door and led him down a series of corridors to the general's private study.

Villacorta was still handsome, though his face had grown lined and his hair was graying around the temples. He was dressed in civilian attire, an exquisitely tailored pinstripe suit over a white silk shirt and necktie, and had put on a bit of weight since the day when he had condemned young Eddie Dawson to a lifetime in prison. There was no mistaking it, though. He still wore the same smug expression.

Remembering that he was meant to be Benson Abbott, to whom Villacorta was a perfect stranger, Idris pushed the old images out of his mind and kept his expression neutral.

"*Señor General*," he said, exaggerating his Anglo accent, "*soy el licenciado Abbott*. I understand you speak English?"

"Yes, I do," Villacorta replied. His English was better than it had been twenty years ago. "I studied at West Point."

"Very impressive," said Idris, or rather Abbott. He wondered if Villacorta knew he recognized the lie and was challenging him to call his bluff. "I was abroad during the war with Spain, and I fear I'm a bit too old for fighting now, should we ever go to bat against the Germans."

"I hope that does not happen," Villacorta said, perhaps challenging Abbott once again. "Let the Europeans fight their wars. We Americans —I mean all the people of the Americas—have our own business to attend to. Our countries have both had their civil conflicts, we've had problems with unruly Indians and rebels, but rule of law will always prevail, and we can now focus on modernizing our respective societies. I understand that is what brings you to my office today."

"Yes, General. My company is in the business of exploration and surveying for petroleum, and it has come to our attention that your estate sits atop what might be some of the richest geological deposits in Mexico. This could be quite profitable for you, and for your country."

"Pearson and Doheny have both surveyed the area already. What can you give me that they can't?"

————

Abbott left the general's house without a signed contract, just a verbal agreement to allow a geological survey to be conducted on his property and any lands under the authority of the Central Army Group of the constitutionalist forces, now the *de facto* national army.

More importantly, though, he had confirmed that this was the right

Villacorta, and he had the chance to observe the avenues of approach to the villa, as well as learn the floor plan of the building itself.

Shortly after midnight, Idris, now in simple sportsman's clothes—lightweight and dark-colored—stepped out of the Cadillac on the edge of the estate. He hopped the wire fence and jogged across the empty orchards, taking care to stay in the shadows, reaching the villa's service entrance in short order.

There was one soldier on duty at the entrance, but he was asleep in his chair, rifle propped haphazardly against the wall beside him. Good. Idris wouldn't even have to climb the trellis onto the veranda as he had expected. Once inside, he found the hallways deserted, as would be expected at that time of night.

Two right turns brought him to the main foyer and the broad staircase to the second story, where the bedrooms would be. Idris had inquired discreetly around Mexico City. He knew Villacorta had a beautiful blonde wife who was currently visiting relatives in Durango; a twenty-year-old son, who was indeed studying at West Point, as the elder Villacorta had never been able to do; and a young daughter just now planning her *quinceañera*. He was said to employ a lovely brunette housekeeper as well, who lived with their children on the first floor, but Idris wasn't worried about those rooms.

He passed the son's room, its door open wide to air it out, he presumed. Enough moonlight shone through the window to reveal an empty bed, its covers cinched down military-style, an elegant desk holding neat stacks of books and papers, and a small wardrobe. Across the hall was another room, its door shut. The size and placement didn't seem right for the master bedroom. Probably the girl's room. Then came a bathroom with porcelain tiles, a French-style commode and bidet, and a lion-footed tub, and, across from it, a lady's reading room furnished with delicate lamps and plush settees.

Finally, he reached the master bedroom at the end of the hall. The door was ajar. Idris slipped through without a sound, but no sooner had he set foot inside than the general startled awake, sitting bolt-upright in his sumptuous canopy bed.

Idris had his .22 caliber Colt automatic in hand and pointed it at

Villacorta's heart before he could even cry out. He would have preferred the familiar feel of a revolver, but the automatic could accommodate a Maxim Silencer. It might take more shots to kill a man, but the magazine held ten rounds and the gun would fire as fast as he could pull the trigger.

"Don't make a sound!" he ordered.

"Mr. Abbott?" mumbled Villacorta, blinking his eyes in disbelief.

"Think harder," said Idris. "Surely you remember seeing me before this morning."

"I don't know many *gringos*," he said, reaching toward the nightstand. "I think I would remember."

"If you think you'll have time to pull a gun out of that drawer, you're wrong. Now think harder about how many *gringos* you know. You might have to go back a ways, maybe twenty years."

Villacorta's eyes grew wide as saucers, shining even in the dim moonlight. "You're the *gabacho* who robbed the gold!"

"Bullseye! The gold you used to buy this house, to buy your estate, your generalship, your *güerita* wife and your *prietita* mistress, your son's studies, your girl's shoes and dresses, everything you have and hold dear."

"They told me you'd never survive in prison!"

"I almost didn't."

"I should have killed you in the mountains like your partner told me to. He said the judge would be content with your corpse, but, stupid me, I let you live. I don't suppose you'll extend me the same courtesy."

Idris took a step back, as if he had been physically struck, as if Villacorta had drawn his gun and shot him in the chest. Frank had not only been in on it, had not only *left* Eddie—Idris—for dead, he had *intended* for him to die. Frank might as well have shot him in the back.

"Courtesy?" Idris spat. "You condemned me to twenty years of imprisonment, of servitude. Twenty years of fighting for my life, twenty years of fear. Twenty years of loneliness, of thinking I'd never see my loved ones again, of wondering whether they were thinking of me or had forgotten me altogether. You spared me a quick death to condemn me to twenty years of hell!"

And yet it had meant almost twenty years of friendship, too. Twenty years of faith. Without Frank and Villacorta's betrayal, Idris would still be Eddie, wallowing in depravity and sin. But that hardly absolved the two conspirators of guilt, did it?

The same God who had used their betrayal to bring about Eddie's downfall could surely use Idris's rebirth to bring justice to the criminals.

"You killed six men!" said Villacorta, as if he had just remembered. "You deserved every day you spent in prison."

"And you sent them to their death." Idris took a step forward, raising the pistol to point at Villacorta's forehead. "What do you deserve?"

"I spared you," Villacorta reminded him, his whole body trembling despite his attempt to appear calm. "You were a stranger to me, and I spared your life because of it, when your own countryman warned me against it!"

There was a certain sense to what Villacorta was saying. He had done no worse by Idris than Idris had done by the dead *rurales*. Perhaps it was premature of Idris to assume he had a mandate to dispense Allah's justice. He would be merciful, for Allah loved mercy, and if harshness was justified, Allah would surely give him a sign. He lowered his gun.

"Don't think to call your men," Idris said. "You wouldn't want their deaths on your conscience, too. And don't try to warn Frank Danger I'm coming for him."

Villacorta laughed. "That *pinche gabacho*? I cut him loose the minute we split our loot. I wouldn't trust a man who'd betray his own friend."

Anger still pulsing within him, Idris turned toward the door. He hadn't taken a step when he heard the rustling of the bedclothes and turned to see Villacorta pulling a revolver from the nightstand drawer.

"Clumsy," he said. "You make too much noise. Come on, if we're going to do this, let's do it right. Stand up."

Villacorta struggled to his feet. Free of his blankets, he looked even older and fatter in his underwear than he had in his elegant suit that morning. He was trembling again, or still, the revolver shaking noticeably in his hand.

"Now you don't have a holster," Idris said, "and my gun is too long to draw like in the old days, so let's just count to three."

"Fuck you," Villacorta spat and tried to steady his aim, but he was far too slow.

Idris's hand shot back up. He pulled the trigger twice, punching two holes in the general's heart, then raised his hand a few inches and put a third bullet between his blinking eyes.

That should be sufficient, even with the little .22 rounds. The silencer didn't muffle the sound completely, but it certainly wouldn't have been loud enough to wake the sleeping sentry at the back door. The daughter might have heard, if she was a light sleeper, though she'd be hard pressed to identify the noise as gunfire.

Idris looked down at Villacorta's body, which was still trembling. He'd probably die within minutes, the way the blood was spreading across his undershirt and pooling under his head, but Idris was taking no chances. With the tip of his boot, he turned the dying general's head to the side, almost parallel with the floor.

He pressed the tip of the Maxim Silencer to Villacorta's temple and pulled the trigger. This shot was almost completely silent, the full force of the explosion absorbed by Villacorta's skull, which cracked like window glass around the entry wound.

Idris opened the French windows onto the balcony, hopped over the low balustrade, and dropped to the ground some ten feet below, his knees flexing with the impact. He moved quickly and silently away from the villa, pistol at the ready in case he ran into any guards, but none appeared. A few minutes later he was at the edge of the orchard. There were no horsemen in sight, so he climbed the perimeter fence and then followed the road until he reached the Cadillac parked a mile away.

"Xavier," he said, "take me to my hotel. I'll be checking out at sunup. There is a steamer leaving Veracruz for New Orleans at six in the evening, and I intend to be on it."

———

Surveying the town of Santa Catalina from the railway station, Señor Tomás Francés could appreciate the progress the town had made over the past several years. The railway station itself was new, with trains stopping every other day en route to El Paso or San Antonio, connecting the dusty border town with the world beyond. All the main streets were paved with asphalt, though the roads leading to nearby farms and ranches were still dirt or gravel, as were the side streets and alleys of the Mexican neighborhoods. The railway station had electricity, as did city hall, and there were some electric street lights downtown, but that was about it. Apart from one Oldsmobile—probably the mayor's—and a few Model Ts on the roads, it looked like life went on in Santa Catalina much as it had during the previous century.

Francés directed his steps toward the offices of the *Sta. Catalina Intelligencer* on the corner of Commerce and Main.

"Good morning," he said to the clerk, a Germanic fellow who he imagined must be responsible for transcribing stories from the wire services while the reporter—Francés doubted there was more than one—compiled stories of local interest. "Perhaps you received my telegram some weeks back. I am Mr. Francés, from Cádiz, Spain. I wired you about locating a certain citizen of Spanish descent."

The clerk shook his head. "I don't remember nothing like that. And I'm the one that reads the telegrams."

Of course Francés had written no such telegram, but in these modern times it would be strange to show up in person without wiring for information first. "It must have been misrouted, then. I knew you would not have ignored my inquiry intentionally."

"No, of course not, sir. Who are you trying to find?"

"I represent the estate of Don Anacleto Hernández y Zaguirre of Extremadura. He is recently deceased, and, unfortunately, left no direct heirs. His closest relatives settled in Mexico before its independence, and, after consultation with a number of genealogists there, it appears that a Mr. Pedro Hernández, resident here in Santa Catalina, may be the principal heir of that branch of the family."

"Hmm. This ain't a big town, but I'd reckon half the Mexicans in town are Hernandezes."

"Yes," said Francés, "Hernández is the most common surname in Mexico, and I would expect it to be common here as well. According to the papers of his late sister in Nuevo León, this Hernández owned a tailoring business on Main Street some years ago. I do not know if it is still there."

"There're a couple sew shops on Main. There's Bob Dixon's place, and Charro Charlie's for the Mexicans. If there's a Hernandez, I don't know about it. You could try the chamber of commerce."

"I'll do that," Francés said and turned to go. Then he turned back, as if he'd just thought of something. "Mr. Hernández has a daughter, reputed to be quite a beauty. Her name is Mariana. Perhaps you've heard of her?"

"Mariana *Montgomery*?" the clerk exclaimed. "Yeah, I think her name was Hernandez. I could look it up in the archives. Everyone in town knows Mrs. Montgomery."

"Montgomery?" asked Francés, his distaste evident.

"Yeah, married Earl Montgomery, a big railroad man in Dallas. He's the only reason Santa Catalina got a station. You want me to find you the wedding announcement? It would have been a good twenty years ago, but the archives go back that far."

Francés was staggering just as he had in General Villacorta's office a few days earlier. He had tried to prepare himself for this eventuality, knowing that Mariana would have married, telling himself that she *should* have married. That she must have believed him dead, that she deserved a normal life regardless, that she deserved happiness, with or without him.

Some corner of his being had hoped she would be waiting for him, like the damsel in a fairy story, refusing to give herself to another man. But he could not be so selfish. If she was safe and well cared for, and, God willing, happy, who was he to oppose it?

"Yes," he said, schooling his voice, "show me the announcement if it is not too much trouble. I don't suppose you have an address for the Montgomerys in Dallas?"

"I don't," the clerk said as he began to rifle through stacks of bound broadsheets behind the counter, "but they are well known throughout the state. I'm sure anyone who's anyone in Dallas will be able to point you in the right direction. Aha!" He picked one volume from the stack and laid it on the counter between them. "This should be it. 1895, if memory serves me right. A spring wedding, May or June."

He began flipping through the pages, careful to avoid tearing the thin newsprint. Francés craned over to scan the pages as the clerk turned them.

"Here we go," he said. "June ninth, 1895. 'Mariana Hernandez wed to Earl Montgomery at St. Catherine's'—"

Francés grabbed the book, more roughly than befitted his role as an estate attorney, and stared at the announcement. There she was, in black and white, his sweet Mariana, young and beautiful as the day they'd said goodbye. And beside her, grinning like the cat that just ate the canary, sat a man Idris knew all too well.

Earl Montgomery was Frank Danger.

10

DALLAS, TEXAS, 1920

DALLAS WAS NO NEW YORK—NOT even a Chicago or Los Angeles—but it had caught up to San Antonio as the metropolis of Texas, and was clearly feeling its urban oats. Still, it was Texas, and Idris Pasha saw as many spurred boots and Stetsons as he ever had on the open range. And Dallas was still provincial enough to go crazy for an enigmatic adventurer like him, ruggedly handsome, rich as an Argentine and a war hero to boot.

Idris scanned the society pages of the *Morning News* on the ride to the Praetorian Building, now the second tallest in Dallas, where the Texas & California Railroad Company had its corporate offices. Rather than staying in the Adolphus Hotel, the *new* tallest building, he had rented a ranch house halfway to Fort Worth. That way he'd have a reason to cruise into town every day in his custom Rolls Royce Silver Ghost—built in England with American-style left-hand drive, as the North American factory hadn't commenced operations yet—instead of walking two blocks. And of course the ranch would be better suited for dinner parties.

"Next week's soirée will be hosted by Col. Jacob Deacon," he read aloud, to no one in particular, "popularly known by his *nom de guerre* Idris Pasha, a decorated veteran of the Near Eastern theater of the recent war and the largest individual shareholder in the Mesopotamian Petroleum Company. Rumor has it that the Pasha, who won his title at the Battle of Jebal el Noor in Kurdestan, is in Dallas to invest some of his considerable fortune in the budding Texas oil industry. He is also quite an eligible bachelor."

Idris laughed out loud at the last line. He had met the loveliest and noblest women in the world on his journeys through the Ummah, from Alexandria to Kordofan and from Mecca and Medina to Azerbaijan. If he had withstood the charms of those pearls of the East, did these people think he would fall for some corn-fed cattleman's daughter?

"Wait for me here," he told his driver, Hayden. "Or drive around the block if you need to."

The receptionist recognized him as soon as he entered the lobby. Idris knew he cut a striking figure, well-proportioned and nicely tanned, still on the youthful side despite his graying blond hair and neatly trimmed beard, and dressed to kill in a three-piece camel suit over a burgundy silk shirt and a richly embroidered wine and gold necktie, both chosen to match his ever-present tarboush with its little golden tassel.

"Railroad office?" asked the operator, a pretty blonde, when Idris entered the elevator. "Fifteenth floor."

At the office of the T&C Railroad, another receptionist greeted him effusively. "Mr. Montgomery is on the telephone with the governor of New Mexico," she said, "but he'll be ready for you in a few minutes."

Idris settled into a plush armchair in the lobby and lit his pipe. He had taken up the habit of smoking the narghile in Egypt, but a standard pipe was more convenient when out and about.

On the wall opposite him were several portraits of staid old men with mutton-chop whiskers, presumably the railroad's founders, whom Montgomery had bought out with Frank Danger's ill-gotten gold. Not right away, Idris was sure. He'd run over the calculations time and again in prison; the whole take couldn't have been much over a quarter million dollars, of which the late General Villacorta had taken a share and returned some to its owners. Frank's share had probably been around a hundred thousand, not nearly enough to buy a railroad.

Montgomery—or maybe he was still Frank back then—might have made some shrewd investments and made his millions fair and square, but Idris doubted it. He was sure Frank had used his take from the robbery to finance some crooked scheme or other, and had only bought or strong-armed his way into the railroad business much later. Idris had done what investigation he could at a distance, but there was still much he needed to find out.

"Sir… or… *effendi*," said the receptionist. "Mr. Montgomery will see you now."

"In Turkey, it is a grave insult to address a *pasha* as a simple *effendi*." He gave her a friendly, even flirtatious smile. "But for you, I'll make an exception."

Smiling back, she opened the door and waved him inside.

There he was, Frank Danger—or, rather, Earl Montgomery—older than the last time they'd met, older even than his photograph, and a sight better dressed, but otherwise not so different from the young man Idris remembered. No, that was not quite true. Perhaps Idris only recognized him because he knew who he was looking for.

Was he so changed, though? Montgomery, for his part, showed no inkling of recognizing that it was Eddie Dawson under the beard and exotic attire. But, then, he probably imagined Eddie was dead.

He wasn't wrong. Eddie was dead. Now there was only Idris Pasha.

Montgomery stood up and reached across his desk to give Idris a handshake, squeezing just hard enough to make it uncomfortable. His skin crawled at making contact with this swine, but Idris controlled his reaction.

"Mr. Pasha!" Montgomery exclaimed, as he motioned for Idris to take a seat opposite his desk. "I've heard a lot about you."

"'Idris,' please. 'Pasha' is just an honorific." Idris sat, allowing his eyes to roam around the office for a moment. "I've heard a lot about you, as well."

"Good things, I hope."

"They say you're the man to talk to about any major infrastructure projects in Texas."

"Right down to business, I like that." Montgomery smiled, that same disarming grin he'd flashed when describing the gold shipment thirty years prior, though his missing teeth had been replaced by porcelain. "What kind of infrastructure are we talking about?"

"As you may know, Mr. Montgomery—"

"Earl."

"Of course, Earl. As you may know, I'm heavily involved in the petroleum industry. To date, my investments have been in the Near East, particularly Iraq and Kurdistan, where I enjoy the favor of both the local *shaykhs* and *beys* and the British occupation authorities."

"I heard you showed Johnny Turk who's boss, like a regular Lawrence of Arabia."

"That's what they say." In reality, he had served in the Turkish army as a medic on the Russian front for only a few months. Then he'd made good on his promise to make the *hajj* pilgrimage to Mecca, which was in Allied hands by then, and he'd stayed there treating stranded pilgrims and Turkish prisoners until the end of the war and through the influenza epidemic that followed. "The Arabs and Kurds did all the fighting."

"If you say so. So you're planning to get into oil here in Texas?"

"Of course. I'd be crazy not to. Near Eastern petroleum reserves are massive, but the oil has to be shipped thousands of miles to market. There's not even a refinery in Iraq yet, so the crude must be transported to Persia by rail, and the refined products by ship to India or to Europe through the Suez Canal. Here you have your own refineries, and you have the biggest markets right next door. Eventually Near Eastern production will surpass domestic, but in the meantime I want to take advantage of Texas's head start."

"I'd love to help, Mr. Pasha, but I'm not an oilman…" He raised his hands, feigning confusion.

"Oh, I am acquainted with several leading oilmen, and will soon meet the rest. My agents are busy securing exploratory leases in several of the most likely oil fields. What I need from you, Earl, is a quick and inexpensive way to get my oil to market."

"You mean by rail?"

"You are a railroad man, aren't you?"

"Biggest shareholder in the biggest railroad in Texas."

"Yes, I mean by rail."

Montgomery forced a hearty laugh. "Of course you do," he said.

"What did you have in mind?"

Idris explained his plan to build custom fuel cars to expedite shipments from wells operated by Mesopotamian Petroleum's U.S. subsidiary, Meso-American Petroleum—Idris laughed at his own cleverness here—in Texas and Mexico. That would give him a leg up on the competition, who were mainly barreling their crude on site and then shipping it in regular freight cars. Meanwhile, Meso-American would build a pipeline along the tracks, paying the T&C a respectable usufruct rate. Other companies were building pipelines as well, but using the railroad's land grants would allow Meso-American to do it faster and cheaper.

Montgomery nodded along, asking intelligent questions at the right times. Idris could see that, while he had almost certainly shouldered his way into the board room through blackmail or intimidation, he had quite a head for business. "It sounds like I'd make out like a bandit here," he said as Idris was wrapping up his pitch. "What's the catch?"

"I'm supposed to say, 'There's no catch,' but we're both too smart for that. You know that getting into the oil business in Texas means competing against Standard Oil. If we try to do this small-scale, Standard will eat us alive. I'm bringing a substantial amount of capital to the table, but I'll need partners. We'll need our own refinery sooner than later, and it has to be approved by the Railroad Commission."

"I got half the Railroad Commission in my pocket already. Won't even take big contributions on your part, just a word from me. Consider it approved."

"There's more, Earl. Ever since the war, refineries have to be American-owned. I'm an American, as an individual, but Mesopotamian Petroleum is incorporated in Bombay—the Brits haven't set up proper courts in Iraq yet—so I need a reliable American partner to invest in the refinery, to be majority owner, in fact."

"Why use Mesopotamian Petroleum at all?" asked Montgomery.

"Why not just create a new company incorporated here in Texas? You short on cash?"

Idris laughed, almost dismissively. "No worries on that account, my friend. I could buy a dozen refineries outright if Rockefeller was selling, but he's not. I can build my own refinery, too, and lease my own oil fields, and build my own pipelines. But that takes time, and in the meantime, Standard will be doing its best to shut me down. They have connections I don't have, with the Railroad Commission, local governments, even the feds. It'll be an uphill battle, but if I have a few well-known local industrialists on my side, it's winnable. I need investors, and no one is going to back Jake Deacon—or even Idris Pasha—but they'll back a multi-million-dollar company like Mesopotamian Petroleum, especially if the Texas and California Railroad is on Board."

"I suppose I could invest a couple million."

"A couple million?" Idris asked, his shock and disappointment evident. "Meso-American Petroleum is already valued at twenty-five million, from Mesopotamian and a few select European investors. If the Texas and California Railroad can only scrape up two million dollars for the most promising investment you've ever been offered, perhaps I should take my business elsewhere."

Now it was Montgomery's turn to look shocked. "Well, damn," he said. "How about you send my accountants a proposal with a number at the bottom and we'll see what we can do?" He stood to offer his hand.

Idris shook Montgomery's hand once again, his skin crawling just as badly as before. "Fair enough," he said. "Anyway, come on over to my place this Saturday. The whole town is invited. Bring the missus. Nothing fancy. Just a simple get-together."

———

It was not a simple get-together. When the guests arrived, they found the ranch house decorated as if for an Arabian wedding, every inch of it bedecked with silk curtains and Persian rugs. There were no Arab musicians to be found on short notice, but Idris had located a Greek ensemble in New Orleans, who kept his party lively with their own folk songs and a series of waltzes, boleros and even foxtrots, played with oriental aplomb on their lutes and tambourines.

The most expensive caterer in Dallas had prepared an eastern feast to his exact specifications: several whole roast sheep seasoned with lemon and garlic, grilled carp, enormous platters of saffron rice, flatbreads and an assortment of vegetables—from artichokes to zucchini—stuffed with rice and pine nuts and baked in a spiced tomato sauce. After the meal, there would be pastries large and small, cheese canapés, candied almonds and dried apricots, and several varieties of coffee and tea, all redolent with exotic spices.

The only thing missing was alcohol. Several of the guests, assuming he had been blindsided by Prohibition, having been out of the country when it was enacted, confided that they had reliable and discreet sources for quality moonshine, or contraband from Mexico.

"No," Idris assured them, "I'm afraid I won't be serving any spirits regardless of the enforcement of the Volstead Act or lack thereof. I am a Muslim, you see, and intoxicating drink is abhorrent to my chosen faith. I don't mind if you drink from the flasks and bottles you all have hidden on your persons, as is permitted in your faith, but I shall not distribute the foul stuff."

"Hear-hear!" said the few teetotalers in the group, especially the women, but others seemed shocked. Whether it was due to the dearth of alcohol at his party, or to his adherence to a foreign, un-Christian religion, Idris could not tell.

Later, one of the ladies—Mrs. Winfield, whose husband was president of the cattlemen's association—asked the inevitable question. "I hear you're a bachelor," she said. "I figured a man like you would have four wives by now."

"*Madame*," he responded, "between fighting the Turks and developing the biggest oil field in the Orient, I am afraid I never had time for even one wife."

"No concubines even?" interjected Mr. Winfield, to the annoyance of his wife, who jabbed him in the arm.

"My friend," Idris said with a good-natured chuckle, "were we not in mixed company, I might describe the pleasures of Oriental womanhood, from the golden-haired Circassian beauties to the stately Negresses of Abyssinia, that the 'peculiar institution' until recently made available to any man of substance in the East, but I fear that might be in bad taste."

It was true that slavery had endured behind closed doors in Turkish territories until the end of the Great War, but Idris had never participated in that unholy commerce. How could he, after hearing Abdallah's account of the Soudanese *razzias*, or viewing the atrocities in Armenia and Assyria with his own eyes? Turning back to Mrs. Winfield, Idris added, "In any case, *madame*, there is only one woman who has ever truly kindled a fire in this heart..."

At that moment, the door to the main hall opened and in strode Mariana Hernández—no, Mariana Montgomery, Idris reminded himself—along with her husband and a handsome young man who must have been their son. If Montgomery had changed little from his days as Frank Danger, Mariana hadn't changed at all. Perhaps her figure was a tad thicker—which only made her more attractive—and her expression a bit more reserved than the girl of nineteen, but her green eyes, accentuated by an emerald evening dress and a mink stole dyed to match, sparkled just as Idris remembered.

He lost the thread of the conversation completely as she walked toward him, guided by her husband, who was only half-heartedly waving to his industrialist buddies as he made a beeline for Idris.

La ilaha illa Allah! It was really her, his Mariana, the only girl he'd ever loved. And fucking Frank Danger with his hand on the small of her back.

Idris clenched his fists. He had the Colt automatic in a shoulder holster under his suit jacket. He could end this right now. He'd go to prison again, or maybe the chair, but he'd survived prison once, and death held no terror for him.

But no, that was not the way to do it. A quick death was not enough. Frank deserved to suffer for his betrayal. And Mariana even more so.

"Idris Pasha!" exclaimed Montgomery. "A pleasure to see you again."

"Earl," he replied simply, taking the proffered hand. "I sent over some papers yesterday, but… how boorish of me to bring up business in front of your family."

Montgomery laughed. "May I introduce my wife, Mariana?"

Idris took Mariana's hand in his, relishing the softness of her skin, the electric tingle in his lips when he kissed her fingers. "A pleasure, *madame*," was all he could say.

"*Enchantée*," she replied. "We've heard so much about you. This is my son, Alberto. Or should I say, Lieutenant Montgomery?"

"Mamá..." the young man began to protest. He seemed hardly more than a boy. If he was a lieutenant, though, he must be at least twenty-one, the age Idris had been when Frank left him to rot in a Mexican prison.

"Lieutenant?" Idris interrupted. "West Point?"

"Class of '18," he replied, taking Idris's outstretched hand. His grip was firm, but not overpowering like his father's. He was wearing an elegant lounge suit rather than a uniform, which would have been considered gauche this long after the war, but his martial bearing was evident. "Missed the war, but I did do some fighting against the Bolsheviks at Archangel."

Idris shook his head. "Nasty stuff, I hear. Couldn't even bury the dead in the frozen ground up there."

"It wasn't so bad most of the time. How was the Turkish front?"

"Just imagine dust instead of snow and you get the idea." They laughed like schoolboys sharing a joke. "Come. I'd introduce you to my other guests, but I expect you know them all better than I do."

11

———

EL PASO AND VICTORIA, TEXAS, 1920

Idris took the seat across from his old friend at the Madrileño, a respectable café in downtown El Paso, popular enough with both *gringos* and Mexicans their meeting was unlikely to draw attention. "I hear you're a general now," he said by way of greeting.

"In Mexico," said Luis Vargas, "anyone with enough money and guns can be a general. I hear you're a count or something?"

"A pasha. In Turkey, anyone with enough money and guns can become a pasha."

They shared a laugh, perhaps the first genuine mirth Idris had felt in years.

"I trust you received the merchandise undamaged?" he asked. His agents had combed the gun shops of little towns across the West and South for good quality Winchesters and Remingtons, and military surplus Springfields, which they delivered to Vargas's men along the border.

"Yes." Vargas looked around to make sure no one was eavesdropping. "The rifles will go far in building a new Conventionalist cadre to oppose Carranza's thugs." Though his intent had been to buy a little ranch and live peacefully off his share of the treasure, Vargas had found that the Mexican army would confiscate any visible signs of prosperity and came close to discovering his hoard when they ransacked his home one night. Since then, he had devoted himself anew to the revolutionary cause, along with his newfound wealth.

"You don't look happy."

"Turco, Carranza has access to modern weaponry, mostly provided by your government now that it's not needed in Europe. Without machine guns and artillery, we'll never be able to hold our own. It will be Celaya all over again."

"God forbid. I'm trying my best. My agents have been buying up heavy weapons in the East, but most of the war surplus has gone to arm the Whites and Reds in Russia, or the competing factions in the Caucasus and the Arabian states. I have a few pieces ready for shipment, but it will still take months to arrive."

"I don't know if we can wait months. Wheels are turning in Mexico City. We'll only have a narrow window if we want to breathe life back into this revolution."

Idris didn't much care about the revolution. Of course he hoped to see the Mexican people—the workers and peasants—freed from poverty and oppression. But all he'd seen after a decade of war was armed factions led by warlords jockeying for wealth and power. Still, it was important to Luis, and Luis was his friend.

A friend who might be of use in the future.

———

The oil business was going better than Idris had expected. Between his own efforts and Montgomery's, dozens of Texas millionaires had been persuaded to invest in Meso-American Petroleum.

His rigs were cranking on farms and ranches from El Paso to Port Arthur—and a few on the Mexican side of the river as well—while Montgomery's fleet of tanker cars was growing daily and their new consortium had broken ground on a refinery outside Corpus Christi.

It was an incestuous business. For every dollar Montgomery and the others invested in Meso-American, they made two back in rent, freight charges, equipment purchases, construction invoices and the like. Landowners reinvested their royalties in Meso-American stock, on the condition the company buy their corn and beef to feed its expanding workforce. Montgomery had agreed to build custom tanker cars on the condition that Idris invest enough in his railroad to pay for most of the work; meanwhile Idris paid the railroad to transport his oil, but the railroad paid him—and Montgomery, as a Meso-American shareholder—for fuel and lubricants. It would take an army of accountants a year to disentangle the web of kickbacks and self-dealing, but it was clear to anyone with a brain that the Texas capitalist class was making a fortune.

Little enough was trickling down to the workers, however. If anything was likely to derail their plans, it was labor problems.

"We gotta do something about these Reds!" Montgomery exclaimed during a private meeting he'd requested. They didn't often deal one-on-one since Idris had brought young Alberto on as regional manager to hold down the fort while Idris was away seeing to the oilfields and the refinery. Montgomery seemed pleased with the arrangement, as Alberto would gain worldly experience in the petroleum business while also serving as his father's eyes and ears on the inside. But when it came to labor agitation, the elder Montgomery needed to make his points in person. "The Railroad Brotherhoods are striking on the Atchison, Topeka and Santa Fe," he continued, "and there's talk the Colorado and Southern crews might join in. It's the Wobblies behind it, no doubt."

"You think your employees will strike?" asked Idris.

"Not my employees," said Montgomery, "unless the Brotherhoods call a nationwide strike like in '86. I'm worried about the oil fields, the pipelines, the refinery."

"I haven't heard anything about an oil workers' strike."

"Not yet, but look who you got working for you. Slavs, Italians, Mexicans! Even Jews! Half of them are Wobblies, and the other half are anarchists and bolsheviks."

Idris choked back his instinctive retort to such racialist nonsense. You'd think Montgomery had never talked to a Mexican, much less married one! He'd let slip in his occasional drunken soliloquies how Mariana was of Spanish conquistador descent, which made her white, and a sort of honorary Texan, like Benavides or Seguín. Anyway, Montgomery's fears were useful to Idris.

"I have the Pinkertons on the payroll," he reminded Montgomery. "They'll root out any real agitators."

"I hope so."

As soon as Montgomery had left, Idris picked up the telephone. "Get me Detective Brewill." A few minutes later, the telephone rang and Idris picked up. "Brewill?"

"Sir?"

"Remember the anarchist you told me about? The Pole?"

There was a pause, while the detective probably consulted his files. "Kowalski?"

"I think so, unless you got another Polish anarchist. You find out anything about him?"

"Funny thing, sir. Seems he's not a polack at all. He's a kraut, named Friedrich Schneider. Probably lied about his nationality to get in right after the war."

"I want to see him."

There was a longer pause this time. "Sir, are you sure that's a good idea?"

"You got dirt on him, right? False immigration records? We can use him against the Wobblies. Get them to show their hand."

"I can work on that, sir. I don't think—"

"Nonsense! I would never have got to where I am without knowing how to deal with fanatics. If I can get Mohammedans to fight their own Caliph, I can get one sorry Red to turn on his friends."

"I'll bring him in, then. Where do you want him?"

"Bring him to the farmhouse in Victoria. Don't rough him up any, just bring him." He checked his Rolex. Two in the afternoon. It was a six-hour drive in the Rolls, perhaps longer as Hayden would have to slow down once it got dark, keeping an eye out for deer and cattle. "I won't be there until late, ten or eleven."

"I'll have him there under guard."

"Bring him yourself. I don't trust your goons not to talk."

"Sir, my men are of the—"

"Brewill."

"Sir?"

"What about the other matter?"

"Good news, sir."

"Good. I'll want you to brief me in person."

He hung up.

———

Idris entered the farmhouse through the back door. A single lamp burned inside, making it easy to keep to the shadows.

"You can go outside," he told Brewill, who was seated at the table across from Schneider. The detective probably wanted to make sure the prisoner didn't hang himself or anything else he'd be blamed for. "I'll take it from here."

Brewill shrugged and walked out. With the money Idris was paying him, he couldn't do much else.

Idris sat across from the prisoner. Schneider was a wiry blond with a handlebar mustache and wire-rimmed spectacles. He was pale, and tapping his toe nervously, but did not appear to have been beaten. Brewill wasn't too bright, but at least he followed instructions.

"My, my," said Schneider, "the boss himself." His guttural German accent was apparent even in those few syllables. Idris had never heard him speak English before. He barely remembered the man, and expected Schneider would not recognize him either, though it had only been a few years.

"Herr Schneider—" Idris began, but the nervous German cut him off.

"I won't rat on my comrades," he said. "You can fire me, turn me in, get me deported—"

"Herr Schneider," Idris said again, firmly enough to shut the man up, "I am fully aware of your subversive activities in Mexico. If I wanted, I could have you extradited, tried and probably executed. Or I could simply have you beaten to death—as Detective Brewill's men were planning to do before I stayed their hands—and your body dumped in the bayous for the alligators. Do you really think anyone would miss one foreign anarchist?"

Schneider sat there wide-eyed, waiting for what came next.

"It is precisely because of your activities in Mexico that I brought you here tonight. I understand you were something of an expert with dynamite?"

"That's what they say," Schneider said, furrowing his brow in confusion. "I confess nothing." He started tapping his foot again.

"Herr Schneider," Idris said for the third time, "this is not an interrogation. There is nothing you could tell me I don't already know, and none of your so-called crimes are of any interest to me."

The foot stopped tapping.

"What I am interested in," Idris continued, "is making use of your skills."

Schneider's eyes widened even more, if that was possible. "You want me to assassinate Rockefeller!"

"No, no," Idris assured him. "I am no murderer, and Rockefeller is of no concern to me. I want you to blow up my refinery."

"*Your* refinery?" The poor German's eyes were about to pop out of their sockets. "Why?"

"Don't you worry about why, *comrade*. Perhaps I have the refinery insured for twice its value. Perhaps I don't. It's not your concern. The bombing will be a great success for your cause, *nein*? Propaganda of the deed and all that."

"You wouldn't be making me your—*wie sagt man?*—fall guy? You get the insurance, I get the chair?"

"No, not at all. In fact, I will make every arrangement so that you may escape undetected. Your life will only be in danger should you expose my involvement in the incident."

Schneider sat in silence for a few minutes, mulling it over. Finally, he shrugged. "Why not? I have spent my life tying nooses for the bourgeoisie. Who am I to say no when one wants to stick his head through the loop?"

"Excellent," said Idris, grinning. "I will leave the particulars up to you. I only have two stipulations. One, it is to be done on the night before the refinery begins operations, when the tanks are full of crude."

"And two?"

"There shall be no needless shedding of blood."

12

GALVESTON AND DALLAS,
TEXAS, 1920

IDRIS STOOD in the poorly lit warehouse, waiting for the workmen to pry the side off the biggest wooden crate he had ever seen.

"What you got in there, boss?" asked the foreman. "Drilling rig?"

"Something like that."

There was a creaking and splintering, and the broad side of the crate fell with a crash, raising a puff of dust from the poorly swept floor.

Inside was a giant steel monstrosity, like a battleship on metal treads, painted khaki with brown blotches.

"Is that a—?"

"British Mark I main battle tank," Idris said. "Captured by the Ottomans at Gaza, used against the Russians before their Revolution. I bought it from the new government of Georgia, now a sovereign state but nearly bankrupt. It is part of an order by the King of Siam. I assure you, all import and export permissions have been obtained."

The foreman shrugged. "I ain't the revenue agent."

The revenue agent would be by shortly, but Idris wasn't worried. He was importing the tank, along with another of the same provenance, three Russian artillery pieces and a dozen machine guns of various types, in his capacity as regional manager of the U.S. subsidiary of the

Royal Siamese Arms and Ammunition Company. The company was real enough; the King of Siam needed to build a native arms industry to maintain his independence against British and French encroachment and Idris had persuaded the King that he was the man to help him do it. Idris had invested a small sum, and had drummed up some interest among Indian Muslim businessmen, but the King was the controlling stockholder. The U.S. subsidiary was a different story. Idris was the sole owner and employee, maintaining only a nominal connection to the Bangkok firm, but that was enough to import and export military equipment legally, as long as Uncle Sam got his cut.

"Crate it back up," Idris ordered after a cursory inspection of the tank. "I'll check the rest, then take it all to the rail yard. I need this equipment to be in San Francisco by Monday."

———

Shortly thereafter, Idris was on the telephone in the Meso-American satellite office in Galveston. "Get me Mr. Montgomery," he said when the local operator had patched him through to the Dallas office. "The younger one." A few minutes later, the T&C operator was on the line telling him to please wait a second, and then he heard the boy's familiar voice.

"Hello?"

"Alberto, I need a favor."

"Sure, ask away."

"I need a private train, Galveston to San Francisco. Can you have your dad's people arrange it?"

"We can probably do that. When do you need it? I think one of the Houston locomotives will be free at the end of the—"

"Saturday. I need it Saturday."

"Idris, that's… three days from now. T&C doesn't have much stock just sitting around, not with the trains ferrying your oil all over the country."

"Our oil, Alberto. You get your Meso-American dividends each month, and we're paying the T&C a handsome rate for transport."

"I know, sir, I'm just saying—"

"Don't 'sir' me, kid. I work for a living. Is there a tanker train headed for California on Saturday?"

There was a rustling as Alberto checked the timetables. "Yes, there is."

"Just add a few cars for me then. I'll make it worth your while. This is a very urgent—and valuable—shipment."

"What is it? Nothing, you know, illicit?"

"No, not per se, but I need your utmost discretion in this. I don't want your dad to worry."

"Of course. You know you can count on me."

Idris did know that, which was why he'd gone to the younger Montgomery rather than the elder. "I've been entrusted with a large quantity of cash—gold, silver and banknotes—belonging to Ali Arslanov, provisional President of the Republic of Azerbaijan. He managed to smuggle it out of his country before the Bolsheviks took over, and has asked me to deliver it to the All Russia Coordination Committee in San Francisco. He hopes to use it to fund a counterrevolutionary expedition to Siberia now that we've withdrawn our doughboys, leaving the White Army in the lurch."

"Good for him!" exclaimed Alberto. "It's a crying shame we pulled out when we did. Happy as I am to be back home, I'd have been proud to kick those Reds' asses back to Moscow, if we'd only had the men and the political will."

"So you'll arrange it?"

"Of course. I'll have a locomotive in Galveston Saturday morning. It can pick up the tanker cars in Houston and San Antonio, and be in California by Monday."

"Perfect. I'm going to have a few more cars in Galveston. Equipment I'm shipping to the Orient. All the trains are insured, right?"

There was a pause as Alberto probably tried to determine the motive behind the question. "The trains themselves, yes. You insure your own freight, just as you always have with the oil."

Now Idris paused, as if considering this information, though he already knew exactly how this was going to play out. "I can't very much go to Lloyds to insure the Azerbaijani treasury and a hundred thousand dollars in armaments."

"The railroad can self-insure," said Alberto, "but we'll have to have an adjuster verify the cargo beforehand, and my dad will have to sign off on it."

"I don't think he'll mind when he sees what I'm paying him. Send someone discreet for the adjustment, though. Everything is in order, but these are sensitive matters, with political ramifications."

"You can trust our people. There'll be premiums."

"Sure. Name your price."

———

Idris put a lot of miles on the Rolls over the next few days, between Galveston, Houston, Victoria, El Paso and southern New Mexico, and finally back to Dallas. When he got to his own office in the new Meso-American Petroleum headquarters in the Kirby Building, he found the newspaperman waiting for him.

"Bertrand Collins, *Morning News*," the man said before the receptionist could introduce him. "You asked us to send someone over."

"Yes, sir. Come into my office."

"Your new refinery is the talk of the business section right now," Collins was saying as they moved from the lobby into Idris's private office, but he waved for the reporter to be quiet.

Once inside, with the door closed, Idris lowered his hand. "What I have to tell you will interest your readers—and your editor—much more than the opening of another refinery. But I must insist on absolute anonymity."

"Mr. Pasha, we protect all our sources—"

"I would have sent someone else to meet with you, but I thought you would give greater weight and urgency to this news coming from me. But I must stress again that I do not want my name connected with this matter."

"As I said, sir—"

"Before I say another word, I will, in fact, require you to sign a confidentiality agreement. All the information I am about to tell you can be confirmed through police records and other sources, which I will provide and which you are free to cite, but my involvement must remain absolutely confidential."

"Mr. Pasha, signing such an agreement would be highly irregular, and I must warn you it would be unenforceable should you disclose any criminal conduct."

"You may go, then."

Collins stood in the doorway, dumbfounded, while Idris settled himself behind his desk and shuffled through his papers until he found the document he was looking for. Collecting himself, the young man strode over to the desk.

"I'll sign."

"I thought you would. Now that that's out of the way"—he pushed the paper across the desk and waited until Collins had signed—"I must tell you that, though it pains me greatly, I have information regarding my partner, Earl Montgomery, of which the public should be made aware."

PART III
JUDGMENT

13

DALLAS, TEXAS, 1920

THIS TIME it was Montgomery's turn to invite the whole town. Alberto had been promoted to captain in the Texas National Guard, skipping first lieutenant entirely. His proud papa—or, more likely, mamá—had gone all out, hiring a decorator, a caterer and a colored jazz ensemble. The wine and whiskey flowed freely too, though the chief of police was one of the guests.

Idris arrived after nine.

"You're late," Mariana chided as soon as she saw him. "Alberto has been looking for you."

"I just drove up from Galveston, Mrs. Montgomery. Honestly, were I not so fond of the boy, I would not have come at all."

"Well I'm glad you did," she said, placing a hand on his arm. "He's very fond of you too, you know. His father is not always an easy man to deal with, and you've taught him so much about business, given him a chance to impress the old man…"

"You know, Mrs. Montgomery, my nomadic life has left me no time for a family. I have traveled the five continents and the seven seas, and I have been content with making money, and spending in the cause of Allah. But sometimes I think back…"

Idris was overcome with a wave of emotion. He turned away to hide the anguish that must be apparent on his face.

"Are you all right, Mr. Pasha?"

He held up one hand, trying to maintain some distance between them. How had he let himself get so close to her? This would ruin his whole plan. To be undone by cheap sentimentality, and after what she'd done! He turned back to her, his expression as neutral as he could manage.

"Quite all right, *madame*. I should not tell you this, but, many years ago, I loved a young woman. Things went rather poorly, and I left the country. But had Allah willed that we stay together, I imagine we'd have a son around Alberto's age. He's a talented young man and will go far in life. It is my honor to assist however I can."

He turned to go, but she put her hand on his arm again, and this time Idris felt as if it burned through the fabric of his dinner jacket and seared the skin underneath. He recoiled involuntarily, barely able to keep from violently pushing her away. Mariana took a step back. Her face was pale with shock. Had she realized—? No, that was unthinkable.

"I am sorry, *madame*," Idris mumbled. "I did not mean to overstep. Let me find the young captain to congratulate him."

He turned away again, and nearly bumped into Alberto Montgomery, looking handsome as ever in his blue dress uniform with its shiny new captain's bars.

"Idris Pasha! You made it!"

"Of course." He gripped the young man's hand and gave him a hearty clap on the shoulder. "I wouldn't miss it."

"I'm to command the armory at El Paso," he said, beaming. "It's practically a federal post, with half the company mobilized at any given time to patrol against Mexican incursions."

Idris thought of General Luis Vargas and his men, patrolling that same desert, perhaps at that very moment. "That's wonderful," he said. "You'll see as much fighting as anyone on occupation duty, but you'll be close enough to visit your poor old mother."

Alberto chuckled and Mariana smiled at them both, apparently recovered from her earlier shock. "If he remembers to stop by after seeing Jeannie Valance," she teased.

Alberto blushed like a schoolboy. "Come," he said to Idris, obviously hoping to forestall any speculation about his love life. "I know you won't take champagne, but have some tea or a Coke."

"I'm afraid I can't stay long. But I would like to see your father before I take my leave. Have you seen him?"

"I can't say I have, not for at least an hour. Have you, Mamá?"

She shook her head, furrowing her brow as she did so. "Perhaps he's in his study. Thomas came by with a telegram for him earlier."

As she was finishing her sentence, one of the staff approached Idris. "Mr. Pasha, sir, they've been calling from your office."

"Calling me here? Yes, I did leave word I might be coming to Lieutenant—I mean—Captain Montgomery's promotion if I made it in time. I haven't called the office since leaving Galveston. I hope nothing has happened."

"I couldn't say, sir. Mr. Montgomery asked to be informed if you were seen here, as well."

"Please," said Idris, trying to sound a bit flustered. "May I use your telephone?"

"Of course," said Mariana and Alberto at the same time. Then Alberto added, "It's in Dad's study."

"Perfect, my boy. Then I'll see your father and call the office in short order, and, *inshallah*, we can get back to celebrating your promotion."

Together they walked to Montgomery's study, down the hall from the ballroom. Mariana rapped softly on the door.

"Who is it?" Montgomery shouted from inside. "Have they found Pasha yet?" He sounded angrier than usual.

"Yes, dear, he's here."

"Send him in. Then get back to our guests. Can't let on anything's wrong."

"Something's wrong?" asked Idris as he walked in. "Your man said the office is trying to reach me?"

"Come in and close the door. Just you."

"If this concerns our business, Alberto should hear it. He's not a kid anymore."

"You're right, Idris," said Montgomery, sighing with weariness. "Come on in, Al."

"I'll leave you boys to it then," said Mariana, and retreated down the hall. Alberto closed the door behind her.

There was an uncomfortable silence, each waiting for the others to speak. Finally, Idris couldn't take it. "What is it then? What happened?"

"The refinery," said Montgomery. "It burned to the ground. A hundred thousand gallons of crude oil up in flames!"

"Impossible!" exclaimed Idris. "I was there this morning. The foreman assured me everything was in order for the grand opening Monday."

"It's still burning. The whole Corpus Christi fire brigade can't put it out. The refinery itself, though—the machinery—completely destroyed."

"The refinery wasn't running yet, right?" asked Alberto. "How did the fire start?"

"Sabotage," said Montgomery.

"Sabotage?"

"Yes, and not just a wrench in the gears. Someone rigged the whole place up with dynamite."

"Impossible!" exclaimed Idris for the second time in as many minutes. "Where were the guards? *Ya Allah!* How many killed?"

"That's the thing. According to the police, there were only a few minor injuries. The first explosion produced a noxious gas that drove all the workers and guards away, then the rest of the dynamite exploded. The whole thing collapsed before the first firemen made it there."

"I'm telling you I was there this morning. The whole place had been inspected by the Railroad Commission yesterday. You're saying someone strung enough dynamite to blow up the biggest refinery in Texas in a few hours?"

Montgomery threw up his hands. "How the hell should I know? I'll tell you one thing though. I'm sure it was the goddamned Reds. You need to get your Pinkertons on the phone and get to the bottom of this."

"I'll ring Detective Brewill right away."

"I've got goons he can use if he needs more muscle."

Idris turned to Alberto. "Sorry, Captain. I need to get to my office, and then I'll probably head to Corpus Christi to find out what I can in person."

"I'll come with you."

"No, please, enjoy the rest of your party. I need you to stay here anyway, hold down the fort if anything comes up while I'm in Corpus." He turned his attention back to the elder Montgomery. "This is a temporary setback. We'll find out who did this soon enough. These terrorists never go undiscovered for long. As long as the wells are pumping and the trains running, we can go on without the refinery."

"Let's hope so," said Montgomery, and Idris thought that, under the fancy clothes and false teeth, he could see the old Frank Danger, ready to unleash violence.

Idris headed out into the night, but he did not go to the Meso-American offices. Instead, he turned the Rolls westward, toward New Mexico. He had a train to catch.

After the station in El Paso, the T&C Railroad crossed the Rio Grande and angled out across the open desert toward Deming, New Mexico. The country there was about as flat as anywhere in the United States, but there were a few low rises, and gullies deep enough to hide men and horses. The Apaches and Comanches had found all these places a century earlier, and used them to such great advantage against the Spaniards that they'd re-routed their Camino Real to hug the river.

Idris's Rolls Royce was more brown than gray after driving all night down unimproved farm roads and cutting through both the Mescalero reservation and the white sand desert. Hayden had been a racecar driver before Idris hired him, but even so, Idris had been afraid that he might not make it to Doña Ana County before the train. When he pulled up, he found Luis Vargas and a hundred hand-picked, seasoned veterans in position.

Vargas would stop the train whether Idris was there or not, but having had to miss the fireworks in Corpus Christi, Idris was not about to miss this.

The sky was red as blood in the east. Idris imagined he could see the flames from the refinery flickering on the horizon. He greeted Vargas with a hearty embrace, then washed up to pray *fajr* while Hayden started up the car and departed for Deming, some ten miles down the road.

"I never understood you, Turco," said Vargas. "You pray to your Allah, then you go kill his children."

"My God told me to fight oppression and injustice. Did Christ not teach you the same?"

"I thought he said to turn the other cheek? If the reactionaries would just do that, the Revolution would have triumphed long ago."

The sound of a train whistle interrupted their conversation.

"Did you bring a horse for me?" Idris threw on a canvas duster over last night's dinner jacket and replaced his usual red tarboush with a cowhand's sombrero.

Vargas pointed to a handsome palomino. "You match, *güerito*. Let's go, everyone! Get in position!"

The men hunkered down behind whatever cover or concealment they could find. The horses were poorly hidden in the shallow depressions to either side of the railway, but by the time the engineer noticed, it would be too late.

They could see the train now, barreling down the track. When it was a little less than a mile away, which looked a lot closer on this arrow-straight track, Vargas gave a hand signal, and his bugler played a single sharp note. Almost a mile west of their position, one of the men pushed the plunger on a blasting machine, and an explosion shook the ground.

The plume of dust and smoke that rose above the blown tracks must have been visible for miles. The engineer must have seen it instantly, because the train's brakes began to squeal and the locomotive coasted to a halt just shy of the breach.

It was a long train, a hundred ten-thousand-gallon tank cars before a boxcar and two flatbeds holding Idris's last-minute cargo. Coupled to the usual caboose was a second locomotive, facing in the opposite direction. No matter, Idris had warned Vargas to expect that. When the train finally stopped, these last few cars were almost right in front of Idris, Vargas and the main body of his men.

The braking noise ceased and silence reigned for a moment, as Vargas appraised the likelihood of seizing the cargo without resistance. A volley of gunshots from the caboose put that question to rest.

As Idris had expected, Montgomery had spooked a little at his insistence on insuring the train, and had added extra guards. Idris would have preferred to do this without bloodshed, but he figured Vargas was fighting for a just cause, and the railroad goons knew what they were signing up for. He'd insisted that the engineer, brakeman and other crew were not to be harmed except in self-defense, and he hoped he could count on Vargas to keep his word.

The *villistas* were firing back now, from behind the slim cover afforded by the slightest rise in the ground. A pair of workmen came out of the first of the boxcars, the one carrying the imported artillery pieces, and tried to uncouple it from the last of the tanker cars, ducking as bullets ricocheted around them. In the second locomotive, the firemen were stoking the engine, judging by the thick black smoke billowing out the smokestack.

Vargas laughed and signaled for his bugler to blow another long note. A mile to the east, another explosion sent a cloud of dust and debris up into the air. The track was now cut in both directions. The train and its guards and crew were trapped, but that wouldn't be the end of the fighting, or the demolition.

"You should hurry up," Idris shouted to Vargas. "This train probably has a wireless."

"You worry too much, Turco. Fort Bliss is thirty miles away."

"They have airplanes, though. A DH.4 can cover that distance in fifteen minutes."

"In that case," Vargas said, waving at the bugler, "charge!"

The bugler played the familiar sing-song call, and the men emerged from their positions to rush the train. A few fell to the guards' bullets, but one of the Mexicans managed to reach the caboose and drop a hand grenade through the window.

The blast blew out all the windows, showering the nearest *villistas* with broken glass, likely killing everyone inside. Probably destroyed the wireless too, if there was one.

There was still sporadic firing from the boxcars, but the Mexicans knew, down to the lowest private, that they couldn't damage these cars, which held the materiel they needed.

Vargas nudged Idris, and they both hopped up from their hiding place and dashed toward the train, pistols at the ready.

The two workmen had surrendered, giving up their attempt to decouple the cars. Behind them, one of Vargas's soldiers was about to blow the door, which had been barred from the inside, with a single stick of dynamite.

"Take the prisoners away," Vargas ordered. "Everyone take cover!"

They all backed away, flattening themselves against the side of the last tank car, as the short fuse burned down. The blast shook the whole car and, judging by the screams from inside, maimed anyone standing directly in front of the door.

One of the *villistas* charged into the car, a revolver in each hand, firing at any hint of movement. Vargas followed, saber in one hand, pistol in the other. He walked from body to body, giving each of the railroad goons the *coup de grâce*, as Frank Danger had done to those other guards so many years ago.

Idris and Vargas inspected the contents of the boxcar, stacks of crates along each wall, some peppered with bullet holes but otherwise unharmed. The artillery pieces occupied the center of the car. Only the first had been scratched up by shrapnel when they blew the door open. As he and Vargas approached the last piece, Idris heard a clanking over the popcorn noise of sporadic gunfire outside.

He held up a hand for silence. There was the noise again, in the back corner, next to the strongbox that Idris knew held the supposed treasury of White Azerbaijan. Vargas gave the signal for one of his men to look back there, but before he could even move, a guard jumped up from his hiding place and started spraying randomly with an MP 18 submachine gun.

The *villista* fell. Vargas ducked behind the Russian gun, the rounds bouncing off its wide barrel with loud clangs. Idris tried to duck too, but too late. He felt the shock—not altogether new—of a bullet striking his shoulder, right around where the *federales'* bullet had pierced his flesh two decades prior.

He stumbled back, keeping the presence of mind to raise his own automatic and crank out half a dozen shots, at least a few of which hit the hired goon in the chest.

"You all right, Turco?" Vargas put a hand on Idris's good shoulder. "The doc will patch you up. Let's see how the men are doing with the last two cars."

The flatbeds had been taken without a fight. In the whole engagement, only a half dozen of Vargas's men had been injured and two killed. All the hired guards were dead, along with the brakeman, who had pulled a gun. The rest of the crew were in custody.

"Keep them under guard until you get to the border," Idris advised as the medic cleaned and dressed his wound. "Leave them in the open, where the air patrol will see them, but off your main route so they can't tell the Army or the *constitucionalistas* where to find you."

Vargas's men had uncoupled the flatbeds from each other while others removed the canvas tarps that had concealed the two Mark I tanks from prying eyes. His engineer pulled the locomotive forward until the gap was wide enough to drive the tanks down. Idris had made sure both were fully fueled when loaded, and that Vargas had men able to drive them. They'd likely see battle against the Mexican army in the next few weeks.

Other soldiers were transferring the crates of weapons and ammunition to wagons Vargas had brought for the purpose, and others still were bringing the horses out of their hiding places.

When his wound had been treated, Idris rose to inspect the ruined caboose. Among the detritus inside, he found what looked like the remains of a compact wireless radio. Surely they would have called for help before the grenade killed everyone inside. The firefight had taken little more than ten minutes, but the unloading was taking too long. The air patrol might be overhead at any minute. There was no remedying the situation for the *villistas*, but Idris didn't need to stick around.

Getting the arms and ammunition to Mexico was Vargas's problem. Idris's goal had been to destroy the train, and that was done.

Almost done.

"You got what you need," he told Vargas. "Blow the rest."

Vargas nodded to his bugler, who sounded three sharp notes. All the men retreated to either side of the tracks and crouched down behind any cover they could find, or simply lay flat on the ground. When the coast was clear, the bugler sounded a single loud note, and someone somewhere pressed a plunger.

Dynamite exploded in a daisy-chain running down the middle of the track, from the first locomotive all the way down the line of tank cars, the blasts so quick one after the other that they made a deafening roar rather than distinct explosions.

The last stick blew under the second tank car from the end—someone must have misjudged the length of the train—and, though red flames and black smoke were already pouring from the rest of the cars as the precious petroleum burned away, the last tank car stood alone, undamaged.

"See if you can handle those guns," Vargas ordered the man in the hatch of one of the Mark I's.

The tank slowly wheeled around until its side-mounted cannons were trained on the surviving tank car. The two six-pound main guns roared, and the car exploded in a massive fireball, as if it had been packed full of dynamite.

A hundred cars destroyed. A million gallons of crude aflame, ten times the quantity lost at the refinery. Almost seventy-five thousand dollars up in smoke.

The flames leapt into the desert sky, from horizon to horizon, redder than the dawn

Idris grinned, and the words of the Holy Qur'an came unbidden to his lips. "Neither the wealth nor children of the disbelievers will avail them against Allah," he recited in Arabic. "They will be fuel for the Fire."

14

DALLAS, TEXAS, 1920

Hayden was waiting for him at a little ranch house a mile outside of town. Idris tied up the palomino, washed and changed into clean driving clothes, and they were off. Every time they stopped for fuel, at Roswell, Brownfield, Haskell and Jacksboro, Idris bought a newspaper.

Even the early papers carried the news of the Meso-American refinery explosion, attributing it to unknown radicals. In Haskell, the afternoon paper was already on the shelves of the local drugstore. It named Polish anarchist Fryderyk Kowalski as the primary suspect, but gave no further details on the investigation.

Good. Schneider should be halfway to Cuba by now, and the fact that only his Polish *nom de guerre* appeared in the paper meant the information came from the Corpus Christi police, rather than Brewill's Pinkertons.

Jacksboro was close enough to town that it got the Fort Worth papers, which had picked up the leading stories from the Dallas morning news. Collins's story was on the front page. "Captain of Industry or Kaiser of Crime?" read the headline. The story repeated almost word for word the claims Idris had made about Montgomery.

Some were true, and well substantiated by the records Brewill had obtained. Montgomery had kidnapped the daughter of the owner of the Texarkana Railroad to force him to sell the company for a tenth of its value—the old man had refused to pursue the matter out of fear or violence or damage to the girl's reputation—not to mention a litany of lawsuits and fines avoided through bribes and intimidation. Others—such as Montgomery's involvement in dope and arms smuggling and white slavery—were just hearsay, but Idris had provided enough detail and a list of secondary sources deep enough to protect Collins from a libel suit.

It was late afternoon when Idris reached Highland Park, and he was not surprised to see a dozen cars parked all around Montgomery's mansion. Newspaper reporters and cameramen lounged outside some of the vehicles, while others likely held detectives or representatives of the various companies and agencies Montgomery was involved with. Idris marched right up to the front door and pounded with his fist, ignoring the knocker and doorbell.

After a few minutes of knocking, the door creaked open and a servant ushered him inside and quickly locked the door behind him. "The boss is out," he said, "but the missus'll talk to you."

Idris gulped. Could he face Mariana alone? And why would she want to see him, anyway? Perhaps she'd guessed he was behind the recent disasters.

The servant left him at the door to the kitchen, where Mariana Montgomery was seated by the stove, drinking a cup of coffee without gusto.

She was wearing a simple house dress, no makeup, her graying hair hanging loose over her shoulders, yet Idris found her even more alluring than when she was dolled up for a party. Perhaps it was the idea that if things had gone differently, if Allah had destined him for a different fate—Allah forgive him for even thinking it!—he might have seen this unguarded beauty every day.

It didn't not bother him so much that Frank—Earl—had Mariana to show off to all his buddies at the country club, but knowing that Frank —Earl—had *this* Mariana, this beautiful, vulnerable, natural Mariana, who had changed so little since she worked the sewing machine in her papá's haberdashery… Frank Danger had taken her away, and now he would pay.

"Mr. Pasha," Mariana began, her tone soft, tentative.

"Please, *madame*," he said out of habit, "call me Idris."

"Idris. I know my husband is not a good man. I know he has a past we don't talk about, and I don't ask questions about his business nowadays either. But he is my husband, for better or for worse. He is Alberto's father."

"*Madame*," he said, trying to keep all emotion from his voice. "Your husband's moral qualities are not my concern, and neither are his conjugal and paternal affections. What does concern me is the state of his finances, seeing as they are a bit intertwined with my own."

"We both know this is not about money."

"Of course this is about money, *madame*. We've both lost a considerable amount of property in the past forty-eight hours, and, with the scandals in today's newspaper, T&C stock is going to crash. We need to figure a way out of this mess. Where is he?"

"Mr. Pasha—"

"Idris, please."

"Eddie…"

Idris's blood ran cold. She knew.

She knew.

She had seen through his flimsy disguise, and how could she not? A beard and a silly hat might fool Frank, but never Mariana.

And yet, she hadn't run to him, embraced him, thanked the stars for bringing him back to her. She'd said, "Good evening, Mr. Pasha," and gone back to bed with Frank Danger!

If there had ever been any doubt, it was gone now. Mariana, too, must pay.

"Where is he?" Idris asked, pretending he hadn't heard. "We can still salvage something of the business."

"He's left town," she replied, her voice flat. "Gone to Mexico to wait this thing out." Her eyes flickered about the room, unwilling to meet his gaze.

She was lying, that much was clear. And if he wasn't home and he hadn't left town, there was only one place he would be. The lodge.

"Haven't you done enough?" she blurted out as he was turning to go. "He's a ruined man. Have mercy!"

Idris turned back to look at her one last time. Her eyes were red and glassy with worry and exhaustion. Idris looked for repentance, but found none.

"Allah is the Merciful," he said, turning away once again. "Ask Him."

———

Montgomery's hunting lodge was on the Trinity River, just a few miles south of town. Even if Mariana called the police, Idris would be able to beat them there in the Silver Ghost. He had left Hayden downtown, preferring to drive himself. There was bound to be bloodshed and he didn't want the boy mixed up in it.

He tore down the country roads like a madman, running through scenes in his head. Scenes from the past—the ambush in the desert, prison, cholera, burying Abdallah alone in the corner of the churchyard, the cave, the treasure, Frank at the party with his arm around Mariana's waist... and then he saw scenes yet to come— confronting Frank, demanding payment for the lost train, voices raised, pistols drawn, gunshots, smoke, blood, Mariana wailing...

There it was, the lodge, a phony log cabin at the end of a gravel drive behind a screen of blackjack oaks. Montgomery's Cadillac was in the driveway, out of sight of the road. Idris pulled into the driveway at speed, then slammed on the brakes to park at an angle behind the Cadillac, blocking it in.

As he drove, he had considered what weapon to use. He had the Colt automatic with the Maxim silencer in the glove box, but what need was there for silence out here? He had a Winchester riot gun and a brand-new Thompson submachine gun in the trunk, but he wasn't here for a massacre. Montgomery deserved better than that—or worse.

Frank Danger's ruination was almost complete, and Idris was there to drive the last nail into his coffin. But there was no telling how Montgomery might react, so Idris strapped on an old-fashioned gun belt, just like he'd worn on that fateful day, except this time he wore a pair of Smith & Wesson .44s.

The belt hung low, the tips of the holsters protruding from beneath his suit coat, so he threw on the duster he'd worn for the train. He supposed that, apart from the beard and tarboush, he now looked more like the old Eddie than at any time in the past twenty-five years.

He banged on the door. There was no answer. He tried the knob, knowing it would be locked.

"Earl!" he shouted. "Your wife said you were here. Let me in so we can figure this out."

He waited a few seconds, listening for any sign of movement inside. Nothing. Might Montgomery have done the honorable thing and ended his miserable life? No, Frank had not been that kind of man, and Montgomery was no different. He was in there, hoping Idris would give up and leave.

There had been a number of burglars in the Chihuahua State Penitentiary, and during the year after the cholera, Idris had learned as much as he could from them, including the subtle art of lock-picking. Now he inserted a bit of wire into the keyhole and jiggled it until he felt the locking mechanism turn. The door swung open.

"Earl!" he called as he strode through the faux-rustic foyer. "Are you here?"

He walked from doorway to doorway, fighting the urge to draw his revolver. Finally, he reached an office, with a desk and a leather swivel chair turned to face the rear window. Though he could not tell if the chair was occupied, the oil lamp flickering in the corner suggested it was. There were papers strewn across the desk—telegrams, bank statements, sums and differences scrawled haphazardly across otherwise blank pages—and, amidst the disorder, a single Colt .44 revolver.

Idris wondered if it was a new piece, or one of the pair Frank Danger had used back in the day.

"Earl," he said, more quietly this time. "Everybody's looking for you. You should probably lock the door."

The chair slowly turned, until Montgomery was facing him. He was haggard, his eyes betraying exhaustion of body and mind. He was still wearing his dinner jacket from the previous night. "No one is supposed to know I'm here," he said, apparently not registering that he had, in fact, locked the door.

"Mrs. Montgomery told me you'd be here," Idris lied. "She might be telling others as well."

"I doubt it," Montgomery said. "Mariana's a smart woman. She only told you 'cause she knows you're in this shit as deep as me."

Idris forced out a laugh. "I suppose I am. It was my crude that burned up, wasn't it? Meso-American stock will be a penny a share by tomorrow morning."

"I'll be lucky if T&C is at half that. Someone did his homework on me."

"I just heard," said Idris. "We all have a past, Earl."

Montgomery gave him a long, hard stare. He'd neglected to put in his partial dentures, and his gap-toothed snarl, more than the gun on the desk, reminded Idris that this was a dangerous man. "What do you want, Pasha?" he growled.

"You lost a train, Earl, but I lost three hundred million rubles in cash and a significant amount of military equipment. I'm ruined."

"Join the club."

"Your railroad insured my cargo for five million dollars."

"I figured you'd come try to pick my bones. You know I don't have five million dollars on hand. When the insurance pays out for my train, I'll pay for your cargo."

"Your train was not insured against acts of war," Idris said. "I checked with your accountants. Given the nature of my cargo, I made sure it *was*, and that it was payable immediately upon authentication of the loss."

"Well you'll just have to wait," Montgomery spat, pounding his hands on the desk. The revolver jumped a little.

"I'm afraid that's not an option. Do you know who my buyers are?

Tsarist agents, former *okhrana*. Secret police. Even Lenin is scared of them. If I don't deliver…" He left the implication of violence unsaid.

"You know," said Montgomery, "I've been in the railroad business a long time. And as you've no doubt heard, I was in some unsavory businesses before that. But I never, never had so many goddamn problems until I partnered up with Mr. Idris Pasha."

Idris narrowed his eyes. "What are you saying, Earl?"

"I'm saying I think you set me up. Maybe you're a Red, or a White, or just a goddamn swindler, but you did this yourself. I'm sure of it."

Idris raised his shoulders in an exaggerated shrug, wincing as he did so. "You can think that if you want, but good luck convincing a judge. Meanwhile I have a signed contract saying you owe me five million dollars."

They stood in silence for what felt like an age, staring each other down. Montgomery's hand inched toward the revolver. Idris peeled his duster back enough to show his gun belt, keeping his hand just an inch above the handle of his own Smith & Wesson.

"You might want to re-think what you're about to do," he said. "Partner."

Montgomery's eyes narrowed, then grew wide as he finally connected the dots. "You're…" he sputtered, "you're that fucking kid! Mariana's old beau, Eddie! You're supposed to be dead."

"Eddie *is* dead," Idris replied, summoning all his willpower to keep from drawing his pistol right then and there. "Your betrayal condemned him to a living death. Now justice demands the same from you."

"Justice?" Montgomery laughed out loud. "You talk about justice, like you're better than me? You came to me for help, looking for a big score. You killed those greasers in cold blood, same as I did. You stole that gold, same as me. Only difference is you were too stupid to hold onto your share. Or your girl."

Idris's body reacted before his brain could. His hand plunged down to grab the pistol grip, at the same time as Montgomery lunged for the Colt on the desk.

Idris dodged to the right as he drew and cocked the hammer.

Montgomery sprung to his feet, upsetting his chair in the process, attempting to cock and aim the Colt at the same time.

Idris's gun was up, and his finger found the trigger.

A car horn sounded, as if from miles away, and both men froze.

"Earl!" called a voice from the front hall. Mariana's voice. "Eddie!"

Montgomery's gun was up now too, aimed directly at Idris's chest. They stared at each other down their gun barrels.

"You told her?" whispered Montgomery.

"She recognized me."

"Dad!" shouted another voice, Alberto's. They were almost at the office door now. "Idris Pasha! I mean, Eddie?"

Quickly, but without suddenness of movement, Idris lifted his finger off the trigger and tilted the barrel toward the ceiling.

A second later, Montgomery did the same. In unison, they lowered their weapons. Idris holstered his, letting the duster fall to cover it, while Montgomery stuffed the Colt in his waistband and buttoned his dinner jacket just as Mariana and Alberto burst into the room.

Montgomery stooped to right the chair. "You surprised me, Marita," he said. "Mr. Pasha and I were talking business."

"Forget business," said Alberto. "I think 'Mr. Pasha' owes us an explanation." He turned toward Idris, who was absentmindedly smoothing his duster where it covered the twin pistols. "Or should I call you Eddie Dawson?"

"That was once my name," Idris replied. "Many years ago, when I was engaged to marry your mother."

"Before you left her," Alberto snarled, "in her hour of need!"

"Albertico," said Mariana, placing a calming hand on his shoulder, but he shrugged it off.

"Your son deserves the truth, Mariana. Why don't you tell him how I was barely out the door before you took up with Frank Danger?"

"I thought you were dead!" she exclaimed, tears welling up in her green eyes. "And who the hell is Frank Danger?"

Idris sneered. "I guess you'd better let your husband explain that one."

Montgomery sighed and opened his mouth as if to speak, but Alberto interrupted him. "Pasha! You're bleeding."

Instinctively, Idris looked at his wounded shoulder. The bullet hole was only noticeable if you knew it was there, and there was no blood visible on the surface of the duster. But when he looked down, he saw a dark puddle forming behind his left foot. He reached over his shoulder to feel the spot where the exit wound was. The duster was dry, but he could feel blood through the bullet hole. The shirt and, presumably, the bandage under it were soaked. He must have broken the stitches during his rush to the lodge.

"It's just my old war wound," he said, trying to keep his voice even. "It's never healed properly."

"You never mentioned a war wound," Alberto said. "In fact, I'm sure you told me you thanked Allah every day for bringing you through the war unscathed."

"Alive," Idris muttered. "I said 'alive'."

"I heard an interesting report from the railroad police," said Alberto, ignoring Idris's explanation. "They sent a man to Mexico to interview the survivors of this morning's bandit attack."

"There were survivors?" exclaimed Idris. "*Alhamdulillah!*"

"Don't play the fool! The survivors said there was a *gringo* with the bandits. A white man with a blond beard, who was *shot in the shoulder* but was seen riding away on horseback before the bandits took the prisoners across the border."

"You bastard!" shouted Montgomery. "I knew it was you!"

He reached for the gun in his waistband, but Idris was faster. Before he could even draw, Idris had planted a round in Montgomery's left shoulder, just about where his own wound was. Montgomery lurched back, slamming against the chair he had just righted and tipping it over again with a loud clatter.

Mariana screamed and rushed to aid her husband, who was groaning and cursing with pain.

Alberto reached into his sport coat to draw his own gun, but Idris trained his Smith & Wesson on the young man's chest. "I wouldn't do that, Captain. Go patch up your dad, before he ends up bleeding out like me."

Indeed, the pool of blood at Idris's foot had grown. If he didn't re-bandage the wound soon, he would die of blood loss and his vengeance would remain incomplete. As Alberto knelt to help his mother, Idris turned and stumbled out the door and toward his car.

15

DALLAS, TEXAS, 1920

IDRIS WAS ONLY a few miles from the lodge when he saw the Duesenberg Straight Eight in his rear-view mirror.

Good. Alberto had decided to come after him, as Idris knew he would. Only when Frank Danger and Mariana had lost what was most dear to them, would justice be served.

It was only fitting. Frank had not only condemned Eddie to twenty years of living hell, he had stolen away the one person Eddie cared about in all the world. Now Frank would feel that same pain.

As he rocketed down the highway, just fast enough to keep distance between himself and the Duesenberg, Idris was surprised to see two police cars driving in the opposite direction, bells clanging. There was no telephone in the lodge, and the closest neighbors were too far to have heard the gunshot. Might Mariana have called the police before leaving her house?

It didn't matter. Idris just had to make it another half mile down the road, where he'd seen a fallow field and a half collapsed barn where he might make his stand.

There. He peeled off the road and down the dirt path leading to the barn, then slammed on the brakes, screeching to a halt in a cloud of dust.

He walked around the car to open the trunk, and pulled out the factory-new Thompson gun just as Alberto flew around the corner in the Duesenberg.

Idris pulled back the bolt, flicked the safety off, and mashed the trigger, peppering the car with bullets. He aimed low, at the tires and engine block, to disable the vehicle and rattle the driver, not kill him.

He'd have to give Alberto a fighting chance.

It only took a few seconds to empty the whole thirty-round magazine. Idris ducked behind the trunk of the Rolls and reached across his midsection to draw the revolver from his left-side holster and turn it around in his hand. He felt that the bleeding from his left shoulder had slowed, but he couldn't move that arm without acute pain, and he feared he'd be unable to draw left-handed without further injuring himself, if at all.

When he peeked around the rear of the Rolls, a bullet split the wood just inches from his head. He scrambled to take cover behind the front of the car instead. A military man, Alberto would know the Rolls's wood and aluminum body was unlikely to stop even a revolver bullet and he would shoot right through it if he could estimate Idris's position. Indeed, a round smashed through the windows just above him, but then he was safely—more or less—ensconced behind the engine compartment.

Idris fired a couple shots over the hood, not aiming to hit Alberto, but rather to provoke him into returning fire. He was rewarded a second later by a crack and the ping of a bullet bouncing off something inside the Rolls's mechanism. Hopefully nothing important, since Idris was planning to drive away from this gunfight.

He poked his head above the hood again, just long enough to draw fire but not long enough to get himself shot. Alberto's bullet ricocheted harmlessly off the chromed metal.

Alberto had two bullets left. Idris had four in this gun and five in the other. He fired two shots blindly, but Alberto wasn't biting.

Idris crawled toward the front of the car, keeping as much of his body as possible behind the wheel well. The Silver Ghost was top-of-the-line, with solid steel wheel covers that might deflect or even stop a revolver bullet. He curled his arm around the grill and just above the headlights, and popped off another two shots. He was rewarded by the crack of a revolver, and the smack of a bullet striking the ground inches from his knee, which protruded a little in front of the tire.

"You got one shot left!" Idris called out. "I got five."

"I can reload."

"I'll walk over there and finish you off before you do." He was bluffing. If Alberto had already started reloading, he'd be done by the time Idris got around the Duesenberg. But he was pretty sure that Alberto was bluffing too, that he hadn't thought to bring extra ammunition. "I got a better idea."

"What's that?"

"We settle this fair and square." He tossed the empty revolver out into the dirt between the two cars. "My other gun is still in its holster. You holster yours, too. We both step out and face each other like men."

"Like old-time gunfighters, huh?"

"Never heard of a duel?"

"Let's go then."

Idris peeked around the front of the Rolls. Alberto had emerged from behind the Duesenberg, but he was still holding the revolver in a two-handed grip, trained on the front of Idris's car. Idris took a deep breath, muttering, *"Hasbi Allah wa Ni'm al-Wakil."* His left arm was useless, and he struggled to pull himself up with his right hand, then steadied himself against the Rolls. He took a few steps away from the car, while Alberto followed him with the pistol barrel.

Idris held his hands open, the right at shoulder level and the left barely waist-high, to show that he had no weapon besides the Smith & Wesson hanging from his right hip, clearly visible with the duster tucked out of the way behind it.

"Now put yours away too," he said.

"Why?" asked Alberto. "So you can shoot me down like a dog?" His voice wavered. "I thought you were my friend."

"I thought the same about your dad, kid."

He *was* still a kid, wasn't he? Had his whole life ahead of him, just like Idris had, way back when he was Eddie. Alberto even had his own Mariana in Jeannie Valance, didn't he?

Idris shook his head to clear away these thoughts. The same could be said of any of the men he'd faced across no-man's-land at Celaya, or the Turks and Armenians he'd treated in the Caucasus, or any of the hundreds of thousands killed in the trenches of France and Belgium, the millions of martyrs lost in battles and skirmishes since the dawn of time. They were just kids, most of them. Young men with their whole lives ahead of them, with wives and sweethearts, maybe even children, with bright futures snuffed out in a moment. Few were guilty of anything at an individual level, yet their lives were the price demanded to settle the feuds and vendettas of powerful men.

Why should this kid be any different?

Idris lowered his right arm, slowly, so as not to spook Alberto, until his hand was parallel to the grip of the Smith & Wesson, though still about a foot away. Just as slowly, Alberto was moving to holster his pistol as well. Idris had known that, even after all that had happened, the boy didn't have it in him to gun him down in cold blood.

His left arm still hung limp, his shoulder hurting something furious now that the fear and excitement was wearing off. Trying not to take his eyes off Alberto, he glanced at the ground by his foot and saw no trace of blood, but he could feel the dampness of it inside his shirt and coat.

No matter. His plan was almost complete. Frank Danger's business had been ruined, and he was likely in police custody. There were enough leads in the news story to keep the cops interested in him for a long time to come, and without his millions he was unlikely to buy his way out of the charges. He'd go to prison for sure, if not the chair. Alberto was the only loose thread. Frank couldn't be allowed to live vicariously through the boy.

Once Alberto was dead, though, Idris cared little enough for his own life.

What was it Abdallah had told him so many years ago? The world is a prison for the believer. Death held no terror for him.

He reached for his gun.

A car raced by on the road they'd come down, its engine choking and brakes squealing as it made a half turn much faster than was safe. Though he should have known better, Alberto turned to see it, leaving himself unguarded at the worst possible moment.

Though he should have known better too, Idris hesitated, squinting to make out the model of the car or who was driving. It was Montgomery's Cadillac.

Alberto turned back to him, and he'd lost his opportunity. Their hands both hovering inches from their holsters, Alberto and Idris glared at each other across the empty field. Idris curled and uncurled his fingers. Alberto did the same.

The Cadillac's driver-side door opened and closed, but neither of the men dared to look away to see who it was, until Mariana rounded the front of the car and into Idris's peripheral vision. She ran toward Alberto, her loose black hair whipping in the breeze, the thin strands of silver catching the rays of the morning sun, but she stopped short, intuiting perhaps that any outburst was more likely to endanger her son than save him.

She halted a few yards away to Alberto's left, and behind him, outside of his field of view. There she stood in silence, staring at Idris with teary eyes, their red rims serving only to highlight their sparkling dark green.

Idris stared back. It wasn't just her beauty, though she was as striking now as the first day she'd looked up at him over the sewing machine in Don Pedro's shop. He'd loved this woman once, enough to throw his life away, and here he was about to throw his life away to hurt her. If only things had gone differently, if only fate had been kinder...

His hand made contact with the butt of his pistol, the movement so practiced he hadn't realized he was doing it, and the feeling of cold metal on his skin shocked him out of his reverie.

He tore his eyes away from Mariana, bringing his attention back to Alberto, whose hand was on his gun now too.

A handsome kid, Idris thought, not for the first time. Looked more like his mother, with the dark hair and greenish eyes. Barely a sign of

Frank there. He imagined how his own son might look at this age, and could not come up with a different image. If only things had gone differently.

But they hadn't. The die was cast.

Idris gripped the pistol tight as Alberto's gun left the holster.

More than twenty years had gone into this moment, and Allah's plan would not be changed. *Qada'* and *qadr. Al-maktub maktub.*

Idris's gun cleared the top of his holster as well, and his arm came up of its own accord, muscle memory ingrained by years of training.

Mariana stifled her scream, and it came out more like a whimper.

Idris looked back at her, though he felt his gun hand continuing its trajectory. She was a wreck, tears streaming freely down cheeks red with pent-up emotion, her graceful hands clenched over her mouth, her whole body shuddering in fear and grief.

His Mariana, his beautiful Mariana. He had done this to her, and for what? Revenge? Jealousy was more like it. She had done nothing but try to survive when he'd left her all alone.

This couldn't be Allah's plan. And if not Allah's...

Alberto's gun was up now, pointed directly at Idris. He only had one bullet, but his aim would be true.

Idris's gun was up, too. He'd known he'd be faster than the boy.

There was only one way out of this mess now.

Idris made a silent *du'a'*, so rushed he couldn't even formulate his entreaty into words. Allah was the Knower of hearts, and he would know of Idris's longings, his sorrows, his thankfulness, his repentance, all without the imperfect medium of human language.

He relaxed his fingers, and the revolver slid from his grip.

A gunshot rang out just as Idris closed his eyes and raised his right index finger.

"La ilaha ill Allah," he whispered.

There is no god but Allah.

The End

ABOUT THE AUTHOR

Jibril Stevenson is an American Muslim who studies linguistics by day and writes Muslim Westerns (and assorted other fiction) by night.

Check out www.jibrilstevenson.wordpress.com for more about Jibril and links to his short fiction in various genres, including DSP Award-winner "Zulfiqar is Coming" (possibly the first Muslim Western in print). Future plans include a series of Muslim Western novels spanning the decades from the US Civil War to Prohibition.

@JibrilStevenson on Twitter, Instagram, and most emerging social media platforms

THE SPATIAL CONDITION

J. AUSTIN YOSHINO

1

———————

Solmaz lived near the outer edge of Baikonur in a communal women-only riad. A few hundred meters beyond her house, the formal structures of the city gave way to clusters of shanties occupied by migrant workers. The Kazakh desert constantly threatened to reclaim this marginal settlement. Musk thistle and wild tulips springing up in the cracks of hastily poured concrete around her house indicated where previous camps had existed only a few years prior. She and Mohsin lived on the edge of the city where it was cheapest and where they could render the most mutual aid to incoming migrants. He lived in a men's riad a couple of blocks away, and only paid for the time that he spent on Earth. It also made it easier for them to save money. His position as a 3rd mate on a Trade Union Collective freighter conferred many benefits, but a large salary wasn't one of them. They were to be married once he had achieved the rank of 1st officer, since the quarters allowed for families to be brought on board. When Solmaz received news six weeks earlier that Mohsin's ship, the *Nightshade*, had gone missing, those plans evaporated.

Sitting in front of her vanity, staring into the mirror through puffy eyes and debating whether or not to apply makeup, Solmaz opted for sunglasses instead. She put on a black abaya over her street clothes, wrapped her head in a hijab and slid the sunglasses on. It wasn't common for a ship to go missing, but it was less common for them to reappear once they had. Ships that disappeared never reappeared. They were either attacked by pirates and destroyed in the process, or they were lost in the void as a result of singularity drive accidents. When she heard the news, she collapsed into tears and remained inconsolable for several days. After another week, she realized that she still needed to survive and returned to her jobs: at the foundry during the day, and at a restaurant at night.

Three days ago, the Nightshade was detected entering Earth's system. It began transmitting shortly thereafter. Solmaz received a voice message from Mohsin letting her know he was ok. This time, her tears were tears of joy. She was headed down to Mina Fada, the starport in the center of the city, because she wanted her face to be the first thing Mohsin saw when he stepped off the jetway.

Getting to Mina Fada from her riad in streetside was daunting. It required taking a series of maglevs and autowalks. As she drew closer, holoboards and vid screens multiplied. Everyone between home and Mina Fada was broadcasting news of the *Nightshade*'s reappearance. Even the Off World Commodities Index had been preempted. The news was being broadcast on every screen on every human colony and in every transport and mining vessel over a thousand lightyears.

From streetside, she could see the suborbital shuttles flying into Mina Fada's spire, like angry hornets buzzing around a nest. At night, it was a bit more picturesque since the exhaust flares of shuttles were all that was visible. "Mina Fada," an old Arabic word for "star port," was more than that. The lower levels contained ore processors and foundries. Each subsequent level contained housing complexes and shops. The higher you went in the spire, the more richly appointed it was. Groceries and department stores became fine dining and boutiques.

The wealthiest families lived even above the shuttle docks, obscured by mist and low hanging clouds, where dropships from orbiting mining vessels would offload their cargo into chutes that carried it down to processing levels. It was a physical manifestation of everything she despised: the wealthiest few at the top and the poor masses at the bottom, begging to be exploited. She didn't count herself among those who envied the rich. None of them knew what it was like to press their heads to the Earth that Allah had created for them, in prostration and supplication. Solmaz thought that those who spent their lives bemoaning their lot, envious of those who lived in the upper floors of Mina Fada, were fools.

Once she got to the maglev stop, she saw someone she knew across the street and tried, discreetly, to avert her eyes and lower her head so she wouldn't be noticed. Fortunately, her sunglasses hid the direction of her gaze, making her attempts to ignore him appear unintentional. While Mohsin had been missing, his friend Hossam had sent her several messages. The house mother at the riad thought it was nice. Solmaz thought it was a bit much. She thought Hossam was a fool too. He was wealthy, and cousin to the Sector 8 Sultan. His father was the Bashi of all operations for the Sultan at Mina Fada.

She met Hossam through Mohsin but she didn't consider him a friend. He always managed to run into her when she was alone in streetside. Sometimes she wondered if it was on purpose. After the *Nightshade* had disappeared, she started seeing him around streetside more. For the first couple of weeks, she was so overcome with despair that she didn't leave the women's riad. But at some point, she had to leave the house to work and shop. She ran into Hossam on the street on her way to her restaurant job. He offered his sympathies and a shoulder to cry on. She didn't take him up on it, but whenever she would see him on the street, she would spare a few moments to commiserate before going about her day.

A maglev was just arriving, but she wouldn't be able to board and pull away before Hossam got to her. Hossam was trying to flag her down but she carried on boarding the maglev in the hope he would feel an aversion to public transportation. She wasn't that lucky. Hossam caught up to her just as she found a seat. He was panting and disheveled, his pores oozing the previous night's drinking.

"Wow, you walk fast." Hossam put his hands on his knees, half panting and half laughing, before planting himself in the seat across the aisle.

"Salaamu Alaikum, Hossam." Solmaz expelled the greeting with some force and a bit of judgment.

"I was just ending a night out when the news came over the feeds. You must be elated."

"Of course I am! How else would I feel?"

"I'm glad he's back. But you must be asking yourself if this is the life you want for yourself. Dodging Corsairs and space fold mishaps," Hossam said dismissively.

"How do you imagine it is any better here? Or streetside? Subject to the inequities of greed. In the Trade Unionist Collective, we work toward a better future for all. Not seeking to enrich the few."

"Oh, yes. What is it they say? 'No one is entitled to anything until everyone has something'?"

Solmaz cut her eyes at Hossam. She hated the way he spoke about those less privileged than himself. His jaw would tighten and his lips would barely move. His tone took on a snappy cadence.

"The rich have money and the poor have each other. And I have Mohsin and we will spend our lives together trying to better the lives of as many as we can."

"Sounds like a fantasy." Hossam said contemptuously.

"Oh yes, Hossam? And what do you dream of?"

Hossam grew quiet. Perhaps he didn't have an answer. Maybe no one had ever asked him before. Solmaz wondered if dreams were even encouraged in a family like his. Or was there just continuity - duty and commitment to maintaining the wealth and status of the family? What else was there? It's not as if he could live streetside like Solmaz and Mohsin. They were happy, but perhaps they had convinced themselves of that because they had no other choice. Hossam had access to all the money and advantage one could ask for, so it was hard for her to imagine he was unhappy.

Solmaz was satisfied that her retort forced Hossam into silence. He had turned in his seat, his legs now firmly in the aisle, and was leaning toward her. She didn't like this. It was common to see these admin nobles on the street, in restaurants, and maglevs, draping themselves over streetside girls in the hope that their wealth and status would impress them. Some were impressed. Others pretended for the sake of politeness. But to an observer it looked the same, as if the poor streetside girls were being taken in by the charms of rich men, who would then use them and toss them aside. And it would go from the eyes of the observer to the ears of the riad house mother. And Solmaz would hear about it.

"Since I'm headed home, I thought I would and offer my congratulations to Mohsin. I saw you and figured you were going to see him, too. I hope you don't mind."

"I think Mohsin would be glad to see you and be grateful for the many prayers you offered on his behalf." Solmaz responded trying to hide her skepticism.

When they got to Mina Fada, crowds and reporters had gathered at the *Nightshade*'s shuttle jetway. As members of the crew disembarked, they were promptly accosted by people. The occasional applause and shouts of the many bystanders made the terminal feel jubilant.

Solmaz and Mohsin had grown up together in Baikonur - what people who lived in Mina Fada called "streetside." Despite Mina Fada being in the center of Baikonur, it was a city unto itself. It had its own police force, its own government. Mohsin's parents had moved to Baikonur from the African Union when he was ten, and he was raised in an AU collective the next housing block over from Solmaz. The balconies of their block levels were close enough that they could talk, and they did, every day. The first time Mohsin told her he loved her, he was still a kid. He was perched on the low concrete wall of his block, and they were talking as the sun was riding low. It was the only part of the day when they could see it at all through the maze of block towers. That summer, Mohsin enrolled in the apprenticeship program, and they began planning their lives together.

Mohsin came out of the jetway. He looked exhausted, but his elation broke through at the sight of her. She ran to him and he picked her up and hugged her. He was tall and lean, with an angular face and eyes that were round with kindness. She covered his face with kisses.

Hossam waited awkwardly to the side as they spent several minutes over their reunion, then stepped forward and patted Mohsin on the shoulder with a rigid formality. Solmaz stopped planting kisses on him.

"I'm glad to see you safe, my friend." Hossam offered stiffly.

"Thank you, Hossam."

"I just wanted to come by with Solmaz and offer my congratulations and express my relief at your safe return. I must be off." Hossam, if nothing else, knew when three was a crowd. Mohsin was attractive and personable. People liked him. Hossam liked him. It was what he hated most about him. But Hossam was no slouch. He was only slightly shorter than Mohsin, and just as good looking, and he had wealth and status besides. It aggravated him that he could never gain Solmaz's affections.

"I want to get you home and get you fed and in bed," Solmaz said. "You must be exhausted."

"The TUC is going to want to debrief me. They got me—us—a room here in Mina Fada until they can arrange it."

"Mohsin, you know I can't—"

"My fiancée can't join me, but my wife can."

"Mohsin…" Solmaz said in weak protest.

"There's a chaplain right here in the starport. We can have a public celebration with our friends later. I just don't want to be away from you again. Not ever." Mohsin put his hands on her shoulders and stared intently into her eyes.

"Mohsin, I still have to work. In fact, I need to get you home and then get down to the foundry. For my shift."

"You don't need to work those jobs anymore. "

"You said we couldn't get married until you made first mate."

I know, or captain." He shrugged casually, pretending it wasn't a big deal, but a grin crept across his face.

Solmaz wrinkled her brow and side-eyed Mohsin, then shrieked and jumped into his arms. They went down to the administrative offices and were married within the hour. Mohsin logged their marriage license with the TUC.

2

THE GALACTIC TRADE Consortium was owned and operated by eight Royal families spanning the Muslim world. Each family governed – and profited from - a sector representing a region of known space. Hossam's father was a high-ranking government official and cousin to the Sultan of the Gulf Sultanate which controlled Sector 8.

Hossam Majd's father was a prominent member of the administrative nobles, a new caste of knowledge that emerged from the new system of peerage. He was the Bashi of all sector 8 operations and served the Sultan of that sector. The emergence of this class solved the issue of looking after the various Sultans' sprawling families, while simultaneously maintaining the familial grip on wealth. Rank was determined by proximity to the Sultan by birth, and occupation was determined by rank.

Hossam's father was originally a high government official, which mostly involved pretending to oversee the vast bureaucracy of the Sultanate while attending lavish state functions and collecting a large salary. But his father had fallen out of favor with the Sultan. His constant public drunkenness and indiscreet affairs with married women were an embarrassment. The official explanation was that Hossam's father needed to be near Mina Fada to manage the Sultan's mining and shipping interests, but in truth, he had been exiled to a place where his drinking and philandering could continue undisturbed. The post was important, but it wasn't something any of the nobles wanted. Hossam was not only embarrassed by this, he was openly hostile to his father when addressed by him, or even merely in his presence.

They lived a good life near Mina Fada, high up in the apartments above the clouds. The streets below, when visible, were so small it was nearly impossible to make out any detail. Despite this, the reduction in status and resources was an affront. While still well paid, Hossam's father did not have access to the same wealth as before. His excesses had left them in generous poverty. Further, their proximity to Mina Fada meant proximity to people of lower status. There was simply no way to get from place to place without "getting one's shoes dirty," as Farouk liked to say. The Sultan's Bashi at Mina Fada was an important and essential position, it was beneath a noble, particularly one as close as a cousin.

Back in Baghdad, Hossam had servants and chauffeurs. He could go from his rooms to school without ever having his feet touch asphalt. Now, in this godforsaken place, he suffered the indignity of having to walk at street level. There were several Mina Fadas around the world; the one his father was assigned to was known informally as "Madinat Mina Fada" or "Space City." Transients called it simply "Mina Fada," but the locals used the old Soviet-era name "Baikonur." It had always been a Mina Fada, a space port. Built more than two centuries prior by the old Russian political hegemony, it had fallen into disrepair until a renewed interest in space exploration and commerce, fueled by the invention of the singularity drive. The eight Sultanates leased Mina Fada as the Russians had before them and built refineries, smelters, and foundries all around it. Every gram of ore and precious metal the Sultanates mined in space came through Mina Fada.

Along with all the industry came some of the attendant vice. But only some. The governor of Baikonur would only tolerate so much. And even then, only if he was getting a cut. Gambling establishments were illegal, though police looked the other way when it came to street gambling and private card games. This is where Hossam eventually found his place. During his first several months in Baikonur, he didn't leave the apartments. Despite the Sultan having given his father an entire floor in Mina Fada's luxury accommodations, they were still paltry compared to what he'd been accustomed to. After some cajoling from his mother and threats from his father, he stepped out into the dreary cold of the city. He didn't understand why his parents were so insistent, as all he found at street level were legions of soot-stained faces and cotton dungarees, heads topped with trapper's hats lined with nutria fur. There were endless barrel fires and barrel grills. He didn't want to know what was cooked on them.

Baikonur was situated in the southern deserts of what had once been the Republic of Kazakhstan. Although the days were warm in the summer and spring, the nights were incredibly cold year-round. The city's moisture collectors, especially those close to the upper atmosphere, condensed what little water vapor could be extracted from the desert air. Some of that condensation evaporated and some of it fell to the ground where it accumulated and drained into automated cisterns for purification and eventual consumption. The vaporized moisture formed fog and clouds and when the temperatures dropped, it would freeze and fall to the ground as snow or freezing rain. It all ended up as dirty slush that washed over the curbs and seeped into Hossam's shoes.

But amongst all the barrel grills, trapper hats, Asian babushkas leaning in shop doorways, and tides of darkened slush, there were games. Those same sooty faced, dungareed workers squatted in alleyways or perched on produce crates with dice and cards. Hossam could have stayed at Mina Fada. He could have shopped in the promenade or strolled and flirted with one of the beautiful local girls. But whenever he came upon a lively game of dice, he even forgot his wet feet.

The day he met Mohsin, he was down at street level. What had once appeared to him a dreary slush- and salt-crusted hell now enthralled him: a lively den of gambling, drink, and women. He didn't imagine the gambling spots here were anything like the parlors back home, the ones his father undoubtedly frequented. There was something headier about these places. Though he wasn't brave enough to eat the food, he often bought unmarked bottles of liquor from corner stores and would use them to get into a game. At first, he pretended to be a simple observer, quietly swigging from his bottle. Then, after a winning hand or roll of the dice, when there were celebratory cheers, he would offer some booze to the winner.

It wasn't long before he became a welcome regular at any one of a dozen games. When his father gave him his monthly stipend, Hossam would head down to streetside. On the coldest nights, while fat flakes drifted slowly to the ground, he would be standing over a game, or next to a warm barrel watching one. He liked to think that these people, who had nothing in common with him, nonetheless liked him. Perhaps even admired him. Hossam convinced himself that, in their admiration and curiosity about his life of privilege, they welcomed him as one of their own.

Deep inside, he knew that wasn't the case, but it was far more convenient and pleasant to believe than the truth. In some strange way, in convincing himself that it wasn't the free booze or habit of losing that made them like him, he felt he had accomplished something despite his privilege. He would be the wayward son, baptized in the streetside alleys, reemerging as half scion of nobility, half adopted son of the proletariat. His hard-won knowledge of the people he meant to rule would serve him and the Sultan in ways his father could never imagine.

One evening, with the aid of drink, he convinced himself more than usual of the imaginary friendship that existed between himself and a group playing dice. Hossam bet and couldn't cover the odds he offered. One of the players was not pleased. He was an older man, smaller, but possibly stronger. At various times while throwing the dice, he pulled up his sleeves in preparation, revealing thin, veined forearms—the type of wiry strength seen in starving laborers condemned to a life of heavy lifting. His beard was dyed so black by soot that it wasn't clear where his beard ended and the dirt began. It looked more like a giant smudge on the man's face, punctuated by mean, greasy lips that had recently feasted on gristly meat. The man reached into his rear waistband and pulled out a crudely fashioned knife with a taped handle. It had jagged and sharpened serrations and looked as if it had been used before.

The man stepped around the others, who still squatted around the crumpled wads of cash, and came toward him. Hossam was terrified, . and it occurred to him that he'd never really been scared before. He knew how to fight, his father had made sure of that. But hand to hand wasn't his strength. He preferred the fencing room to the dojo. Personal safety was never something he had to worry about back home. But he wasn't home.

"Do you know who my father is?" Surely this man would think twice about harming him if he knew.

"Tell me so I can tell him why I had to kill you." Muffled laughter erupted from behind scarves and hat flaps.

"Stop!" A large figure stood framed in the mouth of the alley. Unlike everyone else, he wore a utility jumpsuit like those worn by freighter crews.

"This is none of your business." The man with the knife said with a snarl.

Rather than speak again, the large man reached into a pouch on a utility belt slung over his shoulder and pulled out a wad of bills.

"Does this cover this man's debt to you?"

The smaller man's expression softened to something between confusion and suspicion. He swiped the bills from the man's hand and disappeared into the streets.

People from all over the world could be found in Baikonur, but the man who came to Hossam's aid stood out. He was tall and clean shaven, with very dark skin under a trapper hat with fur on the ear flaps. His jumpsuit was very worn but clean and the utility belt over his shoulder was well cared for. On the shoulder of his jumpsuit was the crescent scythe and spanner of the Trade Unionist Collective.

"Thank you. I'm in your debt."

"It wasn't a gift. I expect you to spread it around."

"You know, comrade, we could just skip all that and you could front me on the next roll. I'll have what I owe plus more for your trouble." Hossam said, trying to sound ingratiating.

"I'm generous, not stupid. Besides, I didn't do it for you." The man responded curtly.

Hossam tried to hide his annoyance. "Why did you do it?"

"I know who you are. Your father would have Sultanate operatives and Mina Fada security down here instantly if any harm came to you. These people's lives are difficult enough without your death on their heads, or you betting against them with their own money."

"Can you at least give me your name?"

"Mohsin."

Mohsin excused himself and went to greet a shopkeeper, a short, heavyset Asian woman wearing a scarf, her cheeks reddened by the cold. She hugged him, greeting him with the obligatory, "Salaamu Alaikum," then began to talk in the local tongue, a creolization of Arabic and Kazakh, which Hossam had not yet mastered. Mohsin took the shopkeeper's hands in his and kissed them. He backed away slightly, took another wad of folded bills out of the pouch on his belt and handed it to her. Hossam waited awkwardly for the exchange to be over then spoke to Mohsin again when he began walking down the street.

"I didn't thank you for what you did for me."

"Like I said, you can thank me by spreading it around."

"You mean like what you just did with that shopkeeper?"

"Yes. People down here don't have much, but they look after each other. That's what we do."

"We?"

Mohsin stopped and pointed at the patch on his arm. Almost everyone down here is or was part of the Trade Unionist Collective. It made sense to Hossam now. The TUC was owned and operated by the employees. They were the second largest mining and shipping group behind the Consortium but were gaining ground every year. He never understood the appeal of wanting everyone to live in poverty.

———

When Mohsin's ship went missing, Hossam was delighted. He'd met Solmaz with Mohsin during one of his excursions streetside and was immediately taken with her. She was tall and elegant with an infectious smile. And she had an engaging quality that made him feel important when she talked to him.

With Mohsin out of the picture, Hossam was free to pursue Solmaz. She would be grief-stricken for a year, but he would make himself available to her as a friend and help her work through those feelings of loss and grief. There was no one else streetside she could possibly be interested in, no more ship's mates or captains waiting to take her off on some collectivist adventure. With Mohsin gone, there would only be him, with the appeal of Mina Fada level luxury and marrying into a good family.

For weeks, he consoled her. Every day, he appeared streetside around the time Solmaz finished work. She confessed to him that she did not want to be at home, even amongst her family, because it made her feel alone. They were kind and well meaning, but never said anything to ease her worry. Ultimately, they all said variations of, "get over it." So, instead of going home, Hossam and Solmaz would walk around the streetside neighborhoods and talk. Despite his moral shortcomings, he could make her laugh. For the first time in his life, he not only felt useful, but he felt genuine joy in bringing relief and some semblance of happiness to another person.

His aims, initially, were less than noble. But as they walked and talked, he began to understand what Solmaz saw in Mohsin. He was selfless and giving, and he believed in something. Hossam had never really believed in anything but his inherent superiority—except when Mohsin was around. Perhaps that was truly the problem he had with him. Mohsin didn't believe he was better than anyone, and this belief, on its own, made him better than Hossam. He asked himself if Solmaz would ever see enough of those qualities in him that she could love him the way she loved Mohsin. Yet he wasn't sure how much it mattered. Perhaps the dream of Mohsin would die along with the person and pragmatism would serve her far better than altruism. Once he plied her with comforts and she felt the ameliorating effects of privilege, the idealism of collective existence would fade, and she would grow not only accustomed to a life of luxury but would come to desire it.

Mohsin's reappearance had ruined his plan. The moment Solmaz learned of his return, she cast Hossam aside. She didn't visit him or request his company on strolls. In fact, Solmaz had gone completely silent, probably holed up in her hovel exchanging messages with Mohsin. Hossam felt more than rejected. He had felt rejected when he first realized she would never want him over Mohsin. What he felt now was a kind of panic, a crisis. The last several weeks had made him believe that they could be happy together if Mohsin was out of the picture. Solmaz deserved someone willing to fight for her and do what was necessary to keep her safe. Mohsin was a commoner who trusted everyone and took her affections for granted. He could not be allowed to leave Earth with her.

                                3
                            ____

As the Justiciar on Mina Fada, Rasoul Damji was tasked with overseeing investigations, regulatory compliance, labor relations, and contract litigation. Despite the implications of his title, his objectives had very little to do with justice and everything to do with making sure the Sector 8 Sultanate's interests were looked after. Rasoul was young for having achieved such a high post. His family, despite being well to do, were not among the administrative nobles. A Justiciar was just shy of administrative nobility, and he intended to make the leap in his lifetime, through an advantageous marriage or gaining his superiors' attention through exemplary service.

While Rasoul was not particularly talented in legal matters, he was greedy and unscrupulous. When Bashi Farouk Majd was exiled to Mina Fada, he made it clear to his staff that this posting was to be permanent. He intended to drive and squeeze every loader, every technician, pilot, crewman, and office worker to produce record profits. His cousin the Sultan would be so overjoyed at increased profits and increased expenditures, that, in his gratitude, he would call the Majd family home. In a bid to ingratiate himself to his new boss, he made a series of proposals regarding labor contracts and pensions.

Although this heavy-handed tactic produced the results the elder Majd wanted, it had the unfortunate side effect of driving parts of the workforce into the arms of the Trade Unionist Collective. Rasoul ordered new personnel to be trained with less favorable contracts which could be terminated before they became invested. Turnover was high but the long term impacts, such as increased liability from accidents, poor maintenance records, and on-the-job injury litigation, would take years before they became an issue. By that time, he expected to be living in a palatial home in Istanbul pretending to work as a high-level bureaucrat.

Rasoul had worked closely enough with the admin nobles to understand a few things, things he believed would help him advance his career and station. The nobles cared more for the appearance of things than the substance of things, except in one case: money. They liked the appearance of their extravagance to be backed up by their wealth, and they would go to great lengths to maintain that appearance even when they fell on hard times. In all other instances, appearance mattered more than reality. All of them had secrets, and they kept each other's secrets. One of the reasons they infrequently mixed with their inferiors was the belief that commoners couldn't be trusted to keep those secrets.

A great example of this was the persistent rumor that the son of the Bashi was spending a lot of time streetside. Rasoul found it both scandalous and dangerous and couldn't see the appeal. The father, though troubled, simply threw up his hands whenever his wife brought up the issue. It seemed hypocritical to admonish his son for his own sins, the very sins that had led to their exile to Baikonur.

But where the father and mother saw trouble, Rasoul saw opportunity. It would be unwise for a reputable bureaucrat and aspiring admin noble to be seen streetside. Someone of his precarious station did not enjoy the same rules of discretion as his superiors, but he felt it would be worth it. He was still a person of significant standing. As long as he could maintain deniability, his reputation would be protected. He would go to street level dressed so as not to be conspicuous. And he concocted plausible excuses that he was running a discreet errand for the Bashi or taking a hands-on role in labor negotiations at any one of a hundred Sultanate foundries down there.

The city of Mina Fada was built on eight struts, each more than two miles wide and nearly twenty miles distant from one another. Together they provided a superstructure upon which the entire city was constructed. And the city itself was said to stretch into space. Though not entirely true, it reached well into the stratosphere. Hundreds of elevators traversed the various levels. Navigating them wasn't easy since each level was restricted for everyone below it. There were times when it was necessary to move laterally to get to another lift that took you to the desired level. Getting to streetside, even for a noble, was daunting.

Initially, Rasoul had thought to wait for Hossam to leave the admin noble levels and then follow him down to streetside. But the massive maze of lifts made the possibility of being spotted, or losing him, too great. He decided on an approach more suited to his talents. As Justiciar, he had unfettered access to data on everyone who worked at the Sector 8 Sultanate's offices in Mina Fada. While requests for data could be traced, in an operation that size, there were thousands of requests every day, and admin nobles didn't care for bureaucratic minutiae. It was beneath them.

Each month, Hossam received a stipend from his father which came electronically and was coded to his biochip. Very few people streetside used biochips, and because they preferred cash or trade, Hossam had to convert electronic currency to physical currency. Most of the time he did this in the upper levels of Mina Fada. From time to time, he did it on his way down to streetside. One thing about nobles was that no matter how convinced they were of their own labors, they were actually quite lazy. It stood to reason that Hossam's transactions were made in the sector of Mina Fada closest to his lift destinations. It reduced Rasoul's legwork, but didn't eliminate it. Baikonur was a city of more than fifty million people. Narrowing down Hossam's point of exit only told Rasoul which quadrant he might be in. It took another couple of weeks of bribing locals and frequenting hostess bars to zero in on Hossam's pattern.

At first, Rasoul observed the young Majd from a distance as he rolled dice and drank in alleys and in rows between market stands. It was unbecoming and almost comical, watching him carry on amongst the live animals and laborers in his expensive coat and shoes, completely out of place. An approach on the street was unwise. Hossam would be suspicious. Rasoul arranged to run into him while pretending to be headed back to Mina Fada by waiting streetside as the massive cattle car brought down crowds of people. It was challenging because he needed to spot him in the crowd. Although he stood out like a sore thumb, from a distance and at night, it wasn't easy. It took several tries, but Rasoul found him. He pretended to be passing on the street and stopped, feigning recognition. Hossam seemed to know him but only vaguely.

"Hossam, right?"

"You'll forgive me if I don't remember your name." Hossam responded, acknowledging Rasoul while maintaining an heir of indifference.

"Of course. I wouldn't expect you to remember. I'm Rasoul Damji."

Hossam was awkward and a little suspicious. "Yes, I think I've seen you around. What are you doing here?"

Rasoul knew he had to be careful with his response, because it could alienate Hossam or buy his complicity.

"Probably the same thing you are." He paused to give Hossam a split second to squirm.

"Business for your father. Last minute amendments to new labor agreements delivered to union offices. I see to this sort of thing personally."

Hossam nodded with relief at the out he was given. "Yes. Haha. My father and his endless errands." He wagged a scolding finger at Rasoul in jest. "None of us are immune."

"I was headed back up to Mina Fada but I'm finding the wait for a lift that isn't packed has made me peckish." Rasoul waited a moment to see if Hossam would take the bait.

"I have to confess that I have, on occasion, eaten at this place around the corner after a particularly difficult day on father's business."

Rasoul leaned in and patted Hossam on the shoulder. "Lead on. Your secret is safe with me."

4

THE ACCOMMODATION PROVIDED by the TUC during their stay in Mina
Fada were nice, at least as compared to living streetside. Every square
inch of their level was lined with autowalks that took them to shops
and restaurants. From time to time, Solmaz felt pangs of guilt at the
indulgence. There were legions of people living streetside, starving and
without shelter, sick and hunched over barrel fires. And here she was,
in Mina Fada, eating at fancy restaurants and living it up in a hotel.
Maybe it wasn't fancy by admin noble standards, but these types of
excesses bothered her. She tried chasing away her guilt with thoughts
of the future.

Life in space with Mohsin would be rewarding, but also difficult.
The wife of a captain was expected to work alongside the crew, so it
meant long hours, and months at a time in space. Hossam wasn't
wrong about the hazards, either. The Corsairs were a concern. But it
wasn't enough of a concern to dissuade her. She felt, as she always
had, that as long as she and Mohsin were together, everything would be
fine. They were always good at working together to find solutions. And
they always watched each other's back.

So much of their relationship was defined by the TUC, by their
politics, by Mohsin's absence. It was jarring to be lamenting his loss

one moment, and strolling through a promenade in Mina Fada holding hands in the next. Her life went from intense sadness to deep calm overnight. Through his hands, his touch, she could sense his restlessness, a frenetic energy that was perhaps lingering adrenaline from almost being killed. Or maybe it was a desire to get back into space. He was thoughtful about it though. Often, when he came home he had to stop himself from talking about some repair or another on the *Nightshade*, or how singularity drive efficiency had improved. If those things were on his mind now, he didn't openly show it. His life was space, and her. Now those two things would converge, which would bring much needed relief to both of them.

The Trade Union Collective had given Mohsin a week of leave, at the end of which he was to report for debriefing. However, on the third day, they were both confronted by Mina Fada security as they walked through one of the shopping districts. There were two of them, clad in Mina Fada pale grey and black, visored helmets. Chrome-plated plasma pistols gleamed in their holsters.

"Mohsin Daoud? Third mate of the *Nightshade*?" one of them said mechanically. Solmaz gripped Mohsin's arm a bit tighter and pressed her head against it.

"Actually, it's soon to be captain." Mohsin responded with a nervous laugh in that easy way he had with people.

"We need you to come with us."

"What's this about?" Solmaz interjected.

"I'm sorry, miss, but that's between Mr. Daoud and Mina Fada security." The two officers remained expressionless and flanked Mohsin, each one taking an arm. Mohsin was frozen with fear and surprise. "I'm sorry, sir, but we weren't given any details. We need you to come with us now."

Mohsin was escorted to the detention level, where the officers put him in an interview room rather than a cell. His repeated attempts to find out why they were taking him there were met with silence. He was relieved, but baffled. He had done nothing wrong but that didn't keep him from being a bit scared, on top of being worried about what Solmaz might think. They had only been reunited for a couple of days, and to have Mina Fada security show up out of nowhere and grab him must have been traumatic.

After a few hours a man entered the interview room. He wore a wrinkled suit and had curly red hair. "Mr. Daoud. I am Mr. Khan, a union representative and advocate from the Trade Unionist Collective."

"Is it normal for them to send a lawyer for a simple debrief? That's what this is, isn't it?"

"I'm afraid not, Mr. Daoud. While the TUC is prepared to log your official statement regarding the Corsair attack on the *Nightshade*, apparently some new information has come to light. They felt it would be prudent to retain my services on your behalf."

"What new information?"

" I am not privy to that information. But I have to advise you that this has been escalated to a formal hearing instead of the usual closed affidavits. The Galactic Trade Consortium has exercised their right to send a representative to preside over the hearings along with the TUC and the magistrate of Baikonur."

"Am I being accused of something?" Mohsin asked desperately.

"No formal charges have been handed down."

5

———————

"WHEN THE *NIGHTSHADE* WAS BOARDED, the captain and the first mate went below decks to help repel boarders. Do you find that unusual?"

"At the time I didn't. The captain insisted. I assumed he had some experience with the situation that he felt was better served in the fighting." Mohsin looked around the hearing room and saw Solmaz sitting in the gallery. She looked like she had been crying again. Hossam was sitting with her, and appeared to be trying to console her.

"And where were you at the time?"

"I was amidships, just forward of the cargo hold." Mohsin replied.

"What were you doing there?"

"Leading a damage-control team. I had hoped to restore sub-light propulsion and maneuver away from the attacking ship. Once I found that impossible, I ordered the helmsman to fire the starboard maneuvering thrusters. Corsairs were pouring into a breach they made in that section, and I thought snapping the grappling tethers would slow them down, perhaps give the captain a chance."

"Did you consult with the captain before giving this order?" the solicitor pressed.

"I tried to, but he wasn't responding. I had to act."

"Tell us about the moment when you spaced your captain."

Mohsin's union representative and solicitor objected. The inquisitor amended his request. "When did you vent the starboard compartments?"

"Several of the crew reported being overwhelmed at critical junctures throughout the starboard side of the ship. The automated boarder-repellant systems confirmed this. I had the choice of surrendering the ship or sealing off the starboard bulkheads and venting the ship. Once boarder-repelling teams reported they were clear of the starboard, I issued the order."

"And in doing so, you killed your captain."

"At the time, I hoped he and the others were still alive below decks," Mohsin responded confidently.

"And you prioritized the cargo above the lives of your captain and first officer?"

It was a trap. If Mohsin were a Consortium officer, this wouldn't even be a question. For the first time, he became concerned that this was a witch hunt.

"I prioritized the lives of my remaining crew over the captain and the first officer. I had no expectation that the Corsairs would simply take our cargo and leave the rest of us alone. "

"How did you escape?"

"I already told you; I had the helmsman fire thrusters."

"You're telling me you escaped a Corsair ship on thrusters?"

"That isn't what I said." Mohsin struggled to hide his frustration. He could see where the solicitor was going and was concerned the magistrate would buy into his interpretation of events.

"The venting of the starboard compartments plus the firing of maneuvering thrusters provided sufficient inertia that the weight of the *Nightshade* snapped the grappling cables. The venting had the fortunate side effect of expelling some of the boarders into space. Many of them were still wearing helmets. I assumed their own crews would bring them back on board before attempting pursuit. That would buy us time. I ordered the helmsman to fire the bow thrusters starboard side to angle the sub-light drive cones toward the attacking ship."

"What did this do?"

"It was a bluff. I wanted them to believe we had restored power to sub-light drives and were preparing to burn them in our exhaust plume. Once I had enough distance, I engaged the singularity drive." Mohsin knew he was beginning to sound desperate and tried to moderate his tone.

"Thank you, Mr. Daoud. You are excused."

Mohsin took a seat in the small gallery available for observers. His union rep looked uneasy, as did the TUC representatives on the panel.

"If it pleases the panel, I would like to call a witness," said the inquisitor.

Mohsin's union rep objected. "This is an informal hearing and a formality at that."

"Witnesses are nonetheless permitted," one of the panelists from the TUC injected.

"Formality or not, the panel's ultimate aim should be to have as much information as possible to ensure things are done appropriately, especially given that several people have died."

Mohsin hoped it was to avoid the appearance of impropriety and had no motive other than that.

"You may proceed, solicitor."

"I would like to call Ghamal Khalil to testify."

Mohsin couldn't hide his shock. Ghamal was nearing retirement. He lived in the crew quarters next to Mohsin and Mohsin often helped him with his chores. It seemed senseless that a man of Ghamal's age and wisdom was still working, but he often mentioned that his pension was too small for retirement. Consistent with the values of the TUC, with his own values, he lent a hand to Ghamal whenever he could. In fact, everyone aboard the *Nightshade* did. Ghamal took Mohsin's place in the chair, but the solicitor didn't ask any specific question.

"Please tell us what you know, Mr. Khalil."

"Mohsin Daoud is a model crewman. He helped me wash the bulkheads and cook when it was my turn. He even filled in for me from time to time on the docks, when my back wasn't doing too good..." Mohsin exhaled with relief. For a moment he was sure there was going to be some kind of ambush. "That's why it breaks my heart to tell you that he is in league with the Corsairs."

"What?" Mohsin jumped out of his chair. His union rep and solicitor stood up to make sure he didn't go any further. "How can you say this, Ghamal?"

"It's true." Ghamal looked up at the panel, an elderly gentleman incapable of lying. "I got suspicious when I was mopping the floors outside his cabin early one morning. I overheard him talking to someone about the cargo and where we would be."

"Ghamal! Why are you saying this? You know it isn't true!?" Mohsin found it hard to conceal the pain in his heart. He had considered Ghamal like an uncle and treated him as such.

"I didn't think much of it at the time, but after nearly being spaced by Mohsin Daoud's recklessness, I had a look at the *Nightshade*'s comm logs. Sure, most of his communications were sent to that fiancée he's always talking about, but there were other messages sent to no place at all."

The solicitor raised an eyebrow. "No place at all? Can you explain further?"

"They weren't sent to anyone along our nav route. Just… out into space where there shouldn't be anyone."

"And do you have evidence of this?"

"I sure do. I kept my mouth shut all those weeks when we were adrift and making repairs. First thing I did when we managed to get home was to bring the comm logs down to the Justiciar's office. I knew he'd know what to do." Ghamal fell silent and hung his head.

Mohsin didn't see the need for any more objections. He had no proof that would controvert anything Ghamal was saying. He just couldn't figure out why Ghamal had accused him. It was possible that *someone* on board was feeding information to the Corsairs, but that person wasn't him. It was also possible that someone had altered the comm logs to make it look like he was the culprit. It wouldn't have been hard, since everyone knew he sent a message to Solmaz before every singularity jump. Maybe his predictability would be his downfall.

"You may go, crewman."

Ghamal nodded, becoming a little teary. "I just want to say how tore up I am about all this. I treated Mohsin Daoud like he was part of my own family. I might have even believed he was for a while. But good men and women were lost to the Corsairs that day and I don't think I can forgive him." The last words were spoken between choking sobs. Ghamal had a gentle way about him, looking at everyone with a wide-eyed admiration. Mohsin assumed it was his way of getting others to take pity on him. Fixing his gaze on the old man, what Mohsin saw now was something else. Ghamal would have everyone believe that was crying from a sense of betrayal, but Mohsin could see that they were tears of guilt, for what he had just done.

"I move for immediate criminal proceedings. The Justiciar's office is satisfied there is enough evidence."

Two bailiffs approached Mohsin and slapped cuffs on his wrists. He winced as they tightened. Solmaz was behind him, crying. As they tried to remove him, he called to her, dragging his feet to slow the bailiffs. Solmaz pushed past several others seated in the gallery to reach the aisle. Mohsin raised his shackled hands in an effort to touch her but the bailiffs were persistent. Their hands missed each other by an inch.

He looked over his shoulder to see Solmaz with her hand still outstretched, tears streaming down her face.

"Mohsin!" she screamed one last time.

The news of Mohsin's conviction and banishment spread quickly throughout Baikonur. As on the day of his triumphant return to Earth, his face was on every feed from streetside to Mina Fada. It was a moment Solmaz remembered from sitting in the gallery. Mohsin lowered his head thoughtfully before answering a question from the solicitor. But the clip had been cropped and darkened to make him look as if he were bowing his head in shame. It was in stark contrast to the one shown in the feeds only weeks ago of a haggard, yet stalwart and heroic Mohsin.

Solmaz spent the morning down at the detention center, trying to find out where Mohsin was being held. The guards wouldn't help, even after she informed them that she was his wife. The rest of the day was spent going from one bureaucrat's office to another, trying to find some way to see him. Streetsiders were no strangers to legal entanglements, but it was usually gambling or street brawls. Solmaz simply had no point of reference from which to advocate for, or even see, Mohsin. She finally gave up when the administrative offices began to close.

She decided to go home and rest for a few hours, then come back to Mina Fada by the time they opened. When she returned to the women's communal riad that evening, she found her belongings packed and sitting outside the gate. The house mother, an older Arab woman, was standing outside with her things.

"What's going on? Who said you could handle my belongings?"

"We thought it would be easiest this way. Everything has been treated respectfully and you will find nothing is missing. I oversaw the packing myself." The house mother said cruelly.

"*We* thought this would be easiest? Who is we?"

"After the recent trouble with your betrothed, we thought it best if you found another place to stay. This is a reputable women's riad."

"You're kicking me out because of something my husband was accused of?"

"You are not responsible for what your husband does. And Allah subhannah wa ta Allah knows we do not abide backbiting. But there are rumors that you conspired with your husband in this evil crime. And now many good workers, many good streetsiders, are dead. Whether this is true or not, we cannot be associated with that."

Solmaz tightened her jaw, holding back tears of rage. It was almost certain that the women of the communal house were gathered at one of the shaded windows that overlooked the gate and whispering amongst each other. She unballed her clenched fist long enough to grab the handle of the cart holding her belongings and jerk them along behind her as she stormed off.

This time, she didn't sit on a bench and cry. She cried as she walked deeper into the city. Solmaz mourned the loss of her beloved. She had been robbed of him and the dream of their life together she had held since she was a child. There were no hostels or hotels this close to the city's edge. It was painful to have to think about where she was going to stay while her world - her heart - was breaking apart. Each step was taken with leaden legs, tears streaming down her face, into an uncertain future.

She was going to be shunned, the subject of gossip and backbiting. The constant whispering and plotting behind her back, especially now, would be too much. This also meant she would likely have to find a new job. Many at the foundry and the restaurant would take the same view as those at the communal house, and commuting to those places from other parts of the city would be expensive and time-consuming. Mohsin's conviction hadn't just upended her life, it tore it out by the roots, and now she needed to put them down somewhere else.

She hadn't been so close to the center of the city in years. When she was a teen, it had held some appeal for her. Now, its only appeal was that she could lose herself in the densely packed streets. She could escape her shame and infamy by becoming invisible.

6

ONCE MOHSIN WENT AWAY, Hossam was certain that Solmaz would fall into his arms. But it didn't work out that way. She spent the next few years mourning him as if he were dead. She quit her jobs and rarely appeared in public. He wasn't sure if it was from shame at being betrothed to a man who had supposedly murdered his shipmates, or possibly to evade the incessant attention from suitors. Once Mohsin's crimes became public, it was sure to bring anyone who was ever interested in Solmaz, calling.

Four years after Mohsin was imprisoned, Hossam's father, Farouk, was murdered along with the sex worker he happened to be with at the time. Apparently, their beverages were spiked with poison. Farouk and his companion died quickly and painlessly. The Sultan was quick to name Hossam as his father's successor. Some said it was in the interest of continuity, but people in the admin noble circles knew the truth. The Sultan didn't want Hossam sniffing around for some cushy post in the capital, especially since stories of his own exploits had reached his ears. He was every bit the hedonist his father was, perhaps more. And given that his proclivities took him to streetside, it would be unbecoming to have someone like him in the professional ranks of the capital. At least the elder Majd had the sense to be discreet.

No one suspected Hossam of killing his father. As far as anyone could tell, Hossam was too busy gambling and carousing to care about assuming official posts. There were plenty of other suspects and there were simply no dots to connect when it came to the crime. There was no danger of disinheritance, and, by his mother's own admission, Farouk passively encouraged Hossam's excesses. Like many other children of the admin nobility, he was content to live in luxury with little or no purpose, not having to work for anything, especially when his position didn't instill any sense of ambition. Besides, the public was assured by Justiciar Damji that they were pursuing several likely suspects and that Hossam was not among them.

He was surprised when he received a message from Solmaz. It would seem his father's death served him in more ways than one. She offered her condolences and said that, as a friend, he could talk to her if he was having a difficult time with his loss. She also mentioned that his absence streetside had not gone unnoticed. Once Hossam ascended to the position of Bashi, he became too busy to visit streetside. Most people took his absence as a sign that he was in mourning, which further reinforced the idea that he had not arranged his father's death, but in reality, he was managing his new position. His father's death had left their house destitute. When Hossam assumed management of Sector 8, he didn't like what he found. His father had lived beyond the means provided by his salary and commissions. Hossam's first thought was to begin liquidating labor contracts and promote unskilled laborers into technical positions, but his father had already squeezed the blood from that stone.

When they met for the first time since Mohsin was imprisoned, Hossam got Solmaz access to the upper levels of Mina Fada. The promenade had excellent shopping, food stands, and restaurants. Initially she didn't want to come but he insisted, giving as his excuse that he couldn't' be too far from work when the truth was, he wanted to dazzle her with a prospective life. Despite her incredible beauty, Solmaz was out of place on the promenade. All streetsiders were. It was full of well dressed, high-level bureaucrats, and boutiques full of items she could never afford. She had worn the nicest abaya she had and it was noticeably faded in areas where the fabric was wearing through.

"Thank you for coming."

"I'm glad I could be here for you during this difficult time." Solmaz gently patted Hossam's hand.

"You know, I would have been there for you, had I been given the chance."

"It was hard enough coping with the loss without spreading the sorrow around."

"Nonsense. Mohsin's crimes are his own. You honored him with your affection. It was he who spread sorrow. He was my friend. I felt betrayed by him." Hossam shook his head with indignantly.

"I guess it's easy to forget we aren't the only ones affected by other people's actions."

"I'm imperfect, but I'm honest in my failings. Makes it easier to keep all the sorrow focused solely on myself."

Solmaz surprised herself by laughing. It was the first time in years. Hossam smirked while trying to hide his satisfaction.

"Enough about Mohsin," she said. "How are you holding up?" Solmaz said, nudging his shoulder with hers.

"One of the great things about the absence of choice, is the absence of choice. My father's death has left me in a bind. I have no choice but to face his mistakes and try to learn from them."

Solmaz's instinct told her that Hossam's vulnerability was an act. She knew he had always desired her. Many men did. But she honestly didn't think he was capable of this level of self-reflection and deprecation. He just wasn't that good of an actor. It occurred to her that maybe the death of his father had matured him. As much as admin nobles looked down on anyone below them in station, it was just as hard for someone from streetside to see them as people. To the people of streetside, the nobles were what they wanted them to see, which was just bags of money and privilege that indulged every impulse.

7

—————

When he was third mate on the *Nightshade*, Mohsin had felt that being away from Solmaz for months at a time was unbearable, but at least then he had been able to communicate with her. Having her taken from him permanently taught him what unbearable really meant. At times, her absence was a void so dense that his wails and sobs were lost in it. At other times it felt like a serrated dagger, a persistent, sharp pain in his chest.

His cell held nothing but a small LED monitor on a swingarm, probably linked to the singularity drive, his bed, a pillow, and a blanket. The bed was nothing but a block of synthetic foam on the ground. The pillow appeared to be made from the same material and had no cover so it irritated his skin as he slept. The blanket was made from fibroweave, similar to the material pallet covers were made from. It was stiff and didn't soften with use. There was no door, but once a day a slot opened and a plastic foam box containing his meals was deposited in the cell. The meals consisted of noodles, synthetic meat, some type of fermented vegetable patty, water, dehydrated vegetables and mushrooms, and a flavor packet. It also contained a spork, a bowl, and a plate. Mohsin didn't have much appetite but after several days he realized he couldn't let himself starve to death and ate.

After three years on the *Damma*, waking, eating, and sleeping, with only the simple tasks of managing the drive section to stave off monotony, Mohsin decided it was time to go. However, his options in terms of suicide were limited. Having been crewman on a ship for two years prior to his imprisonment and a shipwright's apprentice before that, he knew that the compartments were molded alloy. Even with tools, it would be impossible to extract a section of the wall or floor and fashion a knife. Each side was several inches thick. His second non-option was the coolant from the singularity drive's reactor. Assuming he would be able to wrench one of the conduits loose enough to extract some, it was far too painful a death to countenance at this point. Drive coolant was a potent hemotoxin that would liquify his insides, almost certainly cause blindness, and an agonizing death.

He also thought about trying to space himself. As with the knife idea, he faced the same problem: venting the compartment into space would quite literally suck. Or blow. Mohsin spent the better part of a day contemplating atmospheric dynamics of decompression. Eventually, he arrived at the compromise that his body would at first be sucked out of any breach in the hull, but once clear of it would technically be blown as the compartment's air continued to outgas. Hanging was also not an option. He could, in theory, make a noose by stripping his blanket down to its fibers and weaving them back together as a rope, but there was no place to secure a noose on the smooth surfaces of his cell.

After considering all of his options, Mohsin realized that this was part of the prison's curse. On any other occasion, he would be cautiously thankful of the thin layer of alloy between himself and the hard void. But as an inmate, it was the only path to escape or salvation. The only means to freedom, either from imprisonment or from life. Every prisoner eventually arrived at the conclusion that they would spend their entire lives mere inches from freedom. And that realization would shrink their cell to the size of their heads, creating an alloy mask that would serve only to drive them insane.

The drive section was only different from other cells on the prison barge in that it contained a section of the ship's singularity drive that rarely required maintenance. He imagined that if the ship was being refitted or having its drives checked at the required intervals, this cell and the one opposite would be vacated, and the engineers would be able to run diagnostics through the display. Initially, Mohsin saw the panel and LEDs as somewhat of a blessing. It was provided a distraction, something he could interact with. But within months, the incessant flickering disturbed his sleep and became more of a torture. Pulling his blanket over his head while he slept worked for a while, but as time wore on, he swore he could feel the flickering vibrate through the floor and his mattress. There was a storage compartment built into the floor, with the words "in case of emergency" stenciled on it, but he was unable to open it. Likely it was intended for engineers and maintenance crews in the event of a mishap. He preferred the vacuum anyway. There was nothing in the chest or on the suit that would help him escape or end his life.

The one benefit the drive section provided was that it was several degrees warmer than the rest of the ship. The reactor often ran hot enough that, even through its housing, heat radiated into the compartment. Some nights, he would move his mattress closer to the reactor housing in order to get warm. He could always tell, just by the decrease in temperature, when the drive was idle or off. On the days when that was the case, he would move closer. Even when the reactor was inert, the residual heat would still keep him a bit warmer.

On one such occasion, he awoke shivering. Being too cold and too drowsy to bother moving his mattress, he got up and walked a few steps closer to the reactor housing and collapsed onto the floor. When he awoke again, he was reluctant to get up. The cold licked at him, just beyond the blanket. Laying on his side, he could see the cool length of the floor from his head all the way to the reactor housing. The blinking status panel threw intermittent shafts of light onto the floor. After several minutes of zoning out to the pattern, he noticed another pattern within the shuddering light. Being careful not to let the blanket slip off, he rolled onto his hands and knees, keeping his face low to the ground and began to crawl toward the reactor.

What he noticed wasn't so much a seam as a disruption in the grain of the metal. It took almost an hour but he was able to map the entire pattern. Part of it ended abruptly in front of the reactor housing, presumably behind a panel. Someone had welded part of the floor and then ground and sanded it to make the compartment appear to be one molded piece.

But it wasn't a single molded piece. It was a laminate polished over an alloy plate intended to look like a single molded piece. More importantly, the disruption in the metal's grain indicated that it was just part of the welded filler from the seams of the plate that had been ground and buffed over the plate itself. Now that he knew there was a seam, he simply needed to find it and try to separate the welding material from it. Solder and other types of welding material, by their nature, were not going to be as hard as the plates, so chipping away at it, however slowly, might be an option. Mohsin had no idea what kind of fruit this was going to yield, if any, but it would at least keep him busy.

His molded plastic eating utensils weren't going to be of any use. The knife was sturdy, but it was too dull to cut and too well molded to cut serrations into it. In a terrestrial prison, the spork might have been useful to tunnel his way out, but that wasn't the case here. His cup, however, was made from a composite of high tensile plastic and molded ceramic, but it was a single piece and possessed no part or surface that could be fashioned into anything useful.

The reactor housing was actually one of two. The other reactor sat on the other side of the wall from his cell. Mohsin assumed he had a counterpart housed in a similarly configured cell. There were several conduits but none led into the adjoining compartment. That part of the compartment was the darkest. With no way to shine light in that direction, Mohsin ran his hand along the wall and the corners to determine if there was something he might have missed - a pipe, a valve, or conduit that might be useful in his current dilemma.

In the corner, toward the rear wall, he felt a thick conduit running from the ceiling and then curving abruptly aft. It was so cold that the condensation which had accumulated on it had iced over and it seemed to burn his hand. He jerked back in pain and shook his hand violently before placing it on the reactor housing to warm it up. His head and neck began throbbing from secondary brain freeze. As it receded, it deposited an idea.

The laminate layer of the floor was not only thin, but softer than the alloy plate beneath. No matter how firmly welded the two layers were, he believed they could be separated from one another by cooling. The softer laminate layer should contract faster and further than the underlying layer. Mohsin took his cup and began feverishly chipping away at the ice on the conduit. The mug grew cold in his hand, and he knew he wouldn't be able to hold it much longer. Ice from purified water was much colder so, once the cup was full, he set it on the conduit to allow it to further freeze. The conduit was likely full of coolant, venting directly into space. Its exposure to the void made it much colder than it would be otherwise. It didn't take long for the water, ice, and cup to become a single block.

Mohsin couldn't hold the cup without causing serious damage to his hands, so he tore off a piece of his fibroweave blanket, folded it over and grabbed the cup from the conduit. As he walked back toward the section of laminate floor, the cup emitted wisps of white vapor. He stopped and recited a du'a before dropping the cup onto the floor. It bounced an inch or so, then rolled on its side before stopping. He could already hear a low whine coming from it, and backed away. A few moments later an entire section of the laminate separated from the floor at an angle, revealing a row of pristine hex bolts.

The bolts represented another problem, but not a big one. He didn't have a hex wrench, but the bolts were thinner, in his estimation, than the plate that had just come up. They would require time, something he had plenty of, but using the same method forced the bolts to warp. The laminate was thin enough that he could crudely manipulate it. When sections of it were cold enough, he snapped pieces off and used them to grind spaces between the seams of the floor plate and lift the warped hex bolts from their housings. A secondary benefit was that tearing up the laminate exposed seams under the vac suit's storage compartment. He took the opportunity to pull the entire compartment up and gain access to the suit.

Before getting the laminate flooring up, there was no tool to score the walls with. Now that he could break off bits of metal, he was faced with a new dilemma: in order to mark the days, you had to know when one ended and another began. There were no portholes, and even if there had been, they weren't orbiting a sun, nor would there be any recognizable stars with predictable orbits. You simply aged without ever knowing how much. You fell asleep when you were tired and when you awoke, you had no idea how much time had passed. Mohsin thought he could count the passing of days by the arrival of his meal kits but he quickly learned that they were either not being delivered at regular intervals, or his perception of the passage of time has been severely skewed by his time in the cell.

He couldn't be completely certain, but he estimated it took him four months to strip all the hex bolts and grind away the seams on the floor plate. The plate was heavy - too heavy for him to lift out of place. The first time he wedged a piece of the laminate and tried to lever the plate out, the laminate snapped and part of it fell into the space underneath. Mohsin couldn't do that too many more times, otherwise he would have none left. He created a series of shims and used the larger piece of laminate as a shoehorn. He would lift the plate very slightly, then slide the shim down the shoehorn and wedge it under the plate. It took several more days, but he did this until the entire plate was suspended over its groove. It felt like progress but it wasn't enough. He had neither the strength nor the tools to lift the plate completely off. And he didn't have enough laminate to raise the plate high enough to slip under it. It was possible that he would be crushed by the plate or trapped underneath it should one of the shims dislodge.

By the time Mohsin had finished for the day, he was standing in a pool of his own sweat. He moved to the far end of the compartment where it was cool and collapsed onto his mattress. Yet another of the ills of space prison was that after a while he stopped being able to distinguish what was real and what wasn't. Alone in a windowless cage, with no one to talk to, everything could be a hallucination. There were times when he missed Solmaz so completely that he would have waking dreams of her. When she disappeared, he would burst into tears.

This time he was awakened by the bang of metal on metal. Since he had covered the status panel with laminate, the cell was dark. Only the corner of the raised panel was visible in the dim light. For a moment he thought he dreamt the noise, so he closed his eyes to go back to sleep, but a moment later he heard a voice.

"Hello?" Then something unintelligible.

Mohsin sat upright.

"Is someone there? Hello?"

Not dreaming, but perhaps hallucinating. He stared at the small gap in the plate for several seconds. "Hello? Hello?" he shouted.

"Yes, hello! Are you there? I'm under the floor!" The voice was low and raspy, probably from years of disuse.

Mohsin got out of bed and ran over to the suspended plate. He could see a pair of eyes through the gap made by the shims. The eyes were illuminated by some source he could not see.

"Am I dreaming? Are you a dream?" Mohsin said, unsure if he was speaking aloud or to another hallucination.

"Can you not dream a better dream than an old man in your floor?"

"Right. The floor plate is too heavy for me to lift."

"I'm afraid, even with me helping, we would probably just hurt ourselves."

"Suggestions?"

"Go back to sleep and dream of me with this floor plate up?" The man replied dryly.

"Enough about that already! That isn't useful." Mohsin feigned annoyance but was actually intrigued by the man's humor, and the timing of his quips. " Wait. How did you get yours up?"

"One year, there was a drive coolant leak. I managed to get enough of it to freeze out the hex bolts." That also was not helpful. Mohsin paced for several minutes trying not to succumb to the despair of being so close to another human presence. The idea of talking to a pair of disembodied eyes through a thin seam in the floor made him anxious and sad.

Although he'd looked around a thousand times before, Mohsin glanced around his compartment for something that might be of use in this situation. Granted there was now a human on the other side of the plate, but that did not appear to alter the situation enough for anything in his cell to be of use. He went back to his bed and found the fibroweave blanket. Using one of the pieces of jagged laminate, he separated the fibers and pulled them apart. Once he had sufficient lengths, he tied them end to end until he had a crude rope. He handed one end to the man under the floor and asked him to feed it back around the other side of the plate.

"Ah, I see," he said simply and was gone. A second later, one frayed end of the rope slid from underneath the plate. Mohsin took that end and tied it around the center, forming a crude lasso. He went back to the gap.

"I'm going to pull. I need you to push as much as you can. The extra force may help lift the plate."

"Try not to drop it on me," the man said casually.

"On my signal." Mohsin leaned back with his weight on the rope so his heels were pushing down on the floor.

"Go!"

He dropped his hips and began pulling with as much effort as he could muster. Whatever force the old man was applying to the plate didn't seem to be much, because at first it didn't budge. Then Mohsin let out a massive grunt and pulled until he thought every muscle in his body would tear, but instead they turned to pure acid under his skin. The persistent loneliness and sheer curiosity gave him the strength to fight against the pain. The plate whined against its groove and finally began to rise. He felt his heels starting to sweat.

Surprisingly, the old man scrambled through the widened gap. Mohsin had a hard time gauging from where he was but they had raised it enough that the old man wedged the length of his body into the gap in a crouched position, and pushed. He peeked over the edge and said,

"Come! Come!" Mohsin cried out.

Mohsin dropped the rope, hobbled over, and joined the old man in pushing the plate until it hinged over onto its other side, exposing the outer hull. The two of them collapsed into an awkward hug. Mohsin laughed.

"My name is Abbas. Salaamu Alaikum."

"Walaikum Salaam. I am Mohsin"

8

Years of imprisonment had made Abbas gaunt. His prison jumpsuit was little more than rags hanging off his tall, slight frame. His white hair was just patchy tufts around the sides and a long scraggly beard. Abbas' eyes were dark and sunken, but intense. When he moved there was efficiency and deliberateness in it.

Things changed for the better after Abbas arrived. He showed Mohsin the area beneath the floor between their two cells. It was full of pipes and gears and valves, but overall it was bigger than both of their cells combined. It was also a bit warmer and more humid. The increased space alone was enough to improve Mohsin's mood. They had both become so accustomed to being alone that they immediately launched into conversations that lasted hours. Both had much to tell, but reveled in the sound of another voice and therefore had no problems listening either.

Abbas also brought useful prison knowledge with him. The meal kits that were automatically delivered lacked variety. Abbas had figured out ways to hoard specific ingredients, then mix and match them to create different flavors and condiments. They set up a small pantry and kitchen in the outer hull, and used one of the exhaust pipes to boil water and heat their meals. Eating together became a part of the day that they both looked forward to. Though circumstances had taken the desire to pray out of Mohsin, Abbas pestered him until he relented. Praying, then eating, became their daily ritual. During their meals, they discussed how Mohsin came to be imprisoned on the *Damma.*

"We can start with the most obvious question: who would gain from putting you in here?"

"Ghamal was the one who testified against me. It's possible he had some secret grudge."

"Perjury is a long way to go for a grudge." Abbas said skeptically.

"So, you think someone put him up to it?"

"You tell me."

"He wouldn't have had access to comm logs, that's for sure. As much as I liked him, he was barely capable of doing his own chores. And I don't think he had the technical ability to make an alteration like that."

"What about the solicitor?"

"Never saw him before that day."

"Sounds like you angered someone very powerful. Or very close to power."

"Why do you say that?"

"A lot of people you didn't know conspired against you. The sheer number of conspirators has to be a clue. And powerful people rarely do more than plot. The pawns do all the work."

Mohsin sat up, frustrated. "I'm not sure I want to figure this out. What good would it do me anyway, in here? Knowing who framed me, but being unable to act upon it, would only serve to drive me insane."

"The possibility of revenge, no matter how remote, is enough to keep most men alive."

"It's less than remote. We're never getting out of here."

"Maybe. But all things are possible with Allah."

It was hard not to wince. Even the impulse felt blasphemous, but too often he'd seen people succumb to naive thinking with that belief. He believed all things were possible with God too. He also thought winding up on a prison barge was something that would never happen to him, but here he was.

"Do you know anyone powerful who you might have angered?" Abbas asked. "Anyone powerful at all? Someone who might have wanted that captaincy for their own perhaps?"

"I have a friend. Kind of. The son of the Sector 8 Bashi."

Abbas froze, then wrinkled his brow with frustration. "How did this come about?"

"I saved him from getting stabbed in Baikonur. He wouldn't want to harm me."

"You think because you saved him he likes you?" Abbas' tone became admonishing. "Mohsin, he may despise you for saving him. The fact that you had nothing, but managed to bestow him with everything, could make him hate you."

Abbas was knowledgeable, not only about admin nobles, but about people in general. Mohsin believed in dignity and respect for everyone. But most people weren't interested in that. They were only interested in their particular rung on a very tall ladder. He realized that he'd been living his life in an idealistic dream that no one else shared.

Abbas had once served a powerful admin noble family. He had been the bodyguard to the Suleimans, a noble family that had taken to space because they had fallen on hard times and wished to restore themselves to their previous glory. According to Abbas, he had seen to most of their needs, including intellectual and educational needs. Not to mention his physical security.

If Abbas thought Hossam was behind his imprisonment, Mohsin was inclined to trust his judgment, but something wasn't adding up. "You think Hossam framed me for saving his life?"

"No. He sounds too obsessed with his own pleasure to bother with that. Did you take something from him or publicly humiliate him in front of his peers?"

"I was no threat to him. I was about to be a captain. Solmaz and I would have left within a month. Doubtful we would have ever seen him again."

"This Solmaz was your wife?"

"Yes. We had been married in secret, just two days before my inquest." Mohsin stopped and sat up again. "Hossam! He was always hanging around. I suspected he might have desired her, but most men did."

Mohsin didn't want to believe it, but as his disbelief subsided, one possibility after another presented itself. He'd seen Hossam and that Damji fellow streetside once or twice. Rasoul Damji was the Justiciar. If anyone could have used their influence on a solicitor, it would be him. He could have been acting on Hossam's behalf. Mohsin understood now. When the *Nightshade* went missing, Hossam would have been working on making Solmaz his, and when it reappeared, he must have felt rejected. He had been at Mina Fada that day, when Solmaz came to greet him. It must have angered him greatly to see her so glad of his return. Mohsin's captaincy would have taken her from him permanently.

Ghamal would have been caught up in this because of his finances. Hossam or the Justiciar must have offered him money. It was a soft theory with a lot of holes in it, but it was the best working theory he had. And, as time progressed, he and Abbas would fill in the blanks.

"I've got to get out of here."

"It would seem you have plenty of time to figure out how. Only two things are necessary for vengeance, Mohsin: Time and silence. And you have both in abundance in the void."

One evening, Mohsin was working out. He had learned to mark the passage of time by the number of exercises and repetitions he completed. Usually by the time he finished, Abbas would have appeared at the hole in the floor to ask him if he was ready for dinner, but this night, Abbas was still sitting on his mattress, surrounded by scraps of paper and cloth covered in his scrawls.

"What's all this?" Mohsin asked.

Abbas, surprised, jerked upright then hurriedly collected all the scraps and tossed them under his blanket. "A little project I've been working on."

Mohsin was genuinely hurt by Abbas' secrecy. "We've been in this place for years and I still don't know anything about you."

Abbas' shoulders sagged and he nodded slightly. "You're right. We've shared food, prayers, conversation. You've even shared your tragic plight with me. I keep telling myself I am not ready but what does that mean in this place? I am sorry my friend, for holding out on you."

"It's unlikely that we will escape this prison. In which case the details of your life will die with me."

Abbas stood up and headed for the hole in the floor. "I will make us some food. A tale is best told over a meal."

Soon after, he emerged from the outer hull holding a couple of steaming bowls and utensils. He handed one to Mohsin, sat down cross-legged across from him, and took a couple of bites from his food before he spoke.

"I grew up on the streets of Detroit, living in the shadow of massive automated skyscrapers that churned out tug chassis and FTL drive parts. It was a boon for those already endowed with wealth. The same people who had possessed capital in previous eras were the ones profiting from it then. The only other path to some level of comfort, beyond what basic assistance could provide, was vice. And I had no stomach for that. My parents were Muslim, but that was not my problem, since I wasn't particularly observant myself. I just didn't like the prospect of having to exploit or harm others so I could have more.

"There was no shortage of vice." Abbas began thoughtfully. "Almost everyone was on basic assistance, and the vice trade was simply a means of expropriating that money from the people. Food and housing were provided by the bureaucratic remnants of the 'United' States as recompense to the people for having left them behind on Earth while the wealthiest traveled the stars and got rich doing it. And its only function was to be able to buy enough booze, drugs, or sex to anesthetize oneself against the reality of having no purpose. It wasn't enough to buy land, even if you saved for a lifetime. It wasn't enough to buy equipment, start a business, or lease a shop. Not that there were any shop fronts to lease. All of them were occupied by squatter businesses like restaurants and brothels, left by disinterested landlords too busy making profit from off-world booms."

"The other thing there was plenty of were massive holoboard displays with rotating advertisements. Frequently the boards would display a man with immaculately brushed blonde hair and white teeth, smiling and talking about off-world opportunities. Corporations were looking for loaders, pilots, engineer positions for off-world colonies and outposts. Aptitude battery scores would determine occupational specialty and posting. When I discussed the possibility with my friends, they laughed at me. So, I stopped talking. But my mother encouraged me. She wanted more for me than an aimless existence in the bottom of a bottle.

"I went down to the recruitment center and took the batteries. I was aiming for engineer or tug pilot and figured those jobs would be the most likely to land me on a colony eventually. The idea of helping to build something from nothing with a group of newly invigorated and committed people was really appealing. But, no matter how hard I tried, I never qualified for those jobs. The only positions I ever qualified for were loader or combat arms. Looking back on it, my friends were right to mock me. I aced those exams. I know I did. Recruitment was a sham designed to lure people like me in. Disposable people they could herd into specific fields.

"The creation of FTL technology didn't just fuel enterprise, it fueled criminality. The type that was sanctioned and shielded by corporations and unenforceable laws. Claim jumps were as common as new claims. Illegal mining and piracy were also common. Corporations needed cheap ways to secure the bottom line. Weapons were cheap. Bodies were even cheaper, especially if they stopped breathing. And that's what I was herded into. Massive corporate armies were formed faster than any legal body on Earth could regulate them. They barely managed to prohibit the landing of these armies on Earth.

"I spent the next ten years landing on half a dozen planets and countless asteroids to secure or take mining rights by force. Sometimes the landings devolved into protracted campaigns that lasted a year or more. Me and my comrades were little more than broadcast entertainment for the masses on Earth, laying in front of holos and drinking. I marked the years in bodies, but those I worked for at home measured those bodies in stock prices.

"During my last assignment, on a planet with freezing methane snow, I decided I needed to find a way out. I tried to test out of the corporate armies, but that proved to be as much a sham as it was the first time around. Recruiters had quotas, and attrition through transfer was simply not an option. At least not formally. After a several-month stretch in another mindless slog, waist deep in mud, I returned to the rear for bunk time and showers. I was informed that a communique was waiting for me.

"A woman on Earth had taken an interest in me. Apparently, surviving multiple campaigns over a decade and across several systems was a rare achievement. I never noticed that most of the people I shipped out with never survived the campaigns. Everyone was named Steve, or Joe, or Paul. Everyone died. And there was always someone with one of those names to replace them. Or maybe I just called them those names without ever caring if they were right." Realizing he was becoming sidetracked Abbas waved his hand before continuing. "So this woman on Earth worked for the company that owned my contract, so she got on her work terminal and did a search for 'badass' and the computer spit out my name.

"In those days, corporations, authoritarian regimes, and international criminal syndicates had become indistinguishable from one another. Without the legal pretense of human rights, these entities were free to dispense with its trappings. They were brutal, violent, and efficient, and their brutality was not reserved for the most vulnerable. In the race to dominate the stars, entire families would burn in the fires of greed and industry. My new employer understood this. She had lost her husband during an attempt on her life by a professional rival. She was determined not to lose herself or her children to the same fate."

"Yes I've heard stories." Mohsin interjected. "The TUC was founded, in part, to foster cooperation in space commerce and reduce the violence."

"Within weeks, I was back on Earth, but in a much better situation. Instead of the crowded and dark streets of Detroit, I found myself living in a gated compound in Virginia. In the morning I escorted my employer to work in an armored limousine, accompanying her into her building under an armored awning, then returning to the car and the house. I repeated this again in the evening, and often late. In between drop off and pick up, I spent a good part of the day with her children. They had many instructors and sometimes, if the subject interested me, I would sit in on the classes and participate. The kids enjoyed this and grew to like me a great deal as a result.

"I made use of the hours in between lessons and in the evenings. The Suleiman family had access to libraries from all over the world, holo-tutors, and news feeds. When I wasn't being a chauffeur and bodyguard, I was learning. It wasn't just for my own enrichment, though I enjoyed that aspect of it the most. I felt it was important to give myself something I never had before: options. Families were constantly ascending and being destroyed in the newly formed order, and I realized there was work to be had in this line.

"Despite that I had spent most of my adult life up to that point as a soldier, there were aspects to being a bodyguard that you didn't learn in an army. Bodyguards liked to carry vibro-weapons, in case they needed to fight somewhere firearms would do more harm than good. Mercs like me had never cared about collateral damage. So, even as a hardened veteran, I had only the crudest knowledge of their use. The children had a private weapons instructor, and those were among the lessons I sat in on. On the days when there was no martial instruction, I sparred with them to make sure they understood the application of the techniques they learned. I became a formidable fighter and made sure the children were even better.

"Once the children went off to university, it was just me and Ms. Suleiman. I continued with my usual routine, but my days were my own and I spent them much as I had previously, even finding time to take up a hobby or two. The children came home for holidays, including Ramadan, but they had little need for me. They still had need of protection, but with them at different schools and Ms. Suleiman at home, she found alternate arrangements. I was treated more as a revered uncle or family friend than a bodyguard. Sometimes they would seek my advice in personal matters.

"Ms. Suleiman treated me as a friend despite the professional nature of our relationship. I was also privy to the most intimate details of her life. I had to be aware of her whereabouts at all hours and who she was with. It was not uncommon for her to discreetly take lovers. I pored over their lives in great detail. Most importantly, I became intimately familiar with her friends and rivals. If I was going to keep her alive, this was essential.

"One evening, Ms. Suleiman called me into her office to ask for my expertise. To my surprise, it was something from my previous life, regarding astronavigation. Though I was never a navigator during my time in space, she believed my practical experience with asteroids might be useful. She shared with me details of an undiscovered mining prospect, a resource-rich asteroid orbiting a red giant called Adhara. A difficult, yet potentially rewarding prospect. But she was also concerned about the security implications. It was becoming harder and harder to find unclaimed prospects, and many people had taken to stealing information. She was concerned that one of her rivals might try to kill her for what she knew.

"I assured her that I would keep her and her secrets safe. I even memorized the orbital vectors, gravitational constants, and coordinates to this new prospect and, in my spare time, made calculations on how best to approach it. The asteroid was too close to the red giant to mine safely, but the gravity of Adhara was too intense to simply tow the asteroid away. Whoever figured out a way around those particular challenges would become one of the richest people in the galaxy, judging by all the scans they had collected. This fact, I could tell, made her nervous.

"The next several weeks were very tense and kept me on edge. I had never seen Ms. Suleiman so agitated. At time she seemed scared. She was often on calls to the children, admonishing them about their security and made fewer appearances in public herself. It was obvious that this had to do with Adhara. There had been previous prospects, many planetoids, even incursions into rival companies' territories. None of those had rattled her the way this one had.

"The tension subsided a bit when the children came home in the spring for Ramadan. Even I relaxed a bit. Having them all under the same roof made it easier to look after them. Ms. Suleiman was in a festive mood, so she and the children invited me to participate in their Eid dinner. The children entertained us with tales of their college exploits, and we laughed and talked. For the first time I felt like part of a family. Even compared to my own. It's funny how euphoric the absence of poverty can be, but euphoria has its own price. In my time working for Ms. Suleiman, I saw every manner of savagery enacted on and between families, corporate executives, and criminal syndicates. But nothing could have prepared me for the lengths that someone would go to that night in order to get at her closely guarded secret.

"I had seen this before but had never been on the direct receiving end. When I was a soldier, it was common for the various fleets to deploy chemical lasers to soften enemy positions before landing units on an asteroid or planet. This was not an asteroid but there was no doubt in my mind we were under attack. The weapon used was deceptively un-calamitous. The house didn't shake. There was no bright light or explosion. From my seat at the table, I could see down a nearby hallway into a foyer. The door, rails, and windows simply dematerialized. And that dematerialization was moving in a progressively narrowing beam toward us."

"What was it? Was it an orbital laser?" Mohsin sat up and leaned toward Abbas as he continued his tale.

"There was a cracking sound, likely one of the support beams of the house disintegrating and causing part of the structure to collapse. That was Ms. Suleiman's first hint that something was wrong. I jumped into action and grabbed one of the children by the arm. Ms. Suleiman grabbed the other. I pointed toward a pantry and yelled, though I had no expectation they would be safe in there. Turning the table over, I was almost carrying one of them and pushing the others as hard as I could, shoving them into the pantry. I didn't make it in because the floor collapsed beneath me." Abbas paused for a moment and looked down then shook his head as if fighting off the flood of images from that moment, or thinking of something he could have done differently.

"The first time I awoke, I was being dragged by my arms by two people. I couldn't raise my head and my entire body felt like it had been broken. I could only see the immaculately manicured fescue scrolling through my narrowing view, and small plastic rivets in the armored boots of the men who were carrying me.

"The next time I came to, I was in the back of an armored vehicle of some kind. It had small, thick plexiglass portholes, through which I could see the hill where the house used to be situated. Now there was only a tidy blackened crater. Even the trees and grass surrounding the structure remained untouched. Chemical lasers, invisible to the human eye, virtually silent, and pinpoint accurate. They were designed to destroy enemy fortifications. But this was no bunker. It had been a home with a family inside.

"Whoever 'they' were, whatever they were after, they didn't get it. Ms. Suleiman was clearly the target. And the fact that I lived and was being questioned suggests that she and the kids had perished in the attack. I survived only because I'd fallen through the floor and been covered by wreckage from the house. The attack was over before the laser, which I assumed had been deployed from orbit, could finish me. I was hospitalized briefly, during which time I was subjected to an unending stream of interrogations. I responded by asking why Ms. Suleiman would tell me, a servant, anything. I learned a lot through the interrogations about what they were after. As I suspected, they wanted to know about Adhara.

"I also knew that if I gave them what they wanted, they would kill me. They couldn't have someone walking around with evidence of a claim jump covered up by a brutal murder. But they also couldn't kill me. At least not until they found what they were looking for. So they made accommodations for me here, on the *Damma*. I knew that as long as I remained alive, they hadn't found it. And I swore to myself I would never tell them. I mourned Ms. Suleiman and the children and, though I recite a du'a for them every day, I decided to never speak of them aloud. That didn't appear to be a problem here."

Mohsin sat silently with Abbas' tale for several minutes. The statistical probability of meeting another living soul on the *Damma* was astronomically small. The fact that the other person he managed to meet had been imprisoned under dubious circumstances lent credence to the possibility that his own circumstances were somehow engineered. How many others must there be?

9

———

Mohsin was doing squat thrusts when Abbas' gaunt face appeared above the hole in the floor.

"Dinner?"

When they realized that not everyone received the same thing every day, they had begun to combine the ship's automated rations. To increase the variety in their meals and reduce water use, they began cooking stews from the freeze-dried components. They kept the leftover water for a nightly tea ritual, though the tea was actually a weak broth made from ground dehydrated mushrooms. Whatever was left from that was reserved for extra wudu, if the need arose. They even broke down the meal kits into their base components and started a pantry of sorts in the compartment beneath their cells.

If they were together around this time, Abbas would excuse himself, or pop his head up through the hole in the floor and ask if he was ready. He would dump the ingredients into a pot they had fashioned from a gear housing and set it over the provided heating element with some water. Then he would climb back out of the hole, and they would have just enough time to pray maghreb before the food was done. Once they finished praying, Abbas jumped back down into the hole and returned to its edge momentarily to hand off the makeshift pot to Mohsin. Then he grabbed the trays and utensils and hopped up. Mohsin spread his blanket out on the floor, then set the pot in the center. Abbas handed him a tray and began pouring the stew into each. He ate silently at first, then Mohsin caught him staring.

"What?"

"You will need an education if you intend to get revenge."

"I already have an education."

"You have a trade. That is not the type of education I am talking about."

"Then what?"

"If this noble truly is the person who has wronged you, you will need to know how to take your vengeance."

"What is there to know besides showing up and killing him?"

Abbas hung his head and shook it while putting his arm out to lean against the rim of the floor plate. "Sacrificing yourself to kill someone isn't revenge. If you manage to kill this man you will find his death a deeply unsatisfying reward for all the years he has stolen from you and is set to steal from you yet."

"What do you suggest?"

"You need to get close to him and, to do that, you need to understand his world and how to move in it."

"What good will that do?"

"Servants make the best assassins."

"Because they can get close to the nobles?"

"Because they are invisible. I cannot say specifically how this will serve you, but it will serve you a lot more than ignorance."

Mohsin had given up on escape. Their prison was a ship in the middle of space, a ship that never docked and was resupplied by shuttle through an umbilicus. Feeding and water rations were automated, as were welfare checks. He was beginning to wonder if there was any crew at all. It didn't matter anyway, since they had no idea where the bridge was, and, even if they did, there was no way they would be able to gain access to it. He had been completely unsuccessful at opening his own door and imagined it would be similarly impossible to open the dozen or so they would need to get to the bridge and commandeer the ship.

If most of the ship's prison systems were automated, riot-suppression and escape-prevention systems were probably automated too. The *Nightshade* had boarder-repellant and mutiny-suppression systems that worked in concert with the crew. The systems on the *Damma* would likely be engineered specifically to suppress prisoners in the off chance any of them got out of their cells. Abbas had calculated the dates of Ramadan the best he could, and, during this thirty-day stretch each "year", Mohsin and Abbas had gotten into the habit of praying tarawih in the "evenings" and, afterwards, enjoying a game of backgammon while continuing one of their many discussions.

Mohsin had become resigned to this situation and thought it could be worse. He could still be locked in that cell alone, with no one to talk to or play backgammon with. For all the good it did, Abbas had expanded his world by teaching him literature and science, and even expanding his knowledge of their faith. After a long day of instruction, they would play chess, go, or backgammon. It broke up the monotony.

They were in the middle of a game when the ship lurched suddenly. It felt as though the *Damma* had dropped out of sub-light. The ship lurched again, but this time they could hear the whine of the hull stretching under stress. Mohsin was thrown forward onto his stomach by the *Damma's* sudden deceleration. Abbas helped him to his feet and dragged him toward his cell.

"Are we being boarded?" Mohsin asked.

He could hear it now. There were dozens of tiny clinking noises of metal hitting the outer hull amidships. Then there was another loud whining sound like the buckling of metal. Something had clamped onto the *Damma's* aft. The buckling sound was that of tow clamps crushing the ship's drive cones, and the whining was the hull stretching against the cables while the sub-light drives were engaged.

"No!" Abbas shouted. "Hurry!"

Mohsin crawled up through the deck plate and back into his quarters.

"What now?"

"Your vac suit!"

"Wait. Now? You said we weren't being boarded."

"We aren't. Hurry!"

Mohsin eyes grew wide with terror and realization. Panicked, he began putting on his vac suit.

"Abbas! Get your suit on! Abbas!" He pressed the magnetic seal closed on his own suit then mag locked his helmet into place.

To become a crewman, you needed to train extensively before they allowed you to serve on a ship. Space was full of things that could kill you without warning. The various academies and trade schools used simulations to prepare you for all of the possibilities, though some things simply couldn't be taught. A flechette coming through the hull and impaling you was not something you could avoid. However, you could avoid suffocating in a vacuum when a flechette punctured your compartment. Though the current danger was not a flechette, Mohsin recognized the sound. Magnesium augurs were drilling into the hull around the drive compartment and would soon detonate, leaving a drive-shaped hole behind. In a compartment this size, it was possible the two prisoners would be incinerated before the vacuum could expel the heat. And as much as he didn't want to trust that the attackers had made the appropriate adjustment to the augur size, he had no choice.

Abbas appeared at his side from the inner hull compartment, but he wasn't wearing a vac suit.

"Abbas! Why don't you have your suit on?"

"You are going in search of your freedom, my friend. Mine lies here."

"Come with me!" It seemed strange to insist on this, given the likelihood that neither would survive being sucked out into space. And of course there was the issue of pirates if they did. But in Mohsin's eyes, a probable death was better than a certain one. Abbas ignored his pleas and instead pressed his face to Mohsin's faceplate. He held up a piece of paper and stuffed it into the breast pocket of Mohsin's vac suit.

"Peace be unto you my friend, and may Al—"

The shaped charges on the hull detonated, and Abbas was sucked into space.

Mohsin used the rope he had fashioned to tie himself to the intake manifold of the singularity drive before the shaped charges detonated and vented the drive compartment into space. The one thing he didn't expect was for the drive itself to come free of its housing. The *Damma* continued on its now derelict course while the drive floated free out of the breach in the outer hull. It occurred to him now what the impacts were amidships. The corsairs were firing on the cowling in a forward compartment to make sure the drive would separate. It spared the corsair crew the danger of having to board and cut it free with torches, especially with the automated systems active. This was also lucky for Mohsin. If the pirates boarded the *Damma*, they would have killed him outright. But instead, they would have to grapple the drive section and pull it into their cargo bay, and him along with it. He hoped they wouldn't kill him outright then too.

The more immediate problem was oxygen. The vac suit was designed to keep him conscious in the event of a hull breach. It had a small built-in oxygen canister, no larger than a can of soup. Unfortunately, it only held enough oxygen to last a few minutes, long enough to escape a depressurized compartment, but not to survive adrift in space. As Abbas had indicated, the only reason why a non-cargo ship would be attacked by pirates was for the singularity drive. The fact that Mohsin was now tied to it and adrift would indicate he had been right.

There were no maneuvering jets on the suit, so Mohsin had to be careful about untethering himself. If the pirates wanted the drive, they would need to deploy another grapple to bring it on board, which might crush him if he were lashed directly to it. The drive still had a fair amount of inertia on it and any application of counterforce against it might send him hurtling off into space. He loosened the rope enough to allow himself to spin around while still being attached to the drive, which also gave him his first look at the attacking ship. It filled him with a sense of dread, not just because he might soon be among them, but the fact that he was drifting free near something so large. He thought this was how schools of fish must feel in the presence of a whale.

Once he was positioned properly, Mohsin grabbed onto a part of the *Damma's* bulkhead that was still bolted to the singularity drive, then scissored his legs around a bent coolant shaft protruding from the lower side. He unfastened the rope entirely, took up the slack, then tied it back around his waist. Finally, he took the other end and threaded it first around the coolant shaft and then around the swing arm that held the now defunct status display. Whoever was operating the grapple would likely use the ship's cameras and search lights so they could get an adequate grip on the drive. Mohsin positioned himself on the other side of the drive from the ship. He might still be spotted, but he felt he should at least try to avoid detection until the last possible moment.

In space there is no sense of time because there is no sense of movement. Even in the presence of the massive pirate ship, he felt like he wasn't moving at all. Small pieces of the *Damma* occasionally floated past but that only made his drifting feel more interminable. There was also the issue of temperature. Like oxygen, the suit had its own heat, but it was limited. It was impossible to tell how long either would last. Fortunately for Mohsin, his assumption that the pirates would be in a hurry paid off. The searchlights came on, and wandered around him for several seconds before locking onto his position. He peeked around the side of the drive and saw the massive metal jaws of the grapple, flying toward him. Wrapping some of the slack from the rope around his wrist, he braced himself for the impact. Had he remained in his original position the grapple would have pulverized him. He grunted as the impact shook him.

When the grapple deposited Mohsin and the singularity drive onto the cargo deck, it was complete chaos. At first no one noticed him. He figured they assumed he was just a dead body that got tangled with the wires and piping of the drive. But after several seconds someone shouted, "Stowaway!"

Mohsin chuckled softly to himself at the idea that someone would float through space to stow away on a pirate ship. He was lying on the deck when several people surrounded him. He unlocked the mag seal of his helmet and let it roll onto the deck.The pirate crew looked menacing, but none of them made any move to restrain or manhandle him, perhaps because they knew he had no place to go. A few more seconds passed before a large-framed man pushed his way through the rapidly thickening crowd.

"Now that's what I call service. We go out for a singularity drive and we get the engineer for free." Laughter erupted in the cargo hold.

"I couldn't just surrender my drive to you lot," Mohsin replied. He was terrified and couldn't think of anything to say. He regretted it immediately since snark wasn't likely to endear him to his captors.

"Oh yeah? Why is that?"

"We've been through a lot together." Mohsin shrugged as he said this and the surrounding crew erupted into wild laughter.

"We'll take good care of it. Space him." Two nearby crew members flanked Mohsin and grabbed his arms. Mohsin yanked his right arm free and pulled the man on his left off balance, shoving him into the other crewman The large framed man was wearing a utility jumpsuit with the top unzipped and the arms tied around his waist like a belt. A vibroknife was wedged in the back of the makeshift belt. Mohsin grabbed it and held it up, assuming a combat stance. Everyone moved toward him but the man held his hand up to signal that they should stay put. He gestured to a nearby crewman, who drew a vibroknife out of his own sheath and handed it to him.

"I have no wish to kill you," Mohsin said. "I just don't want to die. I'm a skilled crewman and I can work for my passage. You can drop me at the next port."

"Hear this everyone? We can drop him at the next port. Someone get this man a deck chair and a blanket." More laughter. "This is a matter of honor now."

Immediately, Mohsin understood. By taking the man's knife he had embarrassed him. The only way for him to maintain his crew's respect was to kill Mohsin. He didn't fully understand the code, but he hoped there was room in it for magnanimity.

The challenge was in the vibroknife. Had he been able, Mohsin would have grabbed another weapon entirely. Vibroknives were remarkably sharp and could shear off parts of a human body with ease. Likely the first person to draw blood would be the victor and the survivor. Mohsin's opponent widened his stance, then raised the vibroknife with the blade angled up instead of down and balled his empty hand into a fist with his forearm perpendicular to his body in front of him. It was just his luck that he got someone who knew how to actually fight.

"My name is Yacoub."

Mohsin assumed the man wanted him to know who it was that had killed him.

Yacoub started by feinting with an empty hand, slashing low at his belly. Mohsin stumbled back, having briefly lost sight of the blade hand. It came back across Mohsin's body from the opposite direction, which he blocked wrist to wrist. Normally, when blocking a knife slash, he would drag the blade down across the wrist to deliver a cut, but to do so in this case would remove his opponent's hand. The man stepped back, briefly confused, but then lunged. Again, Mohsin parried the blow wrist to wrist. This time he angled the edge of the vibroknife away from the man's arm as he drew back. Yacoub squinted with suspicion and frustration. Then, as if testing a theory, he danced in and lunged at Mohsin several times. Each time, Mohsin blocked and parried without attempting to cut Yacoub.

Mohsin had to end the fight quickly, or else he would end up doing the same thing that precipitated it in the first place by compounding the insult. He threw a feint of his own, which drew Yacoub in. Mohsin blocked with his off hand and threw an elbow with the opposite arm, careful not to cut himself with his own weapon. The assembled crowd gasped. Yacoub fell to the cargo bay deck and hit his head. Mohsin knelt over him and held the knife to his throat. He only needed to flick his wrist and Yacoub would die.

"For sparing my life, I offer you yours," Yacoub said when he regained his breath. "You can join us if you choose."

"If I join, will I ever be able to leave again? I have been a prisoner for a decade, near as I can tell. I don't want to trade one prison for another."

Yacoub laughed. "There are no prisoners here. Everyone who has come to live among us has stayed."

"But you're pirates, aren't you?"

"We are Corsairs! We live out here because we choose not to live under the oppression of unions and consortiums. There is no compulsion in our religion. So why should there be compulsion in our lives?"

"And you survive by preying on defenseless ships."

"Sometimes. When we need to. But we are merely reclaiming lost labor, lost wages, and lost goods. Everyone here was a crewperson, a loader, an engineer. And every one of us was exploited by some mining or shipping entity or another. We take no more than what we are entitled to. And when people feel this life no longer agrees with them, they are free to go where they wish."

"What is the alternative?"

"We space you!" Everyone started laughing and some even began chanting, "Space him! Space him!"

The expression on Mohsin's face changed to one of terror.

"I'm kidding," Yacoub assured him. "It's one of the reasons we don't usually take prisoners. Killing someone in a boarding action is one thing, but spacing them is another."

"You were going to space me a few minutes ago."

"I was actually joking then, too. But then you went for my knife. That was real. We can just put you off the ship at the nearest port."

"I think I'll stay for a while." The people on the cargo deck began cheering.

"My name is—"

"Jawaal."

"What? No it's—"

"Jawaal. Your name is Jawaal. It means drifter. And since that's how we found you…" Yacoub spread his arms out to either side and pretended to be unconscious. "We will call you Jawaal."

"You're just going to change my name?"

"Who you are with us is not who you were out there. It's better for everyone if we are known by new names with each other. Welcome to our ship, the *Hutu*."

10

Living with the Corsairs was nothing like what Mohsin had imagined it would be. For years he'd heard stories about pirates beyond the boundaries of "civilized" space, who would make incursions into shipping lanes, steal cargo, and take the crew as slaves. What he found instead were thoughtful people who cared for each other, and realized that their labor and participation were essential to maintaining collective freedom. They ate meals and spent their leisure time together. When one person seemed to be alienating themselves from the group, they all made an effort to make that person feel welcomed again. There were even entire families among the crew. Most of them prayed together at designated times.

Mohsin also learned that there were many Corsair fleets. There was no true accounting for the numbers and he felt that might be intentional. Sometimes they traveled in groups, and sometimes just single ships. From time to time, they would band together for specific raids then disband immediately afterward. He wondered where all the ships had come from, as it occurred to him that the Corsairs, for all their ingenuity, lacked the ability to build them. All of the stories he'd heard about ships being destroyed by Corsairs or lost during singularity jumps were likely also fabricated. Some people back on Earth might have believed their ships were lost, and perhaps some were, but it was probably convenient to believe that, because it made collecting insurance payouts on lost goods and equipment easier. He also wondered, if this was the case, how much the TUC participated in the fraud.

Although he'd told Yacoub that he would join them, he had every intention of getting back to Earth as soon as possible. The main problem with this was that Corsair ships never docked at Earth ports. Ever. Which meant he would have to make his way to the nearest port, then book passage on a ship and hope it was headed back to Earth sometime soon. The reason he and Solmaz had been so excited about him getting a captaincy was that they would no longer have to be apart for long stretches of time. It took months to mine ore, minerals, and water from an asteroid. Longer for larger ones. Singularity drives, despite being in use for centuries, were not remarkably accurate. You had to use it to jump close to a star system, then spend weeks or months at sub-light getting to the actual destination. Prospectors went out and claimed asteroids, and then mining companies would buy the rights wholesale and negotiate shipping if they didn't have their own.

The Corsairs did occasionally dock at ports, but they spent even longer periods in deep space. They extracted water from asteroids or comets when they needed to, but had no use for ore. They stole it from time to time, but only because the ship they happened to board didn't have anything else. The ore was difficult to sell, especially when you didn't go into port very often. Mostly they were after food, water, parts, and other sundries. The most surprising thing to Mohsin was what happened to the goods once they were taken: they were distributed amongst the other Corsair ships within a fleet. This defied another commonly held belief amongst TUC and Consortium crews alike: that Corsairs only took what they needed. It made sense, because carrying something like ore meant sacrificing space for essentials like water and food.

One of the biggest and most important adjustments Mohsin had to make on the *Hutu* was the expectation that he would participate in the raids. In one sense it was not that much different than having to repel boarders, the main difference being that the Corsairs often had the advantage. Most shipping crews were not comprised of fighters —the crews simply didn't feel the compensation was worth risking their lives, so they were more likely to surrender than resist. But raids still caused casualties, and it was hard for Mohsin to stomach the idea of injuring or killing merchant crew—crew like he and Solmaz might have been—just to take their employers' property by force.

Mohsin was also surprised by his hosts' exceptional discipline. Not only were tasks shared, but they were carried out without delay. Corsair crews would be the envy of any trade organization. The first boarding action he ever did with them was a wonder of collaborative discipline. They were divided into groups by task on a rotating basis, so every crewmember eventually performed every task. The first few times, Mohsin was a boarder. Boarders were required to carry one plasma pistol and one vibrosword. The vibroswords were shorter, but wider than Mohsin was used to, so they could be wielded in close quarters. Plasma pistols were used instead of projectile weapons, which tended to cause unintended hull punctures and also tended to keep going forever. Energy weapons were safer, because they weren't designed to puncture hulls and the energy dissipated quickly, especially in a vacuum.

Boarding tactics varied from fleet to fleet. They used gauss coilguns that hurled small, hypervelocity rounds in ship-to-ship combat. They packed enough punch to puncture the hull and decompress specific compartments. This limited the access of crews to the parts of the ship they needed to defend or repair, without permanently disabling the ship. It took several minutes for a crew to put vac suits on, during which the Corsairs began their assault. Firing cargo grapples, normally used by mining vessels to anchor to an asteroid, they latched onto the ship. Once they were securely anchored, they used shaped charges fashioned from magnesium to burn through the hull. That section of the hull would later be salvaged for use in patching holes in the hulls of Corsair ships. Then they boarded in teams, ten to twenty Corsairs in vac suits, thrust into the breach using the suit's maneuvering jets to begin securing points of access to cargo holds. Finally, loader teams thrust over and began offloading as much cargo as possible. What looked to merchant crews like crazed pirates bent on thievery and vandalism was actually a precision heist designed to minimize loss of life.

From the moment the first grapples were fired to the time the entire crew was back on the *Hutu*, only twenty-two minutes had elapsed, and they had taken enough food and water to last for three months. Initially, Mohsin felt an obligation to be part of the raids. He thought things would go smoother, and there was less likely to be unnecessary killing if he were there. But his presence wasn't needed at all. The Corsairs were restrained, efficient, and professional. No one got hurt that didn't need to be. Although people invariably died during raids, the Corsairs took greater care not to harm the crew of the ships they boarded than the crews' own employers did.

Living with the Corsairs was enlightening and Mohsin believed it had changed him for the better. But it was time he got on with his own plans. Being free from the *Damma* did not mean he was free from the day-to-day task of survival. It occurred to him more than once that he could simply go to Earth and kill Hossam. He even fantasized about challenging him to a fight. But both of those options would end in his death. Seeing the Corsairs in action gave him the beginnings of a plan. By living among them, he had come to see the human aspect of their plight, but they were still universally feared by all of the legitimate shipping and mining operations in the galaxy. He understood that much of that fear arose not from some visceral dread of fanatical pirates, but from the shortfall in quarterly earnings reports occasioned by their raids. At first, he dismissed the idea of involving the Corsairs in the plan he was developing. Their lives were difficult enough as it was, without poking a giant hornet's nest.

11

———————

W_{HAT} C_{HANGED} Mohsin's mind about Corsair involvement was the potential for a mutually beneficial collaboration. His motives were selfish, no matter how much the Corsairs were going to benefit, but he saw no other way. He had been poor before he was imprisoned on the *Damma*, and he was even more destitute now. His only path to revenge was going to be Abbas' asteroid.

The paper that Abbas had stuffed in his breast pocket before being spaced contained the coordinates to Adhara. He needed to convince Yacoub to help him. He wouldn't do it otherwise. They had taken them in and treated him like family. He needed to be honest with Yacoub about his agenda.

"I told you we don't have any need for ore. We only take it when there is nothing else to take from the ships we board. And it's incredibly hard for us to sell on the open market." Yacoub was far more dismissive of the information than Mohsin was prepared for.

"Then I will make sure you get things you can use. Food, medicine, and water. You can't sell ore on the open market, but I can. Or at least I will be able to."

"Despite what you may have heard, we are pirates of opportunity, not politics."

"I think the decision to resort to piracy so you can live the way you choose is fundamentally a political choice."

"What I mean is, we don't take sides."

"I wasn't asking you to take sides. I was asking you to be more discriminating in your targets." Mohsin was becoming visibly frustrated with Yacoub.

"That defies the whole idea of being pirates of opportunity."

"Ok. Let's talk opportunity. I'm offering you one. You say you live out here because you can live how you want. I can make that a lot easier for you if you help me."

Yacoub shook his head doubtfully. "Jawaal, what if this asteroid is just smoke? Is it worth the risk?"

"I can only answer that for myself. We don't even need to take the *Hutu*. We can take one of her tugs, a few solar sails and guide her into open space"

"I owe you a debt. Since no one else will be at risk, then I can honor that debt."

The approach to the asteroid was complicated. They couldn't just swoop in and land. Aside from the star's luminance making it virtually invisible, the intense heat would vaporize them if they got too close. They needed to back into the asteroid and keep it between themselves and Adhara. It would create a heat shadow as well as radiation shield. The *Hutu* would be able to withstand the heat and radiation more readily, but it would still be dangerous, and Mohsin didn't feel it was right to endanger the crew. When he was convincing Yacoub to come with him, they both felt the ship's tug would be more appropriate. Their goal was to latch onto the asteroid with grapples, and reel themselves in. Once they had attached themselves to it, they could deploy solar sails and use Adhara's light to push the asteroid away from it. Once they were close to open space they would transfer the tow cables to the *Hutu* and continue on.

Mohsin was at the helm, and Yacoub was monitoring heat and radiation levels. He could feel Adhara tugging violently at them and the ship. The gravitational eddies were so strong it was like piloting a boat during a tsunami. According to Abbas' calculations, the asteroid was just outside the red zone, so there was little room for error. If they overshot the asteroid by even two hundred kilometers, the tug's engines would overheat and shut off and they would be vaporized. There was also the possibility of Adhara's gravity pulling them into the asteroid, where they would impact and explode. Mohsin trusted Abbas' math, but he had never piloted a ship under these circumstances. And from the look on Yacoub's face, he hadn't either. Mohsin was starting to wonder if this thing hadn't been claimed simply because it was just too damn dangerous.

"Not sure if the tug can take this! Feels like she's ripping in half!" Yacoub was right. He was trying too hard to make course corrections using the ship's sub-light. He was using it as a sort of breaking thruster by accelerating against the gravity of the star.

"You're right. New plan." Mohsin shut off the engines.

"What are you doing? Ya Allah!"

"You were right. The braking is stressing the hull. We'll break apart before we get to the asteroid. I'm going to let gravity pull us in and use maneuvering thrusters to course correct." Yacoub began reciting a du'a. The tug started to accelerate, and the whining of stressed hull bearings became less frequent. Mohsin did his best to keep them lined up with the asteroid but did no fine tuning. He didn't want to overcorrect. Once they got within five hundred kilometers he felt a calm patch on the port side.

He didn't like flying by feel, but he didn't like flying by monitor either. The calm patch was what he was looking for. The asteroid was enormous and created a massive gravity, heat, and radiation shadow. That was the calm patch he was feeling. Mohsin nudged the thrusters starboard and slid the entire ship into that shadow.

"Firing thrusters!"

The asteroid's gravity was far more forgiving, and they rapidly decelerated.

"We're still coming in too fast!"

"I think we're OK!"

"You *think*?" Yacoub was hoping for a little more certainty from Mohsin.

Yacoub was right again. They were coming in fast for the amount of thrust they were generating and, though they were in the asteroid's gravity shadow, they were still being affected by Adhara. If Mohsin increased thrust, the ship might still be torn in half. He was hoping that all of Abbas' lessons on astromechanics would pay off. If he was right, the further into the shadow they flew, the less drag they would get from Adhara. They came within twenty kilometers, and the tug felt like it was sliding on grease. Mohsin ignited the sub-light engines and brought them to a stop above the asteroid.

Mohsin and Yacoub had to work quickly. The asteroid's rotation was mercifully slow because of its enormous size. However, being exposed to the sun side of it would be a death sentence. They needed to deploy solar sails around the equator of the asteroid and the order of their placement was essential. The first sails would be placed at the bottom of the asteroid. The light hitting the sails would cause it to accelerate against its rotation. In the short term, this would give Mohsin and Yacoub more time to place the rest of the sails.

Several mining drones were deployed from the shuttle which flew to predesignated points along the asteroid's circumference and began drilling. Once those were done, they inserted metal collars around the interior of the holes and then placed stanchions inside them that would then be used to deploy and support the sails. Servos in the stanchions would allow the sails to be remotely adjusted by the crew on the *Hutu* to keep them oriented at the optimal angle of acceleration to a progressively higher orbit.

The sails would be bombarded by Adhara's rays which would generate thrust. The increased velocity over time would push the asteroid into a higher orbit and away from the star. They were essentially using Adhara's light to counteract its gravitational pull. It would take weeks for the asteroid to gain sufficient distance from Adhara for the rest of the fleet to safely tow it into open space. Mohsin began scanning its composition, looking for the claim marker. Just as Abbas had told him, though it was expired, the Suleiman name appeared on the marker. And according to him, the claim had never been logged, so it officially became salvage.

"I don't know if you were just people. But know that your ore will be used to a just end. Inna Lillahi wa inna ilaihi raji'un." Mohsin whispered under his breath. Yacoub repeated the words in a whisper.

By the time all of the sails were in place, the composition scan had come back. For the first time, Abbas was wrong about something. The asteroid contained far greater concentrations of ore and minerals than he estimated.

"Look like we got ourselves a ball of ore covered in a fine layer of dirt," Mohsin exclaimed. It was an old space miner's adage that, in this case, appeared to be close to the truth.

"I've never seen that much ore in my life." Yacoub pointed at the monitor. "That vein of palladium right there looks about a kilometer wide. How much do you expect that's worth?"

"More than the entire Consortium combined brought in last year from mining."

"What are you going to do with all this, Jawaal?" Yacoub turned to Mohsin, eyes wide with surprise and joy.

"What are *we* going to do with this? I told you I would cut you and the Corsairs in. But I want to take care of a few things first and I want your help."

Some things did mean more than money. Like revenge. Like love. Like the life he'd dreamed of taken away from him. Mohsin could see this worried Yacoub. Honor demanded allegiance his allegiance, but the silent disapproval was evident every time he accepted a task. Mohsin needed to make this mission worth it for Yacoub, and, if possible, the rest of the Corsairs.

"Until your task is done," Yacoub said, "I am with you. I swear to Allah Subhanah wa Ta'ala." Yacoub touched his hand to his chest and bowed his head slightly.

"I'm grateful for your friendship, my friend."

Yacoub and Mohsin took turns monitoring the asteroid's progress from the bridge. The sails were fully mounted, and the asteroid was yet to achieve maximum velocity but the potential for catastrophe had not quite passed. The first chance they had a little down time they decided to pray Maghreb and have dinner together.

"We've planted the claim beacon and it's begun broadcasting. The claim number and the scans of the asteroid have also been transmitted to Earth." Yacoub said as he entered Mohsin's quarters, washed his oil-stained hands in the tiny basin, then plunked down on one end of the bunk.

"I contacted a few banks in Mina al Fada during my last bridge shift to see if I could get us an advance against the scans. I checked out a couple of banks in other Sultanates as well. I've never done this before, but I wanted to make sure we were paying dividends against an advance and not interest."

"How long did that take?" Yacoub grabbed a pillow and stuffed it between his head and the wall.

"These Earth bureaucracies are needlessly troublesome."

"I kept thinking the whole time about how unequipped we are for dealing with it. We've spent our entire lives mining these rocks, transporting ore and workers, and equipment. We know all there is about mining except how to make money from it. Seems like this would be a lot easier if I were rich."

"You are rich, Jawaal."

"*We* are. But that isn't what I wanted to talk to you about." Mohsin got down on his knees and reached under the bunk to retrieve two prayer rugs which he then unrolled onto the floor perpendicular to it. "You and the other Corsairs have been remarkably generous -"

"You are a Corsair! You're one of us!"

"I appreciate that, and I am proud to call myself one. But I also recognize that this fight is mine. I have no desire to see anyone else hurt over this."

"You are a Corsair." Yacoub's said calmly but something intense grew in his eyes as he said it. "And even if you weren't, you are my friend."

"Do you have any friends that aren't Corsairs?"

"No. But then I don't have any that are." He smiled a toothy grin. Mohsin grabbed his shoulder and laughed.

"One more thing. I need you to open a competitive bid for the mining of this asteroid and the shipment of the ore. Give some small bids to some of the smaller companies. But make sure you get the Consortium and the TUC on the payroll."

"I still don't understand why you would give money to the Consortium."

"An old friend of mine used to say 'greed is a greedy man's weakness'."

Yacoub didn't quite understand, but Mohsin seemed to have thought quite a bit about this.

"What about the refining?"

"We can secure an advance from the banks on Earth and Mars against the claim and the core samples but I don't want any refining done until we have capacity. For now, it's cheaper to outsource it. But I do want you to find some smelters and ore refineries once we are able. Not just in Mina Fada, though I want you to start there. Inspecting my holdings should be a good cover."

"I've grown comfortable calling you Jawaal. I don't think 'drifter' will endear you to the people you mean to take revenge upon."

"I've been thinking of that. The asteroid was discovered by someone with the surname Suleiman, but they were killed before they could file the claim. I'm not a superstitious man, but that is just too bad of a sign. So I've decided to take the name of the star. Adhara."

"Virgin?"

"The chaste. Slightly older interpretation."

12

____

Solmaz did a double take when Hossam walked into their room. He was wearing a new suit, and it looked expensive. It was tailored in the current style, with a banded collar shirt nested in a jacket with a similarly banded collar and large cuffs. But the fabric was different. From an angle she could detect a slight sheen drifting across the fabric. She thought she was seeing things, then realized it was the new electro-pigmented brocade, the latest fashion in the upper levels of Mina Fada. Hossam would be able to program colors and patterns directly into the material, effectively changing clothes without changing them. The pants were fitted and made from the same material and the shoes were real leather, with faint LEDs around the opening. It gave him the appearance of being taller.

His mood was different. She hadn't seen him like this since before his father died. Every day since they got married was filled with tension. His gambling and women had been a problem before, and neither of those things had ceased in the interim. They were going deeper into debt every day. There was also the pressure from his cousin, the Sultan. Earnings were down across the eight sectors but it seemed Hossam's had been hit the hardest.

"Someone's in a good mood."

"I've secured a contract with a new client. Should be quite good for us and it should please the Sultan." Hossam spoke in his usual tight jawed cadence while admiring himself in the mirror.

"Oh? I assume it's a big contract."

"Honestly, it's the biggest one I've seen since being promoted. Others are saying it's the biggest one anyone's ever seen."

"That's good news. I would have expected you to be even happier than you seem. This is awfully restrained even for you."

"Now that mining has commenced, I'm much happier. I was concerned for a while because of all the talk surrounding the prospect."

"What talk?" Solmaz tilted her head and raised an eyebrow.

"The claimant is rather mysterious. Lots of strange stories surrounding him. It makes one wonder what other fiction might be involved."

"Stories?"

"Someone said he was captured and enslaved by the Corsairs and he escaped and was prospecting in the reaches. It's just some nouveau riche types trying to create buzz around themselves. But I hear on good authority that the claim is magnificent. It should keep us in cash for a long time."

"This calls for a celebration."

"Why do you think I'm dressed up?"

Solmaz was confused. She hadn't been notified by either of their secretaries about a night out but then she realized she wasn't invited. "Oh."

"Don't worry. I've gotten a small advance against commissions and deposited some in your accounts. Go buy something nice. I'm sure we'll be receiving invitations once we're flush again."

Hossam had received the communique a week ago from the secretary of a man named Aaris Adhara. "The Chaste" - it sounded like one of those names you chose when you wanted your money to sound old. It was a strange name to take for a guy who'd been captured and enslaved by the Corsairs. Hossam had heard stories about them, too, and what they did to their prisoners. He was skeptical of the man and what he wanted to contract the Sector 8 operation for, mostly because

Adhara's people didn't haggle. Hossam simply put forward his terms and they were accepted. Over time, a large fortune could have been eked out on a single percentage point. He managed to get three. He chalked it up to this upstart being new to the game of wealth.

He was also skeptical of the asteroid's size until he started hearing about it from others. Some said it was more like a planetoid than an asteroid and that it was more ore than rock. This man would be among the nouveau riche within a month and he would be insufferably recounting the stories of his discoveries over dinner for the next year. Everyone would listen and pretend to be interested because everyone would want a piece of this rock. The more Hossam thought about it, the more he disliked the fellow, a buccaneer who thought he could hand out contracts and the nobles would suck up to him.

Yes. This was exactly what would happen. Everyone would suck up to him, including Hossam, to get a piece of that asteroid. But Hossam wouldn't be doing it for just a piece.

13

GETTING BACK to the Terran system from the empty reaches of known space was a challenge. The areas of space where the Corsairs tended to make their homes were well outside normal shipping and commerce lanes. But as one drew nearer to Earth, space became congested. With that congestion came patrols, checkpoints, and even random searches. A Corsair vessel would never be able to get within ten systems. Most of their ships were refits stolen from decommissioning shipyards, or a combination of salvaged and decommissioned ships welded together. The patchwork appearance alone would have every inspector and defense naval cruiser on them the moment they exited space fold. To add to that, Corsair ships had all their navigational beacons and any other electronically identifying markers removed.

There were hundreds of outposts along the edge of known space that were used for registering claims and transferring people and equipment for mining operations. Vessels that wanted to augment their crews for short periods or were dropping others off after mining operations would be docked at these ports. From there it was a matter of navigating a complex web of similar outposts to get to major hubs, and then to the Terran system. Once they got to Gliese, the nearest system with a habitable planet, and a shipyard, Mohsin purchased a yacht. Passenger quarters on frigates were tight, even by Corsair standards, and offered no privacy. He was less interested in the vanity of "new money" than he was in being able to talk and plan openly with Yacoub and the other Corsairs who volunteered to join them. The comfort of a yacht was a bonus.

As yachts went, it was modest. It was older and there was some outer hull damage, but the interior was spacious and contained the only amenities he was interested in. Once they had settled in to their new travel arrangements Yacoub came to visit him in his quarters.

"Jawaal, I know you are intent on carrying out this plan but I came to convince you to give it up. I don't claim to understand why you are doing this or what you've been through, but I want you to consider leaving with us." Mohsin swiveled around in his chair to face Yacoub. "Every single person in the fleet looks at you as a brother. No heart among them has remained untouched by your presence, your willingness to help. You told me once that you joined the TUC to make a difference and I am saying that you have, with us. We have enough money to buy resources and ships, to go where we want and live as we choose. But if this ends badly for you, think of all those whose lives you have and will touch that will mourn you." It was almost enough that Yacoub had managed to summon so much eloquence to make his case. The words and the sincerity tugged at him deeply.

"I will consider what you've said, Yacoub. And no matter my decision, your respect and that of the fleet means a lot to me."

It was one fold from the Gliese system to Terra then another ten days at sub-light to Earth. The whole time Mohsin could feel anxiety building up in him. Every moment he drew nearer to Earth, to Solmaz, and to revenge. Once they arrived, they were put into a holding pattern pending customs inspection. It was something Mohsin wasn't used to but should have anticipated. Cargo ships, especially those transporting ore, were given priority. It's possible he could have expedited things, but money was something else he was unused to. Orbit was good enough for now. He could access the data net from there and set his plans in motion.

The first thing Mohsin did was initiate queries on the whereabouts of Solmaz. There were a lot of possibilities and the one he hoped for was the most remote. She could have died. Or she could have found someone else in streetside and be living quietly there with children. When the first result of the query came back, his chest constricted and it became hard for him to breathe. It was worse than he could have imagined. Any thoughts he had of abandoning his pursuit evaporated. Had the circumstances been anything other than they were, he might have listened to Yacoub, but his reinvigorated sense of vengeance overpowered any desire to leave.

It was perhaps not concrete proof that Hossam was involved in his framing, but it more than strongly suggested it. There was only one person who could begin filling in the gaps for him and that person was the subject of his next query.

Setting foot on Earth again was the most foreign sensation Mohsin had ever felt. He knew what it was to be in space, away from his home, but never for so long and never for this reason. When he arrived at Mina Fada, the first thing he did was go to one of the exterior shuttle platforms. He needed to feel the wind on his face and scalp, to smell the polluted air and the stench of streetside drifting up to him. At this height, there was always a meandering mist that clung to his skin. Feeling Earth's gravity pulling at him made him want to cry. Most importantly, he was close to realizing his objectives.

Yacoub had been busy setting Mohsin's plans into motion before they even arrived. He was constantly sending messages to attorneys, shipping concerns, and outfitters. The Corsair fleets didn't have leaders, but if this one did, Yacoub would have been it. He was more like a fatherly figure, despite not being particularly old. When someone expressed a desire to leave, he would gently counsel them about their decision and respect it either way. He was stern with newcomers, but also patient and instructive. The best part about him was that he remembered everyone, and kept in touch with many of them. The Corsairs were mysterious and invisible. They'd been around since the beginning of space prospecting and mining. Yacoub had inherited the mantle from someone and would eventually pass it on. Each new "leader" would add their own touch.

Yacoub's contribution to their Corsair fleet was this need to maintain the family-like nature of it. But, from that family, he grew a network of informal spies and operatives. The laborers were the real power in the galaxy, and he knew it. If you wanted your ships offloaded quickly you had to know where to look, and you had to treat the people right. Mainly, he used his network to get information on where shipments were heading, get peeks at manifests, and assess the general tone of the various consortiums. It was easier to hit a ship if he knew they had their guard down. Spotting that kind of complacency was easy. And after an attack, everyone would be on high alert, and the spies were great at finding out what measures were being taken to root them out.

The Corsairs weren't just crew people. Often they worked in foundries, ore processing, smelters, loaders—any number of jobs necessary to keep the whole machine operating. The fact that all of them came from or lived streetside meant Yacoub could get information about the comings and goings of people down there. Or one person.

This was how Mohsin discovered that Solmaz and Hossam were married. Hearing that news from Yacoub was like a dagger in the heart. He had expected her to move on. When he was sent to the *Damma*, she was still young, and very much sought after. But finding out she had married someone who represented everything she was against, compounded the pain of it. It also elevated his theory above simple speculation. Yacoub also discovered that Hossam was in considerable debt, despite being elevated to the position of Bashi. He owed money to more than one bank, and to various upscale gambling parlors in Mina Fada, as well as less savory characters streetside. This made the snare of the trap that much larger.

Yacoub also saw to the purchase of the most luxurious penthouse in Mina Fada that they could find. Mohsin had no intention of hosting anyone, but he needed to be seen coming and going from a place that demonstrated his wealth.

"We can't forget our sadaqa, Jawaal."

"You're right of course Yacoub. Arrange for rice, bread and meat to be delivered streetside. But quietly."

There was a time when he wouldn't have needed reminding about his obligation to the less fortunate. It would have been automatic for him. On the journey back to Earth he only prayed a handful of times, and even then never with Yacoub or the other Corsairs. He was so busy plotting his revenge that he would allow days to pass without ever leaving his quarters. It wasn't until now that he realized a giant rift had opened up within him. On one side was the person he had been and on the other was this hardened version of himself. He had one foot on either side, and rift threatened to swallow him. At what point did this rift open? On the *Damma*? During his years with the Corsairs?

Yacoub spent most of the trip back to Earth trying to convince him to leave this life , and he was nearly convinced until he saw the wedding announcement. A small part of him wondered if Solmaz had been in on it. Whether she was or not, he had to know why she married Hossam. Mohsin had to know what his life would have been like if he hadn't been sent to prison, and if any of that life remained for him to claim.

Maybe Yacoub was right. Perhaps he should leave and try and get back to the person he was, or was meant to be. Perhaps Solmaz had found love again and managed to move on. But for Mohsin, time stood still, at least where his heart was concerned. In one of their many conversations on the *Damma*, Abbas had warned him that he couldn't destroy what he hated without becoming what he hated.

Mohsin had already gotten the money and had begun to adopt their ways.

Hossam had destroyed who he was. The way he saw it, he was an anchor that Mohsin needed to untether himself from in order to be who he should. That's what he convinced himself of. It was entirely possible that Hossam would drink and gamble himself to death, just as his father did. That would be a kind of justice, but Mohsin wanted Hossam to pay for what was done to *him*. And he wanted to be the one to exact the toll. He could leave as Yacoub suggested, but knowing that Hossam took everything from him would gnaw at him no matter what remote region of space he ended up in. The two of them could not exist in the same universe. One of them had to go.

He was grateful for Yacoub's reminder, but he wondered if there was another, more personal motive, behind it. Mohsin couldn't remember the specific hadith, but he recalled that charity could be a shield against calamity. Consistent with his political and religious beliefs, he didn't believe in giving for the sake of reward of any kind. Yacoub might also have been concerned that Mohsin's pursuit of vengeance would end in his death.

14

It had been at least twenty years since Yacoub last set foot on Earth. He left his own home, an agrarian planet called Tacitus, when he entered the fleets as an apprentice. He'd only been to Earth a handful of times. His fleet assignments rarely allowed for visits. One thing he always appreciated was how pleasant gravity felt. Artificial gravity was a great simulation, but there was a slight difference. You felt rooted to the Earth, even through the pavement. Back on the *Hutu*, there were times when they would shut off the artificial gravity to move cargo and when that happened, he remembered immediately becoming detached from the deck. There was something comforting about the impossibility of that here.

Earth had dangers other than flying off into an endless void or careening into a bulkhead. Yacoub had been to hundreds of little pirate's coves across the known systems. Earth was no pirate's cove, but it had gambling dens and brothels far exceeding any he'd seen in their shadiness. Out there, in space, you couldn't avoid these places. Many ports of call were just giant dens of iniquity. He was back on Earth and still surrounded by vice. Being a Corsair as long as he had meant having seen every pirate's cove in known space. In truth, aside from the gravity, there was little difference between a gambling parlor on Earth and one on Mars, or Io, or even Tacitus. Where there were people, there was also vice, and those who dealt in it.

Places like Baikonur had formally outlawed gambling, but that didn't mean it didn't exist. It just meant knowing where to look. There were always street games of dice but the higher stakes games would be in secret parlors, likely run by criminal syndicates. Jawaal wanted to come down to streetside himself to handle this, but Yacoub convinced him not to. He didn't want Jawaal to be seen skulking around back-alley entrances to gambling dens and talking to moneylenders in seedy bars. If he was going to infiltrate the upper echelons of Baikonur's elite, he needed to appear squeaky clean. It wasn't that those people didn't frequent such places, they were just part of an entrenched elite. Those he meant to cozy up to might be less forgiving if he were spotted in some of the shadier areas.

It was different for Hossam too. His activities were a well-known secret amongst the admin nobles, as his father's had been, but Hossam's excesses dwarfed his father's. Once he'd been through all the gambling and sex workers in Mina al-Fada, he descended on streetside to continue the party. Yacoub spent weeks playing detective, roaming from one gambling parlor to another, tracking down all the places Hossam frequented. It wasn't particularly difficult, just time-consuming. The Bashi was a hard man to miss. And once you found one disgruntled parlor owner it was easy to find others. Yacoub wasn't going to find them all, but once the scope of Hossam's habit became clear, how much he gambled and owed, he realized they didn't need to.

Two of the Corsairs they brought with them to Earth did the dirty work of tracking Hossam to a few parlors and several street games. Yacoub went behind, took the information and began paying visits to the parlors. The interior of this particular parlor looked to be set up in the bottom floor of an abandoned building. It was a little more sophisticated than many he'd seen. There were several large, round, tables situated in one part of the establishment occupied by players, some with sex workers on their laps. Loud conversations filled the room with words and smoke as patrons exhaled their preferred tobacco.

Just beyond a low, wooden barrier was an array of high-top tables and a wooden bar. This particular establishment had a brothel. A faintly lit stairwell in the rear showed men and women coming up and down, pushing through a thin layer of smoke that had collected there. There was a lingering smell of cannabis with accents of clove, kretek, khat, and a tiny bit of betel nut. In contrast to the offworld parlors, the sweat and humidity were palpable. Yacoub approached a modestly dressed man behind the bar. He was willing to bet all the money he was carrying that this was the proprietor. Bartenders were either snappy in the way they dressed or casual. This man was dressed like someone's father.

"How can I help you?" He while restocking his bar.

"I'm interested in doing a little business."

"Is that right? I have all kinds of services you can buy."

"I'm not interested in services." The proprietor stopped smiling. His eyes darted briefly to something behind Yacoub. Yacoub knew it was probably a bouncer or worse.

"Oh yeah? I got cards and I got sex. I don't do any other kind of business." The man's mouth contorted with annoyance.

"I can make it worth your while. If you don't like what I have to say, then I'll go." Someone was standing so close behind him he could feel their warm breath on his neck.

"Make it quick."

"I want to buy some of the gambling debt you're holding."

"You mean you want to muscle me out. We're done here." The man nodded to whoever was standing behind Yacoub who then grabbed him.

"No. Wait. I'm not here to muscle anyone out. I'm not interested in your books. Just one customer."

The proprietor raised his hand and the other man unhanded Yacoub.

"Which one?"

Yacoub moved closer so no one else could hear. "Hossam Majid."

The man became visibly uncomfortable. "Are you crazy?"

"I'll take every penny he's left you in the hole with."

"What if I were to take this information to him? Someone down here buying up his debt."

"You think he's going to give you a reward? He doesn't have any money. Even if he did, he would be paying you with your own money."

The proprietor nodded as he considered the proposal. "No pennies on the dollar. If you want his debt you take it all."

"Ok. But on one condition: I hold the debt but you still collect."

"If I could collect, I would have already. We can't touch him."

"Who said I wanted him touched?"

Yacoub didn't quite understand what Jawaal was trying to do. He said he wanted revenge but buying a man's debt seemed like letting him off the hook.

15

Mohsin understood the closer you were to Mina al Fada, the more money you had. Even the difference between informal structures like shanties on the edge of the city where it temporarily terminated in the Kazakh desert, and the tiny one person kennels, stacked on top of one another to obscene heights, was noticeable. The apartment he found Ghamal living in was an accommodation that no one with Ghamal's limited pension should be able to afford.

"You're not Mohsin. Mohsin's dead!"

"It would be easier for you to believe that, wouldn't it? Maybe I'm his ghost, returned from the grave for vengeance. Either way you should be worried."

"If you are him, what's to stop me from telling the authorities?"

"You could. But what do you think they will do? Assuming they believe you, do you think they would protect you from me? How do you think the people who paid you to lie would feel about that?"

"What do you want?" Ghamal's demeanor became suddenly and reluctantly conciliatory. "Are you going to kill me?"

"One moment of brutal satisfaction in exchange for a lifetime of imprisonment? No. You owe me more than a life. You owe me the life

I was meant to have. The life my wife never got to have. And the children that never were. Your lie cost them all."

"What do you want?" Ghamal asked again, this time on the verge of tears.

"Admit to me now that you were paid to lie in court, then tell me who paid you and I will leave you alone."

"And if I don't?" Ghamal raised his chin defiantly, all signs of conciliation receding.

"If I have to die a villain then I have no incentive to keep you alive, Ghamal." Mohsin glowered at Ghamal, trying to suppress a sneer. He remembered all the days he'd helped him on the *Nightshade*. All the nights he'd swabbed the deck or took his shifts cleaning the holds because Ghamal was goldbricking. Mohsin treated him like a revered uncle and a friend, and his generosity had been repaid with treachery. "Even as a ghost I can make the rest of your days very uncomfortable."

"I can't tell you. They'd kill me!"

"*I* will kill you."

"Ok! It was a man - a lawyer named Damji - Rasoul Damji. I'm sorry, Mohsin, but I needed the money and he offered it to me. I didn't want to do it but I was broke and scared." Ghamal began sobbing into his hands. Mohsin wanted to pity him but all he could find was hatred. Normally Mohsin would have taken pity at hearing about Ghamal's difficulty but his heart had been hardened since that day in the courtroom. He'd gotten what he needed and being in Ghamal's presence was making him agitated. Mohsin left without saying anything else. As he exited Ghamal's building, he turned off the microrecording device he had palmed.

Another simple query quickly revealed this Rasoul Damji's connection to Hossam. Mohsin remembered seeing him in court the day he was convicted. It all fell into place. The three primary conspirators were all in the court. The public and the courts would have no problem putting it together either. And while this information would clear his name when it became public, he had no intention of letting Rasoul or Hossam see the inside of a courtroom. He wasn't going to let Ghamal off entirely.

The prosecution's case against him rested on Ghamal's testimony. But he wasn't going to kill Ghamal either. Ghamal didn't just owe a debt to him. The people of streetside were owed the truth. Though less of an offense than outright treachery, informing on a crewmate was frowned upon. Lying on a crewmate for financial gain was traitorous. When the time was right, he planned on leaving Ghamal to the streetsiders. They would want justice too, and Mohsin intended to feed him to them.

Mohsin had become so focused on taking revenge on Hossam that he'd nearly forgotten the damage done to his reputation. Streetsiders were peculiar when it came to those they claimed as their own. They would hide you, feed you, even protect you from those whom they considered outsiders, especially authorities. But they didn't take disloyalty lightly. Mohsin had been convicted of transmitting the coordinates of his ship to pirates. Many crewmen, men and women like them, like streetsiders, died in that attack. It had been years since it happened, but people still spoke about it streetside. The fact that Mohsin a rising star in the TUC and so well known in the neighborhoods made it so noteworthy.

Exoneration in the eyes of the law was completely tangential. As far as they knew, he was already dead. Regardless, their corrupt system put him in prison. It was important to him that the people he considered friends and family know the truth. The women who raised him, brought him meals when he put into port, the uncles who taught him how to carry himself on the streets and to be a good Muslim. Those were the people Mohsin wanted to clear his name for. It meant that all the time and love they poured into caring for him was not lost in some get rich quick scheme.

16

NORMALLY THE TUC credit union would have handled all of Mohsin's finances. Once he joined the apprentice program, he was counseled by the administrative offices on how best to allocate his pay to ensure a decent retirement. His pay went directly into his credit union account, which he checked from time to time. Occasionally he withdrew small sums when he had shore leave, but since he had no vices, there was very little to spend it on.

Mohsin never thought he would belong to an actual bank, let alone walk into one in person. Most of the transactions he was about to undertake could be done remotely but he wanted to avail himself of some of the less formal amenities. Before arriving, he had Yacoub transmit the requisite documentation of the Adhara find: a complete spectrographic scan of the asteroid, a digital claim marker, and signatures empowering the bank to receive funds on his behalf. He had opened accounts at a half dozen banks on Earth. It didn't make sense to send all of the money to just one. This one was going to be special.

"I'm honored that you would come all this way to meet with me. I would have been more than happy to come to you."

Mohsin realized there was a difference between being rich and acting that way. He disliked all the deference and fuss people made over those with wealth, but he carrying out his plans was going to require him to do a better job of acting.

"That's alright. I've just come to Earth and I have yet to set up offices and my residence is still being renovated."

The woman nodded, then motioned for Mohsin to have a seat. She sat down at her desk and activated a holo-console.

"We were so pleased to be selected as your bank of choice here in Baikonur. It says here that all of your documentation is in order. What can we do for you?"

"First I am going to need another sizeable advance against the spectrographic scans."

"That shouldn't be a problem," the woman said without pausing or blinking. "We are more than happy to accommodate the short term needs of our clients. That could have been done remotely."

"I wanted to speak to someone because I want this handled discreetly. I want to use the advance to consolidate some large debts."

"That shouldn't be a problem, Mr. Adhara. Given the anticipated size of your portfolio, we can offer favorable terms for a debt consolidation. Can you tell me who currently holds your outstanding debt?"

"Oh. I apologize for not being clear. You're the holder of the debt I want to consolidate. And the debt isn't mine. It belongs to Hossam Majid."

A smirk crept across the bank officer's face.

"Mr. Majid's outstanding debt is considerable. How much of it would you like to buy?"

"All of it."

"I feel personally compelled to warn you that Mr. Majid has been incredibly resistant to collection. His position within his government as well in Baikonur society affords him a level of protection. I tell you this because we value your business and look forward to a long and fruitful relationship."

"Options?"

"His loans bear interest. And until this year he was making those payments." Mohsin scrolled through the debt portfolio on the holoscreen. Hossam was six months in arrears. "We considered petitioning the Sultan in Istanbul."

Mohsin could see how that might work. Hossam had moved his debt to interest bearing, which allowed him to carry more of it while making smaller payments. As opposed to dividends, the Islamic alternative in this case, which was a flat number paid against the principle amount. The size of the debt would be embarrassing to the Sultan. The fact that Hossam was paying interest would be a scandal.

"I like this idea, but a letter to the Sultan is hardly discreet."

"I would recommend setting up a series of shell corporations. Spread the debt out amongst them so it appears to the Sultan that he is being petitioned by a group of debt holders. It won't stand up to scrutiny forever."

"It doesn't need to. Do you have a preferred agent for the incorporations?"

"We have one on premises, Mr. Adhara, and would be happy to help you set that up for a nominal fee."

The bank was more than happy to get debt off their books and Mohsin would use one of his newly-created holding companies to gain access to the bank's debt portfolio. The banks were so eager to unload the debt that they even helped him set up the company and showed him how to access various financial databases. He was shocked when he saw how much Hossam owed. It was a complex scheme of moving money around to satisfy the most urgent debtors. He was always granted favorable terms even when consolidating his debt, which he did from time to time. Mohsin could only guess the reason was because of his position. No one else would ever be able to carry so much debt and still secure loans.

Hossam didn't have a set income, but it remained fairly stable over the last several years. He drew a base salary from his position as the Bashi, and the rest was commission against ore and minerals the Sultanate's facilities processed in Mina al Fada. There was absolutely no way he could sustain as much debt and loan activity as he did with what he made. Mohsin knew Hossam's love of gambling, but the possibility that he was subsidizing all of this with his winnings was mathematically impossible. There had to be another source, and he suspected Hossam was skimming profits from the Sultan. Once Mohsin's petition was sent, the Sultan was going to want a closer look at the books. This would cause another piece of the ground to collapse beneath Hossam's feet.

17

WHEN SOLMAZ MARRIED HOSSAM, she learned what was expected of her. Many people would have considered it a step up from streetside, but she didn't. Back home, she was expected to work and take turns in her collective, making meals, doing laundry, and looking after the young ones. The men were expected to do the same, though many of them shirked their duties in favor of drinking or gambling. But in Mina Fada, servants did all of those things for her. Working or doing chores was suddenly unbecoming. She was expected to dress a certain way, act a certain way, conduct herself at functions in a certain way. It was far more complicated than streetside life and far less satisfying.

The servants, like Hossam, were surprised at how quickly she took to her new role. Honestly, she felt it was beneath her intellect. Ordering new china every year, memorizing the names of important guests, remembering important dates on the social calendar. Servants and computers did most of that work for her. The hard part was pretending to like all of these people. Shaking their hands, offering Salaams, entertaining them, and listening to their endless backbiting of one another. Hiding her revulsion was a full time job.

More recently, Hossam had placed her in charge of throwing an off-season party. She felt it was a bit unwise, given the state of the house finances, but he insisted that she was to spare no expense. He had heard that this Adhara fellow was coming to Earth, and he wanted to throw a party for him. Or rather he wanted to throw a party in the hopes that Adhara would show up. They not only wanted to be seen having an off-season party, they wanted all of Mina Fada to know that their guest of honor was the source of so much newfound prosperity. Who knew, maybe word of this event would get back to the Sultan.

If Solmaz was going by numbers alone, the party was a hit. She couldn't remember a time when there were so many guests. But she wasn't fooled. It had nothing to do with her charm or the Majd name. There were a lot of stories about the mysterious Aaris Adhara, and everyone wanted to get a look at him. Of course there were those, like her husband, who thought they could get into Adhara's good graces, and perhaps his pockets. And there were many young noblewomen who wanted his attention. That was another thing she disliked about these events. They were never just about fellowship or celebrating some good fortune—there were always dozens of competing agendas.

When Aaris Adhara arrived, a hush descended over the room. Solmaz was making small talk with a group of guests. Hossam, surprisingly, rushed over to welcome him, and she thought she should be next to him when he did. Most of Adhara's face was hidden by a heavy mustache and a thick beard, well groomed and fragrantly oiled, which terminated several inches below his chin.

"Allow me to welcome you to my home, Mister Adhara." Hossam bowed slightly, then offered his hand, which Adhara shook. "This is my wife, Solmaz."

"I'm pleased to meet you, madam," Was all Mohsin could manage to say. He felt his chest tighten and his breathing grow shallow and rapid, it was so overwhelming to be in Solmaz's presence after so many years. To be standing so close to her now was intoxicating.

"Likewise." She bowed slightly as well. If she recognized him, she didn't let on.

Rasoul appeared in the foyer, looking quite anxious. Hossam walked briskly across the room to intercept Rasoul. They exchanged hushed but vehement words. Hossam nodded, then motioned toward his office.

He returned to Solmaz's side. "Please forgive me. I have some urgent business to attend to. I won't be more than a few minutes."

"Hossam, please. Adhara is our guest of honor."

"I apologize. I'm sure a man of your newfound stature understands the burdens that come with it. Please enjoy my hospitality until I return."

"Of course. Your lovely wife can keep me entertained."

"I would be glad to." She smiled and led him by the arm into the next room.

Hossam herded Rasoul into his office.

"What are you doing here?"

"The Sector 8 convoys bound for Earth from Adhara have been attacked by Corsairs."

"All I need from you is a temporary authorization for ships to dock in the North American Trade Zone."

"That's a tall order, Hossam! Do you know what it will take to get that much cargo offloaded from that many ships?"

"Yes. That's why I'm asking you and not someone else. There are six ships loaded to the hull with ore. That's enough for both of us to become Sultans ourselves."

"Both of us?"

"Of course, I would cut you in, Rasoul. Look, you've been waiting for this opportunity your entire career. You don't think I knew what you were doing streetside all those years ago—why you helped me kill my own father? This is what being a noble is."

"Stealing?"

"Stealing, killing. Whatever it takes to become and stay a noble."

The Corsairs had been raiding the Consortium mercilessly for months now. A few ships had managed to get into Sector 8 space without being boarded and had formed a convoy. Normally they would dock at Mina Fada, but that just meant all that ore would go through proper channels. It would be offloaded, processed and refined. The fees for it all would go to the Sultan. Hossam got commissions but because so many ships were being boarded, the commissions had ground to a halt. As soon as he heard a convoy had gotten through, he brokered the sale of the unrefined ore and minerals to another party in North America.

"This is a bad situation, Hossam. If the Sultan finds out, he will execute us."

"If I don't do this, I'm dead anyway."

"What do you mean?"

"My debts are being called in."

"What?" Rasoul's eyes widened in surprise.

"The banks I can bargain for more time with, or request an advance from the Sultan. He won't want his Bashi in a debtors' prison. But I also owe money to some unsavory folks streetside who don't care about my station. I have a feeling they would find a way to get to me."

It was much worse than he was letting on. Hossam was really beginning to feel like someone had it in for him. The attacks on his ships were shaking the confidence of crews, and they were rapidly abandoning the Consortium. The Corsairs didn't appear to be targeting TUC ships, so crews were signing with them in order to protect their bonus structure and their lives. It was only a matter of time before his Sultan decided to take his head off out of embarrassment. The part he wasn't sharing with Rasoul was that he had no intention of sticking around to try and fix things. It was beyond repair. He meant to broker this deal then disappear.

"The ships will be on approach soon. Issue the authorizations."

Rasoul nodded.

18

Mohsin's plan was coming to a head and yet all he could think about was Solmaz. Seeing her stirred something in him. It was naïve to think he could separate himself from his feelings until his plans reached fruition. He had changed, but she had not. She was dressed in the finery of admin nobility, but she was still herself. Initially racked with guilt at ever having suspected she had a hand in his framing, it all dissolved that night.

Her expensive perfume mingled with a scent that was only hers and it clung to his clothes, to him. He went home that evening and wept into his pillow while holding his jacket so he could fall asleep with her scent in his nose. She had taken his hand at one point and escorted him around the room to introduce him to the luminaries of Mina al Fada. He was transported back to a time before the *Damma*, before the Corsairs. At various times, she would pause strategically in their conversations to ask him something about himself, then smile as she waited for his response. That's when he knew.

Solmaz was genuinely interested in people. There was nothing beguiling in her but everything about her was mesmerizing. She had a way of making people feel important without being obsequious. In all the time they spent together that evening, she never once talked down to a servant or failed to meet their eye, and she never forgot a name. She hadn't changed.

Solmaz and Hossam lived only a few levels below him in the luxury apartments of Mina Fada. For her to be so close yet not in his arms was torture. And though his plans were unfolding as intended, there was no guarantee that he would live to see them come to fruition. Mohsin needed to see her, as himself, so she could know that he was alive, and so she could know the truth of what happened. It was a risk, but a small one. The Corsairs had been tailing Solmaz, Rasoul, and Hossam since they arrived on Earth. A simple call and he knew Hossam was at his office. He would be notified if that changed.

He took the main lift down a few levels and hurried through the promenade and shopping districts, realizing once he got the residential areas that he was still taking a risk going to see her. Heads turned as he passed, and it occurred to him how conspicuous he was. He was dressed appropriately, though he had removed his beard.

The door was answered by a servant and Mohsin stood there for a moment realizing he didn't know what to say. The woman gestured for him to enter, then disappeared down a hallway. A few moments later, Solmaz emerged into the foyer and froze.

She raised the back of her hand to her mouth and began to shake mouth. Tears streamed down her cheeks. Unsure of her reaction, Mohsin was hesitant to go in for a hug. Solmaz took several teetering steps, then looked at him, the same way she had at the dinner party, though now her eyes were glassy with tears. She reached up and touched his face. They could have been standing in the foyer forever and it would have been fine by him.

"I knew there was something familiar about you. I allowed my reason to override my intuition. I just kept thinking there was no way you could be here." Solmaz began showering him with kisses, which he accepted greedily, almost losing himself in the warmth of her lips and her body. After several minutes of just holding her, Mohsin took her face in his hands and pulled his lips from hers.

"Listen. There isn't much time."

"Yes. We must get away. Just let me pack a few things."

"Not yet. Not right now. But very soon."

"Why can't we just go?"

"I have something that I need to do."

"We have each other again. Isn't that all we need?"

Mohsin looked down without saying anything.

"What is it?"

Mohsin walked from the foyer to the adjoining sitting room where there was a holoscreen. He turned it on, guessing that the news of Ghamal's confession would be everywhere by now.

"Rasoul did this?" She paused and Mohsin could see her connecting the dots.

"It was Hossam. He framed me and had me sent away." Solmaz backed away from Mohsin and gasped. "It's true. Ghamal confessed to being bribed by Rasoul. And while I don't have a direct confession from Rasoul, he and Hossam are thick as thieves."

"Mohsin - I…"

"It's hard to imagine I know. But you understand why I must confront him."

19

RASOUL HAD BEEN under a lot of stress recently. After all the years of being partners in crime, he was beginning to rethink the relationship with Hossam. He remembered thinking at the time that *any* admin noble would be an easy step into the upper echelons of Baikonur society. He was wrong. Hossam's excesses kept them both hustling. There was constant pressure on Rasoul to come up with new ways to skim profits, most of which he never saw a penny of. When he saw his face being broadcast on the news with the caption "Solicitor general implicated in decades-old frame-up" he was overcome simultaneously by anger and terror.

Rasoul was sitting in a small streetside café when the news broke. A large holoscreen behind the bar was broadcasting a drama of some kind only moments before. He happened to look up from his meal and see his face on the screen, which then cut to Ghamal's recorded confession to someone out of frame. Initially, all he could do was stare at the screen and blink. Then the suffocating feeling of all the possible consequences began to press down on him. He was panicking, not from lack of clarity, but lack of options. There were simply no moves for him to make. It was no longer safe for him to be in streetside but Rasoul knew if he returned to Mina Fada he would be greeted by the police. He didn't have the advantage of bodyguards or a high station in life to protect him, and streetsiders were famously loyal to their own.

When he walked out into the cold Baikonur night, he was greeted again by his own face, plastered on holos for as far as the eye could see. And those screens were large enough that he could see them for several blocks in every direction. Seeing hundreds of pedestrians stop to watch deepened his feeling of terror, so he hiked up his collar and did his best to blend in. Even if he managed to blend in, Rasoul realized he had nowhere to go. He was the solicitor general, but there was no guarantee that would keep him safe. He might be arrested the moment he set foot in Mina Fada, he had limited funds on him, and had no idea how to survive on the streets.

As if this were an evening of answered prayers, a pair of scraggly looking fellows suddenly flanked him as he was walking. A third stepped out of a nearby alley in front of him.

"Come with us. We can get you some place safe."

"Why would I trust you?" It suddenly occurred to him that these men might simply be trying to lure him to a more secluded location where they could kill him.

"Feel free to roam the streets." One of them motioned toward all the holoscreens with a wave of his hand. "I'm sure no one will recognize you. If some brave soul doesn't stick you, you might end up in a bag and delivered to the authorities for a reward."

Rasoul relented and mercifully they turned onto a side street. He could still hear the broadcast over the din of streetside. Ghamal had been recorded admitting to lying under oath about the attack on the *Nightshade*. Rasoul's terror compounded itself, enough to eclipse any annoyance he may have felt. He knew immediately he couldn't go to Hossam with this. Hossam said they should have killed Ghamal, but Rasoul convinced him not to. Now Ghamal was implicating him in a crime.

It didn't escape him that Hossam had *him* pay off Ghamal so Ghamal wouldn't be able to identify him. Rasoul was the only link between them, and Hossam might find it easier to kill him and sever that link. Unless the two toughs he was now in the company of beat

Hossam to it. They didn't walk far through the side streets and back alleys, but it wasn't reassuring. One didn't need to go somewhere remote to dispose of a body in streetside. There was so much heavy industry around Mina Fada, so many ways to pulverize, liquify, or incinerate someone.

Rasoul knew where they were. It was the Adhara foundry. To hear tell from the locals, this place was churning out thousands of smelted bars of ore a day which was completely contrary to what he saw.

"Now that you've got me here, what do you plan to do?" The lighting was a lot better inside than out and Rasoul could see the face of the stocky one more clearly. "I know you, you're the servant of Adhara." Rasoul didn't think they could possibly know about the diverted shipments and decided not to offer any information unless pressed. There was no need to preemptively incriminate himself and he could just deny it anyway.

"You bribed that man Ghamal many years ago. Why?"

"That's what you want to know about? Some old burnout that ratted out his friend? What difference does it make? He's probably dead!"

"Not dead yet, Rasoul." A voice came from a poorly-lit part of the foundry floor. A tall, slender man stepped out of the shadows.

"Adhara?" Rasoul squinted to see the man as he walked into the light, recognizing him at first only by his voice. Then, as he saw Adhara's unshaved face, the look in his eyes flickered between confusion and recognition. The face before him was familiar, but weathered and aged. Sunken cheeks and eyes that were sure in their ability to give away nothing. Not dead, but penetrating. Then it struck him. He was staring into the face of that idealist from streetside, whose face had been on holoscreens all over the city. The one Ghamal helped him to frame.

"I want to know why you framed me."

By telling them, Rasoul would be selling out Hossam. He started to ask himself what Hossam would do if their positions were reversed.

"Ghamal's face is all over the news. And now so is mine. Why should I tell you anything?"

"Ghamal is still alive, for now. And you have some of my ore. Enough to live comfortably in exile for the rest of your days. I would say that makes you downright lucky."

The situation was already beyond repair. The moment his face appeared on the holos, Rasoul knew his life in Baikonur was over. So much of this could have been avoided if Hossam had controlled his impulses. Now it was time to look after his own future.

"What must I do?"

"Tell me who ordered you to frame me." Adhara handed Rasoul his comm. "Then message Hossam and tell him to meet you here. Once he's taken care of, you'll be free to go." He stood and ordered his men to leave.

20

Hossam was now locked into his current trajectory. He spent years telling himself there was still time to change his ways. One last game, one last night out. Tomorrow he would reform, for Solmaz. He would pay off his debts, keep his head down, and in time the Sultan would notice and send for him. But his life was catching up to him. He received a communique from the Sultan's finance secretary informing him that one of his debtors had filed a petition of restitution. As a result, they were dispatching a team of auditors to look at his books. Public image aside, they were concerned that his enormous debts could compromise his position. And from the sum of the petition, it was clear he was living beyond what the Sultan provided.

There was a small chance that the shipments could arrive, be processed, and sold before the auditors arrived. The bank might even rescind their petition if a valid purchase order was provided, and then Hossam might be able to talk the auditors out of looking any closer at his finances. He knew that was unlikely. He knew he was going to have to leave. And if that were the case, why pay the banks at all? The Sultan would be on the hook for it, but he could afford it.

Circumstance had removed the need for him to agonize over it, so he took the last of his house funds and headed to streetside to treat himself to one last evening of leisure. When he first arrived, he hated Baikonur, but the city had grown on him. At least the gambling parlors and hostess bars had. Wherever he was headed next would need to have them too. There was a relief in having the decision made for him. At least with the ore he and Rasoul were offloading in North America, he would be able to live lavishly no matter where he went. He allowed himself to feel resigned, and with it a bit of happiness. No more serving that idiot cousin, being under his heel, with the constant pressure of running his operation in Mina al Fada.

His sense of relief and resignation was short lived. His groundcar had pulled up the curb of one of the few establishments where his money was still good. The bodyguard got out first then held the door for him. Hossam had barely made it to the door when he heard gasps and then screams coming from his right. One of his bodyguards was already pulling back toward the car.

"Hossam Majid -!" was all he heard clearly before the loud crack of a gauss pistol drowned out the rest. Everything after that was a blur. Two more shots rang out as he was thrown violently back into the back seat of his car. His bodyguard lay on top of him as they sped away.

On the way back to Mina Fada, he had time to think about what had just happened. A streetsider had tried to kill him. When he thought about all the people who might want to kill him, the gravity of his situation began to sink in. Once word of this got around, there would be reprisals in streetside. But the admin nobles were just as likely to take *his* head. His other crimes notwithstanding, the embarrassment of having one of their own rile the workers to the point of violence set a bad example. And an example would have to be made of him.

Even with the ships loaded with ore being redirected, and now with Rasoul's authorization, it would still be days before it was processed. Hossam couldn't wait that long. Once news of the attempt on his life reached the Sultan, he would order a lockdown. His bodyguards would become his jailers. Closing his ore deal with the North Americans would be impossible, then the auditors would show up and he would have no opportunity to run. He needed to leave tonight. The money he hadn't spent gambling and the small sum in his safe should be enough to get him and Solmaz out of the city. It would be rough traveling as commoners, but it was necessary. And the massive payday on the other side of their journey would be worth it.

When Hossam arrived at his apartments, he called to Solmaz. From the foyer, he could see her in the drawing room. When she didn't respond, he went to see what had her so captivated.

"I need you to pack some things," he said, as calmly as he could. "Only what you can carry. We're leaving." Solmaz calmly looked at him, then motioned towards the holoscreen with her eyes. *'Rasoul Damji, the Justiciar of Mina al Fada is wanted for questioning after this shocking recorded confession has surfaced.'*

"Oh God." Hossam whispered. "That damn fool." He took out his comm and sent a message to Rasoul.

"Please tell me you aren't mixed up in whatever Rasoul has gotten himself into."

"It doesn't matter, we're leaving! Go and pack your things!"

"I'm not going anywhere."

"Suit yourself. I'm sure my cousin will want this place vacated for whomever assumes my post next. So you will have to go somewhere."

Fortunately, there wasn't much of value in their apartments that Hossam felt he needed to take, at least nothing that couldn't be replaced. There was some cash in his safe and a few items of jewelry he'd inherited from his parents. And of course there was Solmaz. She was replaceable, but he did still care for her, and didn't want to be alone in his temporary life on the run. She wouldn't like it, but she'd never really got used to the life of a nobleman's wife anyway.

Hossam opened his safe and began shoving stacks of bills into a satchel. It was the cache of money he used for gambling. It would have to last until he was paid by his contacts in North America. He stopped long enough to check for messages, then picked up the satchel, grabbed his vibrosword from its mounting on the wall and headed for the door. He stopped and looked at Solmaz one last time. She stared at him with indifference. He shook his head and walked out the door.

21

Hossam entered the foundry with his plasma pistol drawn. He and Rasoul were bound to each other through sin, not friendship. And he wouldn't put it past Rasoul to turn on him for the gratitude of the Sultan and a possible elevation in status.

Supposedly, Adhara had been refining ore in this place for months, but it looked completely disused. There was dust an inch thick covering the furnaces and the floor, and it was as cold inside as out. Two figures stepped into view from behind one of the furnaces. They were backlit, so it was hard to see faces, but one appeared to be bound.

"Welcome, Hossam. Have you come to rob me?"

"I don't know what you mean. A friend called me in distress and insisted I meet him here."

The two figures stepped forward. One was Rasoul, gagged, with his hands bound in front of him. The second was a beardless Adhara, pushing him along.

"This friend here?" Adhara tugged at Rasoul. "He's told me everything about your plan to steal my ore. "

"I always thought he was a terrible attorney." Hossam raised the pistol and fired, scorching the front left side of Rasoul Damji's body, killing him.

Adhara ran for cover. Hossam fired again, but missed, the plasma bolt ricocheting off of a furnace cover. He ran to Rasoul's lifeless body to see where Adhara might have gone. Adhara picked up a handful of dust and threw it in Hossam's face as he rounded the furnace. The plasma pistol discharged again, but the shot went wide. Adhara got his hand under Hossam's wrist and wrenched the pistol away.

"You played quite a good game, Adhara," Hossam said, trying to play it cool. "I must thank you. I was getting bored of my life and this little challenge proved quite invigorating. Now it's over." Hossam was backing away while rubbing the dust from his eyes with his palms.

"I'm going to have to disagree with you, Hossam."

"On which?"

"On everything."

Adhara took another few steps forward into a shaft of light that beamed into the dusty foundry through a large bank of windows. Hossam's head snapped up and he squinted while trying to regain his vision. As he did, he saw something familiar. Dark, angular features that he'd known once, but the eyes that stared back at him were not those round, kind ones. They were darkened by age, bitterness, and anger.

"Eh—Mohsin? You're Adhara?"

"Yes."

Hossam started to ask why, but he knew. Mohsin had plenty of time to reason out who had put him in prison. And he'd been to Hossam's home, masquerading as Adhara, so he knew he and Solmaz were together.

"It doesn't matter, the ships are mine. As we speak, they are taking their cargo to a Star Port in North America for offloading. "

"Yes, I know." One of the great things about the Corsairs was they were able to come and go as they pleased. Many decided the lifestyle didn't suit them, and they preferred the oppressive stability of working for the Consortium or the TUC. Yacoub had arranged to find many of them and offer them money to begin working the crews that would mine and ship the ore from Suleiman.

Hossam's grin flattened into a scowl. "How could you know? Those are my ships, my crews."

"They are your ships. But they are my crews. You know what happens when you replace vested crew with unskilled deckhands? Doesn't exactly inspire loyalty in the people who work for you. And, on top of that, you got Rasoul mixed up in this by having him send those false authorizations to ships I control."

"I sent you to prison. Took your woman. Now I'm just going to have to kill you. Far less poetic, but I just don't have the time anymore."

"You thought you would offload the mineral and palladium shipments at an ore processing facility your employers didn't control. Even after the hefty percentage they would charge, you would be able to pay off your debts. Which I also own. Once you killed me, there would be no one who could attest to the missing ore. And now you will be free of the debts as well. I've given you additional incentive to kill me."

Hossam drew his vibroblade and edged toward Mohsin across the concrete foundry floor. Mohsin drew his own weapon, a custom one he'd had made in the fashion of the Mameluke swords of old. It was preferred among many of the admin nobility because of its length and shape. Hossam brandished a kilij not that dissimilar from Mohsin's weapon. Upon activation, they both gave off crystalline howls. Hossam's kilij had a mono-molecular edge. The very air seemed to split and crackle around it. A sane man would be intimidated by its appearance, and the certainty in Hossam's eyes that he knew how to use it. Mohsin was very sane. He was also eager to test Hossam's intention, his confidence, so he stepped in with a series of lunges.

Mohsin felt the ease with which Hossam parried while back stepping. He was almost gliding backwards and resetting very quickly. Mohsin was not winded, but he could see how that might happen. Hossam was smarter than Mohsin gave him credit for. That extra half step was meant to put him off balance and eventually tire him out. He remembered Abbas' teachings about proximity. Hossam would have mastered it, and have had the endurance to use it—or at least deprive him of his.

Mohsin was used to the closed quarters of the ship, and the boarding actions of the *Hut*, as well as the shorter swords the Corsairs preferred. He'd opted for the longer Mameluke sword because he'd learned on a longer blade, but they were more forward heavy than the weapons he'd used more recently. Hossam's skill was effortless, parrying as if not even needing to see where the strikes were coming from. The riposte was so quick that he managed it in the half count after the parry, catching. Mohsin off guard and put him off balance. He took massive galloping steps back to avoid Hossam's blade. The blades snapped loudly and angrily against each other each time he parried.

At this distance Hossam would wear him down and cut him apart. He could simply dance in and out of Mohsin's range.

"Rasoul told me about how you killed your father, Hossam. He told me about how you enlisted him to frame me. I thought you were my friend."

"Friend? You were just a poor kid from streetside that I used to get close to his woman and then make her mine."

Hossam couldn't resist gloating. Mohsin baited him with recriminations about the past and pretended to allow that last statement to enrage him. He charged, knowing Hossam would parry and riposte, then press. It prevented Mohsin from having to chase him and made his movements predictable. He fumbled backward again, pretending to to lose his stance and backed away sloppily, which only encouraged Hossam. This enabled Mohsin to lure him deep between two furnaces.

There, in the tighter quarters, he could restrict Hossam's movements and limit the wider strokes, allowing him to close the distance and keep Hossam from tiring him out. Hossam didn't notice until he parried a blow from Mohsin and immediately countered with a swing that arced wide. The blade cut clear through a furnace exhaust pipe. Hossam looked behind him and saw the long rows of furnaces that stood between him and the open foundry floor. He was still dangerous, but his limited movements made him more predictable. He had less of his repertoire to rely on.

Even in close quarters, it was hard to get past his defenses. Mohsin feinted another lunge, but withdrew his blade and made Hossam miss the parry, hitting the hull of another furnace cover and kicking up a massive cloud of dust. He jerked back and swung wide, hoping to catch Mohsin or at least keep him at bay. Mohsin parried, then brought his blade down on Hossam's hand, severing it completely. Before Hossam could cry out, Mohsin plunged his sword into his chest.

22

———————

IT FELT good to be streetside again. It was one thing to take in the air and the mist of Mina Fada platforms. It was quite another to be home, on the actual ground. There was slush, and trapper hats with ear flaps taped up. There were barrel fires and the smells of cooking food and smoking tobacco. He and Solmaz walked among all this like they had when they were children, and he told her everything. He told her about being framed and being in prison, and spending time with the Corsairs.

"What about us?" he asked her.

"I love you, Mohsin. I never stopped. I mourned you every day, even as others cursed you for your crimes. Ever since you appeared at my apartment as yourself, I wondered how you could have been in my home the night of the party in disguise and not said anything. And I realized it's because it was all part of this plan you had to get revenge on Hossam. And I asked myself, where was I in all of that calculation? Was I just a means to an end? We started out together wanting to help people."

"And we still can—"

Solmaz held up her hand to silence Mohsin. "I understand the revenge. But you made it all about the revenge. Which tells me that you have changed in a very fundamental way. You cannot destroy someone like Hossam as completely as you did, without becoming a bit like him. I have changed too. I will never be that woman again. But maybe I can resume her journey where she left off." Solmaz looked up at him, much the same way she used to when they were together. She kissed him, then walked away into the streetside crowds.

Mohsin's chest was heavy. It had been heavy since the day he and Solmaz were separated. He understood what she was trying to do, and it made sense. Perhaps enough sense for the both of them. Hossam had killed him twice and taken her from him twice. That was enough loss for a lifetime. Yacoub was waiting nearby and, once Solmaz walked away, he approached.

"I've completed the purchase of the *Damma* as you asked. What do you want done with it? It's in drydock being refitted. The prisoners have been temporarily offloaded to a penal colony pending its repair."

"Destroy it. I want to make sure no one is ever held on that ship again."

"What do we do now, Jawaal?"

"Let's go home, Yacoub."

ABOUT THE AUTHOR

J. Austin Yoshino is a Black/Japanese Muslim living in the US. He is the editor of the sci-fi zine "Fresh Pulp Magazine" and is a contributing author to the award-winning collection of essays "Salaam, Love". He has an upcoming paper in the Miptsterze Muslim Futures journal. Upcoming releases include the completion of his novel "Red Mihrab".

@austinyoshino on all social media accounts.

www.ingramcontent.com/pod-product-compliance
Lightning Source LLC
Chambersburg PA
CBHW072005210726
48294CB00013B/1340